<u>Love in the Age of Dispossession</u>

Loretta Buckley Malakie

978-0-9993023-6-1

*Dedicated to my husband, my parents, the American South, and my American generation- the generation they call "X."*

# LOVE IN THE AGE OF DISPOSSESSION
## Table of Contents

**BOOK THREE: THE FUTURE**

**AFTERWORD**

## BOOK ONE: THE FIGHT

*High school is closer to the core of the American experience than anything else I can think of.*
-attributed to Kurt Vonnegut

*I am as suspicious and as prone to take offense as a humpback or a dwarf.*
-Fyodor Dosteovsky, <u>Notes from the Underground</u>

*Tho' I've belted you an' flayed you,*
*By the livin' Gawd that made you,*
*You're a better man than I am, Gunga Din!*
-Rudyard Kipling, *Gunga-Din*

*Full fathom five thy father lies;*
*Of his bones are coral made;*
*Those are pearls that were his eyes*
*Nothing of him that doth fade*
*But doth suffer a sea change*
*Into something rich and strange.*
-William Shakespeare, *Ariel's Song*, <u>The Tempest</u>, Act I, Scene 2

*I know that I shall meet my fate*
*Somewhere among the clouds above;*
*Those that I fight I do not hate*
*Those that I guard I do not love;*
-W.B. Yeats, *An Irish Airman Foresees His Death*

*"And, hast thou slain the Jabberwock?*
*Come to my arms, my beamish boy!*
*Oh frabjous day! Callooh! Callay!"*
*He chortled in his joy.*
-Lewis Carroll, *Jabberwocky,* <u>Through the Looking-Glass</u>

## Chapter 1: Kitty and Mike on the Village Green

New York City is the center of the universe. It is also a sewer. Get out if you can. Gingerly pick your way through the horrors of Penn Station. Stay moving. Don't forget your hand sanitizer, and don't look anybody in the eye. If you're a girl, don't wear a ponytail. Ergonomically-speaking, ponytails are simply handles for attackers. Take the next train heading North. Sit on the right for Hudson River views. At Albany, the train heads West.

The landscape has changed. The Hudson River Valley is wide, spacious, gentle, delicately forested here and there. The farther North and West you go, the scenery grows wilder, lusher, richer, a darker shade of green. Fir trees start to appear among the leafy deciduous forests, and you're reminded you're nearing Canada. The people you see from the train are country people: poor and white. You may ask yourself, Do people really live in those run-down shacks during the freezing winters they get here? Yes. Yes, they do.

As you chug along heading West- unless something goes wrong and you're stopped for hours- you will find you are suddenly looking out the window at a broad slow river, much smaller than the grand Hudson, sporadically overshadowed by clusters of trees. This is the Mohawk River. Welcome to the Mohawk Valley.

Life here is agony for allergy-sufferers, as the valley traps the pollen, but it's paradise for farmers. Something about the pollen being trapped plus the glaciers receding and mineral deposits, and other facts Kitty failed to absorb in Earth Science class, make the valley especially fertile. Fertile for flora and fauna, fertile for people. Kitty's great-grandparents raised fifteen children farming hops in this valley, when this area was the largest producer of hops in the country.

Hops need a wet green environment. They grow in vines twining up tall wooden poles, and hops flowers look like large green buds of clover. They smell like heaven, sweet and ethereal. They flavor beer. Like the tobacco barns of the American South, hops barns have a large airy attic space up-top where plants are hung to dry. The countryside in Central New York is dotted with the ruins of hops barns.

Besides minerals, the receding glaciers also left behind lakes- deep, sunken, dark, and cold. Rimmed with green hills, fields, and forest. Lake Ontario, to the West, is its own mammoth entity. It's wondrous, it feels like a vast inland sea.

From 1810 to 1970, New York State had more people than any other state. New York State's rivers, lakes, and waterways connected Eastern ports and the world beyond with the vast American frontier. In the 1840s they built the Erie Canal alongside the Mohawk River, from Albany to Buffalo as the song goes, and in the 19th century canal cities sprang up. Mills and factories opened. Along the main streets, mansions were built, large enough to house retinues of live-in servants. The canal cities, never lovely, hit their stride around the 1920s- then grew shabbier and shabbier. Today those mansions are community centers, non-profits, or used for refugee housing.

When Kitty's great-grandparents immigrated, and when Kitty's grandparents and parents were born, New York was the most populous state. By the time Kitty was born, New York had fallen to second, and today New York is fourth. Kitty grew up against a backdrop of decline. But today things are different. New York is still in decline, but we are witnessing, not just decline, but the ascent of something new.

Most of the region's WASP founding-stock, gentlemen and farmers, were Connecticut Yankees who moved West from Connecticut into New York State just after the Revolutionary War. The gentlemen WASPs had a penchant for ancient Greece and Rome, and they named many of their new cities- poignantly now- with the grand, dashing names of the cities and heroes from ancient Greek and Latin literature: Homer, Troy, Paris, Ithaca, Odysseus. For the most part, the strain of founding-stock gentlemen and farmer WASPs has long since died out or moved, ceding the region to subsequent waves of Irish, German, and Italian immigrants.

Starting in the 1960s, accelerating in the 1970s, people started to leave New York State. It was the weather, it was the taxes, it was opportunity elsewhere. In the 1980s, the joke went: Would the last person to leave Upstate New York please shut off the lights? That was the 1980s.

The population decline in Upstate New York is worse than the statistics tell because the exodus of Americans from

Upstate New York is offset by foreign arrivals, mainly to New York City. The State government celebrates this demographic replacement of Americans as the best of all possible systems. This is what the French refer to with their characteristic droll wit (which might one day disappear from the earth) as *Le Grand Remplacement*.

Will they still call it The Great Replacement after everybody is gone?

Today the Central New York canal cities' shabbiness has turned into outright destitution, ruin, blight, and…something else. It's not all decline. There is ascent. Amid a landscape of potholes, cracked sidewalks, decaying 19th century mansions, and crumbling brick buildings upon which the faded imprints of painted slogans are still apparent, a new population has taken root.

One civilization's failure is another civilization's opportunity. Through the remains of a canal city that resemble the blown-out shell of a bombed-out war zone, move shadowy cloaked figures trailing broods of offspring. On corners congregate men displaced absolutely from their element, bringing their element with them. Locals avoid certain parts of the city these days.

The newcomers are the replacements. When the WASPs, the Irish, the Germans, and the Italians moved into this valley, they were escaping hardship, generally famines. They got here under their own steam. They paid their own way. They were not strategically installed by entities hostile to America's sovereign interests. They were not being deployed as human weapons of mass destruction.

The replacements are not Western. They are not Christian. They are not European. They are young, fecund, primitive, dull, vaguely resentful, and fundamentally hostile. They are our replacements.

The Catholic school Kitty's father attended is now a center for refugees.

*Full fathom five thy father lies;*
*Of his bones are coral made;*
*Those are pearls that were his eyes:*
*Nothing of him that doth fade,*

*But doth suffer a sea-change*
*Into something rich and strange.*

And indeed the city has undergone a sea change- from a faded industrial canal town to what looks like a Tanzanian port-city bazaar amid the ruins of crumbling, early 20th century, American architecture.

But the countryside is still green and rolling. There are still family farms that date from the 18th and 19th centuries, although many have been lost- and many very recently. "Good luck buying your milk from China," wrote one embittered dairy farmer on a local internet forum.

Outside one shabby canal city, surrounded by the green rolling countryside, there is a small college town- a village, really- numbering not quite two thousand. It's home to a small liberal arts college Kitty's mother calls "a safe place to stash dumb rich kids." A statement which, while a bit harsh, is difficult to disprove.

In the center of this village, there is a village green, and in the center of the village green, there is a fountain. In the center of the fountain, a statue of a nude female child holds aloft a bowl from which cascades a small stream. She looks like Degas's Little Dancer, but unclothed. And although breastless, prepubescent, and sexless, she's been the target of much local merriment. Once, famously, she was stolen by frat boys. It was in the local paper. A reward was offered. She was reclaimed. That was in the 1980s, so no one was required to attend a re-education camp.

Benches and hedges encircle the fountain. Picturesque small shops surround the village green. It looks like a movie set for idyllic small-town USA.

There's the fire station, a brick building with red doors. There's the local inn, a white colonial-style mansion named after the same founding father who also founded the college. There's the café where the kids hide in booths in the back when they skip school. Local legend says it's periodically raided by the principal.

On the other side of the green there's the Presbyterian church and the two Episcopalian churches. The Presbyterian church lost its steeple when it was struck by lightning, and the steeple has not been replaced. One Episcopalian church is actually not a church any more. It has been converted into an art center. How progressive and enlightened is our small college town.

Boomers, when the church was converted into an art center, probably imagined that this was part of the grand coming-together: Our churches will become centers of art where we will all achieve self-actualization. Let the sun shine. When the moon is in the seventh hour, all that. I guess they didn't realize that devolving churches were just a step on our evolution into submission, which is what we're all figuring out now.

This is a village that in 1993, 206 years after its founding by New Englanders, aspires to be New England. Ninety-nine percent of the town is white, and in those days people would have looked at you curiously for pointing that out. Well, of course they're "white." What would you think they would be? Why wouldn't they be white? What's wrong with that?

It's 1993, and when a boy loved a girl, he made her a mixtape. And it happened. And not infrequently.

There were only two genders. There were boys, and there were girls. And they were beautiful. And when a boy loved a girl, he made her a mixtape.

On one of the village green's benches a pale, heavily made-up, teenage girl with dark bobbed hair, wearing a white v-necked t-shirt and a red plaid miniskirt, perches, legs crossed, arms folded, awkwardly brandishing a lit cigarette. Her fishnet stockings reveal skin reddened by the cold, her naked arms are marked by goosebumps. It's April, and it's about 50 degrees in the Mohawk Valley. Where is her coat? She's got on a black velvet choker and combat boots. Underneath her white t-shirt you can make out the outline of a black bra.

This is no accident. In fact, nothing in her appearance is an accident. All is the product of prolonged study, concentration, careful effort, and art.

On the bench where she is sitting, someone has scrawled "Oedipus Schmoedipus!" with a black Sharpie on one of the slats. The observant might note the work of the same flowery hand (with the same marker) on the next bench over, proclaiming "Time For Shitty!" On the bench next to that, the author explores his analytical side. It reads: "Jermaine was not germane to the Jacksons." The girl is an intimate acquaintance of the defiler of park benches. In fact, that was her Sharpie, and she wants it back.

She sits, hunched and shivering, arms crossed tightly over her chest, fumbling the lit cigarette between the two forefingers of her right hand. In her left hand she clutches a pack of cigarettes and a pink slip of paper that says she can go to the library. Few circumstances offer such simple gratification as possessing an official dicta permitting you to go to the library while sitting on a bench in a nearby park, totally not in the library at all.

Despite all her effort- her studies, her hours of preparation- despite the fishnets, the combat boots, the miniskirt, the velvet choker, the black bra, the cigarette- she appears what she is: a wholesome, bright, high-strung little girl, and the beloved daughter of good people.

Her name is Kitty- Catherine Burnes- and she is a senior. She has been accepted early into both top-tier schools to which she applied. She is a legacy, her SATs were phenomenal, she has been working her whole life for this moment, the world is her oyster, and she is skipping school. At this very moment, she is waiting for Mike Connolly, her boyfriend. She's fuming, and she's dying to vent.

And there he was, she spotted him. He too wore only a t-shirt (you can't stop by your locker and grab your coat when you're skipping school, it looks suspicious) and pants whose crotch dragged practically on the ground. Kitty squinted at his advancing form. She never wore her glasses.

Kitty took this opportunity to gauge anew her boyfriend's shoulder to hip ratio.

Kitty had only been going out with Mike for four months. (A drunken hook-up at the Roys' house, he called her the next day- "What's up"- and the affair had formally begun.) Four months ago Kitty had broken up with Peter Park, her boyfriend since the beginning of 9th grade.

Peter's father was a Korean doctor, his mother a nurse and a local farmer's daughter. All the Park children were tall and beautiful and clever. Dr. Park had a deprived, war-torn childhood, and at sixteen-years-old he made it to the US. In this new country and in this new language, he studied and became a doctor. His response to the prejudice or bullying he encountered was to take up boxing and get really really good at it. He married the tallest, whitest, most American, nicest, sweetest wife, and he and she made posh, refined kids who read Milan Kundera, played Bach, and got into Princeton and Harvard.

Except Peter. Peter read Milan Kundera, but he did not play Bach, and, while his grades were very good (for a white boy), he was competing against other Asians, so he did not get in anywhere that great. But the funny thing was that Peter, Dr. Park's least posh, least refined child- the child that made Dr. Park look the least like a success- was the child most like Dr. Park. Peter had the same strong dark streak in him that had propelled Dr. Park into success in America. And Peter's classical violinist brothers, they didn't have that. But Peter grew up in luxury, whereas Dr. Park grew up in poverty, so Peter when he grew up joined the military and went to Iraq.

In 8th grade Kitty and Peter hated each other. Their shared 7th period Earth Science was spent in open warfare. Kitty proclaimed herself a feminist, Peter sardonically mocked her, Kitty snapped back. They were like two puppies experiencing the heat cycle for the first time. In 9th grade Kitty suddenly and violently developed a massive crush on Peter. It was probably the special flavor of contempt he had heaped on her assertions of feminism. Many boys had mocked her, but only Peter engaged with her on an intellectual level with such withering scorn. Also Peter was gorgeous. He was athletic and graceful. He played soccer.

So Kitty developed a crush. Peter, initially puzzled, eventually responded in kind, and in short order was obsessed with Kitty and wanted to do all sorts of disgusting things to her, some of which she let him do. He gave her the combat boots and the fishnets. The velvet choker, her trademark, had been her own idea.

When Peter and Kitty started going out, they were L.L. Bean and J. Crew preppies like the other kids in the Honors classes. Three years later, Peter was stalking through the halls in a black trench coat and army boots, with Kitty bobbing along beside him in a miniskirt and fishnets. Peter was the Pygmalion to Kitty's Galatea.

During the summer before 12ᵗʰ grade, Peter started smoking, because it was punk, so Kitty did too. Sometimes after school, they would go up to the woods at the college and hang out in the Japanese rock garden, by the bridge and the Buddha statue, where they would smoke and look cool. Sometimes Kitty would climb the giant rock in the middle of the garden and, standing on it, recite some of the poetry her mother had made her memorize:

> *I know that I shall meet my fate*
> *Somewhere among the clouds above.*

When Kitty started 12ᵗʰ grade, Kitty's little brother, who was in 10ᵗʰ grade, started hanging out with a group of 11ᵗʰ grade kids, and that's how Kitty met Mike and Holcombe. They were poor kids, and they were wild. They made being poor look fun.

When they went to the movies, one person would buy a ticket, rip it in half, and someone else would use the other half to get in: two entries on one ticket. When they ate fast food, they'd eat half a burger, complain they'd found a hair, and get a burger free: a burger and a half for the price of one burger.

At least once a week, they would raid the fountain on the green for coins, and go buy soda. Every time they collected coins from the fountain, Holcombe would do the same routine. In the middle of gathering coins, he would suddenly, standing in the fountain with his pants rolled up to his knees, hold a coin aloft, and grandly intone with great solemnity, "But this one right here was my wish. And it didn't come true. So I'm taking it back." Kitty, laughing, begged Holcombe to repeat the parody over and over again.

Peter Park, the handsome and perverted son of a doctor who became as time went on obsessed with Kitty, lost out to these poor country boys- who were light-hearted and fraternal. Fun. The problem with Peter Park was that while he was dramatic, handsome, mysteriously brooding, and gratifyingly consumed by Kitty, he wasn't much of a laugh. He could be very funny, but he was never light-hearted. He was dark, he was powerful, he was intense- but he lost out to the boys who made Kitty laugh.

Peter Park had formed Kitty, however, and the ghost of Peter Park remained. This was why Kitty was scoping out Mike's shoulder-to-hip ratio as he crossed the street to join her on the green. Peter Park had given Kitty a slim volume detailing the arts of seduction- there was something like a "body clock," and where you fell on this clock depended on your body shape- principally your shoulder-to-hip ratio. The entire thesis was that in order to find compatibility you had to find a partner opposite you on the clock. So if you were bottom-heavy, you needed someone top-heavy, and vice-versa. This schema had installed itself as dogma in Kitty's head, essentially displacing all human emotion in matters concerning the opposite sex.

So there sat Kitty squinting with concentration at her new boyfriend's approaching form. Kitty was convinced that she was pear-shaped. She had to be a 6 o'clock or a 7 o'clock. Only a narrow-hipped, broad-shouldered superman could redeem her. She needed a 12 o'clock or a 1 o'clock. Was Mike the one?

Sometimes Kitty felt certainty in her heart that Mike was the possessor of this golden ratio, that he could save her. Sometimes Kitty was not so sure. Sometimes a nagging doubt gnawed at Kitty that she had jettisoned Peter Park, who though at times earnest and boring, did have wide shoulders and slim hips- for naught. Mike did not make Kitty's job any easier with his goddam baggy pants. They turned his ass into an empty space above his knees, a space of zen no-ass. And then his posture was so shitty that his shoulders were rounded, it was hard to tell their exact dimensions.

Sometimes, in Kitty's darkest moments, she suspected that Mike's pants and his slouch were merely a ruse to throw her off the scent, that underneath this guise lurked a pair of shoulders and a pair of hips that would only drag her down. Deeper and deeper down into pear-shaped ignominy.

Sweetly sang the muses of the rare and radiant maiden the angels had rather conventionally named "Colleen Perkins." Known by friends, associates, and enemies alike as "Neena," the nickname with which her ("Equally notoriously slutty," muttered Kitty to Holcombe.) older sister lispingly christened her as a baby.

Neena Perkins. Though legend says she appeared one dawn on a crest of foam, more prosaically her accolades remain preserved for posterity in the Harrison Senior High School yearbooks (1990-1993):

8th Grade: Class President

9th Grade: Prettiest Eyes

10th Grade: Class Sweetheart

11th Grade: Everybody's Buddy

(Everybody's *body*," Kitty whispered hotly into Holcombe's eager ear.)

And the literally crowning culmination of a glorious high-school career in which unearthly female superiority was officially recognized and cemented for eternity:

12th Grade: Prom Queen.

"Hey." Mike slouched up to Kitty sitting on the bench by the fountain. He gave her a brief nod.

"Hey," she answered. She was thrilled. Out here in the freezing cold, not even mentioning the fact that they were skipping class. This was living.

"What are you smoking? Vagina Slims?" He grimaced.

Kitty feigned indignance. "Don't say that word!" she squealed.

"Vagina!" Mike shouted.

"Come on." Now Kitty was a bit displeased.

"They call 'em Vagina Slims so the sluts'll buy them," said Mike.

"Why would sluts care if their vaginas are slim?" asked Kitty.

"Tighter," said Mike.

"Mike!" she protested, genuinely shocked.

15

Together, they trudged up the hill to Vincent's to get a slice. They were getting a jump on the lunch-time crowd. Lunch was in half an hour, and Vincent's was about a block from the village green. There were a couple legit ways to get there-meaning basically either walk down the street or you could navigate a dark back alley-way, the latter being obviously a lot more fun when you're 17-years-old and you're going out.

There were two other people already there (Greg Bohling and Ben Ryan, also skipping the same study hall) when Kitty and Mike burst in out of the cold. Kitty's lipstick was all over Mike's chin. Mike casually nodded a greeting at Greg and Ben (Kitty trailed behind Mike, thrilled with her role as voiceless female accessory as only a girl who scored above 1400 on the SAT can be.). They picked a booth, sat down with their slices, and started eating.

This was Kitty's moment. "You want to hear something?" She swatted Mike's arm. "You know what fucking Jennifer Sheffield did to me in gym? I'm sitting around in my fucking *underwear* in the *locker room*, and you know what that bitch does to me?" She blew smoke sideways out of a corner of her mouth, as she'd seen it done. You could smoke in Vincent's. That was part of why people went there.

Incidentally, Kitty never sat around in her underwear in the locker room. Under no circumstances. This had never happened.

Ok, maybe, if one had been really *trying*, one could have stolen a forbidden glimpse of her underwear- possibly even of a duration significant enough to guess what color it was- but, given Kitty's habitual, furtive, speed-of-light, wardrobe transition (slinking her blouse under her t-shirt, whipping off the t-shirt once the blouse was buttoned, putting her skirt on over her shorts, easing down the shorts once it was zipped), this was not likely.

However, Kitty was nothing if not a good pupil, and she had gleaned from the book on the arts of seduction that a casual reference to herself in a vulnerable state of undress was guaranteed to pique the male's interest and render him putty in her hands. So Kitty said the word "underwear" and waited for Mike to be rendered putty in her hands.

"We're sitting around, half-*naked*," Kitty stressed, "and fucking Jennifer Sheffield is giving me all this shit like Neena wants to know why I hate her. It's such bullshit."

"You guys sit around half-naked in the locker room?"

Ah-hah. Interest *piqued*.

Wait, however. The point she was making here was that *she- Kitty-* was sitting around half-naked in her underwear. Kitty was trying to burnish her own allure here, she brokered no free-riders.

She paused a split second and considered. She knew it made for a sultry scenario: a locker room full of half-naked girls. And she also knew that the proper response would have to be a yes, because otherwise that would make her a weirdo sitting there alone half-naked. What was she going to say? "No, it was just me. That's what I do."? But Kitty was understandably loathe to sacrifice her individual half-nakedness to the greater good of general girls' locker room half-nakedness.

On the other hand, Mike was no idiot. If she told him that the Harrison Senior High girls' locker room was like the scene of a Turkish bath house, he was sure to hoot in disbelief.

"No, we don't sit around half-naked..." she began slowly, weighing her words carefully, "but obviously when you're changing, you know, and you're in your underwear, I mean, yeah, you're like, half-naked, but it isn't like we're all sitting *around* half-naked."

"You just said you were sitting around half-naked," Mike said flatly. For some reason he was not being putty in her hands, but was irritatingly bent on factual narrative as though she weren't even an attractive female. He reminded Kitty suddenly of her little brother: annoying.

"Yeah, but I just meant I was changing. Whatever, whatever." Kitty waved her hand dismissively. She wasn't going to let a lousy audience stop her show. She blew smoke, gave her cigarette a theatrical flourish and continued, "So I'm in gym class and fucking Gestapo agent Jennifer Sheffield basically gave me the fucking Spanish inquisition."

"So you're sitting there naked playing Gestapo and Inquisition?" Mike cracked. "Kinky."

Kitty ignored him. She had been waiting to tell this story since 4th period, which was like ten in the morning. The fact that he was not interested was not going to stand in her way. The story was bigger than him.

Anthropologically speaking what was going on was this: Neena Perkins was dominant, Neena Perkins was establishment, Neena Perkins was (drumroll, please) popular. So, to assert her dominance in a kind of head-gorilla sort of a way, Neena Perkins would sniff out unbelievers and send forth her ladies-in-waiting to isolate, interrogate, and force apologies from apostates. Kitty, whether she liked it or not, stood out as a heretic. Hence, periodically, Kitty would have to deal with Neena Perkins acolytes popping out of the shadows for sneak attacks like stealth ninjas. Particularly disarming was that the preferred method of attack of Neena's Army was passive-aggression, a tactic that Kitty was incapable of learning. It went like this:

Kitty was in study hall, or in gym-class, or in the library, or putting on makeup at the mirror in the girls' room, and suddenly, one of Neena's foot-soldiers would appear out of nowhere and sweetly but insistently demand:

"Why do you hate Neena?"

There was no good answer to this. That was the entire point of the question: to make you squirm.

So, invariably, the subject being interrogated would be forced to deny and pathetically remonstrate, entrenching themselves more firmly into a position of weakness. Kitty wondered what it would be like if, faced with one of Neena's emissaries, she responded to "Why do you hate Neena?" with reckless candor.

"Why do you hate Neena?"

"Because she's passively-aggressively sending her drones out to cut down any potential opposition in her path."

"Why do you hate Neena?"

"Because she's the epitome of ordinary, and for some reason that's worshipped."

"Why do you hate Neena?

"Because overlords forcing me to bend the knee aren't exactly my favorite people."

"Why do you hate Neena?"

"Because I can! Because she's there! Because as long as a corrupt, hive-minded, power structure worshipful of mediocrity exists, I will hate it."

But of course Kitty never said any of these things. What she usually did was simply protest weakly "I don't hate Neena!" Then of course Kitty started blushing and stammering because she *did*, rather naturally, hate Neena.

Later, Kitty would find some solace for the torture inflicted by these forced-apology and loyalty-oath sessions, by cursing Neena and Neena's high priestesses in private to trusted acquaintances. The more acute the public humiliation, the keener the private resentment. At second-period gym class that day, Kitty had been set upon by one of Neena's most loyal lackeys, Jennifer Sheffield, and Kitty was still nursing her wounds.

"She's like giving me all this shit, like, you know at first she's playing along doing all this bullshit chit-chat-" Kitty suddenly turned and glanced quickly behind her shoulder. No one was there. Reassured, she went on, "Like all this bullshit, wants to know what college I'm going to go to, etcetera, and then she's like telling me about this party at Neena Perkins' house after the prom, like we're friends or like I would consider going, and she's like, but I guess you wouldn't really want to go to Neena's house because you don't really like her. And I'm basically like, uh-huh, whatever, and then she's like, yeah, Neena said the other day, like, she thinks you're a really great person and, like, really smart- and she- *just doesn't know why you hate her!*" Kitty rolled out the punchline with a magnificent delivery: forcefully stubbing out her cigarette and exhaling smoke from her nostrils. She looked to Mike for his reaction.

There was none. Mike was absorbed in dipping his pizza slice in hot sauce. There was a greasy orange ring of hot sauce around his mouth.

"She doesn't know why I don't like her!" Kitty reiterated impatiently, raising her voice.

"And she fucking does this to everyone," Kitty went on without waiting for a response from Mike, which was good because none was forthcoming. "The minute she senses some *dissent within the ranks* she sends one of her fucking toady androids to go deal with it and wipe it out. And it's so fucking *passive-aggressive. That's* why I *hate* it!"

Kitty delivered this last line as though she had just realized this, and it was the first time she was saying it. In fact, she had been running through this speech in her head since the non-incident happened.

Kitty jabbed her index finger towards Mike's pizza, thumb cocked. "It's passive-aggressive. Like she's all sweet and hurt. Like she wants to be my friend. She's not my friend! And it's totally designed to make me look like I'm this jealous harpy going around hating Neena. I could give two shits about her."

With a hand that trembled slightly, Kitty plucked a Virginia Slim from the packet and lit it with one swift gesture, puckering her lips with the force of the drag. She drew her hand away from her mouth and looked at the tiny cigarette. It was indeed lit, but, my God, it was like a lollipop stick.

She folded her arms, elbows on the table. She looked at Mike steadily and raised her eyebrows, wrinkling up her chin in an expression of world weariness.

"I really could not care less. I don't give a fuck," she said.

"You smoke too much," Mike said. He did not like that she smoked. Kitty liked that about him, that he did not like that she smoked. Nihilistic Peter had loved her smoking.

"Why do you smoke so much?" Mike asked critically.

"I have to make room for my lighter and my inhaler," said Kitty.

Mike looked at her blankly.

"I hate carrying a purse, and I have nowhere to carry my lighter and my inhaler, so I just tuck them into my cigarette packet, see?" She demonstrated, opening the box of cigarettes to show a small lighter and a blue inhaler stuffed inside.

"Why don't you use matches?"

Kitty ignored him and continued in a level and rather pleased, didactic tone. "But in order to make room for both lighter and inhaler, I need to have about ten cigarettes inside, more or less. That means that when I buy a pack, I need to smoke about five cigarettes right off the bat just so I can carry around my inhaler and my lighter. Then, once I have room for them, there's like a golden period where I can carry everything together in my cigarette pack."

Mike was bored. He took a rolled-up *Thrasher* magazine from his back pocket and opened it on the table between them. There was no predicting his mercurial humors. What a fascinating creature.

"You drink, you smoke, you die," Mike pronounced in a strangled voice he called his "retard voice" as he thumbed through his skateboarding magazine. He was mocking straight-edge people. They didn't actually know any straight-edge people, but Mike's cousin who had moved to New York City did.

"And you don't drink, you don't smoke, what happens?" asked Kitty earnestly, almost angrily. "You *don't* die?"

"You become Mrs. Jones," Mike answered sagely. Mrs. Jones was the Health teacher. She taught sex education. The principal's son, after not as much prodding as it really should have taken, had gotten her to admit in class that she lost her virginity on her wedding night. Mrs. Jones was a widely celebrated joke.

Kitty laughed shortly, but only as tribute.

"I'm going to get Marlboros, I can't stand these shitty girly wuss-cigarettes," she declared, sliding out of the booth.

"Get me another Mountain Dew!" Mike called after her.

A few minutes later Kitty returned and set down the soda can in front of Mike. He didn't offer to pay, and she didn't ask.

Kitty took up her lament. "It just really annoys me, all this bullshit. So then I have to be like: No, I don't hate Neena, what are you talking about? And why has she set her sights on me all of a sudden? Remember when she did that to Emily last year? She sent Amy Ford to ask her at golf practice. And then we made that video. OH MY GOD!" Kitty locked onto Mike's wrist with one hand.

"What?" said Mike, "What?" She had his attention now because her nails were digging into his wrist. "Ow. Shit."

Kitty released her hold, gratified to have his attention again, and sat back.

"Dude she must have seen the video! That's why she sent Jennifer Sheffield after me!"

Kitty had suddenly remembered the video she made last year with her friends Emily and Sarah. Emily and Sarah had both been seniors last year. They had graduated, they were gone, and Kitty missed them. They were some of the only girls that were fun like guys were.

Kitty, Emily, and Sarah were always making videos when they were bored- that and driving around slowly playing British dance hits at "decibel pain level" as Kitty's mother called it, desperately trying to make eye contact with boys in other cars and shrieking hysterically when they did.

Last year the three girls had done a video they considered a masterpiece of underground resistance. It was entitled very pertinently "Why Do You Hate Nina?" All three girls had, at one point or another, been asked that question.

Kitty tried to tell Mike about the video they made mocking Neena, tried to convey to him just how awesome it was.

"We did this one skit, it's called 'Why Do You Hate Neena?' Emily and Sarah are sitting at the kitchen table talking. And Emily's like, Yeah I was talking to Neena the other day, and she wanted to know, Why do you hate her? And Sarah's like all scared like, No, I don't hate Neena, why would you say that, not at all. In fact, I like Neena, I like her a lot, I *love* her. And Emily's still like, We know you hate her, why do you hate her?"

"And then *I* show up!" Kitty continued, enjoying herself very much. "*I'm* Neena! And I'm like, 'Why do you hate me?' And the camera cuts back to Sarah at the kitchen table- and she's slumped over *dead*!"

Kitty tapped her cigarette on the ash tray and took a quick drag. She was animated. For the first time that day, Kitty seemed genuinely happy. But suddenly her expression clouded.

"Dude, if Nina finds out about that video, *I'm* dead."

"You want some?" Mike asked, proffering the Mountain Dew.

"It was really funny," said Kitty. "We poured ketchup all over Sarah for blood."

Kitty was smiling to herself. She looked over at Mike, he was perusing his magazine.

"You get it?" Kitty asked. "Killed by Neena?" She tapped the cigarette, took another drag. "They have coffee here, do they?" she asked.

"No," said Mike, "let's go to Dunkin, I'm sick of here anyway."

"Yeah, but we probably have like five minutes until next period, we don't have time."

"What do you have?"

"Health."

"You want to go to Health?"

"Noooo," said Kitty slowly.

"Is it the class where Mrs. Jones passes around condoms and diaphragms and lets everybody feel them?"

"We did that already."

"You know she takes them home afterwards and she and her husband use them."

Kitty laughed. "It's better than if they used them first."

Mike changed his voice to a falsetto, "Now, class, I want you all to put your fingers in this condom. Boys and girls, this is my husband's sperm."

Kitty laughed appreciatively, forgetting to feign shock.

Half an hour later they sat in a coffee-shop booth overlooking the school parking lot, not far from Vincent's. Mike had one donut sitting in front of him, powdered and creme-filled. Half a donut was in his mouth, half a donut in his hand. Kitty, cupping her coffee with both hands, lowered her lips to the rim and sipped loudly. A messy scarlet lip print appeared on the styrofoam. Mike spilled coffee on the front of his shirt. He raised the shirt to his lips and loudly sucked the coffee out of it. Kitty couldn't help watching with disgusted fascination.

"I'm freezing," she said grouchily when he was done. "How are we going to go and get our stuff back from school?"

"No problem," said Mike, mouth full of donut. "We'll just go in after school ends."

"I can never go back there again," Kitty proclaimed theatrically. "Dude, you know that, I can't go back there. I'm not going back to school. Neena must know I made that video making fun of her. Maybe she's even *seen* it. *That's* why she's sending Jennifer Sheffield after me. I'm a dead man walking," she concluded darkly.

"Why do you think they saw it?" asked Mike reasonably.

"We made the video at Emily's house, and we left it at her house, so the video's just been sitting there at the Roys' house, and all the stoners are going there like every day after school, right? It's in the Roy house somewhere. Can you ask Scott?"

Kitty desperately pleaded. Scott Roy was Emily Roy's little brother.

Kitty was not wrong that the Roy house received a lot of traffic. This was due to a combination of logistics and laxity. The Roy kids- Emily, Scott, and Joe- lived right next to the school, and their parents seemed to have a chip missing as far as noticing minor details like groups of kids congregating in their house and filling their son's room with smoke. The Roys' mom had gotten pregnant with Emily her freshman year of college and dropped out to get married. Apparently feeling she had missed out, she decided to devote the rest of her life to self-actualization. Self-actualization meant going back to school to complete her degree, yoga, shopping, gardening, wine-tasting, and ignoring calls from the principal complaining that her children were never in school. Mr. Roy ran a hardware store and was rarely home.

"Yeah, I can ask him," said Mike shortly, "he might not know, but I can ask him."

"Get the video from Scott," Kitty entreated him. "You're going there today, right?"

"Yeah, I might go there today. You have play practice?"

"Yeah, but I could meet you after," Kitty said, forgetting that she couldn't go to play practice without raising questions as to why she'd missed half the school-day.

Holcombe walked in and sat down on the edge of Mike's side of the booth.

"Move over," Holcombe ordered.

In physiognomy, Holcombe was like a cross between a young Ray Davies and a young Harpo Marx. He was wearing a strange, grey, military-issue pea coat he'd gotten from the Salvation Army, bell-bottom jeans, and Converse All Stars. Slung across his shoulder was his omnipresent leather satchel. Thirty years later it would be cool, but here in 1993...

"Are you gay?" Kitty had asked Holcombe curiously when they started being friends.

"No," said Holcombe, staring at her with his large, luminous, brown eyes.

"Are you Jewish?" Kitty countered without missing a beat.

"No," said Holcombe, still staring.

There was something different about Holcombe, that Kitty couldn't put her finger on. She wanted to quantify it.

Holcombe was Holcombe's last name. Nobody called him Justin but his mother.

They would hear it at the beginning of the school year when the teacher called attendance: "Justin Holcombe." And then everyone turned gleefully toward Holcombe, who never failed to meet their expectations.

Gravely raising an index finger, earnestly wrinkling his forehead, he would assert in his deep nasal voice: "That's me. But ahh....." Lowering his hand, clenching the desk before him, and leaning forward, his bright eyes fixed on the teacher, he would say nonchalantly, suavely, as though over cocktails:

"But, ah, they usually call me Holcombe. That is, just the, ah, just by my, ah, family name." And the class would hoot and holler on cue, shouting out what they considered better and more descriptive names for Holcombe and his family.

The teachers' reaction varied by temperament. The more tolerant and patient (younger and weaker) teachers would quiet the class, saying reasonably that there was no reason not to call someone by the name they requested. Elizabeth Jones, for example, wanted to be called Beth. Some teachers were suspicious of Holcombe, and sensed a deeper plot. They saw Holcombe as the class anarchist, inciting others to similar acts of rebellion which would finish with everyone calling themselves by whatever names they chose, some of which were bound to be obscene. So the crusty old teacher might say "All right, all right, that's enough." And go on to the next student.

However, what would invariably happen is that the teacher would start calling him "Holcombe" of her own accord. She would just slip into it. Part of it was the ill-suitedness to Holcombe of "Justin". There was nothing *wrong* with the name Justin. Holcombe had nothing to be *ashamed* of. It was just that it didn't suit him. Justin was the name of the lead singer of the latest boy band put together with re-constituted parts. Justin was the name of the character on "Malibu Heights" who was worshipped by preteens. Holcombe the freaky androgynous oddity just didn't work as a Justin.

For Holcombe himself there was something else at work. He never said "Call me Holcombe, everyone calls me by my last name." It was always *family* name. As though he were displaying a coat of arms or making some kind of solemn pronunciation like one tribal chief upon meeting another. They made fun of him, Kitty and Mike.

"*I am Holcombe, son of Holcombe,*" Kitty intoned. "I am Holcombe of the illustrious Harrison Holcombes, fabled in word and deed."

"Holcombe of the illustrious white-trash trailer-park Holcombes," said Mike.

If prolonged, this made Holcombe angry and almost tearful, his chin puckered slightly. He made as if to go and they stopped him. Even Kitty did not like this, did not go that far. She got a bad little feeling in her stomach, a slight shudder of fear and hurt if Mike said this. Because it was true. But Kitty didn't let Mike get away with it. She would give him back what he was giving, and say, Mike Connolly of the Faggot Connollys. As though what he had just said about Holcombe was on par with getting called a faggot. But while it was pretty obvious that Mike wasn't a faggot, Holcombe really *was* white trash.

Holcombe's father did live in a trailer park. Holcombe saw him every few months. He would come back from a visit full of his father's stories: his travels in the Navy, the time he hung out with Hell's Angels, the time he met Tom Petty. And when Holcombe told Kitty these stories she would think of Mike's teasing: Holcombe of the illustrious white-trash trailer-park Holcombes.

Both Holcombe and Mike were the product of teen romances, and both their fathers were bounders. They both had stepfathers. Holcombe's stepfather, a construction worker, was actually a distant cousin of Kitty's. He was a quiet man who took Holcombe hiking in the Adirondacks. There was no love lost between Mike and *his* stepfather. That was why Mike was rarely home.

"Move over," Holcombe repeated. He was still standing at the end of their booth. Kitty watched, amused. The fun had begun.

"No," said Mike, chewing.

26

"Holcombe, you can sit here with me," said Kitty, egging him on.

"I can't sit with my back to the street," growled Holcombe.

"Why can't you sit with your back to the street, Holcombe?" said Kitty, patiently baiting him.

"I just can't, that's all," he returned grouchily.

"Syphillis," Mike garbled through his donut.

"Um, you would need to be having *sex* to contract syphilis," Kitty suggested in a bright tone.

"Syphilis of the ear," said Mike shortly. "What time is it? Is school out?" he asked, picking up his second donut.

"No," Holcombe deadpanned, "we all just led a revolt and stormed the barricades, that's how we got out."

Mike paused briefly. His expression blank, he faked a glance towards Kitty, and then turned and pounced, lunging across the table at Holcombe, clenching his donut in one fist. Amazingly, Holcombe had already made an anticipatory feint to the left, bumping into Kitty.

"Hey!" she protested angrily.

"I'm gonna go get my skateboard," said Mike, meeting with equanimity his failure to tackle Holcombe. He got up with his donut, leaving all refuse on the table.

"Wait!" said Kitty, "Aren't you gonna go to Scott's house?" She gave him a significant look. "The video," she mouthed across the table. "Get the video."

"I can come back here after I get my board," Mike said.

"No, I have play practice. You wanna meet after play practice?"

"Yeah."

"At Vincent's?

"Yeah."

"I'll be there at six."

He started to leave.

"Kiss!" Kitty cried.

"Move," Mike told Holcombe, who was sitting on the outside of the booth.

"No," said Holcombe grumpily, "I'm sitting here."

Kitty stretched across the table toward Mike. Mike stood at the edge of the table, and they kissed. Holcombe was squashed between them. It was not a quick kiss, and it was not a neat kiss either.

"You are both disgusting," said Holcombe.

Kitty turned her head. "You're the one who wouldn't move, Holcombe." Her lipstick was a red grease stain on her chin. Mike kissed like he ate.

Mike put the hood of his sweatshirt up and sauntered through the door, not looking back. Kitty stared after his retreating back. She felt sure that underneath his slouched skater-rat posture, his shoulders were much wider than his hips.

"Fix your lipstick," Holcombe told her after Mike left, "you look like a woman of easy virtue."

"Actually, I am a woman of difficult virtue. It is very difficult for me to be virtuous!" Kitty crowed. "Heh? Eh? Pah-ritty slick, huh?" She cackled and nudged Holcombe in the ribs. Then, still chortling, she took a cigarette from her packet and tapped it on the counter.

"You are tapping it the wrong way," said Holcombe.

"What are you talking about?"

"You're tapping it the wrong way. You want to tap the filter end. You want to pack the tobacco further back *into* the cigarette, not tap it out of the cigarette."

Kitty put her mouth very close to Holcombe's head, next to the hair that covered his ear. "Shut up," she breathed hotly.

A flush spread upwards on Holcombe's neck. He rubbed his ear. "That's how I got ear syphillis."

Kitty planted a cigarette between her pursed lips. "Look, Holcombe, I need a favor," she mumbled, absorbed in lighting it. She inhaled and drew farther away from Holcombe. They were still sitting on the same side of the booth. She exhaled smoke almost directly into his face, he coughed and swatted.

"I wish you wouldn't do that," he said waspishly. He fanned the air around him with irritation. Holcombe didn't want Kitty to smoke either. For Kitty, smoking was a glamorous self-destructive way of slumming it. For Mike and Holcombe, who had relatives who had smoked and died of it, there was nothing exotic about it.

Kitty squinted at Holcombe through the smoke, one hand posed with the cigarette, staring him down. She ashed her cigarette needlessly and whittled down what remained of the burning cinder, stroking it meticulously against the black plastic ashtray.

"Can I ask you something, Holcombe?"

"You're not fat," he sighed.

"That *actually* wasn't what I was going to *ask* you, Shitty," Kitty hissed coldly, continuing, "Look, I need this favor. I'll buy you a pint [*Kitty means ice cream, not beer. –Ed.*]. There's this video at the Roy house I need you to get for me. Do you think you could? Do you think you could get it for me? Holcombe?"

"What video?" asked Holcombe.

"It concerns..." Kitty paused for effect and tried and failed to raise one eyebrow. "Neena Perkins."

"You want me to go get a video of Neena Perkins at Scott's house?" Holcombe asked curiously.

Kitty had a brainwave. She knew how to make Holcombe actually look for and find the video. "Let's just say," said Kitty, faking reluctance, "it's a video that depicts Neena in a...shall we say a...a rather *compromising* light." Kitty snickered.

"There's a pornographic film of Neena Perkins at Scott's house?" asked Holcombe matter-of-factly.

"Oh, chill out, Holcombe," said Kitty, tapping her cigarette. An idea seemed to occur to her, and she slowly turned her head to face him head on, "Why? Would *you* want to see it?"

"No," said Holcombe.

"Why? You like Neena Perkins?" Kitty knew Holcombe didn't like Neena Perkins. Kitty knew damn well which girl Holcombe liked.

"Why is Neena Perkins making pornos at Scott's house?" asked Holcombe, frowning. "The lighting there is terrible."

"Holcombe," said Kitty, "you are so gullible. Jesus. It's not a Neena Perkins porno. I was just kidding. It's just some stupid video. It doesn't matter. Nevermind. Anyway, it's got like a sticker on it, a white label sticker, with the title on it, it's "W-D-Y-H-N".

"W-D-Y-H-N?" asked Holcombe. "Where Did You Heave Nuggets?"

"Why do you hate Neena?" Kitty explained. "So can you just get it? I'll meet you after play practice, ok? I have to go. Let me out, Holcombe. Let me out!"

Holcombe didn't move, he kept sitting at the edge of the booth, smiling at Kitty. He shook his head. Kitty knew he loved her. It was fun.

"Hey Holcombe, you wanna hear a joke I made up? I made it up today. What do one third of Columbus's crew and the entire population of Harrison High School have in common?"

"Scurvy and a lust for gold."

"No," said Kitty impatiently, "What they have in common is *they all came on Neena*. Get it? Get it? They all *came* on Neena?"

Holcombe got up to let her pass. "That's really stupid," he said disgustedly.

"Niña, Pinta, Santa Maria?" said Kitty, "*Came* on? Get it?"

"I think I'm beginning to catch your drift," Holcombe said solemnly.

"Just get that video for me from Scott's house," Kitty answered. "There's a pint in it for you."

A few weeks earlier Kitty's mother had picked her up at Vincent's, and Holcombe was there, hanging out with Kitty until her ride came. When Kitty got into the car, her mother asked her if that was the "Mike" she had been talking about.

"He's good looking," said her mother, "got a sort of feline quality. Androgynous. Like Mick Jagger."

"Mom, *no*," said Kitty quickly. "That's *Holcombe*. That's my *friend*." Kitty looked out the window at Holcombe with new eyes, and then turned to her mother. "You really think he's good looking?" she asked.

Kitty cast a practiced eye on Holcombe's hips. To her surprise, his shoulder to hip ratio did indeed appear on superficial examination to pass the golden ratio test. Just barely.

# Chapter 3: While Scott's Parents Were Away

Holcombe high-tailed it to the Roy house as soon as he left Kitty; he was intrigued. He took the stairs two at a time. The Roys' old dog was lying in her bed on the porch. She stiffly rose to her feet, and greeted him by sniffing and tail-wagging.

"Hey Cocoa," said Holcombe, "good girl." He knelt down and rubbed her back and then her belly for a while. Then he rose and meticulously wiped his feet off on the doormat. He unceremoniously opened the door. The kitchen was empty, and he could hear strains of hardcore music coming from the living room.

Holcombe put his leather satchel on a chair at the kitchen table. He carefully took off his coat, folded it, and laid it on the back of the same chair. He made a beeline for the refrigerator, threw open the door, and stood intently surveying its contents. Hot dogs, cold cuts, two bottles of chocolate milk, eggs, a package of shredded mozzarella, and-

"Tapioca!" exclaimed Holcombe.

"*Holcombe!*"

"Aaaaaah!" Holcombe shouted, but he didn't turn around, he knew who it was. He snatched the tub of tapioca and cradled it to his chest.

Scott stood athwart the threshold between the kitchen and the living room, his arms akimbo, grasping the sides of the doorway, propping himself up. "I'm with stupid" his t-shirt said. It looked like the words had been scrawled onto a dirty undershirt with indelible pen in a drunken fit. This was indeed the case. His eyes were red.

Holcombe, still holding the refrigerator door open, regarded Scott over his right shoulder, while protectively sheltering the tub of tapioca. "You *scared* me," he said reproachfully.

"I scared *you*! What the fuck, Holcombe? What the fuck are you doing in my fucking kitchen with the fucking refrigerator door open?"

Holcombe was at his most dignified in such situations. He drew himself up. "What are people *generally* doing when they stand with the refrigerator door open? Looking for something to eat, I should think," he answered haughtily.

"Holcombe, you don't *do* that!" Scott insisted, his voice rising to a hysterical pitch. "You don't walk into somebody's kitchen and stand there with the refrigerator door open. Were you *raised* in a *barn*?"

"Christ," growled Holcombe, "What's eating *you*?"

Scott lunged. For a big, stolid, clumsy-looking boy he was very fast. He quickly got Holcombe's head in a chokehold and inserted it into the interior of the refrigerator and held it there. Scott's face was expressionless- actually Scott's face was almost always expressionless- and his attitude was purposeful. Holcombe squirmed, but he couldn't break the chokehold. Scott had about half a foot on Holcombe.

"You just don't *do* that," Scott repeated, in a pleading voice that sounded pained.

"Scott," said Holcombe, muffled. "You're freaking out."

"Out!" shouted Scott. He dragged Holcombe in a headlock to the door, opened the door with one hand, pushed Holcombe out, and quickly slammed the door.

"Good God," Scott muttered, locking the door. He shook his head and ambled back to the living room. Scott had standards.

Mike was in the living room, stretched out on his back on the couch with the bottoms of his feet toward the tv screen. His big toe poked through a hole in one sock. The remote was on his chest. There was a bag of chips on his abdomen. On the floor was a plastic container of French Onion dip, studded with tiny shards of potato chip. "Man, you have to see this," Mike murmured when Scott came in. He picked up the remote, still staring at the screen.

"That was Holcombe," said Scott.

"You have to see this," repeated Mike, without looking away.

"I just kicked him out. Do you know what that fucker *did*?"

"Dude, check this out," said Mike. "Seriously, watch this shit."

"He walks into my goddam *kitchen*, doesn't even fucking bother to knock, just walks in and stands there with the refrigerator door open. What a waste of *electricity*." Scott's voice was getting high-pitched again.

"Yeah," said Mike still staring at the screen. "What's that?"

"What?" asked Scott.

There was another bump.

"That," said Mike.

"Holcombe," explained Scott. "I kicked him out."

A fast insistent knocking began outside the kitchen door. Mike stood up, displacing chips, and narrowly missing stepping in the dip.

"Hey, watch out for the bong," said Scott, moving it out of Mike's path.

Mike walked through the kitchen to the kitchen door, put his mouth to the keyhole, and cupped his hands.

"Your mother is a whore," he enunciated loudly.

The knocking paused for a moment, then continued with renewed vigor. Scott returned to the kitchen to join the fun. Mike unlocked the door and held it open about an inch.

"What do you want?" Mike asked.

"Come on," said Holcombe. He glowered at Mike through the crack in the door. "Let me in. I left my coat in there." Without warning, he thrust his left shoulder and left knee into the space between the door and the frame.

Mike and Scott threw themselves against the door as one. Holcombe gave way, and it shut with a slam.

Scott locked it again. "Was that the Belgium tour?" he asked Mike. He was referring to the skateboarding video.

"Yeah," said Mike. He nonchalantly walked over to the refrigerator and took out a bottle of chocolate milk. They went back to the living room. Mike reinstalled himself on the couch with the remote. Scott sat back in an easy chair, laid the bottle of chocolate milk on the floor next to his chair, picked up the bong, put it between his knees, lit the pot stashed in it, and sucked down a large hit.

"When are your parents coming back?" Mike asked.

Scott couldn't answer, and he didn't. Then: "Saturday afternoon," he exhaled.

"Oh, man, are you going to school tomorrow?"

"Umm, yeah. Right." said Scott, "I really miss it." He snorted.

"I can't believe I have detention all day tomorrow." Mike groaned, staring up at the ceiling. "Baker is such a fucking cock!" He turned to Scott. "Is he in the phone book?"

"I don't know" Scott answered listlessly. "Why'd you get detention?"

"He fucking saw me in the hall with my board after class and then he was telling me it's not allowed in school, like it's an AK-47 or something."

"It's because that of that school shooting in New Jersey," said Scott. "He was a skateboarder."

"I know. Fucking Draper is writing a paper on that shit for Connolly's class. He *interviewed* me in study hall this morning."

There was a thump at the window.

"Shit," said Scott. "What an asshole." He sprang up, put the bong safely away, and drew open the curtain. Holcombe's face glared up at them balefully.

"My coat!" Holcombe bellowed- they could hear him through the closed window- and recommenced pounding on the bottom of the window sill with his fist.

"Shit! The neighbors!" Scott sprinted to the kitchen door.

"Wait!" Mike called after him. He followed Scott into the kitchen, picked up Holcombe's coat from the chair, opened the door, tossed it into the back yard, slammed the door, and laughed. Scott wordlessly pushed past Mike out the kitchen door. He picked Holcombe's coat out of the bushes next to the porch and went around to the front of the house, where Holcombe was still pounding the living room window sill.

Mike went back to the living room and half-heartedly rooted around in the couch cushions for the bong. "Fuck it," he finally said, picked up the remote control, and laid down again on the couch.

Scott and Holcombe came back in together through the kitchen door. Scott was saying emotionlessly, "You are a fucking pain in the ass, you know that?"

"I *want* tapioca," Holcombe insisted. "You *owe* me."

"Pain in the ass," Scott conceded tiredly.

Holcombe returned to the refrigerator. The tub of tapioca was on the shelf where he'd stashed it after Scott got him in the chokehold. The spoon was still buried in it.

"This tapioca isn't the good kind," said Holcombe critically, standing with the refrigerator door open again.

"You'll have nothing and like it or you'll have the door," said Scott from his seat in the living-room easy chair. He looked over at Mike for corroboration, but Mike was staring at the tv screen, mouth slightly agape.

"I'll have the door?" said Holcombe. "What does that even mean?" He laughed.

A couple minutes later Holcombe strode into the living room carrying the tub of tapioca. He was barefoot. He sat down on the other easy chair opposite Scott. He put down the tapioca on the floor, crossed his left leg over his right and began to examine his left big toe. There was a stubborn piece of skin on the cuticle. Holcombe brought his toe to his mouth. Scott jumped up and grabbed the plastic tub.

"Shoes on!" he commanded. "Only tapioca if *shod*."

"Fuck you," said Holcombe indignantly. "You guys got mud all over my coat."

"Your coat is a piece of shit," Mike said absent-mindedly, in a sing-song voice, staring at the screen.

"It's my cousin's," said Holcombe indignantly.

"Your cousin's a piece of shit," came the immediate response.

"That's what *he* said," said Holcombe irrelevantly.

Nobody said anything.

"Did you see that?" Mike turned to Scott. "Infuckingcredible." He pressed "rewind" again.

"You have to be stoned to think that crap is interesting," said Holcombe.

"Holcombe," warned Scott.

"I brought Fawlty Towers," Holcombe offered.

The other two ignored him. He retrieved the tapioca from the coffee table. Scott pretended not to notice. On a shelf next to the tv, there was a row of videotapes neatly lined up. Holcombe got up, walked over to the shelf, and stood perusing the videotape titles while complacently spooning tapioca into his mouth.

"Holcombe," said Scott, casting a glance toward Mike, "Who said you could paw through my videos?"

"This one's mine."

"Holcombe." It was another warning.

"I'm looking for Neena Perkins's porno tape," said Holcombe.

Scott and Mike both turned. Holcombe had their full attention now.

"Holcombe? What the fuck are you talking about?" Scott asked slowly.

## Chapter 4: Holcombe Ruins Kitty's Life

Darkness was falling as Kitty crossed Vincent's parking lot. She was wearing a black shiny plasticky raincoat, belted at the waist. Around her neck was tied a silk, crème-colored scarf. She was freezing her ass off.

"Holcombe!"

Kitty's voice gave the game away. A foreigner might have thought "Holcombe" was a political slogan or that the young girl was yelling "freedom" or "justice" in her language. If the foreigner had understood that the word was a name, then he would have understood that the young girl loved the person whose name she was calling across the empty lot.

"Holcombe!"

Holcombe- leaning against the side of Vincent's, hands in pockets, newspaper under his arm, collar of his cousin's piece-of-shit coat drawn up, plaid scarf around his neck- did not succeed at hiding his pleasure. The scarf had provoked not a few accusations of "Eurofag." He was faintly reminiscent of a photo of Jack Kerouac Kitty had once seen.

"Come to my arms my beamish boy! Oh frabjous day! Callooh! Callay! She chortled in her joy!" Kitty cried as she approached. She could be herself around Holcombe. But when she reached him, her tone became business-like.

"Are you *trying* to look like a Eurofag Jack Kerouac?"

Holcombe stopped leaning against the wall and took his hands out of his pockets.

"I'm freezing my ass off," said Kitty. "Did you get the video?"

"No," said Holcombe, "Scott said that he didn't have any Neena Perkins porno."

Kitty blinked; her eyes widened. "What?"

"He didn't know what you were talking about. He said to tell you he doesn't have any Neena Perkins porno tape."

"WHAT!" Kitty shrieked. She threw her bag to the ground and raised her arms to the sky. She sank to her knees and buried her face in her hands.

Holcombe squatted next to her huddled body. "You don't have to get so melodramatic about it. It's not like it was *your* porno or anything."

Kitty seized the lapels of Holcombe's coat and pulled his face very close to hers. He wobbled, off balance. She violently tugged the collar of his coat. He fell to his knees. Their faces were so close they felt each other's warm breath. Kitty looked deep into his eyes.

"YOU ASSHOLE."

Her teeth were clenched together. She was shaking with rage. She pushed him away violently, and he fell back on his rump. He had an erection.

Kitty dropped her face back into her hands. She rocked her body back and forth.

"You stoopid *asshole*," she moaned. "You told Scott about the video? And you told him it was a porno of Neena Perkins?" Her voice was thick with muffled tears. She gave a little choke. "You told him you were looking for a porno of Neena Perkins," she repeated dully. She was still rocking. She hugged her knees.

"He doesn't care," Holcombe asserted. He stood up. Kitty remained rocking herself in fetal position on the cold cement ground of the parking lot.

"I was just kidding," said Holcombe uncertainly. "I didn't tell him I was looking for a porno of Neena Perkins."

Kitty squinted up at him through tears. "Forget it," she said. She had started crying for real. "Just forget it. Scott is going to tell people I said Neena Perkins made a porno at his house. They're going to find the video we made making fun of Neena. It's all going to come back to me. I'm not going back. I'm never going back to that school. Everyone hates me. You want to run away with me, Holcombe? Just go?"

"Yes," said Holcombe simply. "Where?"

Kitty put her chin on her arm, still hugging her crossed knees. Her stocking was torn, and there were little bits of gravel stuck to her knee.

"California," she said. She looked at Holcombe and spoke in a reasonable tone. "We could go to California. And we could finish high school there. And then we could be state residents and we could go to state schools in California really cheap."

Holcombe stared at her fixedly. "Okay," he said quietly.

"Where's Mike?" she asked.

"He's still at Scott's. He's fucked. He has all-day detention tomorrow."

"Why?"

"Cuz Mr. Baker caught him in the hall with his skateboard. I warned him. It's because that kid in New Jersey shot his girlfriend."

"What? What are you talking about?"

"He was a skateboarder."

"Oh, that's rich," said Kitty bitterly. "That's perfect. American logic. Fucking retards. Guy with a skateboard shoots his girlfriend, so ban all skateboards. I know what we can do, we can talk about how skateboards are corrupting our youth, then we can pray for the souls of the dearly departed."

"He shot her in gym class." said Holcombe soberly. "They were outside playing softball, she was right-fielder, and he shot her.

"Then they should ban gym class," said Kitty. "Here, help me up, would you?"

She gave Holcombe her hand, and he helped her to her feet. She turned her attention to her knees, rubbing the tiny stones out of them, her knees were red and dimpled from the gravel.

"Let's go to France," she said. "Jesus, Holcombe, I told you it was a joke. Jesus Christ, Holcombe, I told you it was a joke, and now, shit.... I can never go back there. I'm never going back to school."

"You want to go to Scott's?" asked Holcombe. "His parents aren't coming back till Saturday, and I think he still has beer."

"Yeah, Holcombe, I really want to go to Scott's house and chill out and drink beer with him now. He either thinks I'm like this rampant lesbian looking for some Neena Perkins porno tape or he thinks I'm out of my mind."

Holcombe shrugged. "Scott doesn't care."

Kitty's troubles flooded back to her. "Now Scott's going to tell everybody I said there was a Neena Perkins porno tape. That was a *joke*, Holcombe! I was *joking*! I just thought you would actually look for the video if I told you it was a porno. It was just this video I made last year with Sarah and Emily making fun of Neena. Which Neena's probably already seen at Scott's house. And which, if she hasn't, she's definitely going to find out about now that you told Scott about it. I'm gonna kill you," she finished. "I swear."

She lit a cigarette. "Why didn't Mike come? What's he doing?" She sounded hurt.

"I told you, he's fucked up and he's watching skate videos. He's probably asleep by now."

"Shit *Almighty*," Kitty moaned. It was her uncle's favorite curse. "There's no way I'm going to classes tomorrow. I'm not going back until this whole Neena Perkins thing blows over."

"Yeah?" said Holcombe, turning to look at Kitty. He sounded hopeful.

## Chapter 5: Kitty and Holcombe Skip School

Kitty had become friends with Mike and Holcombe around the same time. To relate how, a brief comparative discussion of the management practices of slave populations in America versus Brazil pertains.

In America, broadly speaking, the modus operandi for managing slaves from various tribes was to uniformly weaken them by robbing them of all identity, taking away their names, languages, and culture. In Brazil, on the other hand, the general strategy was to emphasize tribal rivalries and play the different tribes off against one another, a sort of "divide and conquer" tactic.

The administrative officials at Kitty's high school favored the Brazilian method. This is the only possible explanation for the high-school intramural volleyball tournament.

In theory, the tournament was supposed to be a friendly competition where half a dozen friends could sign up to become a team and play other groups of half a dozen friends, all in a spirit of healthy sportsmanship and good fun. Whose theory this had been, Kitty was unsure. Absolutely foreseeably, the intramural volleyball tournament's actual effect was to transform casual affiliations who pretty much ignored non-affilates into definite, discrete, warring tribes complete with names, uniforms, and scorecards.

The football jocks formed a team, the soccer jocks formed a team, the Honors nerds formed a team, even the stoners and the heavy metal guys formed teams. And, for lack of a better word, the freaks also formed a team. That was Mike and Holcombe's team.

Each team had a name, which- heartbreakingly- was not permitted to be profane, vulgar, violent, or illegal. This meant that teams had to sit around and think up names that evoked profane, vulgar, violent, or illegal concepts without explicitly mentioning them.

The football team, after a series of rejections for profanity, finally settled on calling themselves "The Champions." ("Lame," Kitty groaned to Mike.) The soccer team did the football team one better by cleverly calling themselves "Battas," which everyone knew meant "Badass" except for, apparently, the teachers. The Honors nerds called themselves "The Hobbits," which was irritatingly typical. ("They should've called themselves 'The Dwarves'" Kitty muttered to Mike. "They should've called themselves 'The Gollums,'" Mike countered.) The heavy metal guys, after having "Kill 'Em All" rejected outright, even though it was indignantly protested that it was the name of a popular album, finally just called themselves Metallica and were done with it. The stoners, in what was either an existential breakthrough or just simple laziness, proposed to call themselves "The Stoners." Mr. Crawford the gym teacher just wordlessly shook his head at them and contemplated early retirement. The stoners ended up calling themselves "Floyd."

For some mysterious reason, Mike and Holcombe's team was called "Polish Wedding," after the sausage. Kitty never knew why. Mike was team captain. Brian Decker, Carson Reeves, Joe Roy, Chris Tanner, and Kitty's little brother were all on the team. Kitty was part of the team, but she wasn't a player, she and Maura had been asked to serve as cheerleaders. So Kitty and Maura gamely showed up in fishnets, miniskirts, and flat basketball shoes- basically looking like Roller Derby girls- to wield some huge black pom-poms and shout encouragement. Their actual function was essentially just to annoy the administration, who hadn't thought to ban the use of cheerleaders.

Holcombe was the team mime. Kitty loaned him her black tights and her black turtleneck. His function was to publicly convey support for the players through pantomime. To their later regret, it hadn't occurred to the administration to ban mimes either.

It was when Kitty handed off her black tights to Holcombe for his mime costume that she realized he was in love with her. She had started hanging out with her little brother's friends a few months before. That's when she and Holcombe became friends. On one of the first occasions Kitty ever hung out with Holcombe, the group was aimlessly killing time, loitering on school grounds after class, when they encountered a group of 2nd grade boys on their way home. They started horseplaying with them- pretending to fight them and swinging them around. The little boys shrieked with laughter, but amid all the shenanigans one boy fell, skinned his knee, and started to cry.

Kitty was surprised to see Holcombe patiently take the little boy by the hand and go with him inside the school to wash his knee. This is a person, she thought.

Kitty showed up to the intramural game with the black tights and the black turtleneck, and asked where she could give them to Holcombe. Someone said he was in the locker room, so Kitty stood outside the boys' locker room holding the black tights and yelling "Holcombe!" He emerged in his underwear. Kitty squealed and flung the tights at him. He caught them with one hand.

"Can I use some of your makeup?" he asked, grinning mischievously.

"Pervert!" Kitty cried, but she dug through her backpack and came up with foundation, lipstick, and eyeliner, and handed them off to him. It was for a great cause.

There was something about the way Holcombe stood in his underwear in the doorway, completely ridiculous, completely vulnerable, large luminous eyes gazing adoringly at her, that made Kitty realize that he was hers to do with what she would. It gave her a thrill of satisfaction. Power.

"Polish Wedding" were playing "Battas" that day, the soccer team. The soccer players had been dressed and ready for about fifteen minutes. They were languishing on the front row of bleachers, waiting for "Polish Wedding." They wore their soccer uniforms, because it was easier than coming up with a new uniform, and they were all on the soccer team anyway.

"Polish Wedding" made their entrance to "Flashlight" by Parliament. The music came from a boom box Mike carried on his shoulder as he strutted in, dancing. He was wearing his characteristic big pants and a lady's bouffant-style wig. Carson was next, wearing a coon-skin cap. Brian came after him in an aviator hat, complete with goggles. Hugh came next, wearing a deerstalker and clasping a pipe between his teeth. Chris followed him in a gorilla mask. He paused periodically to clasp his hands together and shake them in triumph over his head, like a boxer. Kitty and Maura came next in fishnets and miniskirts, shaking black pom-poms. Holcombe brought up the rear: leaping, prancing, and miming away. It is not easy to mime being trapped in a box while dancing, but Holcombe managed.

The whole thing looked like the entrance procession to a gypsy wedding.

The soccer players were sitting at attention now, contemplating their adversaries with mingled contempt, disgust, and outrage. The gym teachers, Mr. Crawford and Ms. McLanahan, had pained expressions on their faces. All they had ever wanted was an easy life and to share their joy of athletics with young people. The students in the bleachers, except for a few boos here and there, cheered appreciatively.

A couple of the soccer players sprang up and ran to Mr. Crawford and Ms. McLanahan. They stood before them complaining bitterly, gesturing toward "Polish Wedding."

"Ok," said Mr. Crawford, getting up tiredly. "No music," he told the members of "Polish Wedding," "No hats. You girls and, uh, *you*," he said with distaste, meaning Holombe, "you can stay but you can't be on the court."

Mr. Crawford deeply despised Holcombe and his traveling mime act, but he was too experienced not to realize that he couldn't publicly admonish him and prohibit him from miming without making himself look silly, and, in a worst-case scenario, provoke an audience revolt that could very well result in having to deal with two dozen renegade mimes instead of just one.

Kitty and Maura were terrible cheerleaders, they instantly lost all interest in the game and started cheering on Holcombe the mime instead. Holcombe mimed chopping wood.

"He's chopping wood!" cheered the girls. They shook their pom-poms. "Yay!"

Holcombe mimed peeling a banana.

"He's peeling a banana!" cheered the girls. They shook their pom-poms. "Yay!"

Holcombe mimed hitting a home run. He swung the bat, dropped it and shaded his eyes with one hand, squinting at the horizon. Suddenly filled with paroxysms of joy, he started trotting across the bases. "Home run!" cheered the girls. "Yay!"

Holcombe mimed unbuckling his belt, pulling down his pants, and sitting down. "Holcombe!" the girls shouted, shocked. Holcombe quickly stood up with a guilty look on his face. He mimed pulling his pants back up. "Yay!" cheered the girls, shaking their pom-poms.

You could tell the soccer players wanted to kick Holcombe's ass, mainly by the number of times they came up to him and told him this. They had utterly no sense of humor about the whole thing, Kitty thought.

Even more frustrating for the soccer players, about midway through, the game came to a halt when six-feet-tall Scott Roy stalked into the auditorium carrying a giant white sheet of posterboard. Silently holding it aloft, he walked slowly and deliberately past the crowd in the bleachers. The sign said merely "FREE ELI." It was a political statement. Eli was in detention.

The crowd went wild. "Free Eli! Free Eli!" the cheerleaders shouted. "Yay!" They shook their pom poms. Holcombe mimed grabbing the prison bars of a cell window with both hands and rattling them desperately.

The day after Kitty decided to skip school to avoid the ramifications of the Neena Perkins porno rumor, Holcombe was in the coffee shop at nine o'clock sharp.

Holcombe's hair was wet and lay in spikes on his forehead. He sat in the booth farthest from the entrance. Holcombe was always broke, so there was nothing on the counter in front of him, just his two hands and between them a book. His fingers were stubby, the nails were bitten and the ring finger of his right hand was strangely thickened by a break that hadn't been treated. This gave his right hand the look of an old man's hand, deformed by arthritis.

The book was an ancient paperback, maybe twenty-five years old. Holcombe seemed to be in a state of deep concentration. The title was in pink swirly letters: "Nana" by Gustave Flaubert. The cover featured a cartoonish drawing of Nana as a can-can dancer, merrily jiggling a gartered thigh as she held open her petticoats, a large and expressly errant lock of reddish hair trailing over her stark white shoulder and enormous cleavage. But there persisted something of the co-ed in this early sixties American Nana with her perky nose and solid white bar of undifferentiated tooth. Underneath the title, the cover claimed "She set Europe aflame!"

"Hey, Holcombe, you *aflame* yet?" Kitty stood over him grinning. Holcombe had been reading Nana for two weeks, and the joke was certainly old, but not yet stale. It was just that there are so many variations one can make with a joke of this kind. Kitty was wearing a black beret, there was a thin leather thong tied around her neck. She had on worn black jeans and combat boots and a brown leather jacket with a hood. For once she looked like she was dressed warmly enough. She was dressed to skip school, and there was no telling where they might go, so it was best to dress for being outside.

Holcombe looked up at Kitty standing over him. "I made you a mixtape," he said with a quiet intensity, shoving a cassette towards her.

"Thanks!" Kitty said enthusiastically. Holcombe's mixtapes were in fact the stuff of legend. She looked this one over. It was entitled "There Is No Accounting for Paste." Holcombe tapes always had genius titles, themes, artwork. He had just finished a series of tapes for Kitty called "Soundtrack to a Movie Never Made Volumes 1-4." She read the enclosed card: The Kinks, The Velvet Underground, The Cars, Steely Dan, The Bonzo Dog Band (natch), Ween, Frank Zappa, Herbie Hancock.

"Thanks!" Kitty repeated. "I'm going to get a coffee. Do you want anything?"

Holcombe wanted a hot chocolate and an egg and cheese on a bagel. He watched Kitty go the counter. Before, they had always skipped school with Mike, but Mike was in detention today.

Holcombe did have a feline quality, as Kitty's mother had remarked. He also had an androgynous quality at odds with his voice, which was deep and tending toward nasal. His eyes were large, soft and limpid, sometimes he seemed to be nothing but eyes. They never pierced or penetrated. They glowed rather, or shined. His nose was of the cute variety. It was flattish and turned up slightly at the tip. There was a mole under the right side of his lip, on his chin. His hair was curly and in a longish-short or shortish-long haircut, like the Beatles circa 1967.

Kitty came back, carrying the coffees and the bagel. "Holcombe, you're such a weirdo you can't buy a normal fucking porno like everybody else? You have to read, like, *19th century* porn?" Again, this was ground that had been covered, but it was too good to let go. "You should go to Adult World and ask them for something that'll set you aflame. I was wondering whether you have anything that would, uh, set me, you know, *aflame*," she muttered, eyes downcast, then looked up and guffawed. Holcombe ignored her.

"Soooo, where should we go today?," asked Kitty. Our options are: the college, the mall, uh, the college, the mall...we could go liberate Mike!"

Holcombe didn't want to liberate Mike. Holcombe wanted to liberate Holcombe. "Are your parents home?" he inquired casually.

"Yes," said Kitty. "Not that."

"Is the station wagon there?"

"No!" answered Kitty ferociously. "And you realize you're never driving it again, right?"

Sometimes Kitty got to drive her parents' station wagon, and, whenever she did, Holcombe would beg like a dog for her to let him drive. On the last occasion Kitty got her parents' car, they used it to drive to go get fast food. It had been Kitty, Mike, Holcombe, Kitty's little brother Hugh, and Brian. Kitty wanted to get a burger and eat it in the car, so she relented and allowed Holcombe to drive.

They were on Route 5, going about 55, when Holcombe suddenly swerved, veered at a 90 degree angle, and, with a screeching of tires, peeled into a parking lot.

"*Bob Mullum!*" Holcome shouted when the car had stopped.

Bob Mullum was a rather bland ordinary kid in their grade, chiefly known for being fat. Kitty, who had been sitting in the passenger seat chattering blithely, immediately panicked, fell to pieces, and began shrieking "Where?! Where?!" under the misapprehension that Holcombe had run over Bob Mullum.

This caused Hugh, in the back seat, to start yelling in return "I'm ok! I'm ok!" under the belief that it was him Kitty was worried about. There was groaning from Brian, who was also in the back. Mike had elbowed him in the head when the car swerved.

When the commotion died down, all the passengers turned as one enraged mob upon Holcombe.

"What the *fuck* are you *doing*, Holcombe?" demanded Brian, who was usually quite even-tempered but who could have had his nose broken and did end up with a very mild version of a black eye.

"He's a palindrome," said Holcombe slowly and wonderingly. "Bob Mullum is a total palindrome. Both 'Bob' and 'Mullum'."

Mild-mannered Brian shot up from his seat, clutched onto the head rest, and began slapping Holcombe on the back of the head.

"The keys!" Kitty bellowed, and started wrestling them out of Holcombe's hand. When Holcombe resisted, Hugh joined in, in a rare moment of Burnes sibling cooperation.

Only Mike was impressed by the epiphany regarding the palindromic nature of Bob Mullum's name.

"Bob. B-O-B. Mullum. M-U-L-L-U-M. How about that," he murmured appreciatively from the back seat.

This was why Holcombe was not allowed to drive Kitty's parents car.

A shuttle service, free for college students, runs from the college in Harrison to the nearest biggest city- the Upstate New York shithole that has been dying on its feet for the past eighty years.

Kitty and Holcombe walked to the college bus stop. It was cold and fresh and sunny. The streets were quiet. They could have by-passed the school, but they didn't bother. It was second period. Kitty would be in English class right now. Holcombe was missing Social Studies. It was April so there were still piles here and there of dirty snow. The sky was blue, their cheeks were pink, and they walked with their hands in their pockets as neither had gloves. The morning tasted like promise, and their brilliant future (this was only the beginning) stretched out before them like their day of freedom, and on into the weekend, promising vague lovely things.

Holcombe, from the wrong side of the tracks, and Kitty, from the right side of the tracks, had a funny thing in common. Although both excellent students and both easily qualifying for the Harrison High School Honor Society in terms of GPA, both had been denied admission.

Kitty thought she knew why they hadn't let her in. The teacher running the Honor Society was Ms. Johnson. Ms.

Johnson, the English teacher, was a diminutive white lesbian whose main passion in life was Alice Walker. A portrait of Alice Walker greeted students entering Ms. Johnson's classroom. On Ms. Johnson's desk stood a row of Alice Walker's books encased in custom leather book-ends. They were all signed by Alice Walker.

All of Ms. Johnson's English students were familiar with the intimate details of Mrs. Johnson's Alice Walker obsession, whether they wanted to be or not (and most of them did not), because Ms. Johnson would regale them with anecdotes about herself and Alice Walker. Ms. Johnson met Alice Walker at a book-signing. Alice Walker smiled at Ms. Johnson. Ms. Johnson felt faint in the great woman's presence.

One of Ms. Johnson's most prized possessions was an actual letter that Alice Walker sent her, in reply to her many fan letters. All of Ms. Johnson's English classes heard about that letter.

Kitty sat in the first row of Ms. Johnson's 11th grade English class. On one occasion when Ms. Johnson was relating the contents of the letter she received from Alice Walker, Mrs. Johnson became so inspired during the course of her own narration that she suddenly stopped in mid-sentence, used a small key attached to a bracelet she was wearing to open a drawer in her desk, whipped out the magical letter, and brandished it before the class.

"And here in the last paragraph," Ms. Johnson said breathlessly, "Alice Walker calls me a lovely person. 'You sound like a very lovely person.' Right here. Towards the bottom."

"Here," said Ms. Johnson, seizing upon Kitty, the nearest student, "Read aloud what it says right here."

Kitty squinted at the letter Ms. Johnson was holding in front of her face. She followed Ms. Johnson's stubby finger to where it was pointing.

"You sound," Kitty slowly read aloud to the class, "like a very *lonely* person."

The classroom immediately erupted in howls of laughter, and Ms. Johnson snatched the letter away from Kitty's blaspheming eyes and held it to her chest.

"No, it *doesn't*," Ms. Johnson responded with energetic hostility. And her deep-seated enmity for Kitty was cemented.

Kitty suspected that this was why, although her grade point average was more than adequate, she had not been invited to join the Harrison High School Honor Society.

Kitty and Holcombe walked slowly, relishing their liberty. They tried to see if they could name every song in the Beatles' White Album in order; they could. Kitty told Holcombe that she was practicing a new sexy walk. It had to do with consciously letting each buttock drop down behind her as she walked, one at a time. She made him stop behind her for a moment and watch her walk from the back. He pronounced it the same as ever, she told him he wouldn't even know what a sexy walk *was*, and they continued on.

The bus dropped them off at the mall. The driver hadn't even asked them for college ID, which was exhilarating. Kitty wanted to go to the new giant super-pharmacy. She had a commission for Holcombe. The pharmacy had just been built and would, a couple years later, get smart and put an alarm system around its "Health and Beauty" department, but as Kitty and Holcombe passed through the automatic doors at the entrance on this April day, there was no alarm in place.

Kitty walked purposefully, her heart beat hard. She had the money in her pocket for what she wanted. But why would she spend it when Holcombe, among his many other talents, was a consummate shoplifter.

The giant pharmacy featured discount products of every variety. They headed for the back, the Health and Beauty section.

"What do you think of the white eye shadow?" Kitty asked.

Holcombe thought it was okay, but not with enough enthusiasm to please her.

"But," she asked him, "do you think it goes with my *type*?"

Kitty had told Holcombe about the book. She told him about her new-found theories concerning body-type clock, compatibility, and the hip-to-shoulder ratio. Holcombe was the only person she had ever told. She would never tell Mike. Holcombe somehow didn't count, she had no need to practice her magic on him. But at the same time, he could provide male feedback- the best kind, in fact, since he was in love with her.

According to this treatise on the art of seduction, females with wide hips were naturally submissive and should wear light colors. Nurses' uniforms were presented as the ideal. Kitty believed in this formula. Without it she never would have snagged Mike, she felt sure.

Kitty and Holcombe walked down aisles of shampoos and conditioners, of hot wax treatments and facial masks. Kitty examined everything seriously. She studiously read labels and compared. When there was something Kitty wanted she gave Holcombe a significant look, set the item she wanted apart on a different shelf, and continued down the aisle. When Kitty next turned around she knew that Holcombe had it, although he looked no different. Kitty paused to consider, selected, and put aside an Australian mud mask for hair, a face mask made of salts from the dead sea, a refill of her favorite lipstick (blackberry), liquid black eyeliner, and white sparkly eyeshadow.

Holcombe left first, Kitty followed. She decided on some items to actually buy, the larger ones: shampoo, body lotion, a loofah mit. She could have simply paid for everything she wanted. That was not what this was about.

Her heart beat hard, but Kitty knew she was okay. Holcombe was the one with the stolen merchandise on his person. When she exited the store, he was there waiting for her. They waited until they reached the parking lot across the street, the parking lot for the mall, before retrieving the booty. It was time to unpack Holcombe.

Black liquid eyeliner surfaced from his left shoe. Liquid eyeliner works like nothing else to give that '60s doe-eyed look, it makes you look like Bambi's little girlfriend, like Brigitte Bardot. Blackberry lip liner was in his right shoe ("Eewh!" Kitty squealed "It'll smell like feet!"). Blackberry is a dark but adaptable color, and lip liner can also be used as lipstick. You trace around the outline of your lips, fill in and, voilà, longlasting stain.

In Holcombe's front pocket he had the small plastic compact of white powder. White eyeshadow- not only "in for spring"- but brightens the eyes and diminishes the appearance or crows' feet. Kitty was very worried about crows' feet with all her smoking. White eyeshadow was retro, Kitty had read. Combined with liquid eyeliner, she could attain that '60's go-go girl, beatnik French prostitute look. "Kitty, she set Harrison aflame."

Lastly, the key to the whole project, without which the ensemble falls apart, cover-up. Cover-up is very very important. Kitty had decided to experiment with a fancy new type of cover-up designed to minimize redness.

Holcombe, after rooting around in his front pocket, pulled out a tube of something green. "What is this?" he asked, frowning and holding it up.

"It's cover-up," Kitty snapped, grabbing the tube from him. "For zits."

"But it's green," said Holcombe. He seemed perturbed.

"Of course it is," Kitty said dismissively. "Because green is the opposite of red on the color spectrum, it cancels out the redness. It's scientific," she added pompously.

Holcombe wasn't sold on the idea. "You're going to paint your face green?" he asked, looking worried. "Wasn't there an ancient tribe that did that?"

"Those were the Picts, and that was blue," Kitty told him with a superior air. "Stick to what you know, Holcombe."

They walked into the mall. It wasn't crowded because it was a weekday afternoon, but it was bustling. In those days people still went to the mall.

Kitty bought a ticket at the movie counter. She then ambled off casually, reconnoitering with Holcombe by the pizza place as agreed. She let him rip the ticket in half.

"The big half, the big half. Give me the big one," Kitty hissed.

Holcombe handed her the big half, and Kitty walked into the cinema alone. It worked. She got in. Which wasn't exactly a miracle since the same girl who took her ticket had just sold it to her. Kitty was carrying the stolen cosmetics in a plastic bag, and she reminded herself nervously that she had ripped off all the bar code stickers and she was far from the pharmacy now. But she still had the jitters.

Kitty passed into Cinema Three and sat down in the back row. There were only a couple other people there, toward the front. Kitty opened the magazine she had just bought. She began diligently reading an article about exfoliation. It was apparently a complicated issue, and she wanted to master it.

The lights suddenly dimmed, and Kitty looked about her anxiously. Holcombe wouldn't make it, she knew it. The first preview was some action movie about racing. Kitty kept glancing towards the entrance. She should have sat in a more visible place. Someone walked in, but he was with a girl; it wasn't him. Fucking Holcombe, she thought, I would have bought him a ticket. The second preview was a horror movie. Kitty was squirming with the discomfort of having to sit through this without providing a running sarcastic commentary. She twisted around in her seat and squinted towards the entrance. A skinny figure entered. She saw its silhouette and knew it to be Holcombe, but she didn't say anything: she watched. Holcombe knew she'd be in the back. She watched him walk up and down the aisle. He found her.

"What took you so long?" Kitty asked coolly.

Both Holcombe and Mike were old adepts at this system of free movie entrance. This was the second time today Kitty had gotten vicarious thrills from Holcombe's behavior while remaining safe in legality.

Before she met Mike and Holcombe, a hamburger was a hamburger, a movie ticket a movie ticket, and a pharmacy a pharmacy. Even the shuttle bus to the mall Kitty had never used before she started hanging out with them, she never would have thought of it. Because Kitty didn't need to. Kitty had never been in a situation where she wanted to see a movie, and she couldn't get the money to go. If she had been without the money, then she would have done without, knowing that the movie was hers to see once she asked her parents for money.

Mike and Holcombe had introduced Kitty to the world of the clever and poor, and Kitty loved the excitement and meaning that this system brought her. Not only were Mike and Holcombe (and she, their patroness) superior to the slow, fat, and stupid they ridiculed, but they had also outfoxed the rich goody-goodies of Harrison, it made her feel like she and Mike and Holcombe had formed a band apart. They were lean, clever, and cunning in a fat, complacent, dull society.

If it were possible to cheat the system and subvert the rules that let ticket-holders gain entrance to a movie, a process Kitty had never thought to question, then maybe other hard and fast rules- exams, curfews, library passes- could all be subject to subversion, and the static, rule-bound world in which her parents had brought her up was more vibrant and dynamic than envisioned.

The movie was about a submarine, Kitty gathered. It was not funny, it was not entertaining, and neither would it further Kitty's knowledge of the seductive arts. She was bored stiff. So when Holcombe snaked his skinny arm around her shoulders, she let him. In fact, it was nice and comforting. There was practically no one there anyway.

Kitty imagined idly that it must feel like some sort of triumph to Holcombe. She was exhausted at the idea of following the complicated, dull story-line. Something about a submarine. Something about the Russians.

Holcombe started kneading her shoulder. She laughed and turned towards him to ask him what the fuck he was doing, and when she turned, he kissed her. She, along with everyone else, had half-suspected Holcombe of being gay, and was amused at his impudence. She laughed again, and he kissed her again. This time she was curious, and she kissed him back. The movie was boring anyway, she thought to herself with a thrill at how jaded and adult she had become.

Kissing Holcombe. Kissing Holcombe was softer than kissing Mike. He smelled different too. Holcombe smelled gentle and human, like a puppy or a hobbit. Holcombe kissing was sweet, too. He kissed the corners of her mouth and her nose. He stared into her face in the darkness with large mournful eyes. His old man's hand reached for her breast, and she slapped it away. He was trembling faintly.

They were tousled when they emerged from the theater into the light. Kitty muttered "I'll be right back," and headed for the ladies' room. After the girl in front of her in line disappeared into a stall, Kitty stood in front of the mirror looking at herself. She looked at herself from the side. She looked at herself straight on, tilting her chin down slightly and staring into her own eyes. She quickly applied some make up to the pimples on her forehead. She redrew her lipstick. When a group of girls entered the bathroom, she fled. Holcombe was waiting for her outside the cinema entrance. He looked a bit dazed, and he smiled at her.

"If you tell anyone I'll kill you," said Kitty. Holcombe nodded happily.

They took the shuttle bus back to Harrison, sitting together quietly at the back of the bus. Kitty held the plastic bag of cosmetics on her lap. Her feet didn't reach the floor.

"Holcombe," Kitty said suddenly. He turned. "You're a pretty good kisser," she acknowledged brightly, like an expert complimenting a novice. "You really are," she insisted graciously.

Holcombe's eyes were shining. "Thanks," he said.

## Chapter 6: People Get Offended, Things Fall Apart

A couple hours later and Kitty was on the pay phone outside the convenience store up the street from the green, smoking a cigarette. Her eyes ran over the phone booth graffiti. Someone had used the phone as a public forum to denounce Heather Morgan as a slut. Heather Morgan was in Kitty's gym class and had one of the most mediocre minds Kitty had ever encountered. If something was acceptable, then Heather accepted it. She doubted Heather had the requisite imagination to be a slut and suspected a spurned suitor.

Underneath the slur on Heather Morgan, it said "Time for Shitty!" in Black Sharpie. Holcombe had been there.

Kitty tried to think of something clever to write and failed. She had to hand it to Holcombe. He was the master of coming up with material on the spot. She contented herself with writing the last line of Huis Clos, which they had just read in French class. *L'enfer c'est les autres*, Kitty printed neatly on the phone booth in stylized black handwriting. Kitty really liked that expression, she thought it expressed a profound truth about the human condition. She thought the same thing about The Smiths' lyrics and John Cusack movies.

Kitty admired her handiwork, and it suddenly occurred to her that it would have been much funnier to write: *L'enfer c'est Mrs. Jones*. But it was too late, and it would be really dumb to use the "L'enfer" thing more than once.

Kitty's mother answered the phone which, shit, meant she was home. No dice. Kitty had to quick think up a reason for calling.

"Hi Mom, I just wanted to let you know that I wouldn't be home for dinner tonight."

"Well, I didn't think so anyway, since it's six already."

"Well, I just wanted to let you know... Are you still going out tonight?"

"Kitty," countered her mother, "Are you *smoking*?"

"Mom, *no*." She dropped the cigarette and stepped on it. "I'm blowing on my fingers, it's freezing out, I'm getting frostbite." Too late Kitty realized the pitfalls of this tactic.

"You don't have your gloves!"

"Oh, here they are! Yeah! I just found them! Okay, bye Mom. Just wanted to let you know I was okay."

"Okay, then, well, bye, be careful." Her mother still sounded suspicious.

Holcombe left the convenience store, swinging a white plastic bag.

"They didn't have Chesterfields," announced Holcombe. "I got you Benson and Hedges instead. So can we get to the old Burnes Family bathtub gin?"

"No dice," answered Kitty. "My parents didn't go out. They're home."

Holcombe opened the pint of ice cream, it was mint chocolate chip. In one hand he held the pint, in the other the container top and the plastic bag. He tried to hand the sticky container top to Kitty. She protested vigorously and refused.

"No spoon," said Holcombe, feeling up the bag. "Those bastards, they don't even know how to run a quickmart."

"It's not a quikmart anymore, it's an xtramart," Kitty pointed out.

"That's exactly what I mean. They're running it into the ground," Holcombe griped. He replaced the top of the ice cream and put it back into the bag, and he went back into the store.

"You give 'em a piece of your mind!" Kitty shouted after him, and turned back to the phone.

She called Mike. He was at home in his room watching a skate video. Winter sucked.

"Where are you?" He asked.

"Nice-n-sleazy."

"Who's there?"

Ah, she wished she could mention the name of a magnificent rival that would smote him with pangs of jealousy. It was just not impressive enough that she, Kitty, was here, and she felt that acutely.

"Who the fuck is *ever* here? Nobody. Holcombe. So, what are you doing later?" she asked casually.

"I'm gonna eat a cheese steak and jerk off."

He never gave a straight answer. It was maddening. She was enchanted.

"Wait, I'll go get a sub, and then we can have phone sex." She played along, and the answer was snappy because she was half annoyed. She made him laugh. She was surprised and pleased.

"I might meet Nick later and get some forties," he drawled seemingly inconsequentially, but his voice was resonant with the full import of his words.

Forties, the gangster contraband. The difference between skulking around in parking lots, moaning with the acute pain of high school boredom, searching for something mean and nasty to do, meanwhile contenting themselves with the torture of Holcombe ("Remember when your mom asked you if you were gay?") and nights of high hilarity. Nights breathless and sparkling with taboo. The world seemed huge and ridiculous, and, laughing, Kitty would reel back on to the hood of an icy Chevrolet confronted upwards and outwards with the whirling bright, cold, starry sky, that you can see so clearly in the middle of nowhere Upstate New York, and she would see the words in her head, black Times New Roman on white: I'm drunk. I'm seventeen. I'm drunk. I'm living.

Once in a while, Holcombe, Mike, and some of the other kids got so bored they would drink a bottle of cough syrup. Kitty had never gotten *that* bored. Just the thought made her want to vomit.

Holcombe emerged from the convenience store swinging the plastic bag and literally whistling Dixie. He joined her by the phone, still whistling. Kitty couldn't whistle and normally would have been impressed, but she was talking to Mike. She turned her back on Holcombe, and he began to sing: "In Dixie land I'll make my stand! To live and die in Dixie!"

"So, uh, when do you want to meet?" Kitty asked Mike, waving Holcombe off. Holcombe sang louder. "Look away! Awaaay! Awaaaay! To dear old Dixie!" Kitty put a finger in one ear.

Out of the corner of her eye, Kitty noticed Marty Wheeler and Jim Schultz loitering nearby, watching them. Marty and Jim had followed Holcombe out of the store, and now they stood straddling their bikes, chugging sports drinks and blatantly staring at her and Holcombe. Holcombe stood to attention for a moment and then saluted them smartly.

Jim Schultz had become something of a legend a couple months ago when he allegedly took nineteen hits of acid at one sitting. The rumor going around school was that he hadn't been heard to utter a single word since. He had never been much of a talker, so Kitty had no idea if this were true.

Marty Wheeler she liked. He was new to the school and hadn't yet fully garnered Kitty's reputation for eccentricity, like the time she ran for 7th grade class representative on the self-styled "Feminist ticket." For many boys Kitty's good grades and general weirdness preceded her, but Marty was secure enough in his masculinity to simply consider her an object, which Kitty found reassuring. She had not beaten them, and now she wanted to join them: she wanted to become a beautiful mask and a piece of ass. Marty was also the rare 16-year-old who was not afraid of eye contact. When he stared at Kitty she blushed. Right at this moment however, Marty was not looking at her, Kitty noticed. Marty and Jim were looking at Holcombe.

Kitty hung up. "Let's go," she said to Holcombe. "Mike said he'll meet us at seven on the green. Maybe he can get beers. Come on."

As Kitty and Holcombe walked away, Jim edged the front wheel of his bike into their path. They silently walked around it. They had to pass by Marty and Jim to get to the sidewalk, otherwise they would have had to circle the gas pumps and walk around the entire parking lot. Holcombe was still whistling. Kitty walked quickly, putting Holcombe between herself and Marty and Jim.

"Hey Holcombe," Marty said abruptly, as Kitty and Holcombe walked by. "I heard your Neena Perkins joke." He paused to casually spit on the ground. "I didn't think it was very *funny*," he added menacingly.

Kitty felt a shock radiate up her neck, make her scalp tingle, and set her hair on end. She experienced a sudden terrifying heightened lucidity, like a bolt of lightning illuminating a dark and stormy night.

Holcombe didn't react and didn't appear to have heard, except that he suddenly stopped whistling. Kitty and Holcombe picked up the pace. Marty and Jim stood silently watching Kitty and Holcombe's retreating backs as the two of them, stiffly and self-consciously, walked away.

"Holcombe, what is he talking about?" Kitty whispered fiercely out of the side of her mouth. "What Neena Perkins joke? *My* Neena Perkins joke?" she hissed, staring wildly and desperately straight in front of her.

"How should *I* know?" Holcombe shrugged with his face, like a Frenchman.

"*Holcombe!*" Kitty turned to glare at him with wide eyes and clenched jaw, but she didn't slow down. Kitty and Holcombe looked like two soccer moms power-walking through the mall, except that instead of swinging their arms for greater cardio-vascular benefits, they held them tight to their sides as they strode along.

In her field of peripheral vision, Kitty's glimpsed Marty and Jim bearing down on them, balanced on little kids' bikes, like witches on broomsticks. The *joke*? The Christopher Columbus Neena Perkins *joke*? Here Kitty was skipping school, expecting people to come after her for spreading rumors about Neena Perkins porn or making a video mockery of Neena, and here it was this pathetic "Neena, Pinta, Santa Maria, ha ha" *joke* that had everyone riled up?

It intensified Kitty's sense of the bizarreness of the situation that the cornball throwaway joke she had almost been too embarrassed to tell even Holcombe would trigger a fatwa.

How did they even *know* about the Niña, the Pinta, and the Santa Maria? Kitty was astonished. She *never* would have predicted these ignoramuses would have that much knowledge of American history.

They probably didn't even get the joke themselves, they had just been given to understand that someone out there was daring to defy the natural social order. Here were Marty and Jim, serving as a couple of goons, the joke police, showing up to enforce penalties for dissent against Neena. But it wasn't really Neena they were protecting, it was the power structure, Kitty reflected. Jim and Marty were merely tapping into a primitive drive to enforce social norms. Dumb people feel good reinforcing the power structure, as it gives them power they wouldn't otherwise have, was how Kitty saw it.

"Hey Holcombe!" Marty called out as he reached them. He vaulted easily and gracefully off his bike, threw it aside, and trotted up behind Holcombe. Jim did the same.

"Holcombe." There was no menace in his voice anymore, but there was no playfulness either. He swatted Holcombe lightly in the back of the head with one hand. "Hey, I'm talking to you, Holcombe," he admonished gently. "We didn't think your joke about Neena was very *funny*."

"Not funny," added Jim.

"Garbo talks!" Holcombe exclaimed.

Jim's expression darkened. He didn't know who Garbo was, and he didn't need to know. He proceeded to kick Holcombe's ass. That's not a metaphor. Jim aimed a powerful stomp-kick at Holcombe's posterior that sent him pitching forward off the sidewalk, stumbling, tripping, and rolling into what ended up as a rather neat somersault across the sloping lawn of the Fowlers, who lived next door to the convenience store.

When Holcombe emerged from the somersault he had almost caught up with Kitty because she had continued to silently scurry on while he was somersaulting. It was funny and terrible. Kitty almost wanted to laugh- especially when Holcombe turned his fall into an actual somersault- but she was scared. Kitty was not really scared for herself because she thought they wouldn't touch her. That would have been completely beneath their dignity, would have shocked everyone and united people against them; she was a girl. But she was also reluctant to test the strength of her immunity.

"Come *on*, Holcombe," she commanded imperiously, as though his dilly-dallying were making her late for an appointment. Holcombe, springing out of his somersault, still clutching the plastic bag containing his ice cream, rejoined her.

And they continued on- upright, jerky, and at hyper-speed, like two little martinets whose puppeteer was on amphetamines and laughing like a maniac. They didn't slow down until they reached the village green. Sometimes there was a police car stationed there, but that was not why they stopped. Just as they all knew Marty and Jim wouldn't touch Kitty, they all knew that no one would beat someone up on the village green. It was a sanctuary. It was neutral territory, like Switzerland. That was understood.

As soon as they step foot on the green, Kitty and Holcombe looked back. Marty and Jim weren't there. They had probably returned to their bikes- laughing their asses off, Kitty imagined. Kitty and Holcombe, without speaking, shocked and ashamed, slowly gravitated toward the fountain and sat together on the Oedipus Bench.

Kitty covered her face with her hands and sank her forehead into her palms. Holcombe the pint out of the bag and started spooning ice cream into his mouth. Suddenly Kitty uttered a piercing shriek.

"*Jesus, Holcombe!* Why didn't you try to *defend* yourself? Why didn't you act like a *man*? You let him *kick* you!"

She had let him kiss her. And there had been a moment when she liked it. She felt sick with the shame. Tears of rage came to her eyes. "You fucking *chickenshit*!"

"I can go back," Holcombe said seriously. He had been randomly thumped on so many occasions in so many different circumstances that he was confused as to why it suddenly bothered her now. It had all happened so fast. "I'll go back and find them."

"Shit, Holcombe, and what the fuck would you do if you *did* find them?" she asked bitterly. "Beg them to kick your ass again?" Her voice grated on her own ears. It was so ugly. "You know what you are, Holcombe, you're a fucking *scourge*. You're a scourge upon the earth, a fucking *plague*. You poison everything you touch." He had touched her, and she was poisoned.

"No, I'm *not*." Holcombe said petulantly. He sounded like he was 5. "I'm *not* a scourge." His lower lip was pushed out, and he scowled darkly at the fountain. He put the lid back on his ice cream and put it back into the plastic bag.

Kitty realized he might cry, and she felt a sore twist in her chest. All she wanted in this wrong and terrible world was a cigarette right now to cauterize the sorrow in her chest with a clean burning. "Give me my cigarettes." Her voice was flat.

He wordlessly handed her a packet of Benson and Hedges out of the plastic bag, and folded his arms over his chest. "You know what your problem is?" Holcombe asked. "Your problem is you're *mean*."

Kitty tore the tin foil off the top of the cigarettes and let it blow away. "I know," said Kitty sullenly, crossing her legs and slumping against the back of the bench. She tapped the cigarette on the box, the right way this time. She turned to face Holcombe for the first time since Marty and Jim had accosted them.

"Do you have a lighter?"

He did, but it was windy, and she had to light her cigarette in the shelter of his outspread arms as he opened his coat.

"I know I'm mean," she said in a clipped tone. "I can't help it."

Then she remembered. *He* was the one who had gotten them in trouble with Neena Perkins joke. *Her* joke. The joke that he had scoffed at. She was sure everyone knew it was really her joke, and Neena's commissar handmaidens would be after her. This was all his fault. She was doubly outraged.

There was a Chinese restaurant on the village green. The only Chinese restaurant for miles and miles- the only Chinese *people* for miles and miles- it brought a little flavor of the big city to this middle of nowhere, with its generic, shiny, glistening photos of shrimp rolls and mu-shu pork, lit up like beacons. If you ordered take-out, what the frat boys usually did, you got the little hexagonal white box. If you ate there, you could read about your Chinese zodiac sign while you waited.

The establishment could have been called "The Peking Duck" or "The Great Wall" or "Mao's" but the name didn't matter because locally it was known simply as "the Chinese restaurant." This did not create any confusion in the town. Just like the family who ran it were called "the Chinese family," and this didn't create any confusion either, even though they were Vietnamese.

At seven, Mike joined Holcombe and Kitty on the green. He had on his mouse-ear headphones, and he was carrying an extra-large coffee in a styrofoam cup. Kitty and Holcombe re-enacted their dramatic encounter complete with recriminations and a mumbled statement of self-defense. Mike laughed. He hung his giant headphones around his neck and slurped loudly from his milky coffee. His eyes were small and bright from sleep.

It relieved both Kitty and Holcombe not to be taken too seriously, and to be rescued from the bad space they were in together by the presence of a disinterested third party. They had been scared. However, Kitty felt that Mike was not joining her in a vigorous enough condemnation of Holcombe. She had whipped herself up into a lather.

"My joke!" she railed. Kitty gestured toward Holcombe with her cigarette. "He took *my* joke, and now there's a fatwa on my head!" Kitty inhaled deeply from her cigarette. She stood next to the fountain, arms folded against her chest.

"What's a fatwa?" Mike asked Holcombe.

"Like a bounty," said Holcombe.

"You know, it must have been a better joke than I thought," Kitty said slowly, gazing thoughtfully into the fountain, "if people are freaking out about it this much."

"I didn't think it was bad," said Holcombe.

"It was ok," Mike said.

"Thanks," said Kitty, turning to them, pleased. "But what about the porno?" she demanded. "That's why I skipped school! I thought people would be pissed off at me because I lied about that Neena Perkins porno tape!"

"Huh?" asked Mike. "Nah. Me and Scott started watching it, but it was just you and Emily and Sarah doing, like, skits and stuff."

"You *watched* the Neena Perkins porno?" shouted Kitty, outraged.

"But it wasn't a porno! There is no Neena Perkins porno!" Mike said defensively. Even Mike was not completely immune to irrational feminine outrage.

"Yes, but you *thought* it was a Neena Perkins porno," Kitty said accusingly. "And you wanted to watch it."

"I'm hungry," Mike said, firmly changing the subject. "Let's eat."

So Mike, Kitty, and Holcombe, in that order, walked into the Chinese restaurant at just after seven on Friday evening. Kitty had been over-ruled 2 to 1, and she was sure that Holcombe was voting against her just for spite. She didn't want to eat Chinese. It was impossible to know how many calories were in each plate. If she was going to splurge on unknown-calorie fat-laden things it was going to be chocolate brownie ice cream, not broccoli and chicken. She had voted for pizza, a known quantity, 300 calories a slice according to her magazine, and she trailed Mike and Holcombe sulking. She was going to get a diet soda.

Mr. Pho greeted them unsmilingly from behind the counter. They were free to sit where they wanted, and they sat down in the booth near the back, close to the cash register. After a frat boy left with his order they were the only patrons in the restaurant. Mr. Pho presented them with greasy plastic menus and retired behind the beaded curtains in the back.

On the wall over their table was a calendar featuring a beautiful round-faced girl in a blue print Haiwaiian dress, a pink lei around her neck. She looked up at the camera, submissive yet playful: Miss June. It was May, Kitty pointed out. It was also no longer 1977, added Holcombe. This initiated a bitter retort from Kitty's side that it might as *well* be 1977, as far as Holcombe was concerned, since he was obviously trapped in that decade as far as dress and musical taste. Lively discussion ensued, during which Kitty's injuries and Holcombe's shortcomings were again catalogued.

Meanwhile, there was proof of life coming from behind the beaded curtains. Dishes clattered, the tv was on, Mr. Pho was engaged in his own lively discussion, with a female, maybe Mrs. Pho. Mr. Pho was doing most of the talking. His voice was loud enough that, if they spoke his language, they would have been able to understand everything he was saying. "Hoo *haw*. Woo *shaw*," Mike imitated him, and Kitty hissed "Shut *up!*"

The curtains suddenly parted, and Tracy Pho stalked silently to their table and hovered there forebodingly. She and Kitty had gym class together every Tuesday and Thursday and every other Friday. Tracy's jaw was pitched forward like a bulldog's, and her eyes never left the notepad. She didn't ask for their order, but stood there mutely hating them like a beaten slave. Kitty, too, kept her eyes fastened to the menu while Mike and Holcombe ordered, like she was looking for something. She raised her head when it was her turn to order and quickly said "Diet soda, please," directed at Tracy's notepad.

Suddenly, out of the blue, like a gunslinger striding through the swinging doors of the town saloon, entered Ditmus Rivera, the only Hispanic in Harrison High School. Well, he wasn't actually, come to think of it, the only Hispanic in the high school, he was merely the only Hispanic who flamboyantly traded on ethnic stereotypes. Actually Ditmus didn't even speak Spanish.

There were several Hispanic boys from New York City, who attended Harrison High School through a special academic program for promising inner-city kids. These boys were almost invariably studious, polite, happy, and athletic, and they gave everybody a good feeling.

Not Ditmus. Nobody felt that way about Ditmus and his brothers. Ditmus had two younger brothers- Jose, who was good-natured and jolly where Ditmus was as touchy as a mafia don, and the youngest brother whom everyone just called "Little Ditmus." This made Little Ditmus very angry, and once in a while he would throw himself, yowling and spitting with rage, at some one twice his age, yelling "My name is *Raoul!*" Mocking echoes would rebound on all sides- "My name is *Raoul!* My name is *Raoul!*"- as Little Ditmus lashed out in a blind and useless fury at his mockers. But Little Ditmus he stayed. He was only 8.

In strode Big Ditmus now, whose fury was not known to be ineffectual, closely followed by two diminutive henchmen. Holcombe, Kitty, and Mike were not aware of his presence. None of the three had ever spoken a word to Ditmus. They hadn't seen him strut in with his rolling pimp-walk, flanked by two nervous flunkies, and they didn't notice him until he was upon them like a wrathful god.

"JUSTIN!"

They froze. "Justin"? They looked up expecting to see the principal.

"Justin! I'm gonna kill you!" The three kids gawked up at him. Had Ditmus gotten Holcombe's name from his school records? Was this official business?

Ditmus pointed at Holcombe with his first two fingers, his thumb cocked back like a trigger, and mimed discharging a gun. Kitty's eyes met Mike's for an instant, and she quickly looked away so as not to laugh. Kitty knew that Mike was thinking the same thing, that he'd also seen that hand gesture, in a rap video, and, hilariously, the rapper was white and embarrassingly lame.

Tracy had disappeared into the back. The two white country-boy flunkies made subdued mediating noises like back-up singers crooning a chorus. "C'mon, chill out, man, it's not worth it, man."

Kitty was embarrassed for Ditmus with his gold chains and gangster pants. She saw him as a victim, forced by society's expectations into being such an asshole. But at the same time as it was screechingly funny, it was scary, too. At what point did parody of gangster behavior become actual gangster behavior? She wasn't sure. She didn't want to find out.

And this use of Holcombe's Christian name, as though death itself had walked through the door for Holcombe, oblivious to any nicknames, knowing only the name that he was given coming into this world, and the name he would be given coming out, as though there were to be a blind and violent reckoning of accounts and only the legal official names mattered. It was unseemly, this screaming "Justin" at Holcombe, as though Mrs. Slawson the school secretary were running amok.

Mr. Pho had silently materialized behind the counter. "I call police," he said distinctly. "You go."

"Dude, we have to get out of here. Hey man, let's go. It's not worth it, man," the flunkies crooned in harmony.

But Ditmus put both hands on the table and leaned in toward Holcombe.

"I heard your Neena Perkins joke, Justin," he said softly. "I didn't think it was very *funny*!"

On the last word his fist came crashing down on the table in front of Holcombe. Holcombe's eyes were bugging out of his head. His brow was furrowed, his lips were pursed, and his nostrils flared. He stared down at his placemat. Mike and Kitty caught each other's glances across the table and quickly looked away again before they started laughing. Kitty briefly wondered why they all used the same stupid line. It sounded like a mafia movie, she couldn't remember which one.

When Ditmus's fist hit the table top, Mr. Pho snapped. He was out from behind the counter and standing very close to Ditmus. "I call police! You go! You go!" The cords stood out on Mr. Pho's neck, and Kitty realized with a sudden shock that in a fight between Ditmus and Mr. Pho, Mr. Pho would win.

The flunkies responded on cue. "C'*mon*, Ditmus. C'*mon*, man." They clapped Ditmus on the shoulders, they tugged on his arms. Ditmus backed slowly away, letting himself be dragged, pointing theatrically at Holcombe, for all the world like a rock star singling out a smitten fan-girl in the audience.

"You're *mine*, Justin," he shouted, and then turned and strode purposefully out the door. His handlers bustled behind him, giving every appearance of hustling him out.

Kitty and Mike looked at each other and broke into peals of laughter. Mike traced a heart with both index fingers in mid-air. "You're mine, Justin," he lisped. Kitty guffawed. Holcombe still looked stunned.

Mr. Pho was taking their menus away. "You go!" he said.

"Hey, we didn't do anything," Mike complained.

"Let's just go," said Kitty. "We're sorry," she told Mr. Pho, "That had nothing to do with us." Mr. Pho didn't answer.

They started to put on their jackets. Holcombe wasn't saying anything.

"What if they're outside?" Kitty asked Mike.

"Nah," he said, "They're not going to be out there if they think the police are coming."

They left the restaurant. It was cold and dark. They walked quickly, three figures hunched forward, hands stuffed in their pockets against the cold. They were silent until they reached the beginning of the road uphill to Kitty's house.

"Justin?" said Kitty in a sweet voice.

"Fuck you," Holcombe retorted bitterly.

"Justin," sang out Mike, "I'm gonna git yoooooo."

"Hey Holcombe," said Kitty. "I think Ditmus likes you. Just from the way he was looking at you." She laughed. "You're mine, Justin." She was laughing very hard. "He probably got your name out of the yearbook."

"Or he called your mom," said Mike.

The three stopped talking as they trudged up the hill to Kitty's house. Suddenly Kitty stopped on the path.

"Do you think Ditmus *knows* about the Niña, the Pinta, and the Santa Maria? Do you think he knows what they *are*?" Kitty pondered.

"He was in my first-grade class," said Holcombe miserably. "It was covered."

"I have to say," said Kitty, "that this whole experience has brightened my view of high-school students' cultural competency. I would've had no idea."

"Make your next joke about Shakespeare," said Mike.

"Chaucerian!" Kitty exclaimed.

"For aught I woot," Holcombe added. He had cheered up a little.

## Chapter 7: The Fight for Neena Perkins

The three of them, Kitty and Holcombe and Mike, could not know that what just happened would escalate. They could not know that Mrs. Pho had called the cops. That the cops arrived, and, due to Mr. Pho's imperfect command of English, got the gist of the story from William, aged 11, who hadn't actually seen Ditmus and his henchman, but who had just seen "Die Hard" on tv. Tracy, who had seen and understood everything, locked herself in her bedroom upstairs. She watched the police come and go from the bedroom window.

Kitty, Holcombe and Mike also had no way of knowing that the pathetic display they just witnessed would be taken up by the local paper. A few months before, a retired reporter from New York City had moved to Harrison to give his kids the kind of wholesome small-town upbringing that would serve as a status symbol when they moved back to the city later on, and he bought the local paper *The Harrison Gazette*.

The following Tuesday (the gazette was published weekly) the paper would feature something a bit more colorful than its usual roll call of local marriages, births, deaths and honor students. The headline didn't seem to belong to Harrison, New York: "Racial Incident at Chinese Restaurant, Owner: "Can't We All Just Get Along?" Incidentally, Mr. Pho had never said that. That was Rodney King.

That weekend the student press at the liberal arts college up on the hill, starved for relevancy in a peaceful small-town environment, seized upon the issue and ran with it. The students staged a demonstration that mainly involved throngs of white kids singing Bob Marley songs. Kitty, Holcombe, and Mike took the shuttle bus up to the college to watch the fun. After the protesters sang "Redemption Song," Holcombe started up a chorus of "No Woman, No Cry" with Kitty and Mike, but it didn't catch on.

The following week the Harrison High School management, eager to demonstrate compliance, staged a school assembly- at which Bob Marley was also invoked, this time by a middle-aged bureaucrat in a suit. Holcombe, in the audience, again attempted to initiate a sing-along to "No Woman, No Cry," and got detention.

And finally, like the tricky matters of human sexuality which ended up in the lap (so to speak) of Mrs. Jones the Health teacher, the issue was relegated to "Health class" and a new unit was added to the curriculum: "Diversity," the teaching of which mainly had the effect of making the sole minority kid in the class extremely uncomfortable for forty minutes.

The following day's event, the follow-up to the Chinese-restaurant incident, also got a mention in *The Harrison Gazette*. The newspaper described it in a rather curious phrasing as "rural gang activity." If all you knew of Harrison, NY was what you read in *The Harrison Gazette*, it would have seemed strange to you that this sleepy little college town was the site of so much racial strife and gang activity.

There were varying accounts of what happened next- the story invariably surfaces at Harrison High reunions, weddings, and funerals. One of the only things everybody always agrees on is the story's title. "Hey, remember 'The Fight for Neena Perkins'?"

In any case, it was agreed by phone, under circumstances that were never very clear to Kitty, that on Saturday afternoon the next day at five o'clock, Mike and Jeremy Clarke would meet on the village green to fight *mano a mano* (location to be announced) until they decided that somebody had won. Mike fought because Holcombe and Kitty couldn't. Jeremy Clarke was a surprise contender. He was the best friend of Neena's little brother.

"Jeremy Clarke?" Kitty's voice reached Mike and Holcombe from the bathroom. Kitty paused while applying her lipstick and raised her eyebrows in disbelief at herself in the mirror.

"Why would *he* fight for Neena's honor of all people?" she asked, looking into her own eyes, "Shit, he's like the only person she probably *hasn't* slept with."

Mike and Holcombe were sitting at the table in the alcove in Kitty's kitchen, waiting for her to finish getting ready.

"You're right," Holcombe to her, "After she banged Mrs. Graham in study hall."

"There's *you*." Kitty emerged from the back hall and regarded Holcombe coldly. "She definitely hasn't slept with *you*."

Kitty was in her standard uniform: white t-shirt, black bra, red plaid miniskirt, fishnets, combat boots, black velvet choker. Her lipstick applied, her eyelashes curled, she was ready.

"Let's go," said Mike. And the three filed silently out of Kitty's house, thudding down the steps in unison. They strode purposefully down the hill to the village green. They walked three abreast, shoulder to shoulder in the middle of the road, because there was no traffic.

Oddly, Kitty was to look back on this moment as one of the best in her life, walking into a fight with Mike and Holcombe at her side- odd because Kitty's entire existence was predicated on the presumption that this was *not* the best time in her life, that she, unlike her inferiors, would move on to bigger and better things. Kitty routinely made fun of the people for whom high school was supposed to be their crowning achievement. People like Neena Perkins.

Kitty felt free, walking into the fight. The lines had been drawn- challenging the establishment was fun, as long as she had her friends. Neena Perkins herself and the whole world, who would naturally be siding with Neena, could be waiting there for them on the village green, and together, whatever happened, it would be funny.

The moment is eternal. It is 1993, forever. Kitty lives in the Victorian house up the hill from the village green, forever. Her father is important and respected, forever. She has been accepted into her first-choice schools, forever. Neena Perkins is the power structure, forever. The nymphet holds aloft a basket from which water flows into the fountain, forever.

Harrison, NY is forever. Just like Paris is forever. Just like London is forever.

Aren't they?

There were about a dozen kids assembled around the benches when they arrived, organized into two distinct camps on either side of the fountain. It makes one laugh now how formal and stylized proceedings were for this sort of thing in high school, how seriously proper form was taken. But really, the practice of *mano a mano* dispute settlement is distinctly Western and deeply engrained. Assuredly, the parents and grandparents of these children had fallen into the same dispute settlement by single-combat formation that the children naturally assumed now. Moreover, historically speaking, these children were young adults. They were at the age when, for most of history, people were marrying, having children, fighting wars, conquering lands.

Jeremy Clarke's group was the smaller of the two- in fact, it was just him and four friends. Kitty looked at Jeremy and wondered again why defending Neena's honor had fallen to this 8th grader.

A series of wannabe gangsters had used the insult to Neena's honor as a pretext to file across the stage and beat their chests, to gang up on harmless eccentric Holcombe and playact mafia. "I didn't think your joke was very *funny*!" But when it came to fighting, 8th grader Jeremy Clarke, the best friend of Neena's little brother, was the only one to stand up.

Maybe, thought Kitty, Neena was not as powerful as Kitty had assumed. Maybe the high-school establishment was not the power structure Kitty had imagined. Maybe, it occurred to Kitty with a flash of insight, maybe Neena was not as well-liked as all that. Maybe *that* was why she sent her minions forth to reinstate the narrative wherever heresy was sensed.

Maybe *everyone* hated Neena.

But what good, thought Kitty, is a narrative if you have no one who will fight? What good are your yearbook titles or your flunkies if you have no one who will stand for you and fight?

Kitty, Mike, and Holcombe joined their group of friends. This was Team Mike. Carson Reeves, Brian Decker, and Hugh stood smoking cigarettes. The Roy brothers were next to them with their skateboards, talking to Chris Tanner.

Actually, Jeremy Clarke's group- which consisted of Eli and Zack Brown and Zack's girlfriend, Maura Carraway- were just as much Mike's friends too, but Eli and Zack had to stand with Jeremy because he was their cousin.

The group assembled on the village green that Saturday afternoon was more or less Kitty's tribe. And just as Kitty will always somewhere in her mind live in the Victorian house up the hill from the village green in Harrison, NY, this will always be more or less Kitty's tribe. In the ensuing decades, Kitty would attend four of their funerals. All, to varying degrees, deaths of despair. Despair is contagious.

But this is still 1993. When a boy loves a girl, he makes her a mixtape.

Others were arriving at the fountain. At the very moment Kitty, Mike, and Holcombe stepped on to the green, Marty and Jim rode up from the other direction, perched on those same little kids' bikes. Kitty guessed they must belong to their little brothers. They looked kind of ridiculous. But Kitty's heart sank as she saw that Marty and Jim trailed Jennifer Scheffield and Jessica Williams in their wake.

Jenny and Jessy's appearance immediately galvanized the proceedings. Another hour of standing around, and the entire idea of a fight would have subsided; everybody present would have been putting their heads together to come up with the name of someone who could buy beer. But, while Marty and Jim stood around with Team Jeremy for a minute and then rode off on their kids' bikes somewhere else, Jenny and Jessy buzzed like gadflies between the two groups, self-importantly relaying pointless communications between the two sides. If the boys had had any doubts about fighting, Jenny and Jessy's female-talk-show-host attempts at psychological counseling only made them more determined than ever that violence was the only way.

Jenny and Jessy's failure at mediation certainly didn't discourage Jenny and Jessy any. It certainly didn't quash their feminine drive to *manage*. Not deterred in the least by rejection of arbitration, they simply moved on to involve themselves in determination of venue. If they could have ordered the event catered and designed outfits for Mike and Jeremy to wear, they would have.

Of course, once it became a matter concerning the fight location, everyone wanted to weigh in. The two distinct camps lost their forms, and it became a group discussion. Anywhere too visible was out of the question. Anywhere near the school would get them in trouble. Anywhere near the Chinese restaurant was immediately rejected due to no-nonsense Mr. Pho. Various people's houses, garages, and driveways were offered, but it was a Saturday, parents were home. Even Mrs. Roy would draw the line at hosting a well-attended fistfight.

74

Finally, Mike walked up to Jeremy alone. He muttered with terse manliness, "Let's do this," like they were workmates on the same crew. Jenny and Jessy looked on, dismayed and at a loss. Mike walked away from the group and motioned Jeremy over. Jeremy left the group and approached Mike. Jenny and Jessy squealed. Someone said gruffly, "Calm the fuck down."

Jeremy and Mike stood apart from the group talking for a couple minutes. No one could hear what they said. Mike was a head taller than Jeremy. Kitty marveled for the hundredth time that Neena couldn't find a better champion than this kid.

Mike turned back to the group. "We're going behind the Grand Union," he announced. This was the supermarket. "Alone," Mike added definitively.

The group on the green watched the boys' retreating backs for a moment and then started to lose interest. It was anti-climactic.

"Come on," Kitty whispered to Holcombe, and they beat a hasty retreat back up the hill to her house. Kitty was terrified that Jessy and Jenny, deprived of material, would move on to her.

About an hour later, Holcombe and Kitty were sitting on the couch in Kitty's living room, trying to watch Fawlty Towers.

"I can't believe Neena couldn't get anyone to fight for her but Jeremy Clarke," Kitty crowed with delight. Then she remembered what was going on, and grew serious. Mike and Jeremy were out there somewhere fighting each other. Over a joke. "I hope Mike will be ok," she said anxiously.

"They should have dueled," said Holcombe, yawning. "Pistols at dawn."

Kitty turned on him savagely. "Shut up! You're the one who should be fighting, not Mike!"

Holcombe looked at Kitty. Her pupils were like pinpricks. His eyes met hers, and they were limpid brown and wide.

"You'll be sorry you're so mean to me," he looked down softly and said.

She was already sorry. She was sorry before she spoke. Holcombe was the unworldly part of herself she hated, that she doubted would survive, that she sensed was helpless prey for the mean mean world, of which she, Kitty, was only a symptom. When you are so far in the wrong, you see nowhere to go but farther.

"You're the one who's mean," she said. "You're making Mike fight for you, because you're too fucking pussy to do it yourself." The wretchedness spilled over. She hated herself, but she hated Holcombe worse. She had to punish him for what he had done to her; this was all his fault. She looked him directly in the eyes, and lifted her chin. "Faggot. This is all your fault. You fucked up getting the video. You fucking told everyone the joke, like an idiot. And then you couldn't even do anything when Jim was kicking the shit out of you. You're *pathetic.*"

Kitty left him alone in the living room. She went to the kitchen and found the cigarettes in the pocket of her coat, and she went down into the cellar near the garage door to smoke. Down in the cold darkness of the cellar she wanted to cry, but she felt too terrible. She winced and let out a whimper, but it wasn't crying. She sat down on the cellar steps. The cigarette made her feel better. It confirmed some inherent wrongness. Something was very very wrong. But it wasn't her fault. It was the system. Together she and Holcombe were defenseless, as this entire episode proved, and they would be trampled and eaten up by the cruel world. She knew that. Mike was fighting for both of them.

When she returned to the living room Holcombe was gone. He had never done that before. His stupid bag was gone, and his stupid Salvation Army coat that reeked of cat piss, his stupid tartan scarf, stupid old man's shoes, stupid old man's hands, stupid big eyes, stupid Holcombe. Where the fuck would he have gone anyway?

She went to the front window and pulled back the curtain, but the street outside was empty and serene. It was already dark. She opened the front door and looked down the hill towards the village green. "Holcombe!" Her voice sounded loud. And desperate. The town seemed completely deserted. A streetlight went out. Kitty closed the door.

Holcombe was gone.

Mike called Kitty a few minutes later, and she met him at Connolly's Garage, near his house. Mike's grandfather owned the garage, and the back lot was littered with the hulks of junked-out cars. There was one abandoned car in particular in which Mike and Kitty had created many fond memories. They got into the back seat.

Kitty thought he wanted to make out, and she furtively peered out through the dirty windows to check the surroundings, more for form's sake than anything else. She knew there was no one there. But sex didn't seem to be on Mike's mind.

Mike sat apart from her in the back seat, slumped, his legs splayed, and baggy pants stretched tight. The back seat was too small for his long legs. He picked glumly at a hole on the back of the seat in front of him with a chewed thumbnail. He was pouting. "That sucked," he said frowning at the hole. "I gave him a bloody nose. He had blood on his face."

In one fast clumsy movement, Mike put his head on Kitty's lap and his arms around her waist. She was pleasantly shocked. She put her arms around him. He was still sweaty, and his head was hot in her lap. His shoulders trembled. He was crying. She stroked his head slowly and gently and brought her mouth to his ear.

"It's okay," she whispered, and she felt a fierce tenderness for him that was larger than herself, that swept her up in itself and flooded her with purpose. This was right. He had fought and won. No one knew that he was crying but her. He needed her. His shoulders had to be significantly wider than his hips, they just *had* to be.

"I love him," she thought, and she saw the words emblazoned before her in black Times New Roman on white.

# BOOK TWO: THE FUNERAL

*He felt that the real Lily was still there, close to him, yet invisible and inaccessible; and the tenuity of the barrier between them mocked him with a sense of helplessness. There had never been more than a little impalpable barrier between them — and yet he had suffered it to keep them apart! And now, though it seemed slighter and frailer than ever, it had suddenly hardened to adamant, and he might beat his life out against it in vain.*
-Edith Wharton, <u>The House of Mirth</u>


*Why did you despise me? Why did you betray your own heart, Cathy? I have not one word of comfort. You deserve this. You have killed yourself. Yes, you may kiss me, and cry; and wring out my kisses and tears: they'll blight you - they'll damn you. You loved me - what right had you to leave me? What right - answer me - for the poor fancy you felt for Linton? Because misery, and degradation, and death, and nothing that God or Satan could inflict would have parted us, you, of your own will did it. I have not broken your heart - you have broken it; and in breaking it, you have broken mine.*
-Emily Bronte, <u>Wuthering Heights</u>


*for Mercutio's soul*
*Is but a little way above our heads,*
*Staying for thine to keep him company*
-William Shakespeare, <u>Romeo and Juliet</u>, Act III, Scene 1

*"I suppose you were in love with this Michael Furey, Gretta,"* he said.

*"I was great with him at that time,"* she said.

*Her voice was veiled and sad. Gabriel, feeling now how vain it would be to try to lead her whither he had purposed, caressed one of her hands and said, also sadly:*

*"And what did he die of so young, Gretta? Consumption, was it?"*

*"I think he died for me,"* she answered.

-James Joyce, <u>The Dead</u>

## Chapter 8: Kitty Comes Home to Find Her Parents Have Moved

When Kitty came home from Spain in July 1999, her parents had moved. They were no longer living in the Victorian house up the street from the village green; they were living in an apartment in mid-town Manhattan. Of course Kitty had known about the move. It wasn't like she came home to find different people living in her house and her parents gone. But it was a wrench all the same. Home was where her parents were, and now home was supposed to be a global metropolis.

Kitty's parents were very happy about moving to Manhattan. It had given them a new lease on life. They had been bored empty-nesters in the Victorian house in the small college town. They were ecstatic about selling the house in Harrison, the house where Kitty had grown up- thrilled to get rid of it, frankly. They were starting a new chapter of their lives in the big city. It seemed it was only Kitty who felt a pang. Her brother Hugh was still in college. Her mother had lived in Manhattan in the 60s, she loved the city. Her father was excited about his new position, he was excited about his work.

And when Kitty came home from Spain in July 1999, she came back with a broken heart.

Benoît was the culprit. He had broken Kitty's heart. He had lied and been seen with another girl. There were scenes of violent anguish. There were scenes of passionate reconciliation. They broke up, they made up, they got back together, everything seemed fine, but soon after, Kitty, driven by some mysterious internal force, left Spain and Benoît.

Kitty stared out of the taxi window on the ride from the airport. Manhattan was a foreign country. The taxi zipping through the streets made her feel like she was living in a video game. Everything looked bright and neat and busy- like Kitty imagined Tokyo. It was a teeming hive of people. Stacks upon stacks of people. Kitty hated people. There was no way to win at this game.

But this was the game Kitty was expected to play. The taxi stopped at the corner of 23rd and First. Kitty's mother was sitting on a bench on the corner. Kitty hurriedly paid the driver and flew into her mother's arms. She hadn't seen her for more than six months.

Her mother was in a lather.

"The closing date's been changed," she said rapidly once she'd hugged and kissed Kitty. "We've got to get everything out."

"What?" said Kitty. It was Barcelona eleven o'clock at night for Kitty, it wasn't New York City five o'clock. And she had woken up at 5 a.m. that morning- on another continent.

"We're up against it," Kitty's mother continued. "It's every man for himself."

These were Kitty's mother's two favorite phrases. It felt familiar, if not exactly comfortable, to be back.

"We've got to get everything out?" Kitty repeated stupidly.

"Of the *house*," said her mother impatiently. "We've got to get everything out of the house before the *closing*. And *you* have got to do your *room*."

So the next morning Kitty and her parents were on the thruway at 7 a.m. and made the five-hour drive (the Hudson River due North, the Mohawk River due West) back to Harrison. Her parents never did anything half-assed. Kitty had spent her whole life wishing they would.

The setting of the sun that evening found Kitty kneeling on the floor of her childhood bedroom staring disconsolately at the mess contained in two closets and a bureau, representing her twenty-three years of earthly existence. There were six empty liquor boxes in Kitty's room for what she wanted to keep and a box of garbage bags for what she wanted to throw. The liquor boxes didn't represent any penchant on Kitty's parents' part. Kitty's mother had determined that liquor boxes made the best packing containers for moving, so whenever they had something to pack she picked up cast-offs from the liquor store.

Kitty wondered if she were going to need more liquor boxes as she surveyed her two open closet doors and the opened drawers of the bureau. It seemed to Kitty that her mother had saved every shoebox diorama, every sock puppet, every award, every papier-mâché sculpture, every scrap of paper she ever doodled on as a child.

Under other circumstances, it might have been very touching, Kitty supposed, but having it all abruptly and ineluctably reverted back upon you in one night made it much less sentimental, and more like psychological assault. Her past was thrust upon her and she was being saddled with it, like the chains of Jacob Marley.

Kitty's room was the first bedroom at the top of the wooden staircase. It was a small room, a corner room with two windows. The window facing the street had an alcove in which there was a window seat. There were closets on either side of the window seat and a large bureau in the corner. The woodwork was white and the walls were pink.

The four-poster canopy bed where Kitty had slept from the time she had left her crib until the time she had left for college dominated, almost filled, the room. She remembered the night she snuck Mike up to her bedroom. Her father had heard something and come to the door, and Mike automatically dived under the bed and remained hidden, while Kitty went to the door and fielded her father's questions about what that noise had been. Kitty had been impressed with Mike's ducking and covering skills. It wasn't planned or anything. He just instinctively slithered under the bed like the stereotypical shiftless lover of story and song. She supposed it was an ancestral memory thing passed down from his absentee ne'er-do-well father.

Kitty sat down on the window seat and surveyed the room. She remembered when they first moved how excited she had been to have a window seat in her room. She was eight-years-old when they moved into this house. Ten years of Kitty's life was in this room, from eight to eighteen. It was still hers until dawn. She had a matter of hours to pack up her childhood and get out.

Kitty felt- as she would for most of her twenties- a vague sense of injustice. She had been cherished and coddled and nurtured like an immeasurably valuable specimen, only to be remorselessly flung out into the world to sink or swim.

Kitty, who had waxed eloquent on Petrarch and Mount Ventoux, reduced to a typing speed.

Kitty, for whom country boys would have died, reduced to speed-dating events. (Praying for the timer to ring, trying to make conversation with a fatty from Queens, whose origins were as unattractively exotic as he was unattractively dull.)

Kitty, whose father was judge in the same county courthouse where his father had been judge before him, whose second and third-cousins were the human flora of this county, whose family everyone knew, Kitty now reduced to a "white girl."

She wondered, not for the first time and not for the last, why it had to be this way. She knew that remaining here would have been an admission of failure. Going to a local school, marrying a local guy, getting a local job: that meant you had failed. Kitty envied those who were allowed to fail.

She started with the bureau drawers. She opened the top drawer and grabbed the nearest thing, which was a clump of letters that Peter Park had written to her when she was in summer camp, secured with a rubber band. They were filthy. In the pornographic sense. And very oddball.

Peter had that summer developed a series of graphic novels centered around Kitty's anatomy. He was actually rather talented, Kitty thought, sitting and looking through his drawings. Here were some sketches of "Clara." Clara was Kitty's clitoris. Peter had given Clara a bubby personality- winsome, always eager to please and up for fun- quite a contrast to her grumpy and uncompliant owner. On the next few pages Kitty found Clara's complement, "Vicky Vulva," smoking cigarettes and wearing a beret. Vicky cut a more mysterious remote figure than Clara (naturally enough). What a weirdo Peter had been, Kitty thought, carefully placing all his letters and drawings into the liquor box she was currently working on.

The drawer where Kitty had found Peter's letters was stuffed with paper. Not only had Kitty's mother evidently saved all the drawings Kitty had done since birth, but she had also saved every composition and essay Kitty had ever written. There was no way Kitty could sit here and read them all. What terrible thing had she done, Kitty wondered, that her mother had decided to relinquish all this material back to her in one night? She was being hazed, Kitty thought grimly- only the result of the hazing would be explusion, not admission.

Kitty found her college notebooks for some of her favorite classes: Nineteenth-Century Intellectual History, The Italian Renaissance, The Herodotean Moment. She had used graph-paper notebooks. She loved writing on graph paper. Her handwriting was tiny, neat, and highly stylized- she gave her lower-case t's a curled tail. She had taken excellent notes; she prided herself on it. She salvaged the notebooks. Into the liquor box they went.

She found a sketchbook she and Holcombe had drawn together in high school. One of them would draw a series of cartoon frames with characters with dialogue balloons coming out of their mouths, and the other would fill in the dialogue. They would take turns. They were kind of dumb, but Kitty threw the sketchbook into the liquor box.

Kitty turned away from the wad of papers stuffed into the drawer. She would do the rest later. She started in on the other closet. Peering apprehensively into its depths, Kitty spied a mysterious shoebox on the floor towards the back. When she opened it, she found a doll made out of a white athletic sock. It had black yarn hair and painted-on blue eyes. It was wearing a piece of one of Mike's flannels. It was a voodoo doll.

Kitty regarded the ghastly thing. She had forgotten all about it. She remembered how she furiously patched it together after Holcombe told her Mike had cheated on her at some party at somebody's house. So embarrassing. It was a good likeness, though, she thought. She had done well drawing the face. It had Mike's hangdog expression and John Cusack eyes. She wasn't even sure anything had ever gone on between Mike and Alison Thomas, Kitty reflected now with chagrin. Holcombe could have very well been lying to break up her and Mike. Kitty shuddered and tossed the doll into the garbage bag.

At the bottom of the same shoebox Kitty found an envelope containing two desiccated frog legs. Her heart skipped a beat. 9th grade Biology: where she and Peter Park had fallen in love. She had kept the frog legs for good luck, but (ah, young love!) Peter had taken her lab rat. Kitty recalled him keeping the rat parts hidden in a jar somewhere in his family's basement for a while. Then he got in trouble for bringing the tail back in to school. Smiling fondly, Kitty threw the envelope containing the frog legs away.

A shoebox in the other corner of the closet was marked "Holcombe Tapes." This was golden. Holcombe was famous for his mixtapes. They were usually soundtracks to movies that had never been made, accompanied by artwork featuring collages and calligraphy. They were the stuff of legend. His 1993-1994 "Soundtrack to a Movie Never Made" series was generally regarded by many of his critics as his best work, but Kitty also really appreciated his earlier, lesser known work. She seized upon the shoebox, and carefully deposited it into a liquor box. That was easy. Sadly, Kitty's collection of Holcombe Tapes had been much depleted by thieving Long Island hippies she had shared a house with in college. Long Island hippies were the worst, she reflected rancorously. They were even worse than regular hippies.

Another shoebox marked "Photos" was predictably filled with photos, random photos spanning decades. Kitty paused at one of Peter Park and her on her 17th birthday, sitting next to each other on the large blue couch in the downstairs living room. Kitty was wearing a blue sweater-dress with shoulder pads and paisley leggings. Peter was in his black trench coat, of course. They were looking into each other's eyes and laughing hard- with embarrassment- as you could see by their awkward contorted poses. Kitty's mom had taken the photo.

Kitty found one of her 18th birthday. She was with Mike and Holcombe in her "uniform" that year: white t-shirt, black bra, black velvet choker, miniskirt, fishnets. Mike was dressed like a skater: over-sized t-shirt, over-sized pants. But Holcombe sported a dress shirt, a tie, a vest. Those vests he used to wear for formal occasions were so crappy. His dress shirt was untucked of course. Kitty was surprised at how *little* they all looked. They looked like kids.

Behind this photo she found a photo of Holcombe that she had taken of him sitting in the back seat of a car. The photo had been taken from the front seat. It was from college, just after they had started going out. His hair was long, he was wearing a leather jacket, and he was staring out the window with a serious thoughtful expression. In this photo too he looked like a kid, Kitty thought, although this was only a few years ago.

Here was another one from college, of Kitty and Holcombe clowning around. It was in Ithaca. Somebody must have taken it from the front porch of the house they were living in that summer. Kitty and Holcombe were on the ground looking straight up at the camera, which was at a height above them. Holcombe was smiling. Kitty's mouth was wide open, laughing. That was the summer they had screwed up. That had ruined everything. They broke up the following winter of that year.

Now that she was back home, Kitty decided she would ask her brother Hugh for Holcombe's number. She had seen Holcombe at the local watering hole in Harrison last Christmas. He was living in Portland, Oregon now. Kitty didn't much see the point of living somewhere different that was still America. How much different could it be?

In her bottom drawer she found her yearbooks. Six of them: 6th grade through 12th grade. Kitty started flipping through them and got sucked into the "Reading Your Old Yearbooks" vortex. She sat on the floor for a good hour looking through them. In 8th grade, Peter Park had signed her yearbook:

*Hi Kitty, You call yourself a feminist, yet by insisting on the equality of women aren't you inherently admitting their non-equality? Don't think about this too hard. -Peter*

The next year, 9th grade, Peter Park had also signed her yearbook:

*Chilly Willy, I love you. –P.*

Kitty smiled at the stark contrast between the two inscriptions, feeling gratified. She felt she had won that one. Peter hated her now, of course, wherever he was. She wondered what he was doing.

She came to her 12th grade yearbook. She and Peter were broken up by then. She was going out with Mike. Mike's inscription was on the back page. It said:

*You are lovely and swank.*

Kitty remembered how thrilled she had been with that simple sentence, how it had seemed to her the essence of under-stated coolness at the time.

She found Holcombe's inscription in the same book:

*Kitty, You are my best friend. Good luck in college. I will come visit you. –Holombe*

Kitty was surprised. She hadn't remembered he'd written that. That was a very normie inscription for Holcombe. No "Oedipus Schmoedipus!" or "Time for Shitty!" or anything. She would ask her brother for Holcombe's number when she got back to New York.

Holcombe *had* visited her in college, true to his word. And then they started going out. She remembered the day it became romantic. He had visited her several times, they had fooled around, no big deal, but then one day Kitty found that she *needed* to see Holcombe. She hopped on a bus and took a five-hour trip because she *needed* him.

They had gone out for a year before they broke up. He had failed her, and the memory was still bitter. Holcombe was too unworldly. He was a loser, he would always be a loser. Holcombe would never change, she thought.

Kitty kept all the yearbooks. She threw them into a liquor box with the letters (a lot of sweet funny letters from her mom, writing to her at summer camp); the notebooks; postcards she had sent home from Paris, Naples, Carcassone; maps of Paris, Florence, and Rome; her baptismal certificate; birthday cards from her grandmother. Her entire life was there, she was exhausted. For the last time, Kitty lay down on the four-poster canopied bed in her girlhood bedroom. She closed her eyes and collapsed into a light feverish sleep.

The next day Kitty was back in Manhattan. Her parents had woken her up at dawn for the long trip back. Kitty's parents' new home, and now Kitty's, was in a large group of apartment buildings next to the East River in the Gramercy Park area. Their two-bedroom apartment was spacious, conveniently located, and had a large window with a view of the river. Kitty stood at the big beautiful bay window. She looked at the sparkling East River, the bustling sidewalks, the Queens skyline, and she was filled with a vast sense of desolation against which she could not win, because it was impersonal, and she was not. She was only a person.

The apartment buildings had been built after WWII for returning veterans and their families. Many of the tenants were holdovers from this post-war urban land-grab: feisty elderly people with strong outer-borough accents. Their children were usually much less colorful creatures, trapped there by subsidized-rent inheritances that they couldn't reasonably refuse.

The elderly original inhabitants were filled with the kind of joy of living that comes with having landed rent-subsidized apartments in prime real estate. They were in Manhattan! They had gotten out of Brooklyn! Their children, however, had faded under the effect of the *ennui* that comes with living your life around your relationship to a subsidized-rent apartment. They were merely Manhattanites near the bottom of a vast pecking order, ruined for living anywhere else.

This was 1999. The city was in that brief sweet spot between Giuliani making entire neighborhoods suddenly livable and September 11th. These were the Seinfeld days: everything was funny. The city was safe. There were lots of jobs. The budget was balanced. Kitty's college crowd had moved all over the country, she had friends in big cities all over: Boston, San Francisco, Austin, Atlanta, Los Angeles, Washington D.C. The possibilities seemed endless. Kitty could have a career. She could be a player. She could work hard and move up. And Kitty was ready, eager, and willing- she just wished she didn't have to be there for it. She wished she could send someone else in her place.

## Chapter 9: Kitty Hooks Up With a Russian Jew at a Gay Bar

Kitty spent the first couple weeks back acclimating to her new environment and wretchedly procrastinating writing her resume. She found the supermarket. She found the pharmacy. She found the library. In the evenings she walked with her parents to the East River. They sat on a bench and watched the ships. Suddenly Kitty burst into tears: Benoît.

By day Kitty's mother took her shopping for work clothes, by night Kitty worked on her resume on the computer in her father's office. Kitty's mother's principal concern in helping select Kitty's businesswear was that Kitty not look the least bit "suggestive." No neckline was too high, no skirt too long. Every time Kitty tried on a skirt and looked at herself in the dressing room mirror, her mother's worried face hovered in the background of the reflection. "You don't think that's too short, do you?"

Kitty ended up looking so un-suggestive that on her way to her interview with the temp agency a young Orthodox Jew stopped her and asked her in Hebrew for directions to a local synagogue. Kitty knew it was directions he wanted because, when she couldn't answer him, he started asking in heavily-accented English.

Kitty was in a hurry. She couldn't be late to a job interview, it was unthinkable, she would die. "I'm not Jewish!" she told the young man bluntly. He seemed offended and Kitty heard him grumble something about not needing to be Jewish to give directions, but, blushing, Kitty sped off.

Great, thought Kitty, she was attracting men from ultra-conservative religious sects. And she was also offending them. She was pretty sure her mother had not thought through all the implications of religious-extremist hemlines. Although, Kitty reflected, her mother couldn't help it if the only people in the city who conformed to her 1950s American standard of modesty these days were Orthodox Jews. The pozz was deep. Deep and lonely.

One of the few things that happened to cheer Kitty up in the few weeks after her return was an unexpected phone call. It was Kitty who picked up the phone.

"Hello! Hello! Hello!" someone chortled on the other end. Kitty was about to slam down the receiver when the voice cried, "It's Zander! It's Zander!"

Zander (Aleksandr) was Kitty's friend from Study Abroad in Paris. He was a diminutive, stout, apple-cheeked, gnome-like madman from the Ural Mountains. His father had come to America seeking religious asylum as a Soviet Jew. All the Russian refugees Kitty had ever met were Jewish, she didn't think there were any other kind. Zander's father settled in Cleveland, married another Jewish Soviet refugee, and Zander had a little American half-brother.

Zander moved to the US to join his father at sixteen, but his mother stayed behind in Russia. She was not Jewish, she was Christian, and she had raised Zander Christian. Incongruously, or perhaps not incongruously at all, Zander had a peasant devotion and reverence for Christianity that was straight out of Tolstoy's short stories. He was very worried about his mother, he confided in Kitty. She was poor, she was going hungry, he sent her money when he could. Sometimes Zander would get wretched and cry with guilt that he was in Paris studying while his mother was suffering.

Zander had a soft, distinctive, charming Russian accent. He spoke six languages: Russian, English, French, German, Italian, and Spanish. His French was divine, he had virtually no accent- which made Kitty very jealous. He was soulful, charming, sensitive, sophisticated. He had the Russian soul and the Jewish sense of humor.

"Zander!" yelled Kitty, overjoyed.

"I'm here in Manhattan!" Zander shouted with glee.

"How did you get my number?" Kitty demanded.

Zander chuckled some more. "I have my ways." He continued seriously, "Listen, Kitty, I have to tell you something."

"You're pregnant?" Kitty deadpanned.

"Close," said Zander. "I'm gay! I just came out!"

There was a silence, then "Congratulations!" Kitty gushed. "That's great!" she said enthusiastically.

So that's why things never took off with Zander, thought Kitty. So embarrassing.

"I wanted you to know, Kitty," Zander continued earnestly, "because you were really inspirational to me. You were one of the reasons I had the courage to come out."

"Well, thank you," said Kitty in a much less enthusiastic tone. She tried vainly to recall anything she could have said or done to turn Zander gay. "*I* inspired you?"

"Your attitude is just so free," said Zander guilelessly. He apparently considered this a good thing.

It was not a sufficient insult from the universe for Kitty to be boyfriendless and prospectless, thought Kitty, she must also suffer the indignity of being accused of turning men gay. The pozz was deep and vast. The pozz was very close now.

Changing the subject, she asked Zander what he was doing in the city. He was living in the East Village with an apartment mate he hated. He was dodgy about what he was doing, just because he was Zander, but it sounded like he was doing marketing for a start-up. Or he was doing a start-up for a marketing company. He was starting something up and he was marketing something, was what Kitty gathered. The best part was that Zander asked Kitty if she wanted to go dancing with him and his friends on Saturday!

So Saturday night, after a couple hours of dancing around by herself, putting on makeup, and sipping wine (preparation was always the best part of any evening in Kitty's experience), Kitty showed up at Zander's apartment in the East Village just below Union Square. She rang the intercom, he answered, and she trudged up the three flights of stairs with a bottle of wine for him. Zander's apartment was tiny. She couldn't believe he shared it with another person, especially another person he loathed the way he loathed his apartment mate.

As Kitty entered Zander's apartment, she caught a glimpse of the apartment mate passing through the living room. He didn't seem especially noxious to Kitty- a tall blonde guy. He was also from Ohio like Zander, and he had also gone to Duke. Zander found him on some online Duke forum. Zander looked at Kitty and mouthed "Nazi" as he walked by, but the flat mate didn't look like a Nazi, he just looked a little annoyed, probably because Zander was having people over. Kitty wished he weren't a Nazi- he was good-looking.

Zander introduced Kitty to his friends. There was Victor, also Russian and also gay, who reminded Kitty very strongly of Peter Lorre- both in looks and mannerisms. There was Robert, Jewish-American from New Jersey- also gay- a painfully sweet boy who reminded Kitty very strongly of Anthony Perkins- both in looks and mannerisms. There was Ellen- a small sharp-faced Russian brunette to whom Kitty took an instantaneous and intense dislike. And then there was a kid with bad posture and his hair in his face slumped next to Ellen, whose name Kitty didn't catch because his voice was so soft. She privately called him "The Kid" because he was younger than them, he was still in college. Apparently he was a programmer. Victor and Robert were Zander's friends from Duke. Ellen and the kid were Zander's Russian friends from Cleveland.

Everyone drank and chatted while Zander bustled about getting ready. Zander had this habit of assembling groups around himself of which he was the star. He had a warmth to which people congregated.

Zander's apartment mate the Nazi occasionally passed through the living room, and when he did Zander would make faces behind his back. This didn't seem out of the ordinary to Kitty. She was used to people who shared housing hating each other.

Once, in college, Kitty and some friends visited another friend at his new place. They were hanging out in his room, and someone asked him where his bathroom was. He said, "Wait," and took out a roll of toilet paper from his desk drawer and handed it over. "Take this," he said.

"You're out of toilet paper?"

"No," he said. "We just all use our own toilet paper. It's easier than dealing with those cheap motherfuckers." System breakdown had occurred to such an extent that everyone in the apartment was bringing their separate rolls of toilet paper with them to the bathroom each time they went.

So Kitty was used to rancorous relations among people who shared apartments: it was the rule, not the exception, in her experience. As they drank more wine the party got chattier- *gayer*, you should pardon the expression. Kitty talked mostly to Robert and Victor. Robert lamented at length the emphasis the gay community puts on physical appearance. Victor and Kitty had a long discussion on the short stories of Tolstoy. They both agreed that Zander exemplified Russian soul. Finally Zander came out and told them he was ready.

"How do I look?" he asked them all coyly.

"Fine! Let's go!" they shouted.

They crammed into a taxi, six people. You could still do that in 1999. Kitty shoved past Ellen to sit on The Kid's lap- the only heterosexual male in the bunch. Tough shit, Ellen, Kitty chuckled to herself as the taxi sped south. Have fun sitting on Victor.

And then they were outside some club. Kitty had only a vague idea of where they were. It had to be the meatpacking district- the streets were wide, there was nothing around. As they waited in line Kitty noticed that most of the people in line were men- fit young men- and a lot of them were gay. Here and there she saw some women. Really decked-out women in really swanky clothes. At least, Kitty thought, looking more closely at them, at least they *looked* like women.

Zander was standing with his back to Kitty, talking to Ellen. Kitty tapped him on the shoulder.

"Zander," she asked him accusingly, "Is this a *gay* bar?"

"I told you I was gay," Zander said calmly without turning around. The bastard. Kitty wondered whether he was rolling his eyes at Ellen.

Kitty poked the computer-programmer kid with the bad posture and the hair in his face with her elbow. They had bonded in the taxi. To her amusement and his discomfort, she had given him a boner.

"Did *you* know this was a gay bar?" she demanded.

The kid giggled softly then abruptly stopped. "No," he said distinctly. He didn't look too happy about it. Kitty assumed the giggling was a nervous tic.

"What's your name again?" Kitty asked him.

"Sasha," said The Kid. "But people call me Sam," he giggled.

"Zander, Zander!" Kitty tapped Zander's shoulder again. He turned around, "What?"

"Sam over here didn't know it was going to be a gay bar either," Kitty said pointedly.

"Nobody said this was a democracy, Kitty," Zander said gently and turned back around. Kitty sensed the steel that lay behind that statement.

"Well, it looks like we're going to a gay bar," she muttered grimly to The Kid. The Kid giggled.

Inside the club was what you would imagine. It was dark and there were a lot of sweaty gay men, some half-naked, dancing away. Kitty had dropped her objections and decided to go with the flow. She signed the roster to get in (unknowingly signing up to have pornographic filth sent to her parents' house, an episode that went on for years) and went merrily through the doors. Their group stood awkwardly for a moment amid the throng, and then awkwardly started dancing. Zander and Victor slipped off to get drinks. Kitty had to admit the music was great, but she couldn't help feeling like she was a bystander at some frenzied worshipping of Baal or something: shirtless men gyrating on each other.

And it was *humid* in there, it was *muggy*. Suddenly Kitty wanted out. Sam, whom Kitty still thought of as 'The Kid," was next to her. Ever since she had protested entering the gay bar he had stuck to her like glue, and she turned to him now.

"You wanna go outside for a cigarette?" Kitty shouted at him, miming the act of smoking, drawing two fingers to her lips.

The Kid nodded earnestly. His eyes were wide with terror. They spotted the nearest door marked "Exit" and struggled through the darkness toward the neon sign. Kitty led the way through the clusters of thrashing bodies, holding her breath and trying not to make contact.

They burst into the open air of the street.

"Whoah," said Kitty. "Whoah."

The Kid giggled in response. She could see his face now. He had tucked his hair behind his ears. He had mild limpid brown eyes and thick eyebrows. He was handsome. He looked like a young Elliot Gould.

"How old are you?" asked Kitty.

"Twenty-one," he said, and giggled.

"So is this like the first bar you've ever *been* to?" asked Kitty. She was joking.

"Uh… Yes," the Kid answered, and giggled.

Kitty laughed.

And about ten minutes later they were passionately making out. "Take that, Ellen" floated through Kitty's mind.

## Chapter 10: Kitty Makes a Multicultural Friend

Soon after the night at the gay club, Kitty landed a temp job working in the mailroom of a consulting firm. An eager cog presenting itself to the machine, she found her way to the building and was issued ID and led into its bowels, down to the basement mailroom. The mailroom boss was a hollow-cheeked and hollow-chested young man his parents had- aspirationally, Kitty thought- named Spencer. He was half-Sicilian and half-Jewish, from Staten Island, and a passionate numismatist. The only time he appeared to come to life was when he was talking about his coin collection, which wasn't very often.

Kitty and Spencer had both gone to Cornell and graduated around the same time. They played the name game: they did not know a single person in common. Kitty's college friends were going to Burning Man and living in yurts in the wilderness until they were rushed to the hospital with giardia (dropped off at the emergency room entrance by dreadlocked people of indeterminate sex who quickly sped away). Kitty imagined Spencer's friends were also like Spencer: colorless functionaries whose passions were sublimated into incredibly boring side interests.

But that always happened with Cornell. Kitty never met anyone else who went there when she did with whom she knew a single person in common. She never recognized a single name in the alumni gazette. Sometimes she wondered if the people she hung out with at Cornell had really gone there, had even existed. Sometimes she wondered whether the time she spent there had actually happened, or whether she had stumbled onto some kind of Brigadoon-type blackhole phenomenon.

Kitty and Spencer had something else in common besides Cornell. They were both Ivy League graduates working jobs that did not even require a college degree. Even as recently as twenty years ago, a competent high-school graduate would have been doing their jobs.

Spencer introduced Kitty to the only other person in the mailroom at the moment: Stephanie, a tall black girl wearing glasses (tortoiseshell, Dolce & Gabbana) and a skirt (tweed, Ann Taylor) who was on her feet busily distributing piles of mail into the different cubbyholes of a wall-grid in the back room. She was statuesque but feminine, with a slender graceful neck and closely-cropped hair. She greeted Kitty charmingly: looked her in the eye, smiled, shook her hand. She had beautiful manners.

Kitty was put to work immediately, sorting the mail next to Stephanie. As they sorted, they chatted. Stephanie had gone to NYU. She was applying to law schools, she had taken the LSAT. Kitty told Stephanie that after college graduation she had studied in Italy for a few months and taken the state language exam in Italian.

Stephanie's reaction was visceral. Her eyes popped. She put a hand to her mouth.

*"Ma anche tu, parli italiano!"* she exclaimed.

At this point, the girls switched to Italian, and the fun began. It turned out that Stephanie had studied in Italy in college, had left behind an Italian boyfriend, and was dying of love. Kitty confessed to Stephanie that she had worked in Spain, had left behind a French boyfriend, and that she too was dying of love.

Spencer actually looked up curiously from his coin catalogue for a moment. "Are you guys speaking a foreign language?"

It was the beginning of a beautiful friendship. Kitty and Stephanie spoke mostly Italian with each other at work from then on. No one in the mailroom minded. All they were doing was sorting mail.

Oddly enough, the people who minded Kitty and Stephanie speaking Italian with each other were the associates sitting in the cubicles up above. The associates were the junior consultants who sat in cubicles and did not have their own offices. Kitty was unclear on what anyone did, not that it mattered, since she did not have to know to deliver their mail.

Kitty and Stephanie often went up together to the upper floors to deliver mail. For this they used a giant mail cart. First they filed the associates' mail in different folders in the mail cart, then they trundled the mail cart through the halls, dispensing mail.

Kitty knew that the company was a consulting firm. From pamphlets, flyers, and posters she saw around the office she also gathered that they provided "global solutions." It was 1999, and people had rather recently started using the word "global." The word "pro-active" was also a very hot one. "Global" was splashed everywhere in the building- on signs, marketing materials, brochures: "global" solutions for a "global" network of "global" connections.

So you would think that with all this "global community" stuff going on, the consultants would be all over a black girl and a white girl chatting away in complicity in a language which was neither's native tongue, right? Wrong. Not at all. The associates eyed Kitty and Stephanie with suspicion. Mailroom employees who were well-educated and well-traveled seemed to render them uneasy. "Probably because their titles and their jobs are full of shit," thought Kitty contemptuously.

Moreover, inter-racial fraternizing amongst those who were effectively servants seemed to trigger extreme tension in most of them. Only a couple white guys and a couple Asian girls were relaxed, friendly, and complex-free.

The first time Kitty and Stephanie went up with the mail truck, Spencer went up with them and introduced them to the associates. Apparently the associates were very delicate people, and a change in mailroom staffing might set them completely off. So Spencer did the rounds with Kitty and Stephanie trailing after him in order for the associates to grow acclimated to their faces. Kitty and Stephanie hung around in the background and waved awkwardly, showing they meant no harm. Some people showed polite interest, some people showed matter-of-fact interest, and a few people were rude.

One young female associate, a Miss Meredith Steinberg, must have been in a foul mood when Spencer stopped by her desk to introduce Kitty and Stephanie. Spencer did his routine where he deferentially explained that, "These are Kitty and Stephanie, they're recent college graduates, and they'll be delivering your mail, so just wanted to introduce you."

Ms. Steinberg looked up from the paperwork on her desk to gaze with some hostility on Kitty and Stephanie. "Where'd you go to school?" she demanded.

"Cornell," Kitty cheerfully volunteered.

"NYU," said Stephanie politely.

"And you're working in a *mailroom*?" Ms. Steinberg snorted with derision.

Stephanie gave a wide smile. "For the summer," she said, sounding bemused. "In the fall I'm starting law school at NYU, and Kitty will be starting at Georgetown," Stephanie gracefully lied.

"Oh. Good for you," said Ms. Steinberg shortly, sounding deflated.

Kitty was impressed with how fast and how flawlessly Stephanie had come up with that. Stephanie was good. She was so good that she hadn't picked Harvard Law School where Meredith Steinberg's degree was from. That's how good Stephanie was.

The other mailroom staff were much less prepossessing than Stephanie- one was a bounder, the other was a drunk- although Kitty couldn't tell that by meeting them and shaking their hands. They had seemed friendly and decent enough at first.

Wellington was the bounder. He was virtually never present. When he was present, though, he was friendly enough, and he had a beautiful lilting accent; he was Jamaican.

Greg, the drunk, was a portly middle-aged black American from Brooklyn. He was usually physically present at work but in a stupor. He was overweight, placid, mild-mannered, and stinking of booze. The consultants adored him. Whenever he brought the mail around, they always heartily greeted him by name. Once Stephanie and Kitty got to be good friends- which was very quickly- Stephanie revealed her passionate disgust for the fondness that the consultants bore Greg.

"They like him because they think that's how a black man should be," said Stephanie angrily. That hadn't occurred to Kitty, but she had observed that the associates were very comfortable and affectionate with Greg, who had an obvious alcohol problem. Kitty didn't mind Greg, but he did not make her want to stand up and cheer.

Stephanie likewise detested Wellington. His beautiful lilting accent made no impression on her. She was Haitian, she could have her own lilting accent when she wanted to.

No one actually saw much of Wellington in the mailroom because he was almost never there. Spencer's boss was a harried fat blonde woman named Elizabeth. She was the real mailroom boss, and she and Wellington were engaged in a constant game of cat and mouse. Oddly enough, Wellington was the cat, and Elizabeth was the mouse.

Elizabeth frequently appeared in the mailroom, greeting everyone with an expression of strained jollity, and casually asking after Wellington, who was nowhere to be found. Once in a while Elizabeth would summon Wellington to her office for a talk. These meetings were much harder on Elizabeth than they were on Wellington. On the mornings of the days Elizabeth had scheduled a meeting with Wellington, she would usually burst into the mailroom and with ferocious and desperate joviality present them all with a tray of baked goods that she would invariably end up eating most of herself.

Sometimes Wellington would not even be there that morning. Then Elizabeth grew very grim indeed. The mask seemed to slip, her jowls and the pouches under her eyes became more pronounced. Because Elizabeth knew that if Wellington skipped a meeting with her without at least a pretext, the situation was drawing closer to intolerable insubordination and some sort of showdown. And Elizabeth knew that Wellington had all the cards. The deck was stacked, and not to her advantage. Wellington was many things, but he was not stupid. If Wellington wanted to, he could risk Elizabeth her job.

So, as the minutes ticked by and the designated meeting time grew closer and still no Wellington, Elizabeth grew increasingly apprehensive. Inevitably, however, Wellington would eventually show. Elizabeth and Wellington would disappear into her office and re-emerge shortly, Wellington sporting the same noncommittal insouciance as ever, Elizabeth fairly sagging with the relief produced by the thought that she could kid herself along for at least a little while.

Stephanie and Kitty would laugh about Elizabeth and Wellington's cat-and-mouse routine over lunch. Stephanie and Kitty ate lunch together every day. Usually they got a sandwich or pizza and went to Bryant Park. Under Giuliani you could now sit in many public parks without being solicited to buy crack rock or forced to watch a homeless person take a dump. It was halcyon.

Kitty told Stephanie about the only romantic prospect on her horizon: The Kid. He was still in college in Cleveland, but he was making plans to visit New York again. Kitty described them as "seeing" each other. She supposed that making out at a gay club and then making plans over the phone to see each other again fitted into what people meant when they used the term "seeing." She told Stephanie he was a Russian Jew.

"You're not Jewish are you, Kitty?" Stephanie asked her. "No offense."

"None taken," laughed Kitty, "I take it as a compliment. They're smart."

"Jews aren't smart," Stephanie answered truculently. "*Asians* are smart. Jews just want you to *think* they're smart."

Kitty was taken aback. Well, this was awkward. She felt somehow that admonishing Stephanie would be the wrong thing to do, as Stephanie- between the two of them- had to be the better authority on multiculturalism. She wished she knew the protocol.

"I don't think it's going to work out with him, Kitty," continued Stephanie, morosely, shaking her head. "I don't see you as being down with their agenda."

Kitty became highly offended at this statement.

"I could *too* be down with their agenda!" she squeaked. Stephanie could be very irritating the way she thought she knew everything. "I went to *Cornell*," Kitty indignantly insisted.

Stephanie chuckled, shaking her head. "I don't know, Kitty. I don't see you as one of them."

Kitty was annoyed, although she said nothing more about it. She supposed it was a backhanded compliment of sorts, but she was a bit irked nonetheless. She could not stay irritated with Stephanie, though, because Stephanie was wicked fun.

While she was temping, Kitty continued to look for a job. After a couple of paralegal interviews, Kitty landed a position in business development for a large law firm. Her new boss's name was Mitch Winner. The name was very apt. He was a partner in a giant "global" law firm, and he was a middle-aged Mormon father of seven from Ohio. Actually, he was the only partner on that corridor who wasn't divorced. Kitty had impressed Mitch Winner in her interview when she told him she subscribed to the Economist. He said the fact she had gone to Cornell and read the Economist was why he hired her.

However, after working at the law firm for a few weeks, Kitty developed an alternate theory as to why she had been hired. Sitting in his office during one of the long boring sessions where he made her watch him make telephone calls, Kitty couldn't help but remark the eerie resemblance she bore to Mitch Winner's wife, whose photo was on his desk. Kitty looked just like a younger version of his wife- they could have been sisters. Kitty was no psychoanalyst, but she bet that had something to do with why she got the job. She also bet that had something to do with why Mitch Winner made her sit there in his office and watch him make telephone calls for hours on end.

Mitch Winner took Kitty out to lunch once. It seemed to make him nervous: he got noticeably more jocular and twitchy. Kitty remained glacially poised. As soon as they sat down, she whipped out a yellow legal pad and fine-tip black pen from her purse and planted them defiantly on the white linen tablecloth in front of her. She certainly didn't want him to get the wrong idea. She was there because she was paid, and she was paid to work. Mitch Winner displayed some visible annoyance, which was unusual for him- he usually maintained his annoyance at a constant roil just beneath the surface.

"You don't have to take notes," he said a little testily.

"Oh, I'm sorry. Of course," Kitty said frigidly and put the pad and pen away. She had made her point.

Only a Mormon could have mistaken Kitty in her Orthodox-Jew hemlines for a whore, Kitty thought dismissively. But then, Mitch Winner didn't really want a whore, did he, it occurred to her. He wanted someone he could pretend to come on to who would remain uninterested.

The partners had corner offices, the associates had hall offices, and the staff sat in cubicled alcoves along the hallways in sets of two. Kitty loved her cubicle-mate Gloria. Gloria was from Colombia, and she worked for a grizzled, elderly, divorced partner who did a lot of South American work. Gloria was overweight but pretty, with soft brown eyes which often looked sad. She didn't smile often, but when she did she was irresistible. She was 33 years-old, she was married, and she had two children- one was 17, the other was 4. She had her youngest child after she married her current husband, her eldest child was the product of an out-of-wedlock teenage pregnancy.

A lot of the Hispanic girls who worked at the firm had lives like that: teenage motherhood followed by getting your act together, meeting someone good, getting married, settling down, and a second child to cement the relationship. In fact, a lot of the uneducated white women Kitty knew operated that way too. Whereas the educated women who got knocked up as teens, they had abortions, and then drank themselves to death, thought Kitty. That was the difference college made, Kitty reflected mordantly.

When the partner was not around and Gloria had no work to do, she was sweet and talkative and kind. She told Kitty about how she'd met her husband, who was Puerto Rican, and she told her about Medellín, where she was from. But when Gloria was typing something up or her boss was near, her face was set, she was serious and focused. She was like a different person.

Like Kitty and Stephanie, once Kitty and Gloria found out that they both spoke Spanish they would chat in Spanish from time to time. A dirty secret of many of the lawyers at the firm was that they would put "Spanish" on their resume, but couldn't speak it or understand it. Mitch Winner, for example, had Spanish on his resume, but, when no one was around, Kitty and Gloria laughed at what he considered "Intermediate Spanish." A lot of the lawyers at the firm reacted to Gloria and Kitty speaking Spanish together the same way the consultants had reacted to Kitty and Stephanie speaking Italian- with suspicion. Fraternization often leads to dissension.

Kitty's job mainly consisted of writing marketing materials touting the mergers and privatizations and other deals the firm had closed. The biggest problem the job presented was that the lawyers never wanted to provide descriptions of their transactions to Kitty because talking to her wasn't billable. It was a great job, however. It involved writing, it involved marketing, it was complex enough that they needed someone educated, it had possibilities, but Kitty just wasn't happy, and it had nothing to do with the job.

Kitty was restless, Kitty was lonely. And this was part of why Kitty's boss was calling her into his office to watch him make phone calls for no good reason: Kitty was emitting flowery inviting pheromones. She couldn't help it. She longed for the one thing that is unattainable for a country-girl in Manhattan: a boyfriend.

Every night Kitty would come home from work, eat dinner with her parents and watch the news. She would stay up late, past midnight, so she could call Benoît when he got up in the morning. Benoît and Kitty burned up the phone lines, generating massive phone bills. Benoît swore he would reconquer Kitty, swore he would come to New York and win her back…

By day Kitty played her *petite comédie* with her boss, by night Kitty played her *petite comédie* with her ex. And always accompanied by the presence of the yawning chasm of loneliness that defined her life.

The first person Kitty called, after her mother told her Holcombe was dead, was Mike.

At 8 p.m. that Thursday night Kitty sat huddled on the floor of her parents' cramped Manhattan kitchen, her knees to her chest, still in her fancy Ann Taylor work clothes.

"I don't believe it," she said flatly, white-knuckling the plastic receiver, pressing it into her ear.

"Believe it," Mike said grimly. He was drunk, she knew. He was in Harrison. People were starting to gather. "Believe it. I talked to his mom."

Exactly two years later, on September 11, 2001, Kitty was to repeat the exact same dialogue with someone else:

*(flatly)* "I don't believe it."

*(grimly)* "Believe it."

This brief back-and-forth seemed to be the magical incantation that introduced an event that would rend the universe from end to end, open the heavens, break the world.

The next day Mitch Winner was sitting in his office at his computer working on a brief when there was a knock on his door.

"Come in," he called out, and he was surprised to see Kitty, who never came to his office except when summoned. He was even more surprised when, stooped and ashen-faced, she closed the door and burst into tears. She was incoherent. Her friend had died, he gathered that, and she was asking to take time off for the funeral. He also understood something about a car crash and something about high school.

Kitty had surprised Mitch Winner, now Mitch Winner surprised Kitty. He stopped what he was doing and gave her his full attention.

"Of course take some time off," he said gently. "Go and celebrate this life," he solemnly intoned, as though he were speaking before an audience in church.

He was being sanctimonious and expected admiration, but he meant it, and Kitty felt that.

"Thank you," she whispered.

Kitty returned to her cubicle, sniffing and red-faced. Gloria did not turn around. She remained rigidly fixated on her computer screen, her work-face on. She would rather have died than poked her nose into Kitty's business right now. Gloria was a lovely person.

Only when Kitty hissed "Gloria" did she turn around. Kitty was standing with her bag, ready to go. She had tidied up her work site, and her computer was off.

"I have to go back home," Kitty croaked. "My friend- from home- he died in a car crash."

"I'm so sorry," whispered Gloria. "I had that happen too. I know what it's like." Gloria didn't offer Kitty a hug or otherwise bullshit Kitty's pain. Her warm soft brown eyes conveyed how sorry she was.

Of course Gloria understands, Kitty thought dully, Gloria's from the ghetto. Urban poor and rural poor are both poor. And everybody knows poor people are reckless, Kitty thought bitterly. Reckless about creating life and reckless about ending it, that was Holcombe.

Kitty walked to the elevator feeling like she was walking into the sea, Gloria's whispered "Good luck" floating in her wake. Alone and enclosed in the elevator Kitty marveled at what was happening. She was leaving work, she was leaving the building, she was leaving the city, she was going back, back home. But what a Faustian bargain. You can only go home again once it's not there anymore.

As soon as she got off the subway at 23rd Street, Kitty bought cigarettes: American Spirit. At her parents' apartment, Kitty put on her best suit. It was not black, it was grey, but it was her best suit. Kitty would live and sleep in that grey suit for the next week. She was like an astronaut strapping on his spacesuit.

Kitty packed make-up, inhaler, cigarettes, a hip-flask that was supposed to be a joke and ended up not being a joke at all, and the cheap black plastic rosary with which she had back-packed around Europe.

Kitty had acquired the rosary under sinister conditions: a gypsy selling fortunes pressed it into her hand outside Notre Dame Cathedral. Flustered, Kitty handed the gypsy a five-franc note and fled. But maybe Kitty's good faith had changed the rosary's luck. Throughout all her travels in Europe she carried it in a special compartment of her backpack. She had brought it to Catholic masses in various Latinate countries. She had clutched it before her as she prayed at European pilgrimage shrines. She had grasped it in terror on plane trips, intoning whispered frantic Hail Marys to the discomfort of those nearby.

Kitty's parents had a collection of dozens of rosaries between them- an almost disrespectful amount, but it was impossible to dispose of a rosary. It was bad luck. Kitty's parents had rosaries from Jerusalem, rosaries from the Vatican, rosaries from Lourdes. They had rosaries from monsignors, they had rosaries from nuns, they had rosaries from their parents. They had cedarwood rosaries, onyx-bead rosaries, rosaries with beads like pearls. But Kitty grabbed this particular rosary because it was hers. It had seen her through some very dark times. Acquired in sin, it had been redeemed through suffering, and she clenched it twined between her fingers now, plastic and string.

Kitty left for Penn Station to take the Greyhound bus North to Albany. She did not know what she would do when she got to Albany, and she did not care.

She stared through the bus window out into the black night, but the black night just threw back her own reflection. All she really saw before her was, in black Times New Roman on white, were the words: "Holcombe is dead."

Floating above Kitty, looking down upon her in her grief, there is nothing anyone can say to her. There is nothing to say. What can you say? "It doesn't get better, but it gets less sore. After a long painful delirium, a stump forms, and the stump is functional. Try not to touch the wound. And don't focus on your lost limb. Focus on the capacity you have left." That wouldn't have helped Kitty at the time.

At around 10 p.m., the bus arrived in Albany. Kitty figured she would take the next bus from Albany heading West, toward Syracuse. In her fancy designer suit, carrying her black backpack, she stepped down the stairs of the bus into the Albany bus station, followed by various unaffiliated drug dealers who had been sitting in the back. She moved mechanically through an alternate universe.

The first thing Kitty saw when she exited the bus was Mike and her little brother Hugh. They had come for her. They had come.

For the first time, Kitty felt as though she had gained some foothold in the alternate-universe alien landscape into which she had just been violently thrust. She hugged them both. They were grim and taciturn and drunk. They were staying at Eli's house. Everyone was at Eli's house. That's where they would go.

Kitty was shocked they had driven all this way to pick her up. Mike had a live-in girlfriend now. And she couldn't remember the last time she had seen her brother do anything for anyone. But when it mattered, they had come for her.

Something about Mike struck her as very odd, and she couldn't put her finger on it. It was only when they were walking to Mike's car that she suddenly understood: he was wearing normal-sized pants. No more big pants. He didn't dress like a skater anymore.

Kitty had realized the second she got off the bus that Mike and her brother were drunk. Kitty was not, she was sober. And, indeed, for the next few days at the funeral, everyone present drank like a fish, including Kitty. But Kitty remained somehow stubbornly sober. As much as she drank along with everyone else, Kitty always remained in her right mind, although her right mind was not where she wanted to be.

Everything at Holcombe's funeral was like that. She was back home, but the one person she wanted to see wasn't there. She kept drinking, but she couldn't get drunk. She was surrounded by attractive guys, but there was no point. She looked beautiful, but it yielded no productive value. Everything was a non-starter. Barren. Fruitless. Sterile.

Mike drove Kitty and her brother to Eli and Zack's mom's place, where everyone was crashing. Eli and Zack's parents were notoriously cool and practiced some esoteric Eastern religion that Kitty had been assured was very mystical. Their mother was a mid-wife, and their father was a college professor. Their parents were divorced, and Eli's mom was away for the weekend with her boyfriend. She was very generously allowing the party of mourners stay at her house.

Mike and Kitty and Hugh arrived in Eli's mom's kitchen around midnight. A group of half a dozen boys was sitting around the kitchen table. In the center of the table was a pyramid they had started constructing out of beer cans. It was unfinished, but by the number of cans they had been sitting there for a few hours.

Eli was there, naturally. His little brother Zack was coming tomorrow. Kitty preferred Zack, who had a sunnier temperament. Eli, despite- or perhaps because of- his aggressively laid-back upbringing, had kind of a chip on his shoulder. He was constantly sarcastic. You never knew whether he was making fun of you or not.

Carson Reeves was there. His father was a Dean at the college, and his brother, who was gay, was a rising star at some famous tech startup. Handsome blonde Carson had dropped out of college and was working as a toll booth operator on the interstate.

Brian Decker was there. Brian had the personality of an accountant, but he had this deep abiding passion for Led Zeppelin that amounted to an obsession. His personality was actually pretty wooden and colorless until it came to Led Zeppelin, the strains of which provoked in him an unnerving ferocity that found its expression in groans, grimaces, and air guitar. Brian and Hugh would end party after party sitting for hours listening to Led Zeppelin. Brian and Carson were Hugh's best friends. Hugh and Brian went to SUNY Albany together.

Benji Russo was there. He had just dropped out of Boston University to be a music critic for a rock magazine. He'd always been full of shit, Kitty thought scornfully. He was wearing a black leather jacket, which she imagined must be requisite for that line of work. Benji and Mike had attended the Catholic elementary school together, they'd been altar boys together.

Chris Tanner was there. He was Holcombe's roommate in Portland, and he had been Holcombe's roommate in college. Like Holcombe, Chris was the first in his family to go to college. Unlike Holcombe, he graduated. He was a mellow, steady, dependable guy, but now his eyes were red and he looked shaken and horror-struck.

Scott Roy was there. His little brother Joe was coming in tomorrow. Scott had dropped out of community college, and he was living in Harrison and working in his father's hardware store.

They were mainly of Anglo, Irish, and German descent, with smatterings of Dutch, French-Canadian, and Italian. Except for Carson, everyone was Catholic. They were middle-class: their parents included an academic, a nurse, a mechanic, an electrician, a teacher, a plumber, a judge, and a janitor. In those days a janitor and a judge were both middle-class. People talked about "upper-middle-class" and "lower-middle-class"- nobody in Harrison, NY referred to anybody as "working-class." In Harrison, NY and other small towns, a janitor and a judge might be close relatives. It happened, and everyone shrugged. The town needed a janitor, the town needed a judge. Both occupations were part of the fabric of the town, and although obviously one occupation was more prestigious than another, there was no rigid caste system.

They were born into late 1970s America, during a dip in the birth rate, and they grew up together in the 80s and 90s. They grew up in an America where mothers didn't work, where divorce was uncommon, where the entire nation watched the same shows and listened to the same music, and some sort of a moral consensus prevailed. They would be the last generation to come of age off the internet. They would be the last generation to come of age in a culturally confident country. They would be the last generation to come of age in an intact America.

They would be the first American generation to do worse than their parents.

There were no chairs left around the table, so Mike and Hugh cracked open a couple of beers and remained standing. Kitty deposited her backpack in a corner of the kitchen, sank down onto the floor next to it, and wept. She had been weeping during the car ride too.

Huddled on the floor, sobbing, she was suddenly flooded with a sense of belonging. This was her tribe. They knew each other's siblings and parents, their siblings and parents knew each others' siblings and parents. They knew each others' formative memories, they knew each other's sexual histories- shoot, they knew each others' *medical* histories. They had come of age together. They knew *her*, they knew Kitty.

New York City and Europe fell away compared with this. This was who she really was. Most of her relationships there seemed ephemeral compared to this. Those people seemed like the ghosts, not Holcombe.

Kitty could pass years away from the people in this room, and it would be the same when she saw them again. Here she was, back from the Ivy League and Europe and New York City, cat-like and svelte, burnished with the glow of city glamor you can't help but give off when you live and work in Manhattan and visit the sticks. And nobody cared. They didn't care. To them she was and always would be Catherine Burnes, Hugh's big sister, known as Katie until Holcombe started calling her Kitty in 12th grade. And they let her sit on the floor and cry.

Scott, Brian, Carson, Chris- even Eli and Benji- they all knew her better than Benoît. What did Benoît know of her? That she was American. That she spoke French. That she was upper-class. That she was witty, that she was fun. For what had she been pining? For what had she been burning down the phone lines? It suddenly seemed to her that there was nothing there.

What did she have in New York? Her Mormon boss? She was nothing to him but a fetching shadow of his pretty wife before he wore her out with child-bearing. The Russian-Jewish kid? What did he know of her? That she was a shiksa? That she was pretty? That she too had been tricked into paying money to get into a gay bar?

Here were her brothers. All those hours of dull monotony, staring at the clock, waiting for the bell to ring and signal the end of class so you could get out of there. All the drifting through a clamorous throng to get to your locker, only to drift through a clamorous throng to get out at the end of the day. All the ecstasy and agony of hook-ups and break-ups. All the ritual humiliations of adolescence. All the boredom and suffering, trapped in that dull institutional brick building. Somehow, without their conscious recognition, time, place, and experience had worked on them like a kind of alchemy. The crucible of high-school had forged a tribe, however imperfect, and this was it.

This was Kitty's tribe- but her counterpart was missing. The only person she wanted to see, the person who most belonged to her and whom she most belonged to wasn't there, and would never be there again.

The boys sat around the table and talked glumly. Periodically one of them cracked open a can of beer, periodically one of them placed a new can on the pyramid, periodically one of them got up to go outside and either smoke a cigarette or take a leak.

Kitty paused her sobbing and looked up with bleary eyes. They weren't talking about Holcombe. They were talking about how Eli had gotten drunk and puked into Scott's sleeping bag on their last camping trip. Kitty couldn't stand it.

"Why did they let him drive?" she suddenly wailed from the floor in the corner. The boys stopped talking.

"Listen," said Eli harshly, narrowing his eyes. He was drunk. "It wasn't anybody's fault. It was nobody's fault."

Hippies were always like that in Kitty's experience. They pretended to be chill, but they'd come down on you like a ton of bricks if you stepped out of their worldview. And it was really easy to step out of their worldview because their worldview was bullshit. It involved pretending a lot of things that were ridiculous to pretend: like they all didn't know Holcombe was a terrible driver, like responsible people didn't stay up with drivers and talk to them to make sure they didn't fall asleep, like responsible people didn't dissuade nutcases from doing retarded things like trying to drive from Portland to San Francisco in one night. But this was Eli's house, and Kitty wanted to stay here tonight.

"Ok," she said submissively. "Ok." She wondered if Eli had slept with the girl who'd been in the car with Holcombe: Angelika. Kitty knew a lot of the boys had. He was probably trying to protect her, Kitty thought.

That was Kitty's entire contribution to the conversation. She continued to sit on the floor in the corner of the kitchen, alternately sobbing and listening to them reminisce about drunk times, until suddenly she realized that someone was addressing her. Kitty raised her head from her hands. "What?" she asked. They were all looking at her.

"He loved *you*," Benji repeated, slightly slurring his words. It was an accusation.

"I know," Kitty acknowledged in a whisper. It was an apology.

Around 2 a.m., Chris and Kitty went outside together to smoke a cigarette and came back into the house to find that everyone else had crashed somewhere to sleep. The only remaining free room was Eli's mom's room, and there was only one bed.

"I'll take the floor," Chris immediately drunkenly offered.

That's what kind of an honorable guy Chris was, Kitty thought. Rather than sleep in a bed with a girl that wasn't his girlfriend, Chris would take the floor.

"Ok," said Kitty. She didn't offer to give up the bed.

Kitty lay down on the bed fully clothed. Chris assembled pillows and blankets and stretched out on the rug, fully clothed as well. They were silent for a minute. Then, out of the darkness, Chris started speaking in a low voice.

"I can tell you how Holcombe died," he said quickly. "I talked to the guy who was in the car with him. He saw him die. He told me how it happened."

"Ok," said Kitty dutifully. She didn't want to know, and she didn't understand why Chris wanted to tell her; but he seemed to think it was important that she know, so Kitty thought she should listen.

The low, rushed, insistent voice coming from the floor proceeded to tell her how Holcombe died.

He was driving from Portland to San Francisco non-stop in one night. He was driving a guy Chris described as a "Phish kid" ("Bum," thought Kitty.) and Angelika ("Slut," thought Kitty.). The Phish kid and Angelika both fell asleep. Holcombe fell asleep at the wheel and drove into the guard-rail. He died at the scene. Angelika sustained a broken arm. The Phish kid escaped without injury.

Chris continued telling the story. His voice was even and rapid, and he spoke with an intensity Kitty had never encountered in him before. Kitty felt powerless to stop him.

"When Angelika got out of the car," said Chris, "she saw Holcombe on the ground. He was dying." Chris paused. "His chest was crushed," he whispered. "So he couldn't breathe, and he couldn't talk." Chris paused again. "He was just gasping," said Chris, "and he made some gurgling sounds."

All Kitty thought was: I know that chest, I know those lips, I know those eyes. Those were the only thoughts she could articulate. Everything else was pain.

"Chris," said Kitty suddenly, "I had an abortion."

She didn't need to say anymore. There was a silence. Kitty waited.

The voice coming up from the floor in the darkness spoke again. "Promise me something," it said.

"Of course," Kitty whispered.

"Don't tell his mother," the voice commanded matter-of-factly. "Never tell her about that."

"No," Kitty whispered, staring into the darkness. She blinked, and she felt the hot tears squeezing themselves out of the corners of her eyes. "No, I won't."

# Chapter 12: Holcombe's Father

The next day Mike, Hugh, Scott, Eli, Carson, Brian, Benji, Chris and Kitty packed themselves into two vehicles and drove out to the Erie Canal Trailer Park to pay their respects to Holcombe's father.

Kitty rode in Carson's car with Hugh, Chris, and Brian. Benji drove Eli, Scott, and Mike. Mike had been avoiding Kitty since he and Hugh met her at the Albany bus station. This was all well and as it should be. Kitty had no wish to fuck up Mike's relationship with his girlfriend, Rachel, who was joining them later today. She couldn't come yesterday because she was working. Rachel Griffin was Maura Carraway's cousin, she had been three grades below Kitty in school, and she was a nice girl.

Kitty had no desire to fuck up any relationships, her own or anyone else's, ever again. She was cursed, and she was happy for Mike that he had escaped her clutches. She wished him and Rachel every happiness.

Kitty got the front seat. She didn't call shotgun or anything, the boys just silently, deferentially ceded it to her, probably because they were spooked because she couldn't stop crying. The boys were just as miserable as she was, and sometimes they wiped away tears. But Kitty had been sobbing on and off since last night.

Hugh, Brian, and Chris crowded into the back seat. Carson was going to follow Benji's car. Mike was directing Benji, and he was the only one who actually knew where Holcombe's father lived.

Kitty lit a cigarette and started playing with the knobs on the radio.

"I have a Holcombe tape with me," Chris offered.

"No!" Kitty said fiercely. "I can't listen to a Holcombe tape right now!"

"Wait," Brian broke in from the back. "This is Zeppelin."

Kitty unwillingly stopped on that station. She liked Led Zeppelin, it was like breathing air where they were from, but Brian was obsessed.

Benoît once, in passing, had mentioned something about Led Zeppelin being English, and Kitty had corrected him.

They're *American*, she insisted. Benoît stubbornly responded: *"Mais ils sont tout à fait anglais!"*

Kitty indignantly refused to countenance this assertion. Led Zeppelin was as American as apple pie, as American as tailgating and pep rallies and keg-stands- American activities to which American Led Zeppelin was the American soundtrack. Kitty was American, and she thought she ought to know what her own country's music sounded like!

"Next you'll be telling me Pink Floyd isn't American either," Kitty scoffed contemptuously, then looked on with ill-humor as Benoît erupted into prolonged uproarious laughter.

"Turn it up," Brian was saying from the back. Kitty turned the knob all the way up and sat back.

It was D'Yer Maker. Hugh, Brian, and Chris started singing along in the back. Kitty and Carson joined in. The song, which had seemed like the staple of every oldies-station rotation, such that she didn't even recognize the song or the band because it was such a part of background noise, took on new dimensions. "I still love you so, you don't have to go." She heard for the first time. She started to get why Brian was obsessed.

How come she couldn't *always* be around people with whom she could spontaneously burst into song, Kitty wondered. Led Zeppelin was the baseline culture where she was from. She could have been riding in a car with almost anyone she went to high school with and they could have all spontaneously joined in the chorus of D'Yer Maker together, depending on the temperament of the car occupants, naturally. What Kitty would have given to live that way, to live among people who'd also grown up with Led Zeppelin as the accompaniment to their coming-of-age stories.

They had entered the trailer park. Kitty had never been in a trailer park before, though she had driven by many. It was kind of cute, this one anyway. The trailers weren't much different from little cheap houses, and they looked clean and neat. There were flowers and yard ornaments here and there. The cavalcade came to a halt in front of Holcombe's father's trailer. There was a sort of patio deck attached to it on which he was sitting, at a porch table under an umbrella, surrounded by some potted red geraniums. He was smoking a cigarette.

Kitty had never met Holcombe's father. She knew he was a ne'er-do-well and a drifter and that he'd been in the Navy. She also knew he never paid for anything for Holcombe, although she didn't know how she knew that, because Holcombe would never have admitted it.

The young people extricated themselves silently from their cars, over-awed with their mission, and shyly walked in a group up the porch steps: eight boys and Kitty in her best suit.

The young men approached Holcombe's dad somberly. He shook their hands, did not get up, but nodded gravely at them, acknowledging their tribute with the comically overdone dignity of a cannibal king. Kitty couldn't help but wonder whether he was enjoying the attention.

They stood around the picnic table awkwardly. There was a brief silence, broken by Holcombe's dad.

"I got more troubles than the law allows a man," he sighed dramatically. He *was* enjoying the attention, Kitty thought cruelly. And what about *Holcombe*, she seethed with silent indignation, what troubles does *he* have, you useless shiftless pud.

Kitty realized, staring at him, that Holcombe's father looked almost exactly like Holcombe, only twenty years older. Same ski-jump nose, same large soft brown eyes, same Ray Davies meets Harpo Marx quality. He seemed nervous, fragile. She sensed in him the same useless contrarian nature and the same otherworldliness that had been Holcombe's. He seemed a bit tougher than Holcombe. Holcombe was a hipster, his father looked like a scrappy little ex-military man. He had the tattoo of an anchor on his forearm, which had to be from his time in the Navy. Like Popeye, Kitty thought.

Chris politely asked Holcombe's father about his motorcycle. Holcombe's father started to talk about his motorcycle, but ended up telling them about how long it had been since he'd ridden his motorcycle because of his hernia. To Kitty's disgust, he started telling them all about his hernia- how his doctors were no good, how much an operation was going to cost, how bad his insurance was.

Kitty regarded Holcombe's father with distaste. How old was he anyway, Kitty wondered, Forty? My God, she had been *born* when her father was forty. Her father had been a young man at forty. Typical white trash, Kitty thought contemptuously, they whither on the vine before the age of *reason* even. So this was what Holcombe would have turned into: this whingeing, self-pitying, white-trash loser without a shred of dignity, whining to utter strangers about his health problems and his poverty, when his own son has just died.

And suddenly Kitty had a realization that was like getting doused with cold water: it didn't matter.

She would have taken it, she thought with a shock. She would have taken Holcombe the white-trash loser, the whingeing, useless, shiftless ne'er-do-well, if only it meant Holcombe alive. She would have married him, she would have cared for him, she would have stuck with him- even if he had turned into this pitiful creature before her. If only it meant he would still be here with her. There in the Erie Canal Trailer Park, this cold hard fact stared Kitty square in the face.

Startling the others, Kitty put her face down into her hands and sobbed anew. Nobody knew what had set her off (an outside observer might have concluded that Holcombe's father's struggles with his hernia had overwhelmed her), but that was ok, she was a female and allowed. In fact, it broke the ice a little bit, reassured the males and reminded them who they were.

When Kitty raised her face, Holcombe's father was regaling the boys with stories of his time in the Navy. He'd been stationed in the "sugar islands" among "the colored people."

"The colored people," Holcombe's father pontificated slowly "are the same as you and me." Above his head, the boys caught each other's glances and grinned. Kitty experienced a wave of irritation. She felt sure Holcombe's father was being deliberately politically incorrect for comic effect. She also felt irritated at the boys for egging him on. This was supposed to be about Holcombe.

They didn't stay long. Holcombe's father's wife, or girlfriend, started calling to him from inside and asking him questions, nagging. She never came out to say hello. She probably resented them coming. They took the hint, said their good-byes, and trooped silently back to their cars.

As they were getting back into Carson's car, Chris said to Kitty, "I know it's been hard for you, being the only girl. I know-we don't cry… and I know it's hard for you," he finished clumsily.

Kitty was surprised Chris had picked up on this.

"Tomorrow other girls are coming," Chris reassured her. Tomorrow was the wake.

## Chapter 13: Holcombe's Mother

That night, Friday night, Kitty and Chris went to pay their respects to Holcombe's mother. Everybody else chickened out.

Chris drove, from Eli's house in the village, along backroads out into countryside. It was a dark night, the moon was only a crescent. You could only dimly see the cornfields, the woods, and the cemeteries. But Kitty knew every twist and turn of the winding backroads to Holcombe's house. It had been such a pain to pick him up, it was so far out in the country. Holcombe was always trying to get people to pick him up at his house and bring him into the village. He was also always trying to get people to come out to his house and hang out with him when he had to babysit his little brothers.

When Kitty was a senior, Holcombe's little brothers had been about 3 and 5-years-old, and they made it very difficult to reach Holcombe by phone. Holcombe's room was in the attic, when he was home he was usually up there. Whenever the phone rang, his little brothers would seize upon it with delight. But that was the extent of their telephone skills. They were very good at getting the phone off the hook when it rang, but that was about it.

Kitty's heart sank whenever she called Holcombe, and a small baby voice answered sweetly, "Hello?"

"Tucker? Tucker is Justin there?" Kitty entreated.

Tucker was 3-years-old.

Sometimes, if Tucker was feeling magnanimous, he might answer softly in the affirmative. This gave Kitty hope.

"Tucker! Tucker, you go get Justin?!" Kitty would coach him encouragingly, as though playing "fetch" with a puppy.

There was a clatter. Tucker had put down the phone. Kitty waited with a sinking feeling, the receiver to her ear. Soon she heard Tucker playing nearby. He was making truck sounds.

"Tucker!" Kitty shouted desperately into the receiver. "Tucker!"

Kitty usually had slightly better luck with Cory, who was five. Cory you could at least try to negotiate with. But he too often forgot what he was doing, and Kitty could hear him in the background blithely going about his business, while Kitty shouted enticements regarding candy into the receiver until she went hoarse.

They parked in the driveway, and Holcombe's mother came out of the garage to meet them. She embraced Kitty, and the two of them held on to each other very tightly, crying, for what seemed an eternity. It didn't seem strange or awkward at all. Here was the person whose grief was more wrenching and more primal than Kitty's own. Night-time out in the country was dark, vast, and silent. It felt for a moment like it was just the two of them in a black empty world.

Then Holcombe's mother quieted. She greeted Chris, and thanked him for coming. She was a small woman with a pretty heart-shaped face that always wore a sad expression. Now her face was puffy from crying.

She invited them in. They walked through the garage and into the kitchen. Everything looked just the same. When they used to visit Holcombe, he would do what he called "Tours of My Mother's Insanity." His mother's insanity assumed a very innocuous form: she collected owls. She had little glass owls, ceramic owls, owl plates, owl dishtowels, crocheted owls, owl flowerpots. So a "Tour of My Mother's Insanity" consisted of strolling through the house, counting the owls they found in each room. It was very boring, and they usually made Holcombe stop before too long.

Holcombe's mother invited them to sit down on the orange couch in the living room off the kitchen. Then she disappeared up the back stairs in the kitchen, the stairs leading to Holcombe's room in the attic. Kitty caught a glimpse of Cory and Tucker sitting and watching tv in the next room. They were big boys now, school age. She marveled at how big they were. It hadn't occurred to her to keep in touch with them. She didn't want to greet them, she didn't want to infect them with her terror.

Kitty and Chris slunk over to the large orange couch and sat down. The "Circle of Love" family photo stared at them from the wall across from the room. Holcombe had been ruthlessly mocked over that photo.

The "Circle of Love" consisted of a circular formation of five photos: Holcombe, his mother and step-father, and his little brothers. Holcombe's mother and his stepfather looked happy, smiling, and relaxed. In real life Kitty had never seen them look like that. Tucker and Cory looked like nineteenth-century greeting-card cherubs: blonde curls, rosy cheeks, bow lips.

Holcombe, for some obscure reason, looked like Quasimodo. He appeared to be a hunchback. It had to be the weird vest he was wearing. Classic 70s-era white trash, Kitty thought, a butterfly collar and a vest. His face was also strangely twisted into an expression somewhere between a grimace and a leer. One eyebrow was raised, one was lowered, and his teeth appeared clenched. Kitty guessed that what had happened was that a photographer had put an awkward 16-year-old on the spot, had humiliated and patronized him, and, finally, appealing to filial duty, had exerted psychological pressure- and this was the ghastly result.

"The Circle of Love has a missing link!" Kitty would tease Holcombe.

Holcombe's mother emerged from the kitchen, cradling a stack of large portfolio-sized faux-leather-bound books in her arms. Kitty recognized Holcombe's sketchbooks with dread. Holcombe's mother sat down on the couch between Kitty and Chris.

The last thing Kitty wanted to do was peruse Holcombe's sketchbooks, some of which she had collaborated on. She didn't understand how people had the desire at this moment to listen to his tapes, study his artwork, read his poems, or watch his videos. Peering into the vast chasm of horror to try to inventory the loss seemed like a very bad idea right now. It was probing a serious open wound; it could be fatal.

But Holcombe's mother didn't seem to be interested in showing the artwork to Kitty. She sat between Kitty and Chris, carefully turning the pages of her freshly dead son's sketchbook. She seemed a bit awed. Kitty wondered if she had waited for Kitty and Chris's arrival to study them, so that they could serve as interpreters.

Each time Holcombe's mother turned a page, she paused and gazed wonderingly at what she found, as though somewhere in these notebooks she could come across some explanation for the horrifying mystery of what was happening. Kitty and Chris sat nervously bolt upright on either side of her.

She seemed scarcely aware of their presence. She was absorbed, she was searching for clues.

Holcombe's mother paused for longer than usual at the next page. Kitty leaned in to see what she was staring at. It was a page filled with bottoms. A proliferation of round, curley-queued, swirled buttocks crowded the page: an army of asses like angels' wings. Beneath the asses, printed in a small stylized hand, was a short poem:

> *and sex and sex and sex*
> *and shattered*

Holcombe's mother stared silently at the page for a while. Kitty and Chris sat frozen. Finally, she turned to face Kitty.

"Was Justin…was Justin *gay*?" she hazarded.

That was not the question Kitty had expected. She was flooded with relief. Here was a question that she could easily answer.

"Oh, no, Mrs. Collins!" she replied earnestly. "No, he wasn't gay! My goodness, not at all, he-" Behind Holcombe's mother's shoulder, Chris caught Kitty's eye. His eyes widened, and he gave an almost imperceptible shake of his head.

"No, he wasn't gay," Kitty concluded in a more somber tone. "Girls loved him," she added gently.

"I never understood him," his mother murmured faintly, the sketchbook open on her lap. "I didn't have to," she added sorrowfully, closing the book.

She turned and looked at Kitty. "He loved *you*," she said wonderingly. It was not an accusation. It was spoken like the dazed survivor of a natural disaster who, surveying the ruins, makes an attempt to quantify what remains.

## Chapter 14: Holcombe's Wake

Holcombe was dead. There he was. Kitty waited silently in the line of mourners at his casket. No one spoke. She was wearing her grey suit of course, and she wound her fingers through her black plastic rosary.

And now it was her turn. Kitty scrambled into a kneeling position on the prie-dieu, clutching her rosary that looked like the kind of trinket you'd win as a duck-duck prize at the county fair. She was so grateful that she had been brought up to know how to operate these tools, to be conversant in this language. Form was astoundingly comforting in the face of this horror, and she fell back into its arms: "Hail Mary," she murmured, "Full of grace...."

For any mourner praying at a casket the question is: Do you look up? Kitty had been to wakes before. Usually, she did not. Usually, she just cast a quick glance at the face, after having prayed and before she left the casket, because it seemed the respectful thing to do. It seemed disrespectful to ignore the body completely.

This was different. Kitty stared. It was not Holcombe, of course, Holcombe was gone. It was his dead body. And it smelled funny- like industrial-strength cleaning solution.

She stared at Holcombe's dead face, his dead hands, his dead chest. Did his chest seem uneven? She remembered with horror what Chris had said: Holcombe's chest was crushed.

There was the mole above his lip. There was the finger he had broken that had never properly healed. His lips had the same curve. Was that makeup? Fancy not seeing Holcombe for a couple years, and then meeting up with him like this, she thought numbly.

This was her last chance to memorize everything before they put it into the ground. It reminded Kitty of the night she had cleaned out her room. Again she was being granted one brief moment to retain what she could.

Kitty felt like if there weren't all these other people here, if Holcombe wasn't saturated with whatever chemical was causing that smell, if she was just allowed to *get* to him, she felt sure she could reach him. Holcombe would have done anything for her. Maybe there was still the faintest trace of him left in there somewhere, maybe it would respond to her, maybe she could connect, if only she could get closer.

And all of a sudden, Kitty was being led away.

She stumbled alone past the line of waiting mourners, still clutching her rosary, and burst through the doors of the funeral home and into the sunlight. The funeral home was across the street from the village green, and the green, the fountain, the church, the art center, the fire station- everything looked as pretty and bright and shiny and new as a movie set. Cars passed by. Saturday afternoon.

Her pack of cigarettes was in her pocket, with her inhaler and a lighter stuffed inside, the way she had done it in high school. With trembling hands she pulled the yellow cigarette pack from her pocket. She took out a cigarette, put it to her lips, put the cigarette pack and the rosary back into the pocket of her suit blazer, cupped her hand around the cigarette, and stopped.

In the bright sunshine she could see the blue veins in her pale hands. She could see the life coursing through her veins. These were the mottled trembling hands of a live person, unlike Holcombe's hands, which were a dull monocolor now, which had become *objects*. The life running through her veins seemed a rebuke to her. It seemed incongruous. She was not here, she was with Holcombe, yet here she was, still on the other side. The people she saw around her also seemed like a rebuke. It seemed very unfair.

They talked about disadvantaged youth, Kitty thought wildly, they talked about people with disabilities, they talked about people with special needs. Holcombe was at a severe disadvantage compared with everybody now, his disability so great as to render him defunct, his needs so special nobody could even tell what they were. And her own life and everybody's life around her seemed a monstrous privilege, a mocking injustice to Holcombe, lying there misunderstood and deprived.

As Kitty's eyes began to process the scene around her, she spotted Carson sitting alone on a bench by the fountain, across the street on the green. Kitty, still holding her cigarette, bounded across the street, prompting a honk, and made a beeline for him.

Carson sat with his back to the funeral home, staring into the fountain and smoking a cigarette. He looked very pale and very young.

"Can I have a light?" Kitty asked although she had a lighter. "My cigarette's gone out." She wanted to direct the situation toward the quotidian, tangible, and definite.

"Sure, here you go," he said, handing her a lighter.

As she lit her cigarette, he said rapidly, still staring at the fountain, "I'm scared." Carson looked up and met her eyes. "Have you seen him?" he demanded, frowning.

One time during Kitty's senior year, she and her little brother and Holcombe and Carson were hanging around making prank phone calls. They were picking names out of the phone book and competing to see what they could come up with.

Suddenly Kitty's little brother shouted with joy.

"Look!" he said pointing. They read the name he was pointing to: "Ron Bleenis."

"No way!" they all said. It was too great. It was so great that it was impossible to do it justice.

"Me," Carson said quietly. "This one's mine."

So Kitty and her little brother and Holcombe all stood back and listened, while Carson picked up the phone in Kitty's mother's sitting room and dialed.

"Hello?" It was a man's voice.

"Ron *Bleenis*, your *penis* is the *cleanest*!" Carson chanted sing-song in a choir-boy falsetto.

The effect was all they could have hoped for. "You're gonna *die*!" they could all hear the man bellowing with rage.

Legend.

Now Carson was frowning at Kitty, and she saw he was trying not to cry.

"It's not him," Kitty told Carson gently. "It's his body. He's not there. He's gone."

She wiped her eyes with the back of her left hand, and took a drag on her cigarette. "I was scared too. But there's nothing there to be scared of in there. It's his shell. He's gone. That's the scary part. That he's gone."

126

"Kitty!"

Kitty heard a female voice calling her name. That was never good. She didn't turn around. "Kitty!" the voice called again. "Who is it?" she hissed at Carson. Carson shrugged. She turned around. On the other side of the green, three girls were getting out of a parked black 1992 Cadillac Deville. The Long Islanders had arrived.

Kitty left Carson, and went to meet them. She knew these three girls. Improbably, their names were Jamie, Julie, and Jenny. They were Holcombe's friends from SUNY Albany. They were all half-Jewish and half-Italian, and they had all slept with Holcombe- Kitty knew that too. They were part of a cavalcade of Holcombe's college friends that had driven up from The Island. They must have driven at least six hours to get to the middle of nowhere- the hinterlands. There was another car of them pulling up, Kitty could see.

Jamie, Julie, and Jenny emerged stiffly and stretched themselves. Jamie and Julie lit cigarettes. All three were wearing black sunglasses and dressed in black.

These days many people do not know how to dress for a funeral. They do not even wear dark colors. And many young women these days interpret any formal occasion as an opportunity to dress like a whore. Kitty had already observed a few backless sundresses in the line of mourners. With any young crowd at a formal occasion that sort of thing was to be expected.

Not Jamie, Julie, and Jenny. Say what you want about Long Islanders, but they typically know how to dress for a funeral. The three girls were swathed head to toe in black, including black stockings and large, sensible, black, Doc Marten-style shoes. These were no little black dresses. There was absolutely nothing sexy about their getups. They were disfiguring, as the occasion demanded. It looked as though they had raided their Sicilian grandmothers' closets.

The last time Kitty had seen these girls they had been wearing sagging, voluminous, skater pants and tiny midriff-baring t-shirts emblazoned with band names, the better to show off their bellybutton rings. Their eyes were rimmed with liquid eyeliner. Their hair was blue, their hair was purple. They had nose-rings, they had tongue-rings. They had tattoos.

All that was gone. Only the Doc Martens remained the same.

No tattoos were visible, no body jewelry. Kitty saw the hole in Jamie's nostril where her nose ring had been. Their hair, healthy dark brown now, was pulled back and fastened. They wore no makeup. They looked fragile and sallow. Under their sunglasses, their eyes were red-rimmed, puffy, shadowed with dark circles.

The three girls embraced Kitty, and they wept. They keened. Kitty was astounded by their transformation. Their hipness had fallen away. In their grief they had cast it off. They stood now reclaimed by the Old World.

Because their mourning was Old World. It was distinctly Mediterranean: the long black garments, the sallow complexions, the wailing. They resembled nothing so much as a group of Sicilian fishermen's widows participating in a time-honored village ritual of descending *en masse* to the harbor to lament to the gods, rend their garments, and hurl imprecations at the sea. Ellis Island, Brooklyn, Queens, Long Island; their snappy two-syllable American names; their hipster aesthetic- all had just fallen away.

They were good girls, as it turned out.

After they had embraced, Jamie, the shortest and most talkative of the three, took a pack of cigarettes out of her purse, handed one to Julie, and offered one to Kitty. "No, thanks," said Kitty, "I've got some."

Julie, the tallest and least talkative, took a hip flask out of her purse and passed it to Jamie, who took a slug and offered it to Kitty. "No, thanks," Kitty repeated. "I've got some."

Jenny was the driver, she wasn't drinking. Kitty seemed to remember that Jenny was studying to be a librarian. Jenny must be the sensible one, Kitty thought.

"Julie got the cops called on her Thursday night," Jamie blurted out, like a proud mother who couldn't bear to keep her child's achievements secret any longer. "She trashed her apartment when she found out he was dead."

Kitty didn't know whether to act impressed or concerned, so she made some noises that she hoped conveyed both. Personally, she couldn't relate to that level of self-indulgence.

Julie seemed oblivious to what Jamie was saying, she seemed far away. She reminded Kitty of a chihauhua: high-strung, with large, brown, nervous eyes. She seemed jittery, but spacey at the same time, and Kitty wondered if she were on something.

"I like to think he's in Africa," Julie said hoarsely. "Like he's living there now. We won't see him again but he's there."

This Kitty understood. She nodded. She had the same desire to fantasize that he was simply away. She had even fantasized about the same location- Africa. Probably because of the Toto song, Kitty thought. Julie may have been unhinged, violent, and on drugs, but she and Kitty were on the same page when it came to the big picture.

"He loved *you*," said Jenny suddenly. The sensible one. It was another accusation, like Benji had made.

"Yes," Kitty acknowledged. She wasn't about to apologize for this to Jenny, that was for sure.

"Is that the funeral home?" Jamie asked, pointing toward the other side of the green.

"Yes," said Kitty.

"Have you seen him?" Jamie demanded abruptly.

"Yes," said Kitty. She said the same thing she'd just said to Carson: "It's not him."

"I'm getting a tattoo," Julie whispered to Kitty. "Just: Holcombe. In his handwriting." She slowly drew her hand across her upper arm. "Right there," she said softly.

"That's a great idea," Kitty said in a tone that she meant to sound soothing. The idea of getting a Holcombe tattoo seemed redundant to Kitty. She felt like she was a walking Holcombe tattoo. She was marked for life.

From the second car, a 1988 Pontiac Fiero, emerged Holcombe's buddy Eric. Eric was the only Scandinavian from Long Island Kitty had ever met. He was Holcombe's opposite: stolid, positive, definite, steady, placid, determined. His girlfriend came out of the passenger side. Tall, blonde, massive: she looked like she could have been his sister.

Mild-mannered Eric was red-eyed and uncharacteristically distraught.

"Is Aaron here?" he demanded. "He's not, right? I left him all these messages, he hasn't returned any of my calls." Aaron Kaufman had been Holcombe's freshman-year roommate.

Inwardly Kitty marveled at Eric's naivete. Of course Aaron wasn't going to drive six hours out of the city to attend the funeral of the white-trash drop-out he'd happened to be roomed with freshman year.

Kitty remembered meeting Aaron when she visited Holcombe at college. Aaron was excited to meet her because she went to Cornell, it gave him a higher opinion of Holcombe. Kitty didn't dislike Aaron, he was pleasant enough, but people like Aaron made Kitty nervous. They made her feel like she was in a hostage situation. She wanted to give them whatever they wanted, just concede to their ulterior designs, and get away from them.

But when Eric asked angrily, "Where's Aaron, why hasn't he bothered to show up?", Kitty didn't bother to offer her two cents.

If Eric, being from Long Island, didn't understand why, then it was nothing that Kitty could explain to him. Aaron was undoubtedly moving up some ladder somewhere. There was no advantage to Aaron of taking a break from moving up that ladder for the funeral of a white-trash clown. If what you valued was status, then you really had no use for Holcombe. And Kitty knew that underneath it all, for people like Aaron, she and Holcombe were the same.

Kitty didn't blame Aaron, it was just his nature. Aaron was worldly, and Holcombe was otherworldly- now more than ever.

Kitty watched them walk off toward the funeral parlor: the three Sicilian widows and Eric the Viking and his shield maiden. She lit another cigarette and was struck anew by the blue veins in her pale hands: life mocked her.

All at once, a thought struck Kitty and she sprang up and examined the bench on which she had been sitting. This was it. This was the bench where Holcombe had scrawled "Time for Shitty!" It was only a few years ago. Where was it? All the benches around the fountain had borne messages from Holcombe. That bench over there, it should say "Oedipus Schmoedipus!" on the back, she thought. And "Jermaine was not

130

germane to the Jacksons!" should be scrawled on the back of that bench over there.

Kitty surveyed the bench. She walked around it. She knelt on the ground and peered up at the underside of it. But it didn't say "Time for Shitty!" on it. Not anywhere.

Kitty felt a rising panic, she tried to stay calm. She walked over to the next bench. It didn't say "Oedipus Schmoedipus!" on it. It had no writing on it anywhere. Maybe she had gotten the benches wrong, she thought. She checked the other two. She circled them, looking them over carefully, she knelt down on the ground in her $300 suit, and peered up at them from below, ripping the pantyhose on her left knee. There was nothing written on any of them. Kitty stood up, feeling her heart pounding. Everything seemed too bright and too real. She took another drag on her cigarette.

As she did she spotted one of the three widows- it was Jenny, the librarian- leave the funeral home alone, her arms folded tightly across her chest. Jenny crossed the street, huddled into herself, reached the fountain and sat on a bench, where she flopped down and put her head between her knees, clutching her ankles. Kitty approached and stood over her. "Can I help you?" she asked politely.

"I'm ok," Jenny replied in a muffled voice.

Kitty remained nearby but looked away towards the funeral home in case Jenny didn't want to be stared at. Jenny said something else that was muffled.

"What?" asked Kitty.

"I'm the only one he didn't sleep with," Jenny repeated.

"Oh," said Kitty politely. Kitty had less than zero interest in this particular line of conversation at this particular time.

Jenny sat up and wiped her eyes and smoothed back her hair, tucking it behind her ears.

"Can I have a cigarette?" she asked Kitty. "I quit," she laughed ruefully.

Kitty said "Sure," and handed Jenny a cigarette and her lighter. She wondered how many cigarettes Jenny was going to bum from her. She hated it when people who didn't want to buy a pack bummed all their cigarettes from you.

"We had this agreement," Jenny said, lighting the cigarette quickly and expertly. "That if we got to thirty and we

131

both weren't married, that we would find each other and get married." She laughed ruefully again, and her laughter quickly turned into sobs.

"I'm sorry," Kitty said and hugged Jenny mechanically. Kitty knew that it was she who would always have first dibs on Holcombe's affection- and everyone else knew that too. But let Jenny believe she and Holcome had this special secret understanding if it made her feel any better.

While the girls were hugging, a bright yellow school bus, brighter in the strong afternoon sun, lurched into view and roared past. It got both the girls' attention, and they looked up. As the bus passed, in the back window, they saw a little face with a ski-jump nose and two large shining eyes looking out at them from under the rim of a floppy newsboy cap. Just like the newsboy caps Holcombe used to wear. The little face gleamed brightly at them, a little hand waved, and then the bus was gone.

Kitty and Jenny sat on the bench together looking after the bus as it drove away. They didn't say anything for a moment. Then Jenny turned to Kitty. With a sound between a laugh and a sob she said, "I'm glad you saw that too."

## Chapter 15: The After-Party

Holcombe's mourners stood grouped into clusters around the entrance to the funeral home. It was five o'clock and visiting hours had ended, but no one wanted to leave each other. The girls were crying, the boys were ashen-faced.

Holcombe's was the first funeral in their circle. Subsequent funerals would have progressively fewer attendees, and the attendees were progressively less bereft, progressively more distracted, progressively more resigned.

In fact, Holcombe's funeral brought out the tribal in his mourners like none of the other funerals to come would. Maybe because his was the first tragic death, so it was a shock. Maybe because everyone was so young. No one had spouses or children of their own, everyone had just been expelled from their university cocoon into the world of impersonal relationships. Holcombe's death had summoned them back. But maybe it was simply because of Holcombe. He had been their poet, their shaman, their wizard, their jester, their Druid, in a world where such things seemed to have gone extinct.

Holcombe's death, although it occurred two years previously, would always be associated in Kitty's mind with 9/11. Both events shattered Kitty to pieces, flattened her with shock, overwhelmed her with tragedy.

And both were only the beginning.

They were not isolated events as they seemed at the time, they were dramatic prefaces that ushered in a new chapter. They starkly punctuated the beginnings of general trends which- ten, twenty later- are just a way of life, and many people now know no different.

Holcombe was the most difficult loss for Kitty, but he was only the first friend she lost to an accelerating trend of white working-class Americans dying deaths of despair. Just as 9/11 was one of the first instances of another accelerating trend.

Such that, almost two decades later, what seemed most remarkable to Kitty about Holcombe's funeral and 9/11 were the responses to them at the time. The events- a death through recklessness born of despondency and an attack on American soil- in hindsight do not seem as notable as the reaction to them. 9/11 galvanized the country with a patriotism that almost two decades of fruitless war later, would be hard to recreate. Holcombe's funeral brought his friends together to mourn him as a tribe. Today it's not the tragedies that seem unusual: it's the patriotism, it's the tribe.

Kitty stood smoking a cigarette in a group that included Carson, Brian, Benji, and Eli. Hugh, Mike, Rachel, Scott, and others stood in a huddle nearby. Kitty saw Jessica Williams officiously flitting among the bands of mourners- taking a moment to stand with each, listening and nodding, a hand on cocked hip, before flouncing off self-importantly to another group. The more things changed, the more they stayed the same. The only thing different was that Holcombe wasn't there with Kitty to mock Jessica Williams, and never would be there again.

Kitty had gone back inside the funeral home once more before viewing hours were over. She had to see him one last time. She waited in line again and approached the casket again. This time she wasted no time looking down, but- muttering Hail Marys which continued in her head even now- she tried to fix it all into her memory: the knuckle of his left hand that hadn't mended right, the mole above his lip, on the right side, the curve of his lip, the slope of his nose, his brows, his lashes. And again someone led her away. She had taken too long.

Her black plastic rosary was in her blazer pocket. It stank of formaldehyde. The smell of formaldehyde would never come off that rosary.

"What are we doing?" Kitty asked the boys. She was exhausted, but she wanted to stay with the group.

"I think we're going to the rock garden in the glen," said Carson. He had seen Holcombe. He was pale but composed.

"Sanger Glen" was the woods behind the college, named for Jedidiah Sanger, the Connecticut Yankee who founded the town. They were Northern woods: maples, birches, spruce. In the middle of the forest, there was a clearing with a stream running through it, and the college had made this a meditative space with a Japanese rock garden and a Buddha statue. Naturally, local kids went there to smoke pot.

"Where are you guys going?" Jamie broke into the group.

"Sanger Glen," said Brian. "It's the woods at the college."

"We don't know where that is," protested Jenny the sensible one. "We don't know where we are."

"You're his *college* friends?" Scott growled at them. Like most everyone else, he was drunk. He glowered at the three girls in black. Kitty envied Scott his drunkenness. She had been drinking too and, despite her best efforts, remained lucid.

"Have you met Julie, Jamie, and Jenny?" Kitty asked Scott politely.

"Yeah, well, we're his *Harrison* friends," he snarled, slurring his words. "We're his *hometown* friends. Because this is his *home*."

Kitty, while pretending to disapprove, felt grateful to Scott for making this distinction. She was gratified to have it spelled out, and it made her feel magnanimous towards the girls.

"Come with me," she told them. "I can ride with you, I can take you where we're going."

Kitty felt a responsibility to do right by the three Sicilian widows. They had come so far and in such good faith. They loved him. So Kitty rode with Jenny and directed her up to the college, Eric following closely behind. A flotilla of cars snaked their way up the hill through the pretty early 19th century New England style campus, to the parking lot by the woods.

Kitty wished she were riding with her high-school friends. These were their old stomping grounds. Kitty remembered the time when Carson got diagnosed with ADD senior year. The day Carson picked up his meds, they had all taken Kitty's parents' station wagon up to the glen. The boys crushed Carson's Ritalin into a fine powder and snorted it off the hood of the car, and then they went and played bongos in the woods. Kitty wondered whether the others remembered.

People were getting out of their cars and congregating in groups. Some of the boys wore button-down dress shirts, some wore polos. All the girls wore skirts or dresses. Bands of mourners started leaving the parking lot and entering the woods by the path next to the trail marker. It felt magical to watch the bevy of formally-dressed young people disappearing in twos and threes into the woods in the Indian-summer dusk.

They walked the trail single-file, a long line of people marching through the woods, to the Japanese rock garden in a clearing by the stream. There were a couple benches facing the giant rock and the Buddha statue in the center of the garden.

Some girls sat on the benches, the boys stood. It was twilight in the wood. The sun would not set for about an hour.

A steady hum of conversation permeated the group. There was a lot of catching up to do. There were people who hadn't seen each other since high school. There were also people who had never seen each other who suddenly wanted to see a lot of each other, and the conglomeration started to take on a cocktail-party atmosphere as the buzz of conversation grew more intense. Someone lit a joint, and it started to make the rounds. Kitty refused. She wanted to be able to communicate with Holcombe's mother, and she was afraid that if she smoked pot she wouldn't be able to connect with her. Someone broke out a bottle of whiskey and started passing it around. Kitty didn't pass that up. She took a swig, burned her throat, and dulled her senses a little.

Kitty passed from group to group. She could talk to anyone there, she knew everyone. But there was no group that was hers where she belonged. Holcombe had been her group. Mike and Holcombe had been her group. Mike sat with his girlfriend. And that was fine, Kitty was happy for him. Mike was trying to construct something in this world, he had something he was trying to protect, and Kitty respected that. She was still grateful to him, would always be grateful to him, for meeting her at the station.

In the fading daylight, Kitty stood for a moment apart from the others and looked at the crowd filling the forest clearing. Everyone there was really just bits and pieces of reflections of the only person who most belonged to her and to whom she most belonged- and his body was lying back down the hill in the funeral home off the village green.

It occurred to her that soon all of this would be over, that everybody would go home. There would be a diaspora of Holcombe mourners. And she would spend her life like this, moving easily from group to group, not really belonging to anyone, no one really belonging to her. She took another swig of whiskey. The Sicilian widows were sitting on one of the benches, and Kitty made her way over to them.

"Wait, I want to tell you guys something," said Kitty, "Chris and I went to Holcombe's mother's house last night, and Holcombe's mom got out all his sketchbooks." The girls stared at her solemnly. "So Holcombe's mom is looking at this one sketchbook page full of asses- you know the curlicues he would draw when he was starting to trip? So Holcombe's mom looks at me and she goes..." Kitty paused for effect. "'Was Justin *gay*?'"

Peals of laughter rang out. "I know, right?" said Kitty, smirking. "And I'm like, Uh, no, I'm not sure what you want me to say, but no...." The girls laughed together. Holcombe was notoriously heterosexual; he was at the mercy of females.

The light was getting dimmer and some of the party, chiefly the SUNY Albany crowd, wanted to leave the woods. Some of the locals, drunk, wanted to relocate to somebody's field where they could have a bonfire. The mourners made their way through the darkening woods, back to their cars, and it was decided that their destination should be the local dive-bar, Ron's Dock.

Ron's Dock was a famous Harrison attraction. It was a sloping decrepit shack of a watering-hole that contained what many locals fiercely maintained was the most excellent jukebox in America. A few dedicated local eccentrics unironically considered it their life's work to cultivate, hone, refine, and burnish the body of work available in that jukebox. The bartenders were chosen for musical sensibilities. Any change to the jukebox roster was preceded by lengthy and lively discussion that might end up involving everyone in the bar. Kitty had been there during the discussion of the motion to include Phil Collins Genesis alongside Peter Gabriel Genesis. Purists finally succeeded in tabling the motion by loudly denouncing the lack of quorum, but she felt sure the Phil Collins faction had probably managed to get their way by now.

It was always what Kitty's mother would call "pitch-black" inside. There were dart boards and a pool table in the back. Occasionally college kids, slumming it, would frequent The Dock. They stuck out, they did not fit in. Kitty knew that she could walk into The Dock any night of the week and find someone she knew- knew their first name and last, their occupation, where they lived, their relatives, their high-school GPA, criminal and medical history- and who knew the same about her. Whenever anyone was in town, they came to The Dock to find people.

Holcombe's mourners flooded the establishment, displacing some college kids and a couple of locals, who retreated to stools at the bar. Kitty had caught a ride down the hill back to town with Chris. She wanted to be with the Harrison people. She walked into Ron's Dock with Chris, Carson, Brian, and her brother Hugh. Hugh went to the bar to get some beers, and Kitty ducked into the Ladies' Room.

You could have done an anthropological survey of the graffiti in The Dock's bathroom. It was like Icelandic sagas in there. The loves and the hates of Harrison, NY were recorded there for the ages, decades of graffiti, sometimes scribbled, sometimes painstakingly etched, sometimes ornately inscribed with three-dimensional shading, and embellishments and flourishes. You could find people's *parents'* names on those walls.

The last time Kitty had been in this bathroom, Holcombe had been with her. Last year she came home from Spain for Christmas, she went to the Dock with her brother, and Holcombe was there. He affected to be cold and distant with her, which Kitty found ridiculous. But if that was what he wanted, then she could do that too.

Little did Holcombe know that after they had broken up, Kitty had discovered her element- her soulmate- and it wasn't a person. What you saw of Kitty now was only the tip of the iceberg, a vast unclaimed territory lay out of sight: a territory where Kitty spoke other languages- became a different person- became different *people*. The unseen presence hovering about Kitty was the entire mighty continent of Europe- the Old World. Kitty had gotten lost in it, had lost herself in it, and what she found was an American. The people, the streets, the food, the architecture, the history- and the addictive sensation of being a foreigner. Finally, as a foreigner on the *vieille continent*, Kitty made sense to herself.

But you couldn't expect Holcombe to understand any of this. This was the lunatic who'd dropped out of college and used his financial aid money to travel to Wales. Really. What kind of a white person would something like that even occur to, thought Kitty contemptuously.

Kitty had called him after she arrived home from Europe. She wanted to tell him everything: about Madame Hoffenberg and Rue Daguerre, about the Basque country and Normandy. She went to a party on a houseboat in Amsterdam, she saw a bullfight in Spain, she met mafia in Naples, she toured Christiania in Copenhagen, she got swindled in the Czech Republic, she hitched a motorcycle ride along Norwegian fjords. All the long discussions they had together on their long walks, all the dreams and plans- here was Kitty topping them all, and she expected Holcombe to want to know.

But he hadn't even asked her about her nine months in Europe, the boor. Instead, he told her about his own trip to Wales. He hadn't been impressed with the people. He was disappointed with the "big-hair girls" he found there.

"Aren't you going to ask me about Europe?" Kitty had asked him indignantly.

"Oh, I never ask anybody about anything," Holcombe responded airily. "I always figure they'll tell me what they want me to know."

Kitty was infuriated with Holcombe. When she got off the phone, she told her mother what he had said, and her mother replied, "Well, I kind of agree. People do generally tell you what they want you to know." And then Kitty was infuriated with her mother.

That was the last time they had spoken until they saw each other here at The Dock last Christmas. Holcombe was frosty, Kitty didn't care. Let him be contrarian and pretend they didn't know each other, she thought. It didn't matter. But she was irritated nonetheless. She left her brother and Holcombe and Benji at the bar and went to the Ladies' Room.

As she opened the door she sensed someone behind her, right on her heels. She was jostled to the side as Holcombe rushed past her into the restroom. He stood in front of the sink, his eyes wide, his head rotating back and forth like a tourist at the Sistine Chapel. "So this is what it's like," he breathed wonderingly. "I've never been in here."

It *was* pretty spectacular, really. The earliest graffiti dated from the early 70s, and the parents of several people Kitty went to high school with were featured- and not always coupled with their subsequent spouses, either. There was a Led Zeppelin tag, a Pink Floyd tag, a Who tag, a Def Leppard tag. Chiefly, there were declarations of love: "I [heart] Matt" and complaints: "Matt

Curtis lies." or "Matt Curtis cheats" or- and this is the kind of stuff the males really cared about- "Matt Curtis has a tiny little dick." It was a bit like the opening lines of Anna Karenina: The love graffiti was all the same, but the unhappy graffiti was unhappy each in its own way.

One of the most famous lines was a scrawl above the toilet in the first stall that read: "I NAILED TRISH HATFIELD RIGHT HERE. 10/21/89." It was a catch-phrase that kids would drop on each other once in a while, but substituting the current date: "I nailed Trish Hatfield RIGHT HERE! Four sixteen ninety-three!" Or whatever the date was. The "RIGHT HERE" was the funniest part.

Holcombe banged open the stall door and stood holding it open. "I've never actually even seen the Trish Hatfield one," he said enthusiastically. "It's supposed to be over here, on the wall right above the toilet, isn't it?" He frowned, studiously scrutinizing the wall, like an archeologist deciphering the hieroglyphics over an Egyptian tomb.

The pause in the proceedings allowed Kitty to overcome her shock, and she regained the power of speech. "ARE YOU NUTS?" she bellowed. "You are gonna get kicked out of here, and you're gonna get me kicked out too!"

"Not at all," said Holcombe coolly.

"I have to *pee*," Kitty growled.

"Nobody's stopping you," said Holcombe impudently, fishing around in his back pocket. He pulled out a Sharpie. "I've always wanted to do this," he said, uncapping it with satisfaction.

"Ok, but I have to pee," pleaded Kitty. And she laughed. She couldn't help it. What an asshole Holcombe was.

"Be my guest," said Holcombe graciously.

"My God, you're *such* an asshole," said Kitty. She darted past Holcombe into the stall, pushed him out, and shut the door against him. "Don't look," she ordered him fiercely.

As Kitty peed she heard Holcombe over by the sink, murmuring "I…nailed…Harvey…Keitel…right…here…" in a singsong voice. She knew what he was doing.

Suddenly Kitty heard the door to the Ladies' Room swing open, someone bustled in.

"What are you *doing*?!" screamed an outraged female. It was Mrs. Dawes the lunch-lady.

Kitty hastily pulled up her jeans and buttoned them, flushed, threw open the door to the stall, said, "I'm so sorry, he was bringing me my inhaler- asthma attack!" took Holcombe by the arm and dragged and pushed him past the fuming woman and out the door, while Holcombe protested that he wasn't finished. He had only managed to write "I nailed Harvey Keitel." When they returned to the bar, he began hatching plans for how he could add the "right here."

And here was Kitty, only about nine months later, emerging from the same stall in the same bathroom. She regarded herself in the mirror.

Her Banana Republic pearly grey suit was holding up fantastically- was it Day 3? She believed it was Day 3- she'd taken a shower at Eli's that morning and washed her hair. It was loose and down, frizzy and wild. Her eye makeup had smeared of course, but messy eye makeup always became Kitty for some reason. She was pale, but she was always pale. She was thinner than ever, thanks to New York City and misery. And something else. She was no longer a kid.

She gazed at her reflection coldly, without love. She had the doomed haunted beauty of a TB victim. She turned her head. She was beautiful.

It was beyond a cruel joke. All the Health classes she had sat through, having a litany of STDs drummed into her head. Kitty's generation was taught to see the specter of AIDs looming around every corner. They were taught that the only reasonable moral dilemma regarding sex involved a piece of latex. Throughout her entire adolescence the institutional establishment had shouted at her through a megaphone: "Safe sex!" It was dogma.

There was nothing safe about sex, thought Kitty bitterly. There was nothing safe about sex or love or friendship or anything to do with other people. "And sex and sex and sex and shattered," Kitty whispered to her reflection in the mirror.

How could she have known when she got pregnant in college that this was it? That this was Holcombe's only chance at life?

Calling it ironic was like calling Hiroshima a bomb, she thought to herself illogically. She was trapped in a dystopia that had taken her by complete surprise. And now, staring at her lovely haunted face, Kitty was flooded with panic. The rest of her life stretched out before her, and it looked like this. Kitty the murderer, alone with her crime.

Kitty remembered the summer after freshman year, the summer before she got pregnant, she and Holcombe had dosed together. When the acid started to hit, Kitty became frantically verbose, and what burbled out of Kitty were panicked plans for what she could do with her life. I think I can get an internship with our congressman in DC, Kitty said, wringing her hands. I could definitely work for him, my dad told me. I'll apply to law school, she said hopefully, looking at Holcombe. I bet my dad could get me into Georgetown, she said. As the acid kicked in, Kitty's life stretched before her as a big problem that expected her to solve it, and she didn't want any part of what some mechanism buried inside her required her to do.

It was no different when she was sober. "If only I could just do it and not be there," thought Kitty, "my whole life. Go to law school. Be a lawyer. Marry one of the guys from law school. Just accomplish it all, but not have to be there for it."

But while Kitty was desperately disposing of a future in which she wanted no part, Holcombe had been her present. If she just had that moment to do over, Kitty thought, staring at herself in the Ron's Dock bathroom mirror. She wouldn't have spent that time fixating madly on climbing some phantom corporate ladder in DC. Now that moment was the past, and this moment was the present.

Kitty supposed she had thought of Holcombe, like Jenny did, as a safety net, as someone she could fall back on. But in Kitty's mind, issues between her and Holcombe had been ongoing- and now they were not. Now they were over.

But here in the Ladies' Room at Ron's Dock, it still felt like Holcombe was about to burst in again, brandishing a Sharpie. The entire time she had been in Harrison everything felt like that- like Holcombe was just out of reach, just out of sight. Kitty lay her hands flat on the wall beside the sink and began scanning the graffiti, letting her hands run over the surface of the wall, as though it were Braille and she was blind.

"I…nailed…Harvey…Keitel," she murmured. And she couldn't find it. And it was useless and stupid to have supposed she could. Like the "Oedipus Shmoedipus" on the bench, it was gone. Kitty, feeling the panic rise in her chest, wanting a cigarette, left the Ladies' Room.

At the table, the boys had been joined by the Sicilian widows. Kitty pulled up a chair and asked loudly, "Anybody want to do shots?" "Yeah," said her brother, "I do." "Yeah, I will," said Carson and Brian. Hugh pushed the beer they had ordered for Kitty over to her, and got up to go to the bar.

"Hey, Brian," said Carson, "Remember that time you guys had that house party and Holcombe wrestled those black kids?"

"I remember," Jamie offered. "I was there."

"Me too," Jenny laughed softly.

"Holcombe and Chris had this house party," Jamie told Kitty. "We were on the stoop and there were these little black kids- maybe 8-years-old- from the neighborhood- who kept riding by on their bikes and checking us out. And then all of a sudden Holcombe calls out to them, and he's like, Hey you wanna hang out with us. So the kids get off their bikes- and Holcombe started kind of play-fighting with them in the front yard." She laughed. "They were running at Holcombe, and he was doing these kung-fu moves on them. It was so stupid. They just kept attacking him, and he was throwing them around. Everybody left the house and came out to watch." Jamie laughed again and rubbed her eyes forcefully with one hand. When her hand came away from her face, her expression had become serious again.

"No new material," Jamie said dramatically. She shook her head. "That's what I'm going to miss. No new material," she repeated. "When I met Holcombe," she drunkenly declaimed to the bar room at large, "I was just a dull girl from Queens."

Kitty was surprised. She was used to being thumped over the head with native-New-Yorker-status as *per se* evidence of being a superior fascinating creature. She had met people from the city whom *she* considered dull, but she didn't think she'd ever met someone from the city who considered *themself* dull. The party line went that New York City was a vibrant cultural mosaic, which made New Yorkers interesting. That's what Kitty had been taught at college.

Kitty spotted Hugh making his way back to the table from the bar, carefully balancing a tray of shots. Once he reached the table, he gingerly positioned the tray in the center of the table before quickly selecting a shot glass for himself.

"Guys," Hugh pronounced solemnly to the gathered assembly. "I would like to make a toast."

Everyone at the table looked at him expectantly. Hugh didn't look back at them. He stared straight ahead, into space, and said slowly, "Holcombe told me once that if he ever died-" Everyone's eyes were glued to Hugh, everyone was frozen, no one moved. "- that he wanted Brian to suck Carson's dick," Hugh continued just as seriously.

There was a brief silence before the others started laughing. Scott applauded, a slow methodical clap.

"Wow," said Carson reverently, "That was awesome."

"Wait!" said Scott abruptly, holding up his hands. "I'll be right back." Without waiting for a response, he bounded from his seat and sped over to the jukebox. The table watched him go passively. Hugh remained standing, holding his shot glass. Scott at the jukebox was more purposeful than Kitty had ever seen him. He didn't even have to flip through the song selections, he just punched in the number from memory, and was back at the table again.

Scott slid into his seat and slapped twice in quick succession on the table top with the flat of his palm. "Let's toast!" he said, "To Holcombe!" His jukebox selection began to flood the room. An immediate cry of protest went up from the girls.

"Is that 'Poison'?" asked Kitty scornfully.

"Yeah, I'm not toasting to this," Jamie said flatly.

Scott turned to them with a mild, injured expression. "You're wrong," he admonished them gently.

Kitty and Jamie and Jenny rolled their eyes at each other, but joined in when Scott, Brian, Hugh, Carson, Eli, and Benji clinked their shot glasses together.

Eli quickly downed his shot and slammed his shot glass down on the table. "To Holcombe!" he said thickly. "To Holcombe," everyone echoed.

Scott began to sing with feeling and an utter lack of self-consciousness, "I listen to our favorite song playing on the radio…" Eli chimed in.

Hugh started singing, and then Carson and Brian. The girls watched them, laughing. But before long, Kitty and Jenny and then even Jamie, started to sing along- ironically, giggling and making faces at each other. But as they kept singing, something changed. Soon they were all, even the girls, completely unironically belting out the cheesy 80s rock ballad that they all knew by heart.

The college kids in their polo shirts and chino shorts sitting at the bar looked over at Holcombe's friends curiously. They weren't clowning around, they weren't distancing themselves from the corny lyrics. They were meaning the words, and singing it like the sad ballad it is. Like Russians, Kitty thought. Soul. They had broken through irony and reclaimed emotion. How had Scott known, she wondered. How had he known it would be this way?

When the song ended, the spell was broken. Hugh asked the table if anyone wanted more beer. There was a scramble to get out money and hand it over to him, and then he left. Eli, Scott, Carson, and Benji got up to play pool in the back, leaving Brian alone with the girls at the table. Kitty asked if anyone wanted to go out for a smoke.

"You're so pretty," Jamie retorted sharply. She meant Kitty. Kitty turned to Jamie, and found that Jamie was staring at her, not in a hostile manner, but not in a friendly manner either- appraisingly. As Kitty looked at her, Jamie announced matter-of-factly to the table in another total non-sequitur, "I have to find someone to sleep with. I'm not sleeping alone tonight."

With that Jamie unsteadily rose to her feet and tottered off toward the pool table. Kitty was sure she'd have luck. The ratio of guys to girls among Holcombe's mourners was about three to one. Kitty was kind of embarrassed for Brian, who had been sitting there at the table with them while Jamie made her declaration, and whom apparently had just been passed over as inadequate by a succubus in search of simply a warm body. But he didn't appear to notice or care.

"Remember," said Brian, not so much to Kitty and Jenny who were still there, more to himself, "last summer when we were playing Spin the Bottle, and I landed on Holcombe so I pretended to kiss him, and he goes"- Brian paused and mimicked Holcombe's gruff nasal voice- "You call that a kiss? That's not a kiss!'" Brian chuckled.

"Last summer? This past summer?" asked Kitty. "Holcombe was here? When?"

"July 4th weekend," Brian answered.

Kitty's mind reeled. That was the weekend she had taken the overnight trip back to Harrison to empty her girlhood room. She had been here. He had been here. They had missed each other. She had been at loose ends- unemployed, bored, lonely, miserable. They could have met up, they could have gotten back together, he could still be alive right now. Everything could be totally different.

Hugh was back at the table with beers.

"Why didn't you *tell* me Holcombe was in town July 4th?" demanded Kitty with rising hysteria. "I was *here*!"

Hugh shrugged. "You didn't ask," he said dully. "It's not like that matters now."

Kitty grabbed her purse and rushed from the table, past the dart-boards and the people playing pool, out the rear entrance, to the parking lot. The clearness and stillness of the country night seemed to rush at her. The night sky was full of stars. The streets were empty. The village was silent.

Holcombe's body was only up the street, lying in the funeral home, Kitty thought. She wished she had rights over his body. She never would have let them pump him full of formeldahyde and put makeup on him. She would have stayed up all night with the body, as you're supposed to. She would have put coins over his eyes. She would have observed all the most beautiful rituals. If she'd had rights over Holcombe's body, however, perhaps that body would still be alive.

It was so lonely to think of Holcombe lying just up the street from all his friends. A fragment came to Kitty from far away and long ago, and she spoke softly into the dark night, "For Mercutio's soul is but a little way above our heads."

"What?" croaked a hoarse voice coming from the back door of the bar. Kitty jumped. It was Julie, her favorite of the three Sicilian widows, the three fates.

"I just came out for a cigarette," said Kitty. She didn't want to explain what she was doing or what she meant.

"I have a lighter," Julie rasped. She clicked the small orange Bic in her hand and offered the flame to Kitty.

"Thank you," Kitty whispered. She put the cigarette in her mouth and leaned towards Julie's light, cupping her hands around the fire. Julie's hands trembled slightly, and so did Kitty's.

"He loved you," said Julie shortly. Kitty looked at Julie. It was not an accusation. It was a gift.

"I know," said Kitty miserably.

"I want you to know something," said Julie. Oh no, thought Kitty. She steeled herself. It didn't matter, none of it mattered now, but she didn't want to hear all about how Julie had slept with Holcombe. Everything was already sordid enough.

"I want you to know something," Julie repeated.

"Ok," said Kitty. She resigned herself.

"One time maybe a year after you guys broke up, I did acid with Holcombe," said Julie.

Oh God, here it comes, thought Kitty. She was irritated. She knew Julie had slept with Holcombe. Did she really have to hear about it? And she hated hearing about people's experiences on acid, it was quite as bad as having to listen to people relate their dream sequences.

Julie went on, "And Holcombe had this book of photographs called The Family of Man."

"Oh," said Kitty faintly, "I gave him that book." Kitty's parents had a copy of it when she was growing up. Some of her earliest memories were of those photos.

"We were looking at that book, and we started to trip," said Julie. "And there was this black and white photo of this little girl from like the Great Depression. A little girl in a sleeveless dress standing in front of this shack. A little, like, sharecropper girl. And Holcombe thought she looked just like you." Julie tapped out her cigarette. "And she *did*," Julie insisted. "She had the same eyes, the same eyebrows. Holcombe just kept staring the photo, he just sat there staring at it, and he kept saying, 'That's Kitty, it's Kitty.' He wouldn't stop."

Julie grabbed Kitty's arm. "I just want you to know he loved you," she said earnestly, looking intently into Kitty's eyes. "Because he did."

# Chapter 16: Holcombe's Funeral

The pallbearers were Hugh and Mike and Chris and Scott and Eli and Brian and Carson and Hugh. The boys dressed up in funny Salvation Army outfits like they had for Polish Wedding, their intramural volleyball team only five years ago. Kitty wasn't sure what the intended effect of clowning it up with silly clothes for carrying Holcombe's casket was supposed to be. The actual effect was unbearably awful. Kitty found it grotesque. It seemed to mean something for the boys, though, they seemed to be think they were fulfilling a fraternal pact with Holcombe.

Kitty wished again that she had some rights over personal decisions concerning Holcombe's interment. Brian had told her that Holcombe was to be buried with his plastic model of Boba Fett. Brian found this piece of information somehow wonderful. Kitty went along with it, anything to make anyone feel any better, but she found it distasteful and demeaning. She would have done better, but she had relinquished all formal rights to Holcombe, she had severed them and thrown them away.

Whether notice was too short, or Holcombe's mother lacked the connections, his funeral was not held in the village church where he had had his first communion. It was held in a nearby Catholic Church with a strange priest who did not know Holcombe and summed up his personality as "liking music."

"He didn't know him," Maura Carraway sobbed angrily after the mass. "He didn't even know him!" She and Maura had stood next to each other. It seemed fitting that the Polish Wedding cheerleaders should come together to mourn their mime.

And then the mass was over, and Kitty, feeling, like Maura, that she had been cheated out of the kind of tribute she wanted, walked down the aisle toward the door. There near the door she saw the only person besides Holcombe who could have made her feel better. Her mother was here.

With a sob, Kitty sprang into her mother's arms. What happened then was astonishing. For the first time since she learned that Holcombe died, Kitty felt some comfort. And it was not anything her mother said. It was in the warm soft body of her mother- who miraculously even smelled the same as when

Kitty was little. Kitty was amazed that although her mother was 60, she was still the primal mother, still the same presence that had been central to Kitty's babyhood and was central to her being. Why didn't they hug like this all the time, Kitty wondered.

She rode along with her mother to the graveyard. The grave was in a cemetery linked to their local village church, a village cemetery, filled with local names. It was a beautiful cemetery, just outside the village, surrounded by farms and corn fields, on the way to Holcombe's house. Kitty's own paternal grandparents were buried there.

And near the entrance, on a small hill which would have a beautiful view of sunset, there was a freshly dug hole in the ground.

The hole struck terror into Kitty. They would put him in the ground and leave him? But wouldn't he be *lonely*, she thought stupidly. And then she couldn't sob enough. There was nothing she or anyone could do. She cried with pure pity for Holcombe.

Holcombe's mother had arranged a buffet at the VFW up the road after the burial, and most of the mourners re-assembled there. It was Sunday, and most of the out-of-towners were going to drive back home that day. Holcombe's cousins wanted to do shots with Kitty at the bar, but she just couldn't drink anymore. She couldn't eat either. All she could do was smoke.

She passed by Mike sitting alone at a table. He was still wearing his silly pallbearer outfit: a 70s, butterfly-collar, button-down shirt, a wide paisley tie, and 70s bell-bottom polyester pants. She stopped.

"I didn't appreciate him," Kitty said wretchedly.

"I did," Mike answered simply. "I appreciated him."

Kitty remembered what Mike had said when she told him about the abortion, soon after it happened. "What a cool kid." That's all he had said. He meant the baby.

This was the first time they had spoken since he picked her up in Albany. She knew his girlfriend, or his girlfriend's friends, must be watching them speak from somewhere in the room. She didn't want to talk long.

"I'm going to write it all down," Kitty told him with a frantic intensity.

"You think that's going to do something?" Mike inquired in a tone of mild surprise. He wasn't being rude. He seemed detached.

"Yes," said Kitty forthrightly. She felt her way through her emotions, stumbling and then righting herself again. "If we write it down we can keep him a little," she said. Mike didn't respond. Kitty repeated, like a mantra, "We can keep him a little. We can write it all down."

Mike looked thoroughly unconvinced. Kitty didn't know the stranger who sat regarding her coolly. He was someone else's boyfriend now.

"I have to go," she said. "I'll see you."

Mike nodded. "Ok," he said, "See you later."

Mike had never said "He loved you," Kitty noticed. He didn't need to.

Kitty let her mother go back to the city without her. She would stay an extra day, take an extra day off. She never wanted to go back. She was scared. What would happen when she was not around a group of people who understood? What would happen when she was alone? Already, her life had been lonely. What would her life be like when she was alone and all she had of Holcombe was the grave on the hill in a country cemetery.

She tagged along with the crowd who was staying, back to Eli's house. The three widows had left just after the burial, which was poetically fitting. They had put on their black sunglasses and gotten into their black 1992 Cadillac Deville, and were on their way back to the city to be a librarian, a paralegal, and a bartender: Sicilian widows no more. Eric and his girlfriend had left too, they both had jobs. Most of the Harrisonians stayed.

They went back to Eli's mom's house. Someone got beer, and someone put on old videos Holcombe and Mike had made in high school.

"I can't watch," said Kitty, and she went out on the deck to smoke a cigarette.

Eli's mom was back, she was sitting outside on the deck with a cup of coffee. She was a slight woman with large blue eyes and masses of long grey hair, like a witch.

"You're too Irish," Eli's hippie mom told Kitty, by way of greeting. Kitty didn't know what to say. She figured Eli's mom must be Irish too or else why would she say that. People were always most critical of what they were themselves, Kitty had observed. Hippies were always coming down on you, she thought to herself again. Very judgmental people.

After delivering this pithy assessment of Kitty, Eli's mom silently rose and went back into the house. She was an odd woman, Kitty thought, but she had been so kind in letting everyone stay at her house. She must be sick of it, Kitty thought.

The impetus and cohesion were starting to go out of the mourning party. Some new couples had formed, people were making travel plans. It was anti-climactic.

Kitty walked back into the house, into the kitchen. The kitchen was full like it had been Thursday night, but this time it was all girls sitting around the table. The boys were watching videos in the other room. There were some girls there Kitty had not seen at the wake.

Amid the half-dozen girls sitting at the table she spotted a girl with her arm in a cast. A fresh cast. A brand-new, gigantic, white cast, as eloquent as the newly dug hole in the ground in the cemetery.

Kitty stared at the girl. She was pretty but nothing special, just as Kitty has imagined she would be. There was nothing particular about her to indicate that she was an agent of death.

"Do you have a problem with Angelika?"

Kitty jumped. It was Eli's dumpy Russian-Jewish girlfriend from Queens. Kitty didn't rise to the bait.

"No, not at all, I thought she was someone else," Kitty said nonchalantly. "I thought she was Alison Talarico. They look alike."

Eli's girlfriend was not to be so easily put off. "Oh, because you were staring at Angelika like you were angry at her," she said loudly, loudly enough for Angelika to turn around.

"Why would I be?" Kitty asked simply, and walked away. If that fat bitch wanted drama, she wasn't going to get any from Kitty. People like her- city people- they never understood people who didn't take the bait, just walked away, and didn't care. Worldliness was all they knew.

It was their handicap.

She went out on the deck to smoke another cigarette.

"You're in this one," someone came out on the porch and told her. It was a video she and Mike and Holcombe had made her senior year. She bet she knew which one, she bet it was the one where Holcombe prank-called a stable and told them he had a horse that needed inseminating. The stable owner hadn't caught on until Holcombe had insisted on the necessity of plying the filly with fine wines beforehand.

"I can't watch," Kitty repeated grimly. Someone else came out on the porch and said they were ordering a pizza and asked her if she wanted any.

"This should have been his wedding day, not his burial," Kitty responded, and the person was nonplussed and went away.

The funeral was over for most of the mourners, but it was not over for Kitty.

"Sometimes I see him," Kitty told Stephanie on the phone a couple weeks later. She was in her parents' apartment in Manhattan, looking out the window at the East River. "Sometimes I set a place for him or I pour out a separate cup for him. But then I drink it for him, because he can't drink it himself, because he's dead."

"Hm," Stephanie mumbled in response. "Uh, wait just a second, Kitty," she added casually. "I'll be right back." Kitty waited patiently for a couple minutes, and then Stephanie returned to the phone.

"Ok," she said, "My mother says you're not crazy, this is normal. Good thing," said Stephanie. "I thought you were cracking up."

Kitty felt reassured, Stephanie's mother sounded nice.

After Kitty got off the phone with Stephanie, she made a decision. If she was going to live the rest of her life as an exile, she would make it official. Since home was gone, she would go somewhere that did not remind her of home. She would return to Spain.

# BOOK THREE: THE FUTURE

*Deliver me from bloodguiltiness, O God, thou God of my salvation: and my tongue shall sing aloud of thy righteousness.*
-Psalm 51

*Tell me not, in mournful numbers,*
*Life is but an empty dream!*
*For the soul is dead that slumbers,*
*And things are not what they seem.*
-Henry Wadsworth Longfellow, *A Psalm of Life*

*I balanced all, brought all to mind,*
*The years to come seemed waste of breath,*
*A waste of breath the years behind*
*In balance with this life, this death.*
-W.B. Yeats, *An Irish Airman Foresees His Death*

*The apparition of these faces in the crowd:*
*Petals on a wet, black bough.*
-Ezra Pound, *In a Station of the Metro*

*Tho' much is taken, much abides; and tho'*
*We are not now that strength which in old days*
*Moved earth and heaven, that which we are, we are;*
-Alfred, Lord Tennyson, *Ulysses*

*Midway upon the journey of our life,*
*I found myself within a forest dark,*
*For the straightforward pathway had been lost.*
-Dante Alighieri, The Divine Comedy, *Inferno*, Canto I

*Showing up is 80 percent of life.*
-attributed to Woody Allen

## Chapter 17: The Shabbos Goy

It was Friday night, and Kitty was shabbos goy.

This was great fun and did not entail much work at all, required no special effort, really. It required being born a goy, of course, which Kitty had successfully accomplished almost three decades ago. That prerequisite met, the tasks basically involved turning on and off a few light switches here and there and being receptive to hints.

Actually, Kitty wasn't that stellar of a shabbos goy. Often her friends had to reiterate their hints in raised voices until she finally caught on and, chuckling sheepishly, turned on the lights for them, or whatever it was they wanted doing. Her friends weren't allowed to explicitly ask her to do things, they had to hint at what they wanted- that was part of the fun.

In any event, it made for an amusing situation, which was Kitty's main goal in life. Being shabbos goy was like having superpowers, only your superpower was that you could turn on the lights when no one else could.

Paul was Kitty's fellow shabbos goy. He also could turn lights on and off on a Friday night. Kitty did not feel threatened in her role as shabbos goy by the presence of another one. In fact, it took some of the heat off. Kitty liked to needle Paul by telling him they were just like the butler and the housekeeper in Remains of the Day.

"You're Anthony Hopkins, and I'm Emma Thompson," Kitty would say with a wink. Paul sighed. "You're kind of the stiff-upper-lip, very correct shabbos goy," Kitty continued merrily, "totally in love with his fellow warm, down-to-earth shabbos goy, but you'll never ever tell her because you're way too repressed."

"Yes, that's it," Paul deadpanned. "You got me. And Yitzhak is an English aristocrat Nazi sympathizer. You figured it out."

The shabbos goy gig was why on 4 o'clock on Friday afternoon Kitty was knocking on the door of Paul's Union Square apartment, carrying a six-pack of Corona in a brown paper bag. Neither of them had class on Friday afternoons. Ah, the lifestyles of the idle and indebted.

Actually, even if Paul did have class that day, he would still probably have been found at home. To say Paul was an indifferent student would have been a vast understatement, "pathologically self-sabotaging" would have been more on the mark. He had failed his first year of law school and- unheard of- rather than dropping out, had repeated it. He was in his second year now, while Kitty and the others were in their third and final year. Paul was almost always home, Yitzhak unkindly but rather accurately referred to him as a "shut-in."

As a matter of fact, Kitty had been sent by Yitzhak to Paul's apartment to ensure Paul made it to shabbos dinner, although she would have stopped by even without Yitzhak's irritatingly bossy texts. Yitzhak was like the Jewish mafia boss she had never had, Kitty often remarked laconically to Paul, and sometimes to Yitzhak. Yitzhak would grin when Kitty said this, flattered.

Yitzhak spent the hours before sunset on the eve of a shabbos dinner frenetically bullying his acolytes with instructional texts, knowing that in a short while he would be powerless to do so. So Kitty had gotten a text instructing her to, among other things, pick up Paul and not be late, to which she had responded "Ok, mafia boss" which she intended to be sarcastic, but Yitzhak had promptly texted back a terse but satisfied "Thnx." Madly annoying, Kitty thought grouchily. But, she reminded herself, soon he would be powerless, desperately sending out hints that his cigarette needed to be lit. In a few hours, the axe would be Kitty's to grind.

Yitzhak was a very practical person, and he was correct: If Paul was not bearded in his den and smoked out, so to speak, chances were great that he would not materialize at the gathering. Texts urging him to get off his ass and join them would be ignored. So there stood dutiful Kitty knocking on Paul's door rather in the capacity of a sort of nurse-warden, as well as fellow shabbos goy, and, of course, friend. Kitty wore many hats.

Paul answered the door in a brown, silk, paisley dressing gown secured by a tassled drawstring. Kitty saw he was wearing seersucker oxford pajamas underneath it.

"Why are you wearing the curtains?" She asked with buoyant obnoxiousness, bounding past him into his apartment. Paul sighed heavily.

Kitty glanced around. Paul's one-bedroom apartment was adorable, Paul's slovenly housekeeping notwithstanding. It belonged to his father, an investment banker, and his stepmother, an Eastern-European ex-model.

One of the best things about the apartment was that, miraculously, it overlooked Union Square- an asset lost on Paul, as his blinds were usually drawn. Paul couldn't have lived in a cooler neighborhood, and he had turned his apartment into a dysfunctional-male man-cave. Lucky, Kitty thought happily, that Paul had a friend like her to force him out of his shell, try to see that he got some air, and encourage him to enjoy his prime location.

Paul's place was the same as ever. The light was dim, the blinds were drawn, and the air was stuffy and stale and reeked of cigarettes. There were large messy piles of magazines, mostly The Economist and National Geographic, assembled here and there, as well as the odd prospectus, academic journal, and work of non-fiction. A total fire hazard, Kitty repeatedly warned Paul, given the smoking.

Behind the blinds, you could see it was bright day outside in Union Square, where a vast spectacular farmer's market was just wrapping up, right outside a giant Whole Foods with a bustling outdoor café. Kitty walked to the window, propped open the blinds with one hand and peered out. Healthy dynamic vibrant people living healthy dynamic vibrant lives were out there, flocking to buy antioxidant-rich vegetables. She let the blinds close. Kitty preferred Paul and the Orthodox Jews. They made more sense to her.

"The place looks great!" Kitty told Paul enthusiastically and made a beeline for the kitchen. She rifled through his kitchen-counter drawers until she found a bottle-opener (which she had gifted him for her own use, Paul rarely drank and never beer), took a Corona out of the six-pack and stuck the others in the fridge. She took a swig and set the bottle back on the counter. Out of her giant Michael Kors brown leather bag Kitty pulled a pack of American Spirits and a lighter. She grabbed the Corona, and headed for the futon in Paul's living room where she lay down, deposited the Corona on top of a pile of magazines on the coffee table, and, rolling over and using her arm to prop herself up on one side, awkwardly lit a cigarette.

"Aaah," breathed Kitty, crossing her legs, lying back, and blowing smoke up towards the ceiling with satisfaction. "Let the weekend begin!"

Paul sighed again. He had been standing near the doorway during Kitty's preparations, now he ambled back to his desk near the window.

An Apple laptop sat on Paul's desk, deeply ensconced in a nest of detritus: a plethora of near-empty drink bottles that had been turned into ashtrays, a couple empty fast-food cartons, a rainbow assortment of plastic lighters, some of which did not work, a glass pipe, and a dirty bong. Most of the bottles on Paul's desk were exotic organic concoctions whose labels (studies in copywriting savvy) claimed they contained vital enzymes, vitamins, and various fauna and flora rumored to confer health benefits, but which were now reservoirs of dirty ash-water. One time Kitty had tried to calculate the ratio of oxidant versus antioxidant among of the objects on Paul's desk and had determined that they pretty much canceled each other out. Only once had Paul mistakenly drunk from one of the ashtray bottles, as far as Kitty knew.

Paul sat down at his desk, but facing away from it, towards Kitty sitting on the futon. "Can I get you a…" he began absently. Paul was unfailingly polite, with prep school manners. He seemed to rifle through his mind for something to offer Kitty for a brief moment, until his imagination failed him, and he quietly subsided.

"I ran three miles at the gym!" Kitty crowed happily and dragged on her cigarette.

"That's nice," said Paul mechanically. He rose and placed a near-empty bottle whose label said "Vitamin B6: Tranquility" on the coffee table in front of her.

"Thanks!" Kitty said enthusiastically, and tapped out the cigarette into the bottle.

Paul lit himself a cigarette, frowning. He was a pale, freckled, red-headed, pear-shaped young man who looked middle-aged, although he was only twenty-three. His manner was unfailingly deferential, formal, diffident, and mild until he was goaded into a mordant sarcasm, which Kitty always regarded as a personal triumph. It took a lot of goading to make Paul lose his deferential formality, which Kitty not only enjoyed, but felt did Paul some good, put a little life into him.

"Three miles," Kitty repeatedly smugly. She gestured with her cigarette to the latest edition of The Economist lying on the ground near Paul's feet. "You read that yet?"

"Not entirely," said Paul pompously. The Economist was what had initiated Kitty and Paul's friendship. Kitty had spotted Paul with a copy in class and struck up a conversation. They both had subscriptions.

"I was checking out this article on-line, wait, let me show you," Paul said. Paul always had interesting things to talk about, that was part of why everyone liked him. He turned around to his computer screen and started navigating through The Economist's website.

In the ensuing silence, Kitty, staring up at the ceiling, cried out in sudden agony, "I want a boyfriend!"

Paul ignored her, continuing to search the site for the article he wanted. He had two sisters, which had immunized him to a large extent against female theatrics.

"I want a boyfriend!" Kitty keened pitifully from the futon.

Paul sighed noisily and turned around with an air of resignation.

"Why don't you get a dog?" he suggested reasonably. This was not the first time he had made this suggestion. Nor was he the only person who had made this suggestion to Kitty. Her face set grimly, and she stared stonily at the ceiling. Kitty was prepared for this.

"Tell me NOT in mournful numbers!" Kitty bellowed at the ceiling. "That I should just get a DOG!" She sounded like a marine shouting "The Rifleman's Creed."

Paul sighed again and returned to perusing the Economist website. There was a brief silence which was broken again by Kitty.

"I want a baby!" Kitty shouted at the ceiling from her prone position on Paul's futon.

This was a new one. Paul turned and looked at Kitty, disconcerted. "Well, wouldn't you need a husband first?" he asked primly.

"I want a *baby*!" Kitty insisted petulantly to the ceiling.

Paul paused and seemed to reflect. "Why don't you get a *picture* of a baby?" he suggested gently, tapping out his cigarette on the rim of an energy drink. "Why don't you just get a picture of a baby and carry it around with you and see if you can take care of it for a month?"

Kitty fell silent. She visualized a torn, folded-up, stained, smeared, tattered, scragged baby picture. She visualized herself on her hands and knees, hunting about under her couch for it. She felt extremely guilty.

However, a few seconds later, after Paul had returned his attention to the screen, Kitty came back to her main theme. "But I *do* want a boyfriend," she piped up.

Paul ignored her, scrolling along.

"I say," growled Kitty. She yelled, "I say I want a *boyfriend*!" She sounded like a spoiled child demanding candy in the supermarket checkout line.

Paul didn't turn around from the screen. "Do I have to be here for this?" he murmured patiently. Kitty chuckled.

Paul's phone, lying on the desk, beeped, and he picked it up and looked at it. "It's Yitzhak," he said. "He says not to be late and to bring rolling papers."

"The *cheek*," said Kitty archly, smiling contentedly up at the ceiling. Yitzhak only had a couple more hours to bully them by text. Sunset was at around 6:30 p.m. If they were late, there was nothing he could do about it but sit at home and impotently fume, she thought with satisfaction.

"Sunset's at 6:30, right?" Kitty asked Paul. "So at like 6:00 you should send him a text like 'Fuck your rolling papers.'" She chortled and took another drag on her cigarette. This was her time off. She worked hard, she played hard, Kitty told herself.

Paul looked shocked. "I wouldn't do that," he said indignantly.

"Oh relax, Maiden Aunt," said Kitty, exhaling smoke. This was what Kitty called Paul: "The Maiden Aunt." Mild-mannered to a fault, Victorian in his sense of decorum, able to

160

convey gentle remonstrance with a single sigh: The Maiden Aunt.

"We'd better get going," said Paul dutifully. He got up. "I guess I'd better get dressed," he said awkwardly.

"Oh don't mind me," said Kitty airily. "Plenty of reading material. And if I get hungry I'll just grab a spoonful from the half-empty mayonnaise jar in your fridge."

Paul flashed a smile, Paul's smiles were always disarmingly charming, and disappeared into his bedroom. As soon as his bedroom door was shut Kitty sprang up and took his seat at the laptop. She set the bottle of Corona among the health-drink ashtray receptacles on his desk, went to Youtube, and typed in "Hurt Johnny Cash."

"I'm sorry, Paul!" Kitty yelled, loudly enough so it could be heard through his closed bedroom door as she started the video. "I have to do this!"

She thought she heard Paul moan something about not playing it more than four times from the other side of the door. What was he going to do? Come out and stop her in his underwear?

"I hurt myself today!" Kitty brayed. She couldn't hear Paul's sigh through the closed door, but she felt it.

"What have I become, my sweetest friend!" Kitty boomed, like an old sea dog belting out a sea shanty. She thought she heard the Maiden Aunt behind his bedroom door protesting something about "the neighbors."

Kitty got up and walked to Paul's bedroom door. She shouted through cupped hands "I'm going to use your bathroom, ok? There better not be any surprises in there!"

"Just watch out for the Honduran family living in the bathtub," she heard him say.

Kitty grabbed her purse, and went into Paul's tiny bathroom. It was fine, it looked clean- well, fairly clean, it was hard to tell because every surface was covered with magazines. In fact, there were more magazines, professional periodicals, and academic journals in the bathroom than in the entire rest of the apartment combined.

Once Kitty found some kind of fruity face-wash on Paul's counter, with which she immediately confronted him upon emerging from the bathroom. He claimed his stepmother had planted it there. Kitty suggested he transplant it to his desk where it could take its place as another antioxidant ashtray.

Once, looking for Advil, Kitty opened Paul's medicine cabinet. She was appalled by the number of prescriptions bottles for neurotic, what Kitty thought of as housewife-type mental afflictions- anxiety, depression. Kitty attributed it to Paul being rich and from New York City. If he'd been poor and from Harrison, NY, or if he'd been from Ireland or something, he wouldn't be on all these drugs, she thought. Outside of New York City, Paul would have been a harmless eccentric allowed to do his thing. There was nothing wrong with Paul. Kitty blamed the city- the demands of the flattening, homogenizing, Procrustean bed that was the city.

Kitty immediately regarded herself in the mirror upon entering Paul's bathroom, as she did when entering any bathroom. She looked stunning. She was in her prime. She was almost thirty. Inevitably, her next thought was that she was also a rose wasted on the desert air, with no boyfriend in sight. The romantic-interest landscape was a wasteland. She vaguely resented Paul for not being boyfriend material, but it was out of the question. She doubted he was gay. She had spotted a Gina Gershon lesbian movie among his things, and immediately gleefully chided him. But she very much suspected him of still being a virgin at twenty-three. He was also shaped like a weeble.

The other boys in law school were dreadful- either total pricks or total nerds. Her best friends were Paul and the Orthodox Jews. Kitty's mad, bad, and dangerous-to-know college friend Orla was now attending Columbia Law School and was always berating Kitty for hanging out with Orthodox Jews.

"It's not normal," Orla would say unpleasantly. "I mean, you go to their parties, you're their shabbos goy. It's not healthy. It's weird."

Yeah, well, according to Kitty, Orla's friends were the weird ones. They apparently wanted to exist in a lawless society (which claim Kitty couldn't take seriously as most of them were going to law school), their diets were way screwier than keeping kosher, "dumpster diving" was apparently a thing for them, and a couple of them literally stank.

The Orthodox Jews were cool, Orla didn't know what she was talking about. Some of them were obnoxious, sure, but they were who they were. They weren't looking past your ear while you talked to them, scanning the area for someone more important and more worthy of their time, which the Long Islanders in law school did constantly. At least, Kitty's Orthodox friends didn't do that.

The Orthodox were normal down-to-earth people. They married young, some of the law-school students were parents, some of the girls were pregnant. They reminded Kitty of the small-town proles of Harrison, as a matter of fact. They weren't going anywhere. They were rooted. Their hometown just happened to be Manhattan.

Kitty dismissed Orla's criticism as just one of the many chips on Orla's shoulder. Orla probably didn't like Kitty's friends because she was always going on about the Palestinians. She was also always going on about feminism. And anarchism. And banner drops. Orla's solution to everything was a banner drop. Once when Kitty and Orla were discussing a mutual friend having problems with her live-in boyfriend. Orla had, and Kitty believed she was serious, suggested executing a banner drop to get the message across. Orla started describing with messianic fervor how they could stage a banner drop from the roof of their friend's apartment as the boyfriend returned home from work. Orla was not a stable person, really.

"You can't just *banner-drop* your way out of every situation," Kitty told her with some exasperation.

In fact, Orla was going through life looking for pretexts to banner-drop, Kitty thought. That was why she was so into feminism and anarchism; she was only in it for the banner drop.

Kitty absolutely dismissed Orla's assertion that hanging out with Orthodox Jews was not normal. Her Orthodox Jew friends were infinitely more normal than Orla's friends. Kitty had gone to a law-school party at Orla's place a few months ago. Virtually all of Orla's law-school friends described themselves as anarchists in conversation. Kitty kept trying to explain to them the inherent contradiction in their existence; they were studying law with presumably the intent to practice it while professing to espouse a lawless system. They did not care. They were total superficial assholes.

Upon Kitty's arrival at the party, Orla warned her in hushed tones that her apartment mate was bulimic and very sensitive about it, so under no circumstances were they to bring up anything related to bulimia. "I was hardly going to bring up bulimia," Kitty grumbled, leaving her coat in Orla's bedroom. Kitty kept her purse with her, she didn't trust Orla's friends. She barely trusted Orla.

"Funny," Kitty muttered to Orla after meeting the apartment mate, an ordinary-looking girl, "she doesn't look that thin."

"Shhhh! Bulimics *aren't* thin," Orla hissed back at her. "*Anorexics* are."

"What was that?" Paul asked politely. Kitty had dragged him along.

"Orla's roommate's *bulimic* and she's very *sensitive* about it," Kitty stage-whispered to Paul, and then briefly mimed gagging herself with an index finger. Orla shook her head frantically and looked desperately over at the apartment mate.

"Really?" asked Paul curiously. "She doesn't look that thin."

"Those are *anorexics*!" hissed Orla angrily. "Anorexics!"

By this time, Orla's apartment mate had started glancing over at them.

"Oh God, there she goes," Kitty muttered to Paul. "Any minute now she'll be purging. We'd better get to the pizza before she binges it all." Cruel Kitty had zero sympathy for those with eating disorders.

Yes, Kitty's Orthodox Jewish friends were infinitely more normal than Orla's friends. There was no comparison.

For example, Orla's friends' diets were much weirder than Kitty's Orthodox Jewish friends' diets. Kitty didn't know the ins and outs of what made things kosher, but there was a kosher restaurant they went to sometimes, and the food was good. Whereas among Orla's friends, bulimia was one of the most garden-variety of their dietary proclivities. Many were vegan. At Orla's law-school party one girl had fainted from anemia. They put her on the couch, where she soon came to, completely unfazed. Apparently this was just a common thing for her, and she considered perpetual fainting spells a small price to pay for the rarefied status she imagined veganism conferred upon her.

On the other end of the spectrum were Orla's friends who were always bragging about their dumpster-diving. They knew which restaurants got rid of which kind of food on which night. They compared dumpsters. They bragged. It was very similar to the restaurant snobbism exhibited by a lot of the law students at Fordham, but instead of "I know an exquisite little sushi place where on Thursday nights they serve the best California rolls," it was "I know an exquisite little sushi place where on Thursday nights they leave out still completely viable California rolls."

Orla's friends, like Orla, were also constantly attending rallies, banner-drops, and protests. None of them seemed to have what Kitty considered a real job. They worked at various non-profits, coffee shops, book stores, and community gardens. They were dog-walkers and babysitters. Some of them made money enrolling themselves in medical studies. Kitty had been surprised to learn that that was legal. None of them had offered themselves up for organ-harvesting yet, as far as Kitty was aware. But she had no doubt that, to avoid the necessity of getting a 9 to 5 job, they would have jumped at the chance.

Yes, Orla's friends were insane- and very easily riled. Encountering the slightest deviation from their lunatic-anarchist worldview set them off. You had to deal with them like you would a wild animal- no sudden movements. Orla herself was also insane, Kitty reflected, but intelligent, and she could be funny. It was Kitty who had told Orla to go to law school. Orla was working as a computer programmer for a startup when one day she decided she was going back to school to become a nurse. Kitty reacted incredulously. She couldn't imagine Orla as a nurse. She could imagine Orla *causing* someone to need the assistance of a nurse, yes, but she could not imagine Orla actually *nursing* someone.

"Go to law school, if you're going to go back to school," Kitty told her. "You majored in Computer Science, you'll ace the LSAT. You're a natural for it."

And Orla had indeed aced the LSAT and was now at Columbia Law while Kitty was at Fordham. Kitty didn't mind that Orla had gotten into a better law school. The Columbia students made the Fordham students look great. Fordham was more meat and potatoes, Kitty thought confidently, the Columbia people were flakes.

The Fordham students, except for the Orthodox Jews, were virtually all coarse, ambitious Long Island strivers. (Kitty contemptuously referred to almost anyone from the tri-state area as a "Long Islander.") Maybe they weren't so charming and elegant, but they were going to make competent lawyers. The Columbia students Kitty met were either superficial flakes or impossible nerds who couldn't navigate life outside the nerd matrix.

But Kitty wasn't friends with any of the Long Islanders. Paul was her only non-Orthodox Jew law school friend. She couldn't relate to the Long Islanders, they were city people. The Orthodox Jews reminded Kitty of the people from her small town: they weren't going anywhere. Their worldview encompassed thousands of years of precedent. They didn't want to do away with all laws, they wanted to understand the separate system of laws that governed the country they were living in; they carried within themselves a deeper system of law. Kitty felt comfortable with all this. It made intellectual sense to her.

The Orthodox Jews also reminded Kitty of people from her small town in that they settled down and married young, they had kids, they had families. They were normal people with normal lives. The Long Islanders were all single. Kitty supposed that after graduating from law school, passing the bar, moving up the corporate ladder, the Long Islanders would settle down with someone at around 35 and after a few years pop out a kid or two (with the assistance of fertility medicine) whom they would pay to never see. This seemed to be the lifestyle they wanted because it was high status. The Long Islanders were all about status.

And there was another thing about the Orthodox Jews that made Kitty feel comfortable. After spending four years living in Europe, she was used to being a foreigner. She was a foreigner here in the city. Being a foreigner felt natural.

Among the Long Islanders Kitty felt like a foreigner too, but there was no good *reason* for it. There were law students who were not from Long Island who ran with the Long Islanders and

166

fit in seamlessly. Kitty did not. She just did not have the same values. She was just not that materialistic. The Long Islanders made her think of the metaphor of crabs in a barrel, clawing and squirming their way to the top. She felt the difference between her and the others rather like a physical defect or a deformity.

Unfortunately, the law students with which Kitty had the most affinity were the diffident, bitter messes- students who, like Kitty, half did not want to be there, and had a poetic streak that in the law-school context was positively perverse. Kitty avoided those people like the plague because they would drag her down.

Among the Orthodox Jews, Kitty encountered the same attitude toward foreigners like herself that she had encountered in Europe. Most people tolerated you, but considered you not really human. Some people were actually rude to you, some were nice, and a few people were willing to be friends.

That was the way it was too with the Orthodox Jews. Actually, it had all centered on Yitzhak. Yitzhak was the only Orthodox Jew who ran with both with the Orthodox and the Long Islanders, probably because Yitzhak smoked a lot of pot. He had an affable, sociable, carefree personality, but in class he stood out for perspicacity and doggedness, and was always arguing with the professors. Everybody liked Yitzhak. He was like one of those kids in high-school everybody gets along with- the nerds, the jocks, the geeks, the freaks. He was the baby of a large family, and it showed. He was often obnoxious, but people forgave him because he had *charm*.

Avi was Yitzhak's best friend. He was a beached whale of an Orthodox Jew, who was a lot of fun. Unlike Yitzhak, Avi was a terrible student. He belonged to the miserable-with-a-poetic-streak category of law student. When finals neared, he would show up to classes with a Graham Greene novel in hand that he read during class. Kitty was also novel-reading, but she studied as well. Avi was like Paul- diffident, absurdist, otherworldly, half in the game, half out of the game.

Avi was half German-Jewish and half Sephardic. Kitty had been impressed to learn that his Sephardic ancestors had been in Manhattan since the 1630s. How many Americans were still living in the same place their ancestors had been in the 1630s, Kitty thought.

Kitty envied the Orthodox Jews. She envied them their sense of place, their history. They were like the Amish, but unlike the Amish, the world they lived in was the world everybody wanted to live in. They lived in and were of the worldly world.

Most of all, she envied the Orthodox Jews their community. They got to stay where they were. They got to live in their hometown. They got to get married and have children- they were *encouraged* to get married and have children. The girls were encouraged to look for husbands, and the boys were encouraged to be husbands. While gentile girls in the city couldn't even find a *boyfriend*, Jewish girls were finding husbands. Kitty didn't find it unfair, because it was their place, after all, not hers- she'd had to leave her place- but she envied them this most of all. Kinship, place, community, and shared history. How lucky they were to have all that.

And they were not so alien either, the Jews. "Jews are our ancestors," her father told her brother and her when they were little. They had laughed and made fun. "So is Mr. Goldstein our cousin?" But the Jews did seem like cultural ancestors to Kitty, and she had no problem sitting down with them and observing their prayers on the Sabbath. At yoga, Kitty refused to bow down to the Hindu icon they wanted you to venerate at the end of class, but she had no problem sitting silently and respectfully for the Jewish prayers.

Kitty peed, hovering in a crouch over Paul's toilet seat as she always did when not at home or at her parents' home. She was pretty confident Paul was pure, but who knew what Paul's stepmother or sisters could be up to. Better safe than sorry. She scanned the piles of reading material on the floor for anything interesting. She'd already read all the New York Magazines and the Economists she saw, and she didn't much care for National Geographic. There were some technical journals that looked totally boring that she didn't know what he was doing with.

Kitty checked her makeup again in the mirror. It was perfect. She had been going out for going on fifteen years now, so she knew what she was doing. She sighed. Kitty had a gang to hang with on a Friday night, but no boyfriend. It had occurred to her that Friday nights were a logical time for the secular population who was her natural pool for mate selection to frequent public spots. But instead of trailing herself invitingly around public spots on a Friday night in the hopes of luring in a boyfriend, she was participating in someone else's holy observances as a foreign menial employed for simple tasks, accompanied by a mild-mannered dysfunctional neurotic. Kitty got it. She was under no illusion as to what was going on.

But it was just that her friends were so nice. They were normal. She wished she could find a Christian group just like them. Why didn't Christians get together for dinner and prayers once a week? Why didn't Christians marry young and stick together?

A few months ago Kitty had attended a Bible study group at a fancy Uptown church with a celebrity preacher. The group was very nice, and obviously they were all Christian and into the Bible, but they were strangers, from all over the country, in a territory that was strange to them. They lacked the social cohesion that comes with place and time. Kitty had known that kind of social cohesion briefly, growing up in her small town. But of course her group was scattered to the winds. Because it had to be that way. There were no jobs in Harrison, NY. And no opportunity. When you grow up, if you have anything going for you, you leave your small town, and you get thrown into an urban environment where you have to make your way. If you're industrious and steady and lucky, maybe you find a job that recompenses you enough to have a family, maybe you find a person to have a family with. But the industrious and steady and lucky are not everybody, and many drift, fall by the wayside, and are dissipated. Isn't this how American life works?

There was no boyfriend material in law school. They were the same Long Island strivers with whom she'd attended college- only worse because at least in college there were some dreamers and some hicks. Law school was a distillation of the Long Island striver: the specimen boiled down to its essence. They had a place, those people, Kitty was sure many of them would make excellent lawyers. Of course, she had much more respect for her fellow Fordham Law students than she did for Orla's Columbia Law students, who were neither fish nor fowl. A lawyer was like a dentist, a trade, and you wanted your lawyer to know what they were doing. Orla's law student friends were more like the Woody Allen short story about the dentists as impressionists: attempting to turn something bloodless, prosaic, and bourgeois into an art. Ha.

Kitty supposed she should be using a dating website. Once in a while, she would make a half-hearted attempt to sign up with one. She would painfully slog through long boring surveys with questions like: How many times a week do you go to the gym? All of a sudden, a future spent turning the lights on and off for observant Jews and hanging around Paul's apartment perusing his back-copies of The Economist didn't look so bad. The dating websites invariably matched her up with some outer-borough Catholic guy named Steve who was a public school-teacher and liked to go to the gym.

"I was bored before I even began," Kitty would sing as she cancelled her online-dating account.

Anyway, now the bar exam was on their doorstep. There was no way she would be able to start dating anyone now even if she wanted to. The yawning maw of death that was the bar exam was a romance killer.

In fact, Kitty, who didn't care much about the others in law school, couldn't help but notice that as the bar exam loomed all the boyfriend/girlfriend couples that had formed were either getting engaged (or married) or splitting up. It was like people needed a definitive relationship status going into the bar exam situation. And, oddly enough, Kitty also couldn't help but notice that a lot of the split-ups that were happening were among the couples that were black and white or Jew and gentile. The marriages that were occurring were mainly among Jews (but then perhaps the majority of white students were Jews), getting their houses in order before the big push.

Yitzhak and Hannah had married last May, a few weeks before finals. Paul was Kitty's "date." It had been a huge wedding in Queens. Kitty and Paul took the subway to an unfamiliar destination in Queens and promptly got lost and ended up walking down empty streets lined with sinister-looking warehouses. Paul said it felt like he was getting taken somewhere to get whacked.

"I'm sorry, Paul! I'm sorry! They made me rat you out!" Kitty yelled, and made a theatrical display of bolting from the scene.

In the vast wedding party, Kitty and Paul were shuttled off to the side with the other non-Orthodox Jews. Kitty recognized Yitzhak's cool friend Polly, so she went over to say hello. Polly was something of a renegade Orthodox Jew. Kitty remembered a party at Polly's apartment where she sported a homemade t-shirt that said "JDate Gave Me Crabs" and drank vodka straight from the bottle. Polly and Yitzhak had grown up together, and apparently everyone had assumed Yitzhak would marry Polly. Kitty didn't really see that happening. Polly was too spirited. She'd yell back at Yitzhak when he yelled at her. Kitty didn't think he wanted that.

As Kitty and Polly stood chatting, two different women stopped by to express their surprise at the fact that Yitzhak was not marrying Polly.

"I've been getting this all day," Polly told Kitty comically after the second woman had left.

They were standing together when Yitzhak and Hannah were carried in on chairs.

"At most weddings, you kind of assume they've already slept together," Polly muttered to Kitty. "At this one, you genuinely don't know."

Before eating, the two girls went to walk through the line to congratulate Hannah. Polly told Kitty that it was tradition for the bride to give single girls her blessing, so they would get married too. Kitty figured it didn't apply to her because she wasn't Jewish, but she wanted to congratulate Hannah, so she went with Polly through the line. Hannah seemed a bit glassy-eyed and shocked. She'd been fasting, Kitty knew. Kitty had a second to tell Hannah "Congratulations!" and then she was through the line and it was over. Polly was through the line too.

"Did she give you her blessing?" Polly demanded.

"No," said Kitty.

"Me neither," laughed Polly. At that moment an elderly lady approached them.

"Polly, I thought this was going to be *your* wedding!" she exclaimed. Polly looked pointedly at Kitty. Kitty giggled.

That was last year. Now Kitty stood regarding herself in Paul's bathroom mirror and remembered resentfully how Hannah had not given her a blessing to get married. "I look gorgeous," Kitty thought. "I look gorgeous!" she shouted fiercely at her reflection.

"Can we go now?" Paul's voice pleaded mildly from the living room.

Kitty threw open the bathroom door. "Can I have one more beer and listen to 'Hey-Ya'?"

Paul was sitting on the futon wearing a navy blazer over a light-blue oxford shirt, khakis, and a pink bow-tie. Brooks Brothers. Kitty would never understand people who dressed like this to party with friends.

Kitty dramatically stopped dead in her tracks. "Is that a pink bow-tie?" she screeched.

Paul looked down at his throat. "How did that get there?" he muttered.

"I'm sorry," said Kitty slyly, "I was under the impression we were going to go sit shabbos with some Orthodox Jews, I had no idea we were participating in a Book TV panel discussion tonight." She guffawed. "Look, can I have one more beer and listen to 'Hey-Ya'?" she demanded again. She sounded like someone's obnoxious kid brother.

"I guess so," Paul conceded reluctantly.

"You're just jealous," said Kitty haughtily, walking to the refrigerator. She opened another Corona, shouting to Paul from the kitchen, "You're jealous of my vibrancy and dynamism! You wish you had rhythm like me!"

"Yes, that's it," Paul answered sarcastically.

"Ok, fine," said Kitty re-entering the living room, "I'll play a song by a white person. Would that make you happy? You fucking *racist*!"

"No," said Paul. "That would not make me happy."

"Dancing With Myself," said Kitty.

"No," said Paul.

"Radio Free Europe. Final offer," said Kitty.

"Ok," Paul sighed.

Kitty strode to the computer purposefully. She searched Youtube, and selected a video. It became quickly apparent that the song was "Hey-Ya."

"Just one song! Just one song!" Kitty yelled, shimmying wildly.

Paul lit a cigarette and attempted to cover one ear with his hand while smoking it and looking through a copy of the New Yorker.

About twenty minutes later, Kitty and Paul were standing on the Union Square subway platform among throngs of other partygoers. It felt great to be out. If Kitty had been on a date right now with Steve the Catholic public-school teacher from Long Island who frequented the gym three times a week, she would be frantically fighting a sinking sensation and trying to make pleasant entertaining conversation, feeling like she should be getting paid for the effort, and wondering whether any of her friends were out and if they could meet up.

Instead here she was trading quips with the Maiden Aunt, enjoying herself. From the comfortable vantage point of their cozy fraternal spinster/bachelor relationship, she could spot some couples on dates trying to make small talk. The only real boyfriend/girlfriend couples you ever saw, Kitty thought, were Jewish. Everyone else was too stressed to really settle down. It was a Jewish town, Kitty was under no illusions about that. It was their town: they got to procreate, they got to settle down and have families. Everyone else was on foreign turf and had to carve out their way in territory which was not their own.

There were no heterosexual white men in the city, at least not any worth a damn, that was for sure- except, like, firemen. Kitty's tastes had been forged in the crucible of *education sentimentale* that was Harrison Senior High School, Harrison, NY. Many of the males she encountered in higher education just seemed "gay" to her. She didn't mean "homosexual," she just meant effete. New York City firemen were notorious for being handsome and manly, but a lot of it came from the fact that they were some of the only white heterosexual red-blooded guys in town. They must be all dating supermodels or billionaires, Kitty thought.

White girls in the city were all strung out, driven insane competing over a scant supply of resources, the quality of much of which made Kitty wrinkle up her nose with distaste. Actually, black girls had it as bad if not worse, Kitty thought. "Sex and the City" tried to pretend being a single woman in the city was a fun, glamorous lifestyle. It was not. Single girls in the city were not happy, they were desperate. Meanwhile, Kitty noted drily, while portraying a desperate single girl adrift in the city, in real life, Sarah Jessica Parker had found a nice Jewish boy for herself and settled down to raise a family.

But this was the hand Kitty had been dealt. She had visited friends in other cities: Orla in Austin, Micah in LA. But all large American cities seemed inadequate to Kitty compared with New York. New York was the most international, New York had a standard of correctness to which outsiders conformed. All the other cities seemed "soft" to Kitty: fatuous, self-indulgent, small-time. And so she returned to New York. Above all, although Kitty wouldn't admit it to herself, Kitty returned to New York because her parents were here. Being able to go to her parents' for dinner and chill out and watch tv with them on their couch was paramount.

Kitty and Paul took the L Train West. It was full of Brooklynite hipsters stepping out in Manhattan for the night. Kitty and Paul looked rather conservative among them, Paul in his Brooks Brothers blazer, Kitty in an Ann Taylor leather jacket. At 8th Avenue, they took the C Train uptown. There was a more varied assortment of people on the C train, and it was crowded: people heading home from work to the Upper West Side and Harlem, no observant Jews on the train because it was near sunset.

Kitty and Paul passed their time on the C Train gently making fun of Hannah's cooking. They knew Orthodox Jewish cooking could be really good because at the diner they went to with Yitzhak and Avi the food was excellent. But everything Hannah made was almost inedible. And the whole focus of her reason for being was supposed to be domestic. It was odd.

It wasn't that they didn't like Hannah. They liked her. She was nice. And Hannah liked them. Well, Hannah tolerated them. Hannah tolerated them as a temporary mania that Yitzhak was going through, part of Yitzhak sowing his wild oats, a sort of *rumspringa* for Orthodox Jews (Kitty had come up with a parody of "Rumpshaker" she called "Rumspringa," inspired by her Orthodox Jewish friends.). But Kitty and Paul knew well enough that although Hannah accepted their presence with good humor, she had no use for them. Kitty she actually, rather naturally, resented.

174

Kitty had gleaned from conversations at parties that Hannah was supposed to have moved up in the world by marrying Yitzhak. Hannah was from a humble family from Brooklyn, whereas Yitzhak's father was a rabbi in Manhattan and a diamond dealer. And Hannah loved Yitzhak. Whom Hannah loved happened to coincide with whom Hannah *should* love; Kitty envied her that. So Hannah tolerated the shabbos goyim, who were harmless losers in any case- that was how Kitty suspected Hannah felt- because they amused Yitzhak, for now.

The shabbos goyim got off at 86th Street, and then they had to walk.

"Yitzhak needs rolling papers," Paul obediently reminded Kitty.

"Oh fuck Yitzhak and his rolling papers," was Kitty's merry rejoinder. But it was bravado; they stopped at the next bodega they saw.

"Let's get him mint-flavored ones," whispered Kitty naughtily as they perused the array of rolling papers behind the glass counter display.

Paul disapproved. He was never any fun.

Kitty briefly considered getting mint ones in addition to regular ones, just as a Yitzhak-tease, but she didn't feel like spending the money.

Yitzhak's apartment was only a couple of blocks away. When Paul and Kitty got there, they pressed the intercom button for Yitzhak and Hannah's apartment. Of course Yitzhak and Hannah couldn't buzz them in- the sun had set- so Yitzhak would come to the door to let them in. After they pressed the buzzer, they heard a "*Pssst*," and they saw a head silhouetted along the top of the building. They were up on the roof. Yitzhak had landed an extraordinary deal, as usual: he had found an apartment with a rooftop space. They had to share the rooftop space with a neighbor, but the neighbor hardly ever used his part of the rooftop. Yitzhak and Hannah erected a tent and set up a grill up on the roof. In the summers, they hung lanterns out, and everyone hung out up on the roof for hours in the evenings and far into the night. It was glorious. It was one of the only times Kitty really enjoyed the city.

Paul and Kitty waited patiently at the front door. Yitzhak had to take the stairs down because he couldn't press a button. Several minutes later, Yitzhak opened the door with a grin and ushered them in.

Paul pressed the button for the elevator; his first shabbos-goy act of the evening. They all got in and rode the elevator up to the 12th floor.

Hannah and Avi were waiting for them. Hannah had fixed the dinner beforehand and then left it in the oven to stay warm. Sometimes she used timers and tried to time-cook the dinner. Kitty wondered if that were part of the problem with her cooking. It couldn't be easy to have to work under such strictures.

"We got the papers," Paul told Yitzhak dutifully.

"Well, now I have a better idea," said Yitzhak mischievously.

"Yitzhak!" admonished Hannah. Yitzhak ignored her. "Follow me," he told Kitty and Paul and brought them into the living room where a 3-Liter soda bottle was sitting alone on the coffee table.

"A bong would be nice," Yitzhak told them.

"You want us to make you a *bong* for shabbos?" Kitty squealed.

Yitzhak answered by flashing a wide grin, but he quickly became serious again.

"Bongs need water," he remarked obliquely.

Hannah stood by the living room door. "Yitzhak," she said worriedly. Yitzhak ignored her. Avi stood next to Hannah, chuckling.

Kitty and Paul hovered by the coffee table nervously, unsure of whether an exercise of their shabbos-goy powers were appropriate in this situation or no.

"There's tin foil in the drawer," Yitzhak observed mildly. "And toothpicks for holes."

"I'm not being a part of this," Hannah said angrily, and she walked down the hall to the bedroom and closed the door. The others silently watched her go.

"Ok," said Yitzhak, breaking the silence. "The bottle needs holes. Scissors are here."

"This is a job for you, Paul," said Kitty. "I've never made a bong before."

"Well, neither have I," Paul huffed.

"Useless," muttered Kitty under her breath. She and Paul tended to play-act an old, married, grouchy couple when they were among the Orthodox. "Fine, ok, give me the bottle," said Kitty. "I don't even like pot," she complained to the party at large.

"I hope I don't stab myself here," Kitty muttered before puncturing a hole in the side of the bottle.

"Not too big, not too big," Yitzhak murmured with concern, hovering behind her. Kitty rolled her eyes heavenward and sighed.

"Foil," Yitzhak prodded gently. Kitty picked up the disk of foil, put it over the neck of the bottle, and poked holes in it. Then Kitty put a bud of marijuana on top of the foil and lit it while Yitzhak sucked the smoke out of the bottle. Kitty felt vaguely guilty, even though it wasn't her tradition, and they weren't *her* laws. She sensed that Hannah was in the right. There was a subtext to Hannah's disapproval that Kitty didn't understand. This was worse than just lighting Yitzhak and Avi's cigarettes. Kitty thought maybe it had something to do with the water in the bong. She got the sense some special kind of taboo was being broken, and that was why Yitzhak was so excited and Hannah was so mad.

# Chapter 18: The Intrepid

The night Kitty and Paul clumsily jimmy-rigged a bong for Yitzhak was Kitty's last stint of shabbos-goy duty. After that night, everyone had to buckle down for finals, and, of course, after finals, there was: "The Bar." Then, after the bar, events conspired to make shabbos-goy duty impossible. The spell was broken. Camelot had ended. Kitty always looked back on that last night as peak shabbos goy. She hadn't known it was the last time.

The following Saturday morning Kitty got a call from Peter Park. There was nothing so very extraordinary about that.

After Kitty broke up with Peter senior year, his parents took him skiing in Vermont for a week. When Peter came back from Vermont, he avoided Kitty. She avoided him too. Then they graduated from high-school, and never saw each other again. Kitty went to Cornell, Peter went to Bowdoin.

But after Holcombe's death Kitty was filled with a messianic zeal to seize upon and round up the people who had been important to her (actually, it was more like people to whom *Kitty* had been important, although Kitty did not admit that to herself). She made a list of significant people from her past, and she dutifully tracked them down- googled them, contacted family members and friends of friends- and called them and checked up on them. But she lost track of most of them again before long. Holcombe was still dead, who had really mattered. We are always fighting the last battle.

However, there were three people on Kitty's get-back-in-touch list, with whom she actually stayed in touch: Peter Park, Orla, and her college friend Micah from L.A. She never saw her high-school friends except when her brother was in town, although Brian Decker was living in Brooklyn, and Benji Russo was living on the Lower East Side with his girlfriend.

Kitty had seen Mike Connolly, her skater ex-boyfriend, last year for the first time since Holcombe's funeral. At Eli Brown's funeral. Eli had died of a heroin overdose- or something they said was stronger than heroin, what he was using had been laced with something, they said. Kitty had never even known Eli was using heroin. He had been on her list of people to keep in touch with, she had called him a couple times, but without the group, they had nothing much to say to each other, and they lost touch.

Mike was messed up at Eli's funeral. Beyond the "I'm messed up because my friend just died" state that everyone was in at Holcombe's funeral. They were older now, nobody except Mike showed up drunk to the funeral. People were better dressed than at Holcombe's funeral. Now they had actual work clothes (or at least interview clothes) that could convincingly double as funeral attire. They no longer had to raid their parents' closets for something dark and tasteful.

Some of the girls were pregnant. Kitty looked enviously at them. The reward for never going anywhere and staying put and being a mediocre student with mediocre life-goals meant you could have children. It wasn't fair.

Kitty tried to talk to Mike, but he seemed out of it. He told her defensively, slurring his words, that he was working on getting membership in the carpenters' union. He didn't have to be defensive with Kitty, he didn't have to prove he wasn't a loser, Kitty didn't think about her high-school friends like that. Why the hell would she have left the city to take the train to travel five hours Northwest for the funeral of an obscure heroin addict if she thought that way?

Kitty couldn't really get through to Mike. The spark wasn't there. He seemed doped. She didn't know if he was drunk…or something else. He and Rachel had broken up a few years ago, Kitty knew that. And now Rachel was married to someone else and had a baby, Kitty knew that too.

The funeral services were held at a Unitarian Church. Kitty was surprised. Eli's parents were these hippies, and Kitty hadn't been sure *what* religion, if any, they were. She had heard they were Buddhist. Eli's sister was apparently named after a Babylonian fertility goddess. Eli's brother Zack had told her their parents were into a mystical Islamic sect.

Kitty supposed a Unitarian Church was where residually Christian boomer-hippies went. She couldn't see a cross anywhere. The minister was a woman. Despite the swinging multicultural dynamic going on, the service was even flatter and more stilted, more unsatisfying, than Holcombe's funeral services in a Catholic Church had been.

In her eulogy, Eli's mother seemed resigned. "I've been expecting this," she said matter-of-factly, unflinchingly facing the mourners, dry-eyed. That was the first line of her eulogy. Then she told some parables about Buddha.

Eli's father had evidently *not* been expecting this. He was broken. He had been a kind, reassuring presence at Holcombe's funeral. Now, when Kitty went through the receiving line and offered him condolences, he hugged her desperately, and his red watery eyes begged her for something that no one in this world could give him. He is not going to be all right, Kitty thought, looking at him.

Eli's mother did not cry once during the funeral. She stood, dry-eyed, silent, and furious, in the receiving line. A small, slight, erect figure with masses of frizzy iron-grey hair. She still looks like a witch, Kitty thought affectionately.

"I'm not happy to be here," Eli's mom had snapped at the mourners during the eulogy. It was an odd turn of phrase, like something you might say if you were unnecessarily hauled into court to pay a parking fine. But Eli's mother was much easier to deal with than his father. She acted like she considered that she had been handed a shit sandwich, by whatever gods it was she believed in, and she was *pissed*. Eli's father just seemed lost. It was much easier to countenance someone who was angry than someone who was broken.

That was the last time Kitty had been back to Harrison. For another funeral. Things seemed even poorer, more dilapidated, more run-down. When you got off the train, there were shady people loitering around; that hadn't been the case before. Harrison, the cute college town, was looking shabbier and shabbier. Some of the houses on the main street had peeling paint. There were a lot of For Sale signs. There were a lot of For Rent signs on houses that hadn't been rentals before. The supermarket had become a dollar store. They had let the famous Ginko Biloba on the village green die.

That was the last time Kitty saw Mike, and she thought it might be the last time she ever saw him. She expected that the next time she heard about Mike it would be in form of a phone call and another funeral.

So Peter Park was the only high-school friend with whom Kitty still kept in touch. A couple weeks after Holcombe's funeral, Kitty, riding the crest of her messianic zeal to reclaim the past had, armed with her list, done the unthinkable. She called the Park household- she knew the Parks hated her- and when Peter Park's mother answered, Kitty had been emboldened enough that it wasn't his stern Korean doctor father, to ask her for Peter's number.

And Mrs. Park, to Kitty's surprise, gave it to her. Kitty was upfront with Mrs. Park, who had always been nice to her; she told her that Holcombe's death made her want to reach out to former friends. Mrs. Park didn't sound too thrilled to hear from Kitty, but she was bone-decent (or maybe she didn't hate Kitty so much after all, maybe Peter's subsequent girlfriends had made Kitty look comparatively not so bad) and she gave Kitty Peter's number. He was in North Carolina.

Peter, rather brilliantly, had joined the military after college, thereby constructively channeling his dark homicidal impulses into a societally acceptable framework.

On the day that Kitty happened to call Peter, after having not spoken to him for seven years, he had just failed out of the Air Force. That day. He sounded stunned. All he had wanted to do was to be a pilot, he kept repeating vacantly. He wanted to fly, he kept saying.

Peter took Kitty's call in stride, but he seemed struck by the coincidence that she was calling him on the very day his world had been destroyed. Kitty tried to make him feel better, but she was at a loss as to what to say. Their conversation was friendly. Peter had a girlfriend, of course. They lived together. Her name was Autumn, Peter lovingly described her as a "Florida cracker." Kitty was jealous.

Peter complained about training. He said the army had published a brochure with photos from his training period, and for the cover they used a photo of a guy who dropped out of training after a few days. Meanwhile, Peter, who completed the initial training period with flying colors, had his photo featured in the portion of the booklet devoted to the army chaplain. Under a caption reading "Sometimes soldiers need some help," there was a photo of Peter talking to the chaplain. "Like a giant pussy," Peter remarked bitterly. That had been the only occasion on which he had ever even *spoken* to the chaplain, he insisted to Kitty. It was a group meet-and-greet, he complained. He just *met* the guy. Meanwhile, Peter noted, the cadet who dropped out on Day Three was featured on the cover scaling a mountain with all his gear. Kitty was appropriately sympathetic.

Peter also told Kitty that the army had assigned him to tutoring the other enlisted men in Math. Kitty was shocked.

"But you're *terrible* at Math!" Kitty protested. "You didn't even make it into Honors Math! Even *I* got into Honors Math! My God- is it because you're *Asian*?! They made you tutor Math because you're *Asian*?!"

"That's the most likely explanation," said Peter sardonically, and Kitty broke out into peals of laughter.

After that they spoke pretty regularly, every few weeks. Kitty noticed, as any female would, that Peter seemed to call her when his girlfriend wasn't around. But Kitty was no threat to Peter's status quo. She was far away; she was living her life, and Peter was living his. They were friends. They had the past in common. They had Harrison, New York in common. And they had in common a shared sensibility that was at once cynical and romantic. So they kept in touch. He complained about work and his girlfriend, she complained about law school and her inability to find a boyfriend.

Therefore, Kitty wasn't surprised when Peter called that Saturday morning. She figured he was going to the gym. He tended to call her on his way to the gym. Peter was intensely disciplined about his diet and gym regimen. He didn't drink, he didn't smoke, and he monitored his weight, his lifting capacity, and his speed like a hawk. Kitty was allergic to people talking about their diets, and this was her least favorite aspect of their conversations. She tuned him out and muttered "Hm" a lot when he started to tell her about his diet and exercise regimen. People describing their diets and physical fitness routines was right up there with people narrating their dream sequences as far as level of boredom.

Peter had been obliquely complaining about Autumn for months. He was always complaining that Autumn had gained weight since they started living together. Peter lamented that this invariably happened to him: as soon as he started going out with a girl, she gained weight. "So disrespectful," Peter said with distaste. Kitty snickered.

"It's because you're too nice," she responded cheerfully. "You're not keeping them on their toes."

Peter had gotten Autumn a gym membership and some running shoes, but she hadn't taken the hint.

But in the last couple of months Peter started complaining that Autumn wanted to get married. She had always wanted to get married, but when her cousin got engaged, that had galvanized her. She was *planning*. She was subscribing to wedding magazines, and she was leaving them around the house.

"Nothing says 'I own you,' like fucking *wedding* magazines everywhere," Peter told Kitty bitterly. Kitty was sympathetic. She knew what he meant.

Today when Peter called Kitty, he had news: he and Autumn had broken up. Kitty was, of course, thrilled. Even in the abstract, the news that Peter was back on the market was cheering. It is a truth universally acknowledged that a single man in possession of any potential at all must necessarily cause a single girl in the city to rejoice.

A couple days ago, he and Autumn had a big fight, Peter told Kitty. Autumn wanted to get married; Peter did not. Autumn had threatened to call the cops and accuse Peter of domestic violence. Peter told Kitty she said, "Who are they going to believe? Me or some half-breed?" Peter left the house to stay at a friend's.

Kitty's eyes narrowed when she heard this. "Don't go back," she said grimly. "You cannot be in a relationship with someone who is looking to *jail* you."

"You have a point," Peter said coolly.

"Yeah, I know I have a point!" Kitty responded with vigor. "That's nuts! She's going to call the cops on you? Are you crazy? What the hell is going on with you guys? Sorry, but she is not on your side."

"I'm going to Iraq," Peter said abruptly.

"You're WHAT?!" shouted Kitty.

"Relax," he answered. "I'm more likely to die of a heart attack from the greasy canteen food than anything else. It's not Afghanistan."

"You're WHAT?!" Kitty shouted again. "Does your MOM know you're doing this?" she demanded, as though they were back in high-school and he'd just told her he'd gotten a piercing. It somehow hadn't occurred to Kitty that Peter was in the army after all, and getting deployed had always been a possibility. When it did occur to her, she recalled every Hollywood movie she'd seen about the Vietnam War, and her tone suddenly changed. "I'll drive you to Canada," she said wheedlingly. "Six hours to the border from here."

Peter politely declined. "I'm going to be back Northeast before I go," he said. "I'm going home to see my parents."

"Visit me here in the city!" Kitty yelled. Obviously, with Autumn out of the way, Peter would be hers, she thought, triumphantly. She didn't think beyond conquest. What *was* there beyond conquest?

"As your lawyer," Kitty told Peter, "I advise you not to marry Autumn. Things only get worse after you're married. She's threatening you with the cops and you're not even married."

Peter was noncommittal.

"And as your lawyer," Kitty continued, "I'll drive you to the border."

"You don't get it," said Peter evenly. "This is what I signed up for."

"You're right," said Kitty miserably, "I don't get it." She had never understood Peter Park. There was a pause.

"Iraq is better than Afghanistan?" she asked him timidly.

"Oh yeah," Peter answered flatly. She couldn't tell if he were being brave or honest. "No comparison. Iraq is nothing. Afghanistan's bad. Not Iraq. Like I said, my major problem will be not getting fat."

"I think *I'd* rather to go Iraq than take the *bar*," said Kitty wretchedly.

"You'll do fine," said Peter. "You're the Aging Champ."

That was Peter's nickname for Kitty: The Aging Champ. He called her that because he said she reminded him of some old movie he'd seen about an over-the-hill prizefighter who knows he's gonna lose some day, but keeps on fighting.

"I hope you're right about everything," said Kitty doubtfully. "Well, let me know if you're going to be in the city.

You can stay with me. It will be fun," she added sweetly. By "fun" she meant "sex." The really amusing thing was that the two of them had never even *had* sex. Three and a half years they had gone out in high school, and no sex. Three and a half years of foreplay.

After Kitty got off the phone with Peter, she studied herself in the bathroom mirror. She was more beautiful than ever, and he would be captivated. This was amazing. After all these years, she was going to have sex with Peter Park. Three and a half years of groping and heavy petting and dry humping and onanism. Seven years of not speaking. Five years of casual friendship. The Florida cracker's loss was her gain. She just hoped he timed his visit for after the bar exam. The bar exam. Kitty felt a wave of panic encompass her. She met her eyes in the mirror.

"The Aging Champ," Kitty murmured to her own reflection.

Kitty took the bar exam in the shadow of the Intrepid. That's not a metaphor. Kitty was assigned to sit the bar exam in a warehouse-like building on the Hudson River next to the USS Intrepid, the World War II aircraft carrier. The day before the bar, Kitty's mother drove her to the exam site to check it out. Kitty warily regarded The Intrepid. There it was, looming over the proceedings. It mocked her puny human endeavor with its solemn bulk. It spoke of a better time and a better people. Better than Kitty, anyway. Kitty did not feel intrepid. She felt extremely trepid.

After dutifully and seriously completing her bar exam course, Kitty lost her mind completely about two weeks before the exam and started reading novels. She was smoking heavily, of course. The night before the bar exam she drank three Corona Lights and went to sleep on the couch. She woke the next morning without an alarm and sat bolt upright with terror.

Kitty dressed hurriedly, slung a rosary around her neck, and sallied forth. She had more rosaries in her purse in case she ran out. She couldn't articulate how she might "run out," but extra rosaries on hand made her feel more secure. She grabbed a coffee at the deli across the street, washed it down with a couple Vivarin, and met her mother who was sitting idling in her Park

Avenue Buick outside Kitty's apartment building, like the getaway car for a robbery.

Unfortunately, somehow, near the Roosevelt Island tramway, her mother took a wrong turn and they found themselves forced into a stream of traffic, and then the terrible realization dawned that they were crossing a bridge, they weren't sure which bridge, but all of a sudden they found themselves in Queens.

"Make the sign of the cross at the other drivers so they know it's life or death! *Make the sign of the cross!*" Kitty's mother shrieked as she performed a U-turn across eight lanes of traffic.

Kitty showed up at the exam site about twenty minutes later, trembling and shaken. As soon as she got out of the car, she saw someone else also wearing a rosary slung around his neck, a boy who looked Hispanic. They nodded at each other in passing, in recognition of a kindred "We who are about to die salute you" spirit of desperation. She felt sure his mother was probably as much of a nervous wreck as hers.

Kitty walked into the vast hall filled with thousands of students and promptly sat down in the wrong seat. A nice Indian girl whose seat it was calmly corrected her, and Kitty, apologizing profusely and starting to sweat, moved.

The exam session itself was a blur, a kind of out-of-body experience. Kitty began regurgitating information as frenetically and urgently as a newly freed hostage trying to communicate details about his captors. Then they were breaking for lunch. Kitty gravitated in a daze toward the daylight she saw through the open doors. She marveled vaguely at the stolid peasants around her, taking out apples and carrots to sensibly snack on during the break. Soulless people, she thought, without rancor. She envied them. She needed a cigarette.

She rushed towards the entrance, past rows of metal seats, and stumbled out of the building into the light of day, when suddenly, improbably, wonderfully-

"Avi!" Kitty shouted. "Avi!"

It was Avi. He too had been assigned to the shadow of The Intrepid.

She had never imagined a Diamond-District-looking Orthodox Jew could look so much like home. She ran to him.

They didn't embrace or anything, they just stood and beamed at each other. Here, in the midst of hell, was some sort of oasis.

"I've been reading Graham Greene novels!" Kitty burst out. "The past two weeks! I lost the plot! I've been novel reading!"

"Me too!" Avi returned. "Me too and Graham Greene!"

"The Power and the Glory!" cried Kitty.

"The Comedians!" Avi shouted.

Something happened at that moment. Some dynamic changed between them. They walked down the pier together and looked at The Intrepid. There it sat: Intrepid while they were not. They sat down together on a bench to admire the view.

"The Intrepid," murmured Kitty.

"I know," said Avi, shaking his head, "I couldn't believe it either."

It seemed to Kitty the narcissist that she and Avi were the only bar exam participants to appreciate the poetic symbolism. The other students had minds like steel traps, she thought contemptuously. It didn't seem admirable to Kitty to have a mind like a steel trap, it seemed simple and insensitive and foreseeably cruel. The others were inside now, obediently grazing on vegetables like healthy herd animals, Kitty thought with a sneer, performing whatever other rituals their self-help manuals had prescribed: stretching, deep-breathing. Avi lit Kitty's cigarette and then his own, and they sat for a moment, contemplating the aircraft carrier's majesty and their own wretchedness.

Then suddenly it was time to get up and go back inside and continue the exam, and they did, but stronger and brighter from having found each other.

On Day Two of the bar exam (two six-hour days the bar exam was), when it was lunch break, Kitty rushed past the carrot-snackers straight to the entrance. Avi was waiting for her there.

In the manner of everyone at the bar exam when reconnoitering with friends, Avi and Kitty narrated to each other in meticulous detail all the actions they had taken in the interim since they last saw each other: what they had eaten, how they had slept. It was like meeting up with surviving family in a prisoner of war camp. The camaraderie was intense.

And, again heartened by their meeting, they resumed their assigned places in the phalanx of metal chairs and returned to the examination. Only the afternoon session remained.

And then suddenly Kitty was out in the open air again, at liberty, and it was over. It was over, whether she passed or whether she failed, she did not have to stay in that building anymore. She had imagined she'd feel happier. She felt exhausted. She felt like she'd just been liberated from a prisoner of war camp, and she should feel ecstatic, but she was too spent and too traumatized.

Avi was on the phone with Yhitzhak. Yitzhak and their friend Dylan Zellner were together at another exam site. A bunch of people were meeting up at a bar near Penn Station. "Ugh," thought Kitty vaguely, "Why go out there?" but she tagged along with Avi to go meet them. Yitzhak was not going because he was taking the New Jersey bar the next day. Passing both bars made you even more viable of a job candidate. Kitty shuddered in horror: one bar was good enough for her.

Dylan was the one of the coolest of the Long Islanders. Like Yhitzhak, he was friends with everyone. He was an easy-going, pretty, superficial boy who reminded Kitty of one of the young men from Satyricon: sexy in an androgynous way.

Last spring Kitty had gotten an email from someone at the law firm where Dylan had "summered," inviting her to Dylan's birthday party. It was going to be held at a strip club, and the idea in the invite seemed to be that they were all going to hire strippers to celebrate Dylan's birthday. Without stopping to think, Kitty fired off an outraged response. She was certainly NOT going to a strip club to hire strippers!, she railed indignantly.

She immediately received a fawning, contrite reply from the host, a young Jewish guy who worked at Dylan's firm. But he misunderstood her anger. He thought she was pulling an SJW on him, he thought she was pulling PC rank. He apologized profusely and included some placating bromides to feminism.

But Kitty hadn't thought about it that way. She just didn't want to go to a strip club. Did they think she was a whore? Or worse, a whoremaster? Was she really going to go hang out in some den of sin and pay some poor Midwestern girl who had dreamed of becoming a dancer to perform like a slave?

It wasn't a feminist issue, it was a morality issue. It was a *slavery* issue. It was a using-people-as-chattel issue. But these Long Island guys, they just didn't see it that way.

Yitzhak had taken her to task about it later. He thought she had been uncool and rude, he thought she was being a prude. Kitty thought that was rich coming from someone whose womenfolk couldn't even show their hair, but she didn't say that. She just shrugged it off. Yitzhak could say what he wanted. Kitty knew the score. They were her friends, but she wasn't going to participate in that.

"You realize it was Zellner's *girlfriend* who was organizing the party, right?" Yitzhak sneered.

"I don't care," Kitty answered implacably.

"She goes to strip clubs all the time, and she gets lap dances, it's no big deal, it's fun," Yitzhak said airily.

Kitty wanted to answer "Then why don't you let Hannah do it too?" but she held her tongue. She was intrigued.

"Zellner's *girlfriend* gets lap dances?" said Kitty incredulously. What the hell *for*?"

"Because it's *fun*," Yitzhak answered irritably.

"Well, that's not my idea of fun," said Kitty grimly.

Avi and Kitty met up with a group of about twenty other law students in a dive bar near Penn Station. Everyone looked terrible: bedraggled, pale, strung out. But the camaraderie was still strong. Kitty chatted and celebrated with people she hadn't been able to stand for the past three years. It was like Christmas in the trenches in World War I.

"I haven't eaten a vegetable in weeks," Kitty confided to one of the people she hated, a Chinese girl who had made Law Review.

"My parents kept asking me if I was eating vegetables," said the girl, laughing. "And I was like 'I had broccoli on my pizza last week!'"

It was like that. Everyone was on the same side.

Kitty was engaged in a spirited conversation, chatting about plans for post-bar trips, when all of a sudden she found herself lying on the floor. She gathered she had fainted. That was interesting, thought Kitty, she had never fainted before. When was the last time she had eaten a solid meal? Kitty wondered, and she thought it might be two days ago.

Someone was stroking her hair and crooning to her. Kitty blinked blearily upwards and recognized the frosted tips and Cleopatra-style makeup of Zellner's girlfriend. The strip-club maven had apparently taken charge of her while she was unconscious. Kitty watched passively as Zellner's girlfriend ordered people to get Kitty a glass of water. She also commandeered people to help Kitty up. She was obviously enjoying herself.

Kitty let herself be led to a booth, where she obediently sat with her head between her legs as Zellner's girlfriend told her to do. Zellner's girlfriend sat down next to Kitty and started telling her an anecdote about how she had gotten drunk and shit herself at a party. She seemed to think this would make Kitty feel better.

"I have to get away from this person," Kitty realized with alacrity as the blood rushed back into her head.

She looked up and saw Avi across the room standing with a group of people. Kitty mumbled thanks to Zellner's girlfriend, muttered something about needing a cigarette, and headed towards her friends.

"Are you ok?" Avi asked.

"What, that? That was nothing," said Kitty nonchalantly. "I just haven't eaten in two days, that's all."

"Order some fries from the bar," said a down-to-earth girl from Staten Island.

"You are all right," said Kitty pointing at her. "You have a good head on your shoulders."

Kitty ordered some fries from the bar and then took a taxi home. She dropped into bed with her clothes on and fell into a dark dreamless sleep that was like oblivion.

A couple weeks after the bar exam, Avi called Kitty and nonchalantly asked her if she wanted to go to a movie. Like that was normal. That was not normal.

They hadn't seen each other since the bar exam, but the same feeling of closeness remained. The movie was terrible, and after the movie they went back together to Kitty's apartment, like that was normal. That was not normal.

"Can I kiss you?" Avi asked. And that was definitely not normal. She said yes.

What followed was an affair. It was an affair because it was illicit. There was no future in it. No good future, anyway.

"Of all the bar exams, in all the city, in all the state, he walked into mine," Kitty muttered rancorously to herself.

She contemplated the deep, rich, bitter irony that the only boy she had organically fallen in love with in the city was an Orthodox Jew. The unfairness. Romantically, Kitty was used to always losing, but she wasn't used to coming this close to winning only to lose.

After the bar exam, Kitty went back home to Upstate New York. Her parents rented an apartment in Harrison, which was shabbier every time she visited. There were familiar faces, but Kitty didn't see any friends.

But the village was peaceful. Kitty stayed in the apartment with her mother. They spent the days reading and watching tv. It was quiet.

It was the "done thing" to take a trip somewhere after the bar exam, and Kitty decided to do the done thing. She decided on Iceland, she had always wanted to go there. It did not disappoint. Iceland was utterly beautiful and otherworldly, Reykjavik seemed like a large village. It was August, and always light.

Her first day in Reykjavik Kitty went to the main tourist office. She called her mother, she called Orla, she called Micah, she called Avi, and she called Peter Park.

That night Kitty went out to a pub alone and brought a book. You could do that in Scandinavia. The men were gorgeous and totally cool. You could sit at a bar with a book and read just like a man would do, and it wasn't assumed you were a prostitute. That by itself made Scandinavia a very attractive destination.

A young Irishman was sitting at the bar, and he and Kitty started talking. They were both traveling alone. They were very frank with each other, as strangers at a bar who are never going to see each other again can be. He told Kitty he was an atheist, she strongly disapproved.

"What do you think of the Icelanders?" he asked Kitty. Opining on the natives inevitably became a topic of conversation among foreigners in a strange city, Kitty had noticed.

"I think they're lovely," Kitty said. "The girl at the hotel who checked me in was beautiful. This is a beautiful country, and the people are beautiful."

"*I* don't think the people are beautiful," the Irishman abruptly contradicted her. "They all look alike," he sneered.

Kitty was taken aback. He had been baiting her, Kitty thought. He only asked her opinion because he wanted to give his own. She looked over at the bartender, who was Icelandic. He didn't seem to have heard.

"They do," the Irishman insisted with a wild look in his eye. Kitty guessed he had been mulling over his theory for a while, and she was the lucky person to whom he had decided to disclose it. Sometimes traveling alone could make people weird.

"Good God, take a *look* at them," he commanded her fiercely. "They all have the same face." He leaned in closer and loudly whispered, "Upturned nose and pointy chin!"

Kitty frowned at the Irishman. He was rather a rude person with rather an odd turn of mind, she thought. She looked over at the bartender again. He did have an upturned nose and a pointy chin. At the other end of a bar there was a couple drinking beers. Yes, they had upturned noses and pointy chins. Kitty turned around. At the table behind her were a group of girls having a girls' night out. A girls' night out with their upturned noses and pointy chins.

Kitty turned around. "You're right," she told the Irishman tersely. "Ok, you've just ruined Icelanders for me."

The next day Kitty went on a tour. She picked the tour where you got to see where the Vikings held the world's oldest parliament, where the tectonic plates of North America and Europe met. She couldn't imagine anything more romantic.

There was a horrible obnoxious American family on the tour bus, a mother and father and two teenage daughters. They immediately asked Kitty where she was from and became electrified when she said New York City. They were from Florida. They had gone to Galapagos last year. Galapagos was better than Iceland, they told her.

By the end of the tour, the tour guide, who was knowledgeable and enthusiastic, pretty much openly hated the American family. They didn't seem to care or even notice. They treated him like a menial non-entity as he imparted the history of his country. The parents kept talking while he was talking, and the daughters didn't even pretend to care what he said- they kept their headphones on the whole time.

Kitty did her best to convey to the tour guide that she hated them too and that they didn't really represent Americans, without getting into too much detail. She was used to being in such situations. There were a lot of rich obnoxious Americans like this abroad.

The tour bus stopped, and they all transferred into a special truck that was designed to ford rivers; they were going to see a waterfall. Kitty vigilantly avoided sitting near the American family.

The waterfall was magical. They even had the opportunity to walk behind it. After about an hour, most of the group was back at the bus, standing around, when the tour guide suddenly yelled, "Stop! Come back!" No one understood what he meant, then he gestured toward the waterfall. On the high cliff above, they saw a small slight figure. It was the Japanese girl from their tour. She was taking photos. Kitty could not imagine how she had gotten up there.

"Come down!" yelled the tour guide. The girl nodded politely and, smiling, disappeared from view, presumably to clamber down the same way she had clambered up. Kitty was terribly impressed. The Japanese were so hardcore.

Kitty and the Japanese girl went out to dinner that night. Kitty invited her to dinner by miming eating, and she happily agreed. It was rather a frustrating meal since they couldn't speak with each other, but convivial nonetheless.

The next day was the music festival. Thousands of Icelanders converged on Rejkavik. The streets were thronged, very different from the previous couple nights. As she scanned the crowds of Icelanders, the Irishman's observation came flooding back to Kitty. Masses of people, and they all had the same face. *The apparition of these faces in the crowd*, thought Kitty. *Upturned noses over sharp pointy chins.*

It was easy to meet people, Kitty met some Americans, she met some Australians. They all went pub-hopping together and met friendly, cheerful, good-looking Scandinavian men who all seemed to be into Metallica. It was interesting, Kitty thought, how passionate Scandinavian men were for death metal; she connected it somehow with their pagan, berserker, Viking past. With the re-paganization of the West, she reflected, everyone was reverting to tribal type.

After that late night she had one day to recover, and then it was time to go home. Armed with bottles of Icelandic spirits and a volume of Norse sagas, Kitty took her seat on the plane. Kitty hated flying, although she had done so much of it. Her fear of flying was growing worse with each trip. She sat down and pulled out a pack of Benadryl from her purse and downed four of them. "That's a good idea," the nosy woman beside her said appreciatively.

The minute the plane began circling the runway preparing for take-off, Kitty slipped her rosary out of her purse, and, clutching the rosary with one hand and her arm rest with the other, closed her eyes and began muttering Hail Marys. If the woman next to her thought this was a good idea, she didn't mention it.

Then they were air-born and climbing. A stewardess stopped by with the drink cart. Kitty stopped muttering Hail Marys long enough to croak, "Whiskey, please."

The woman seated next to Kitty did not tell her this was a good idea, but she did not tell Kitty this was a bad idea either (which would not have surprised Kitty at all). The woman pursed her lips and read her paper, she had dismissed Kitty. It was the rosary that had put her off.

But despite the Benadryl and the whiskey(s), Kitty could not sleep. She white-knuckled the rosary and the arm-rest all the way to JFK.

And then she was back, and it was like she had never left. Her new job would start in a few weeks. It was not just a job but a fantastic opportunity, the launch of her brilliant career. Kitty wished she could get someone else to live her life in her place- brilliant career and all the rest of it. She wished she could just go back to Iceland.

And when Kitty got back, she got a call from Avi. They started going out on dates, an odd couple. They would go see a movie and then go back to Kitty's apartment and make out. No sex, obviously. Avi was a virgin for religious reasons, and Kitty didn't want to (a) ruin his life and (b) anger God any more than she already had.

Oddly enough, Kitty seemed to have a lot more qualms about Avi's spiritual life than she had about her own. Kitty felt conflicted, tortured really, about her own spiritual life, whereas Avi's path was clear-cut. It was too late for her, she felt, but maybe it was not too late for Avi. The thought of corrupting him and causing him to stray from the path filled her with fear.

This unconsummated affair with Avi sounded the death-knell for Kitty's shabbos-goy tours of duty. No more shabbos-goy nights hanging with the Orthodox crew. Kitty couldn't face Yitzhak and Hannah, she was ashamed. She had been given access to their community, only for this to happen. They had shown her hospitality, she had been their guest- and she had turned a wholesome situation into a *histoire de fesses*. She didn't blame Avi at all, she blamed only herself.

Her relationship with Avi was not making Kitty happy. She was haunted by a conversation she once had with her cubicle mate Gloria at the law firm where she had worked. The previous lawyer Gloria worked for was also Irish-American, so when Gloria was sharing a cubicle with Kitty, she kept relating Kitty back to her former boss, because her ex-boss was the only other Irish-American Gloria knew.

When you're somebody's secretary, you get to know everything about them. Gloria's boss was the mistress of an Orthodox Jew, a diamond dealer.

Kitty remembered being surprised when Gloria related this anecdote, because she didn't typically associate "Irish" with "mistress." An Irish-American woman, wondered Kitty, throwing her life away to be somebody's mistress. It sounded so funny. Who would want an Irish-American mistress, anyway? Irish didn't seem like mistress material at all.

Now Kitty recalled this casual gossip and wondered. She loved Avi, in a comfortable way, and he loved her, in a comfortable way. She could see the writing on the wall, and she could see herself ending up like Gloria's boss: a career-woman and somebody's mistress.

She would live in infamy, in the shadows, Kitty fretted. Apparently she could not have both a man and a baby in this city. No family for shabbos goyim. Even if she did have an illegitimate child with Avi, any child she had with him would be a misfit, would renounce her, would be ashamed of her, would reject the half of itself that was her.

Kitty thought of her friend Jen, one of her housemates in college. Jen's father was Jewish, her mother was not. Kitty remembered someone mentioning that Jen wasn't really Jewish because her mother wasn't (such conversations were not uncommon at Cornell), and Jen bristled, was really hurt, and asserted in a wounded tone that her mother had converted to Judaism, had kept a kosher kitchen. Which hadn't prevented Jen's father from leaving Jen's mother later on, Kitty recalled.

Second-class citizenship. That's what Kitty was looking at. Not only for herself, but for her children.

Kitty remembered this guy named Isaac she met at a party Orla took her to at some community-garden co-op on the Lower East Side. Isaac had just gotten back from an Irish-language immersion program in Donegal. He spoke fluent Irish. He had studied all the greats: James Joyce, Synge, Sean O'Casey. Much respect, Kitty felt. She was impressed.

Isaac told Kitty he had just come from dinner with his priest that evening. Isaac kept throwing around the term "my priest," the way Hunter S. Thompson dropped references to "my lawyer." He seemed to relish the reactionary shock-value the words "my priest" had, in the context of a party at a Lower East Side socialist collective. He was being contrarian, Kitty thought.

Something was off about Isaac, Kitty could feel it. He was trying too hard.

"Are you entirely Irish?" Kitty asked innocently.

Well, no, Isaac admitted. His father was actually Jewish (his parents were estranged).

Immediately Kitty was flooded with an almost psychic impression of a neurotic Irish mother competing for ethnic dominance and cultural hegemony with the Jew with whom she had mated, turning her son into a seething battleground.

This was the future Kitty foresaw for her progeny should she mate with Avi, which would be the foreseeable result of sex with Avi, naturally.

And Avi was the boy that Kitty had found the most natural affinity with since she'd been in New York City. This was her New York City homeboy.

Kitty contemplated her future as a stressed-out middle-aged lawyer- either a childless mistress, or a desperate single mother paying for her only child to study Irish in Donegal for the summer with the futile hope he would not deny her side of the family, that he would not abandon his mother's people.

Was that a better future than simply being alone? But at least she would have a child, Kitty thought desperately. Even if it wasn't really hers.

# Chapter 19: The Chambers

Then it was time to start her new job. Through her family's connections, Kitty had landed that most coveted of law-school graduate opportunities: a clerkship. Judge Jackson was a Republican, like Kitty's connections, and she was an African-American woman. That was how she had been appointed despite being a Republican. And she was a brand-new judge, she had only been appointed a few months ago.

Kitty had interviewed with the judge in her chambers. Naturally, Kitty was a nervous wreck, eager to impress. Judge Jackson was very pleasant, refined and soft-spoken, but seemed subdued and rather wistful- kind of depressed, Kitty thought. Kitty suspected Judge Jackson wanted to be a judge the same way Kitty wanted to be a law clerk: not at all, really, but supposing it her duty to take advantage of the opportunity.

On her first day of work, Kitty bounded into the chambers early and eager and found the reception area empty, as it had also been when she interviewed. Judge Jackson had greeted her at the door that day. There was no secretary sitting at the big desk near the entrance this morning, and Kitty assumed that the secretary hadn't arrived for work yet, but later she learned that no secretary had yet been assigned to the judge.

There were two rooms off the reception area. Kitty, eager to make a good first impression, strode into the room on the right, no one was there. A hoarse voice called "Over here!" It was coming from the room on the left. Kitty changed course and headed into the room on the left.

There, calm and alone, a young black woman sat behind a desk and expressionlessly tolerated Kitty's effusive greeting. Kitty's greeting was more effusive than usual to compensate for her surprise at the absolutely enormous head-dress upon the girl's head. It was gigantic, bright, and multicolored, and seemed to be composed of a number of differently patterned scarves. Kitty saw a leopard print pattern, one seemed to be turquoise, there was also gold. The effect was magnificent, Kitty had to admit.

When Kitty had interviewed with the judge, the judge had been alone in the chambers. Kitty had never seen Ludivine before. She would have remembered.

Kitty looked directly into Ludivine's eyes in a desperate bid to avoid staring at the vibrant display of colors festooned about her head and held out her right hand with ferocious joviality. Ludivine calmly looked down at Kitty's out-stretched hand and then back up at Kitty.

Kitty remained with her hand extended. She was not going to back down. Good God, she had to hang on to her sanity. In the face of such aggressive assertion of tribal identity, Kitty strengthened her tenacious hold on convention with a fierce determination.

Ludivine reluctantly extended a hand and granted Kitty a perfunctory limp-wristed handshake. This was enough. Kitty had established formal, respectful relations with whatever situation it was she was getting into here.

Thank God in Heaven Kitty had not committed the unpardonable sin of assuming that Ludivine was the secretary. No, Kitty was too clever for that. She was too well-raised. She had lived in New York City too long. Moreover, Kitty surmised at once that this was her fellow law clerk because most secretaries wouldn't have dared, or even wanted, to walk about wearing a giant spangled multicolor turban. In comparison with the turban, the startle factor of Ludivine's nose-ring and lip-ring faded in comparison.

Kitty was not really sure why a conservative Christian judge had a law clerk who was, well, probably not conservative, or at least not conventionally conservative, but Kitty soon learned that Ludivine was as serious, dutiful, and hardworking as her headdress was large, multicolored, and spangled. That was why Ludivine got away with a giant headdress, because she did her work. Kitty was also to learn that Ludivine was the only member of the chambers to access the judge. It was, in effect, Ludivine's chambers, Kitty was to learn.

Ludivine seemed to churn out memos for the judge at a good rate. Whenever she finished a memo, she would bring the memo to Kitty and ask her to proofread it. Kitty would proofread it and propose grammatical changes (Ludivine was comma-happy and indulged in convoluted run-on sentences), which Ludivine would invariably ignore. Ludivine's prose was clunky and pompously legalistic, which Kitty didn't mention, obviously. Kitty didn't understand why Ludivine was even asking her to proofread her memos since she never paid attention to Kitty's feedback. Kitty had only graduated from law school a few months ago, so she didn't feel in a position to assess Ludivine's memos on their legal merits, but they seemed ok to Kitty.

Kitty, for her own part, despite fevered enthusiasm and all the good will in the world, was writing precious little. She had only graduated from law school a few months ago, and she had no idea what she was doing. Her longest conversation with Judge Jackson was during the job interview, and they mostly talked about opera. She had no idea what the judge wanted. Sometimes she wondered whether the judge did either.

And Ludivine was no help. Kitty soon learned not to ask her questions. Ludivine's response was invariably a self-possessed, wide-eyed, innocent stare, and in a composed, aloof tone, Ludivine would hand Kitty's question right back to her.

Ludivine repeatedly informed Kitty that the judge did not wish to be disturbed. Judge Jackson spent almost the entire day locked in her chambers. Kitty never saw her. And, unlike most of the other judges, she logged hours and hours at work. She was there when Kitty came to work and still there when Kitty went home every night. She must be spending sixty hours a week at the office, Kitty thought. And ninety percent of the time, she was locked in her office, not wanting to be disturbed.

Once Kitty, toiling away on a lengthy memo on which Ludivine apparently couldn't provide guidance (Kitty had asked), decided she had had enough. "That's it," she spoke aloud. "I'm going to go ask the judge."

"I wouldn't do that," Ludivine responded quietly. Kitty froze. Why not? Was it Judge Jackson who wouldn't like that or was it Ludivine?, Kitty wondered miserably. But Ludivine had returned to her screen with composure, and gave no clue. Ludivine was obviously the boss around here. Ludivine was the only person the judge talked to, and the judge never talked to her. What could Kitty do?

Judge Jackson wasn't just toiling away inside her office, Kitty knew that. Sometimes they would hear the cheery rhythmic tones of an exercise video going on in there. Occasionally, they heard opera. But the longer Kitty went without speaking to the judge, the harder it became to speak to her.

Kitty began to be filled with social anxiety regarding the judge. She was paralyzed by doubts. What if she knocked on the door at the wrong moment and the judge was in there in leggings doing exercise routines? Kitty didn't think she could overcome the embarrassment. She didn't blame the judge. Judge Jackson seemed just as much a hapless prisoner, if not more, of the system as everyone else.

Each time Kitty brought up asking Judge Jackson a question, Ludivine would solemnly shake her head, saying only "I wouldn't do that."

But one day, Ludivine was not in the office, and Kitty screwed up courage enough to knock on the door of the judge's inner sanctum. "Just a minute," came the soft-spoken reply, and after several long minutes the judge opened the door.

Judge Jackson sat down behind her desk and motioned Kitty toward the chair across from her. "Sit down," she told Kitty. Kitty was desperately grateful. She plunged into the details of the memo she was working on, spilling her guts like a penitent on his deathbed. The judge said nothing while Kitty talked. She appeared thoughtful. Eventually Kitty trailed off. The judge still said nothing and still appeared thoughtful.

"So," said Kitty hesitantly, "I could go with either the first option, or I could go with the second."

The judge continued to say nothing and appear thoughtful.

"Or not," said Kitty nervously. "Or I could incorporate both options into the memo and just leave it open-ended."

"Yes," the judge said faintly. "Why don't you do that." And that was all. "Thank you," she told Kitty politely, letting her know she was dismissed. Kitty got up, left the inner sanctum, closed the door softly, and returned to her desk, feeling that, although the meeting hadn't been overwhelmingly rewarding, at least she had touched base.

When Ludivine returned to the chambers, Kitty didn't tell her about her meeting with the judge. Ludivine doesn't need to know everything, Kitty thought smugly. But then, shortly after her return, Ludivine received a call from Judge Jackson, summoning her into the office. Kitty watched Ludivine enter the judge's office with some trepidation. It wasn't unusual for Judge Jackson to summon Ludivine, but Kitty had a wild idea it had something to do with her own earlier meeting with the judge. Ludivine returned in a few minutes.

"Judge Jackson wants me to take over the Roberts memo," Ludivine told Kitty impassively. Kitty felt herself blush. So apparently the judge had been unfavorably impressed with their little tête-à-tête.

"Oh, ok," said Kitty miserably. She wondered what she had done wrong.

Ludivine took over the memo and had it finished the next day. On the next occasion when Ludivine was out of the chambers and Kitty was there alone, Kitty retrieved the memo and opened it. She wanted to know what she had done wrong, and she didn't dare ask Ludivine. She wanted to see what Ludivine had corrected. To Kitty's astonishment, Ludivine had changed almost nothing. The memo was virtually the same document Kitty had brought into the judge's office to ask her about.

"Judge Jackson hates me," Kitty thought wretchedly. Kitty lacked the maturity to consider the matter from the newly-appointed judge's perspective. Judge Jackson was just starting out, she wanted clerks to know what they were doing, and insecurity on the part of a clerk made her insecure. Unfortunately, Kitty was just starting out too. They were a bad match.

Kitty never asked the judge another question. Ludivine had been right, of course. It wasn't a good idea.

A few days after Kitty's ill-fated attempt to consult Judge Jackson, Kitty and Ludivine were joined by a third addition to the judge's orbit. Kitty and Ludivine were sitting at their separate desks, working, when a loud voice interrupted their work saying playfully "Knock! Knock!"

They looked up in astonishment. A short, Mediterranean-looking, elderly man stood before them, grinning demonically. "Rumpelstilskin," Kitty thought idiotically. His dimensions were dwarfish, a large head and a stunted body. On his head he wore a jauntily-tilted black fedora. He was carrying a purse, a large leather purse- it wasn't a man-bag, it was quite definitely a purse. He looked like the Truman Capote cameo in Annie Hall, and Kitty reminded herself to mention this to Ludivine later.

"It is I!" the man proclaimed.

The girls, who had been staring blankly at the outlandish-looking visitor, now glanced nervously at each other.

"Her Honor's new secretary!" the gnome-like man announced joyfully. "Massimo Zucchero. Max!"

Kitty suppressed a wild desire to play a drumroll on her desk and announce "È arrivato Zucchero!" à la Giulietta Masina.

"Oh," said Ludivine, getting up from her desk, dutifully rising to the occasion with the passive fatalism of a gazelle getting taken down by a pride of lions.

Ludivine led Max to the desk in the foyer. Neither Ludivine nor Kitty was surprised that Judge Jackson had neglected to tell them they were getting a new secretary. The judge's chambers ran like a dysfunctional family, Kitty thought, on an unhealthy system of covering up and enabling. Personally, Kitty hadn't even seen the judge in a couple weeks.

Kitty remained at her desk and let Ludivine handle Max. Ludivine was the senior clerk, so she felt it was Ludivine's role to acclimate the new secretary.

Ludivine confronted the desk. It was bare, except for a computer, and empty. She checked the drawers: nothing.

"This would be your desk, but I'm sorry we haven't had time to set everything up," Ludivine explained politely. Kitty inwardly sniggered. "Haven't had time"- they had had no idea they were getting a secretary.

"You just leave it to me," Max chuckled at Ludivine, rubbing his hands. His chuckle sounded as diabolical as his grin had looked, Kitty thought. He resembled a gargoyle: squat, hideous, and filled with devilish glee. Kitty pretended to look at her screen while surreptitiously keeping an eye on Ludivine and the new secretary in the other room.

"Oh, I'll manage," Max chuckled again. "I always do, you know!"

Kitty was suddenly possessed by the mad conviction that the judge's new secretary was the devil. And she didn't commonly go around forming sudden mad impressions that people were the devil, either. She wondered if he really *were* the judge's new secretary. This felt like a Twilight Zone episode.

He was asking Ludivine something now. Kitty pretended to be reading and listened with interest.

"She's a champion, you know," Max was confiding in Ludivine. Kitty imagined he meant the judge. Everyone was always flattering the judge, it was just part of how things worked.

"She's retired now, from showing, but, you know, she's not a diva at all." Kitty was puzzled. The judge was not a diva, that was true, she was more of a hermit and a recluse (Kitty had started to mentally refer to the judge as "Boo Radley") but what did he mean she was "retired from showing"? Did he mean she was hidden inside her office all the time?

"She's trained," Max went on. She's *trained*?, Kitty wondered. Trained in *what*? Those exercise videos? Is she doing martial arts?

"And she placed at Westminster in 2003," Max added. Placed at *Westminster*?, thought Kitty stupidly. He's talking about a *dog*?

"So," Max prattled on, "I don't think it would be an inconvenience to Her Honor, and in fact it would be an asset to the chambers and really be a mark of distinction to allow Helen of Troy to spend her days with us in the office."

Ludivine, standing behind Max, facing Kitty, caught Kitty's eye. Her expression remained as impassive and composed as ever, but the whites of her eyes had enlarged, like those of a nervous horse, her jaw was clenched, and Kitty knew she was trying desperately not to laugh. Max chattered on obliviously, painting a halcyon picture of a utopian office-setting, full of cheerful hearts of one equal temper, united by their love of a champion beagle that cast its benevolent energy from its position under Max's desk.

"We would *all* bask in her reflected glory," Max insisted to Ludivine. Ludivine nodded, trapped.

Max had been previously working for a female judge who had just retired, who had allowed him to bring Helen of Troy to work. Max couldn't stress enough how glorious this made the entire office situation for all involved.

Ludivine tried to change the topic of conversation to office supplies, making a courteous show of offering to ask the court administration for whatever Max would need.

"Oh no," he chuckled, "I can ask them myself. I'll write up a memo. Don't worry, I'll manage. I always do, you know," he added. Ominously, Kitty thought.

Ludivine, through the door between the two rooms, gave Kitty a significant look. This was why Max was being fobbed off on their judge- a new, unseasoned, unconnected appointment with zero social skills, who was, moreover, a Republican. Max was insane, and they were palming him off on the newbie. Every bureaucratic administrative structure in New York contained people like this: those that could not be gotten rid of (because unions) so they floated around within the bureaucratic system, and people desperately handed them off to others, like a game of hot potato. And now Max had been handed off to them. All that was conveyed in Ludivine's expression.

Trying to turn on Max's computer, Ludivine realized it didn't work. Max had no paper in his desk, no pens. In short, Max had almost nothing of the materials which he needed to do his job as the judge's secretary. Ludivine surveyed the extent of the problem. It was overwhelming.

"Ok, I can make a list of materials you need," Ludivine said flatly, with a marked lack of enthusiasm.

"Oh that's all right!" replied Max cheerfully. "I can get it out of them! You'll see! I'll manage! I always do!"

And he gave a terrifyingly leer, of a kind that Kitty had only ever seen before above a floating buttress. She shuddered with a superstitious dread, and resisted the urge to cross herself.

And Max did manage, it was unnerving the way Max managed. This was why, when another judge invited Judge Jackson and her staff to his chambers to celebrate her birthday only a few weeks after Max's arrival, it was unanimously decided by both chambers that Max would handle the preparations. Max pounced on the opportunity with alacrity.

Since arriving in Judge Jackson's chambers to find an empty desk and a broken computer, Max had procured an amazing treasure trove. In fact, compared with Kitty and Ludivine's room, his office space now looked like a Turkish seraglio. Of course, the Turkish rug was his, he hadn't ordered it from HR the way he had almost everything else.

Every day, in fact, since his arrival, Max had been churning out multiple memos to HR, requesting everything from an ergonomic keypad arm-rest (physical therapist recommended) to a refrigerator (for medications which had to be kept cold) to a humidifier (sinuses) to a coffee machine (therapist-recommended) to a neck-pillow (he presented a note from his chiropractor).

The truth was Max was more prolific when it came to memos than either Kitty or Ludivine. Every day he was writing multiple memos, while Ludivine was writing about one a week, and Kitty one every two weeks. It felt like the actual business of the chambers was riding on Max's scoliotic but capable shoulders and consisted of stockpiling as many comforts as possible on the taxpayer dime.

Max possessed a drive and determination to his memo-writing that Ludivine and Kitty could only feign. Every day he thought of more requests for HR. At first, Kitty and Ludivine happily delegated to Max any material lack they came across (which wasn't much, all they were supposed to do was to sit there and write), but soon they were carefully avoiding mentioning anything the office might need for fear Max, a gleam in his eye (diabolical, thought Kitty), would seize upon it, and make procuring it his next cause.

The crown jewel, however, still eluded Max, and the crown jewel was the office presence of Helen of Troy, the retired champion beagle. The judge, from deep within the bowels of her inner sanctum where she was possibly wearing leggings and stepping to Jazzercize ("Sweatin' to the Oldies," Kitty muttered under her breath), softly but firmly kept refusing Max the company of his dog.

Kitty had to laugh. The previous judge Max had worked for had been a rarefied, Ivy-League educated Democrat from Brooklyn who easily acquiesced to Max's request for an "emotional support animal." Judge Jackson had put herself through law school at a state school, attending classes at night while she worked. She was from a small town in Alabama. She did not want a dog in her office.

Max was crestfallen, but naturally not completely deterred. About once a week a memo was presented to the judge regarding Helen of Troy. The possibility occurred to Kitty that the judge might realize that Max was in fact the best memo-writer of them all and start assigning him cases.

Because the truth was Max's memos were genius advocacy. They did the job, Kitty suspected in part because the memos revealed a writer so completely unhinged, manipulative, and insistent that people would rather surrender what he wanted than deal with him face to face. But, whatever it was, the persistence, the self-righteousness, the hint of vindictiveness, the familiarity with the system, Max had a special talent for wrangling favors out of bureaucracy that made him uniquely suited to his world. He also, Kitty uneasily reflected, would have come in handy during World War II rationing or life in the Soviet Union.

Accordingly, when Max was informed that he was to be in charge of the material preparations for the judge's birthday party, his relentlessly acquisitive mind immediately began avidly formulating HR requests. His first request was that the event be catered. HR returned an answer very quickly responding that that was out of the question.

Max, who was Italian, immediately took vicarious umbrage at what he considered a racist slight against African-Americans. Both judges to be involved in the event were African-American. This was a blatant display of racism, Max decided.

Mild-mannered self-effacing Judge Jackson herself would *never* have considered the denial of this outrageous request as evidence of racism, Kitty thought. But then, the judge, unlike Max, wasn't focused on extracting as much as she could out of the system.

Once denied catering services, Max's next memo re-submitted his request for catering services and moreover submitted a motion for change of venue. Max wanted, if not a courtroom itself, then one of the boardrooms reserved for meetings.

This was denied. Max was affronted. He immediately dialed HR and accused them of treating the judges like "the help." Kitty and Ludivine, overhearing this, looked at each other aghast. "The help," Ludivine mouthed silently at Kitty. Kitty raised her eyebrows in response.

Judge Jackson, they both knew, would be mortified if she knew what Max was doing in her name. Judge Smith, the judge who was holding the birthday party, was a different story. He was the opposite of their judge in every way. They were both African-American, that was about it. Where Judge Jackson was reticent, Judge Smith was brash. Where she was halting, he swaggered. Where she was wistful, he was on top of the world, and where she was proper, he was not at all.

Ludivine had clerked for Judge Smith her first two years out of law school, and she had some wild stories. She told Kitty that the judge's mistresses were constantly calling the chambers and leaving messages with the staff. Judge Smith apparently had a system with his mistresses where they used the names of major cities for their code names when they left messages. So the judge's staff was constantly taking messages such as, "Tell the judge Dallas called." Or: "Tell the judge it's Chicago and it's urgent." Or Kitty's personal favorite: "Tell the judge Boston's open for business." The judge always received these messages from various American cities in a grave and dignified manner, quite different from his usual puckish demeanor.

Judge Smith had two clerks: his senior law clerk, a nerdy young Jewish woman, and his junior law clerk, a nerdy young black man. His female law clerk was the kind of person who advocates for all sorts of abnormal lifestyle choices, in part, Kitty thought, because she lacked the dimension or passion that would render them a temptation to herself.

She was the kind of person who's pro-choice because she supports a woman's right to choose, but she herself was never at risk of having to choose because she was so sensible about risk. She was the kind of person who's pro-drug legalization, because she was the kind of person who's too status-conscious and straitlaced to stray from the straight and narrow. In short, she advocated for all these sinful proclivities because she herself lacked a soul that could be imperiled by them.

The sensual sins she advocated held no attraction for her, and in fact, would end up generating business for bean counters like herself. Degenerates were client material. More degenerates meant more business. She was pro-degenerate. It was kind of akin to the old doctor joke: You don't make money from a well patient, keep 'em sick.

Judge Smith's junior law clerk was the polar opposite. Whereas the senior law clerk was a nerd who confidently navigated the politics of degeneracy and thrived on it, his junior law clerk didn't confidently navigate anything. It would have been more difficult to find a more socially awkward character than Lawrence the junior law clerk.

Ludivine referred to Lawrence as "Enigma." Eliciting a greeting from him was a big deal, and it usually came in the form of an offhand wave in passing while he fled for the nearest exit. A handsome young man, he wore a three-piece-suit every day. Felt, but not seen, in every interaction with him was the presence of his mother. She had probably been dressing him in suits since he was born, thought Kitty.

Kitty liked Lawrence well enough. Lawrence reminded Kitty a bit of Kitty's judge. She tried to imagine what would happen if Lawrence clerked for Judge Jackson. They would operate in parallel socially isolated universes, Kitty thought. Complete stasis.

Kitty and Lawrence had memorably shared an elevator together once. Lawrence had been riding up to his chambers on the fifth floor, and Kitty hopped in at the last second. It was just the two of them. Lawrence knew that Kitty worked for Judge Jackson, and Kitty knew that Lawrence worked for Judge Smith. Their judges were friends, and they had been introduced. Kitty said hello. Lawrence appeared not to have heard. He remained stony-faced, staring with absorption at the elevator buttons. When Kitty pushed the third-floor button, Lawrence adjusted his gaze and stared fiercely at the elevator wall.

In fact, people as socially maladroit as Lawrence brought out something very jocular and expansive in Kitty. They put her at ease, in a way, because she figured they were more scared of her than she was of them. She also felt she had to broadcast friendliness extra-hard in order to compensate for their lack and reassure them. Kitty, faced with Lawrence's extreme gaucheness, became almost dangerously jocular and expansive.

"Fifth floor?" Kitty asked Lawrence heartily. "Hey, aren't you one of the clerks for Judge Smith?" she chuckled.

Lawrence immediately and not totally unreasonably interpreted Kitty's heartiness as an attack and adopted the best defense: a counter-attack. "And aren't *you* one of the clerks for Judge Jackson?" he asked sardonically.

"Yes!" exclaimed Kitty with ferocious good humor. It felt like the Ghost of Christmas Present was filling the elevator with his festive presence and about to burst into song. "Ha ha! Yes, I am!" she boomed.

At this point they reached the third floor, and Kitty stepped out. "Bye-bye!" she sang out, waving merrily, like an extra in a Busby Berkeley musical number.

In response, as the elevator doors closed between them, Lawrence silently flashed what looked to be the Star Trek sign, holding up his palm, his fingers split into two factions. Kitty's grin faded into an expression of bewilderment. What did he mean by that?

Kitty asked Ludivine about Lawrence flashing a Star Trek sign as soon as she got back to the chambers.

"That's why I call him Enigma," Ludivine laughed mirthlessly. Ludivine suggested that Kitty flash the sign back at Lawrence in an effort to provoke some response that would shed further light on its meaning.

"Who can figure that guy out? He's got two white noise machines in his room so he can sleep," Ludivine remarked in a dry tone. "Not just one but two. He should just rent a room next to JFK so he can hear the planes taking off. There isn't enough white noise in the world for that guy."

"How do you know he's got two white noise machines in his room?" Kitty asked curiously. She thought she might need a white noise machine too, it sounded like a good idea.

Ludivine shrugged. "I slept over at his place last Saturday," she said wearily.

"You did NOT!" squealed Kitty. "But I thought you had a boyfriend!"

"Semi-boyfriend," Ludivine corrected her. "We're seeing each other but we're not dating." These distinctions were always lost on Kitty. All the secular goyim Kitty knew, they all talked this way. They also all seemed to use different definitions of "dating, "seeing," "going out," and they all seemed very confident of their own particular definition. The absence of such unsettling nebulousness concerning human relations was one aspect of the Orthodox Jewish community that Kitty appreciated.

Kitty couldn't believe Ludivine had had sex with Lawrence. She couldn't see it happening, even if both parties were falling-down drunk. Why had Ludivine slept with

Lawrence, whom she didn't even like, Kitty wondered. Strait-laced nerdy Lawrence whom Ludivine made fun of, whom she disdained. Why?

Kitty's first impression of Ludivine had been that she was wild. It was nothing personal. It was the giant ornamental headdress. The nose ring and lip ring were really nothing in comparison. Judge Gonzelez's law clerk was from Nigeria, and she wasn't going around wearing a giant spangled turban, Kitty thought sourly. And there had been a few Jamaican girls like Ludivine in law school- they didn't wear ornamental headdresses. Ludivine didn't always wear a turban, only when her hair wasn't done. When her hair was done, she came to work with neat pretty little braids.

But after this initial impression, Ludivine's serious demeanor and work ethic had caused Kitty to respect her. This was a good worker; she was really smart and got the job done. However, after a couple weeks of spending eight hours a day locked up in a small space with Ludivine, Kitty's second impression ceded ground again to the first. It was like the Zen koan, Kitty thought: First there is a mountain, then there is no mountain, then there is. First there is a turban, then there is no turban, then there is.

Ludivine, although productive, spent an inordinate amount of time at work on the phone dealing with family issues. She was the oldest of six; her mother was a single mother to six children by four different fathers. Ludivine was like a de facto mom to her siblings, and they were always calling her at work. Ludivine told Kitty that when her mother wanted a break she checked herself into a psychiatric institution. Kitty didn't laugh, she didn't think Ludivine was kidding. Sometimes Ludivine took home office supplies for her little sisters- paper for them to draw on or rubber bands for them to play with. Kitty envied her for having little children in her life.

One day Ludivine spent all day on the phone because her younger brother had been caught shoplifting. She was frantic. She was afraid he was going to fall into the criminal justice system and never get out.

"I'm so sorry," Kitty told Ludivine.

"Want to adopt a 14-year-old black boy?" Ludivine asked Kitty sarcastically.

"No," said Kitty sadly.

"Well, apparently no one does," said Ludivine hoarsely. She laughed, a short sharp bitter laugh like a bark.

After a couple weeks working together, Ludivine asked Kitty if she wanted to go out after work. The evening started out normally enough, they got sashimi rolls in a Japanese place in the East Village. From there they decided to go to a soccer bar. They did shots of saki at the Japanese place, and on their way to the soccer bar, Ludivine nipped into a bodega and bought half a dozen miniature bottles of Bourbon. At the soccer bar they met up with Ludivine's "semi-boyfriend," a Russian Jew, and the three of them ended up at Ludivine's place at one in the morning, with Ludivine leading Kitty and the semi-boyfriend in a call-and-response Jamaican choral arrangement. It took Kitty longer than Ludivine would have liked to learn the harmony part.

After a few weeks into the clerkship, Kitty was going out with Ludivine every weekend, which, Kitty reflected, seeing as how Ludivine was a raging alcoholic, was kind of a commitment. You couldn't go out with Ludivine and have a mild, innocuous evening. Every night out with Ludivine started out pleasantly enjoying sashimi rolls at her favorite sushi place and ended in a bacchanal.

But while Ludivine drank a frightening amount, she never seemed to get drunk. She got more talkative, but she remained basically the same: pessimistic, cynical, world-weary, with wild flashes of brilliant humor.

Once Ludivine brought Kitty to a club on the Lower East Side for karaoke competition night. They went to the liquor store beforehand and stocked up on sample-sized bottles of rum. They wanted to try a karaoke act together. It was a rap club, so it had to be rap. Conveniently enough, Kitty practically knew Tribe Called Quest's "Midnight Marauders" by heart. They got up on stage and performed "Electric Relaxation." Kitty knew the song better than Ludivine, as it turned out. Kitty, lit on the tiny bottles of rum, gave the introduction. It was concise and accurate. "We're lawyers and we're drunk!" Kitty told the audience.

Some guy came up to Ludivine later and wanted to know where they worked (Kitty could just imagine the type, a nosy little busybody.). Savvy Ludivine dissembled and fled.

Kitty was not doing well. During the day, she was failing at work. After failing at work all day, she was failing at romantic relationships and dissipating herself with Ludivine at night. Kitty didn't understand what had gone wrong. The bar exam was over, she had passed. She had a job that was universally coveted. Only a few months ago, Kitty had imagined passing the bar exam and getting a job would solve all her problems. But things were worse. Both her work situation and her personal situation were tortured and unsustainable.

At work, the combined effect of Boo Radley the mysterious hermit judge, Ludivine the desperately troubled clerk, and Max the rather satanic secretary was driving her insane. After work, Kitty was serving as the booty call of a morbidly obese Orthodox Jew.

The last straw came one Friday night. Kitty was sitting at her desk on a Friday evening, trying to write a memo on a subject she didn't understand, when an administrative clerk walked into the chambers and handed Kitty a packet. On certain days new immediate requests for orders fell to either Kitty or Ludivine. It was Kitty's turn. None had ever come to Kitty before. This was the first time.

She looked at the packet. It was a request for an injunction against an election it contended was being held in a racially discriminatory fashion. It was actually routine, brought by the same activist group year after year, but Kitty didn't know that. Kitty was young, untested, unseasoned, inexperienced, and on her own. She did not know how to begin dealing with this.

"What do I do with this?" she asked Ludivine urgently, in a non-deferential tone.

Ludivine looked at her expressionlessly and shrugged. Kitty felt a spark of irritation flare within her. For fuck's sake, she thought, Ludivine can't even direct me to where I can begin to research, can't even tell me how to begin thinking about this, can't even lift a finger to help me out, when she's been clerking for more than two years, and I've only been clerking for a month? The judge, unusually, had left the chambers at five that evening.

"I'm gonna call another chamber and ask someone," Kitty said abruptly. "I'll call Jen in Judge Smith's chambers, she'll know." She took the court directory out of her desk, found the number, and picked up the phone. Suddenly Ludivine was at Kitty's desk. Ludivine took the receiver out of Kitty's hand and hung up the phone. Ok, this is very weird, thought Kitty.

"I wouldn't do that if I were you," Ludivine said evenly.

"Ok," said Kitty. "Ok." She quietly gathered her things and left work, left the request for the injunction lying on her desk.

When Kitty got home from work she called her father. "I need to talk to you," she said. She and her dad met at a coffee shop near her apartment on Saturday morning.

"I've got a problem. I am getting zero direction, and I'm crashing and burning," she told her dad. "The judge doesn't know what she's doing, no one in that chambers does, they won't offer me help, they prevent me from trying to get help." And she told him how Ludivine took the phone out of her hand and hung it up.

Her dad wasn't much help either. "You do the best you can," he said laconically.

"Yeah, I'm *doing* the best I can!" Kitty returned with some exasperation. She needed more than bromides, she was going down. *He* had never had to deal with affirmative action politics, Kitty thought sourly, or at least he had never had to work with it.

Nepotism has made a failure of my career, thought Kitty bitterly. On paper, landing a clerkship with a federal judge looked great. If that judge had been appointed a few months ago, didn't yet know what she was doing, and you were the white man out and not allowed to receive instruction, it was not so great. It was disheartening that her dad didn't understand. He didn't.

Her second heart-to-heart that weekend was equally unsatisfying. It was with Orla.

Kitty met Orla in Brooklyn for dinner on Saturday night in a new Moroccan restaurant. Orla was sitting waiting for Kitty in the back when Kitty entered. Kitty sat down.

"I'm a self-actualized person, and you are too," Orla began.

Kitty was amused but nonetheless flattered.

"You think I'm self-actualized?" she asked Orla coyly.

Orla was positive.

Over lamb, couscous, and red wine, Kitty told Orla about her situation with Avi. They were going on these "dates," they were going to movies together, then Avi was coming over, they were making out, heavy petting- no farther because the wrath of God and all that- and it was all very tortured and unhealthy.

"He's exploiting you," Orla sneered.

"No, he's not," Kitty started to protest, and then she stopped. He *was* kind of exploiting her. They all knew what the deal was.

"Remember Austin?" Orla asked Kitty pointedly. "Let me return the favor. Intervention. Nip this shit in the bud."

"Austin" referred to an intervention Kitty had performed on Orla five years ago. After Holcombe's death, during Kitty's comprehensive inventory of friends, Orla had been living in Austin, Texas. Kitty, before she left for Spain, decided she should visit Orla as part of her grand reconnaissance tour. When Kitty had arrived in Texas, Orla was doing computer programming for a small tech startup and living in a cute little bungalow with her boyfriend Billy. As in hillbilly. As in drunk-ass hillbilly grifter.

Kitty arrived to find that Orla's house was a mess, like a pigsty. "Maybe you can clean up a little while you're here," Orla mumbled absently by way of explanation. Typical Orla.

The minute Kitty stepped foot into Orla's household, she knew something was very wrong. Orla was living in squalor, Billy was a drunk. They all went out together. Billy was three sheets to the wind, Orla was disaffected, Kitty was puzzled. Billy came on to Kitty, Orla didn't even care. In fact, if anything, Orla was favorable. She obviously wanted to get rid of him- if Kitty was a port in a storm, so be it.

The next morning Kitty and Orla went to brunch at a trendy Austin diner. They sat across the table from each other over French toast and coffee.

"Orla, what the fuck are you *doing*?" Kitty demanded right off the bat.

Orla didn't pretend not to know what Kitty meant. She was relieved.

It turned out that a few months earlier Billy had impregnated Orla, and Orla had decided that an abortion was in order. For so many reasons. Billy had no job, Orla's job was uncertain, Billy and Orla weren't married, Billy was a big drunk. Etcetera. Unfortunately, the giant reasons not to have an abortion were not as obvious to Orla.

Hyper-intelligent "self-actualized" Orla the computer programmer had a very interesting reaction to her abortion. She reverted to type. Orla confided to Kitty that after the abortion she had developed this problem: she kept repetitively and obsessively reciting the Hail Mary.

"That's not a problem, that's a solution," Kitty said implacably.

"No, it's a problem," Orla answered. She was reciting the Hail Mary thousands of times a day, she told Kitty. She had been to a therapist, and the therapist told her that she was "too Irish," that that was her problem. High-IQ Orla sat crestfallen at this professional verdict.

Kitty asked critically, "What was the therapist's last name?"

Orla paused and tried to remember. "Flanagan," she said, "Why?"

"Because the only person who'd tell you you're 'too Irish' is somebody Irish. You need a Jew," said Kitty matter-of-factly.

"You're right," said Orla, wonderingly. "She *was* Irish."

"Sure, only a fucked-up Irish would tell you you're 'too Irish', that's ridiculous,'" Kitty remarked calmly, sipping her coffee. "She was probably raised Catholic and she's got all these issues about it. It's not you, it's her. Get a Jewish therapist!"

"As for Billy," Kitty continued grimly, "Get rid of him. Change the locks. I don't know what you're doing here, but this isn't you."

Orla nodded with relief.

So when Orla said "Remember Austin?" that was what she meant.

"Yeah, I don't know what to tell you," said Orla. "You're being exploited. Just like the Palestinians."

"For fuck's sake, Orla," Kitty said, disgusted, rolling her eyes. "Always with the Palestinians. Next you're gonna tell me we need to do a banner drop."

"I'm actually saving my banner for the march in D.C. next month," said Orla coldly. She was offended.

"How's the anarchist bookstore doing? Still problems with the trannies?" Kitty asked solicitously, smoothing Orla's ruffled feathers.

"Oh, all right," said Orla briskly. Orla was in charge of the feminist component of the bookstore collective where she volunteered, and she was constantly battling trannies, whom she perceived as elbowing their way onto her turf.

In more candid moments, Orla admitted to Kitty that she did not like the trannies, and she resented them trying to take over the feminism department.

"They're not *women*," she would tell Kitty sourly. "They're just pretending." This was a step too far, however, and Orla would be shocked by her own transgression. If they were in a public place, she'd glance around furtively to see if she'd been overheard.

If no one who might care seemed to be around, Orla would continue, emboldened. "I just don't see transgenderism as a feminist issue, and I don't see how transgenders fit into feminism, why don't they just have their *own* branch of activism."

Orla was always complaining to Kitty about the trannies, because Kitty was Orla's only friend who would tolerate this sort of apostasy. Kitty was used to hearing such confessions. With most of her friends at Cornell, she had played the square. Everyone else was trying to one-up each other at virtue-signaling, and they loved a foil. Kitty was happy to serve as their straight man. She was the Archie Bunker in every room.

Good, thought Kitty, when Orla started complaining about the trannies again. She's distracted.

But soon Orla returned to the subject of Avi. "Look, when you came and visited me in Austin, you told me 'This isn't you.' I'm telling you now 'This isn't you.' What the hell are you going to do? Join the harem of some diamond merchant?"

"He doesn't sell diamonds," Kitty protested miserably. "He's really unsuccessful," she added in a sulky tone. "I mean, he failed the bar."

This was true. Avi had failed the bar. This hadn't really surprised Kitty. At Yitzhak's post-bar-exam party, they started comparing answers, and Avi's were consistently different from everyone else's.

"So you're going to join the harem of the only Jew in the tri-state area to fail the bar exam?" Orla laughed.

"You know I have strict standards," Kitty deadpanned. But Orla's arrow had hit its mark. "There have got to be other Jewish guys in the tri-state area who failed the bar," Kitty objected weakly.

Orla snorted with derision.

"Look he's just like the failures we like to date," said Kitty, "only he's an Orthodox Jew. He's like an urban redneck, a Manhattan good old boy."

"The rednecks we like to date," said Orla evenly, "can you eat with them? Do they consider you unclean or inferior?"

"No," Kitty answered sullenly, "but the rednecks we like to date don't read Graham Greene." Kitty suddenly changed tone. "Anyway," she squeaked peevishly, not kidding at all now, "I didn't *mean* to like him, it just happened!"

This was true. Kitty liked *les gars du coin*, and her *coin* was in Manhattan.

"It's not going to get better," Orla said seriously. "It's not. Ten, twenty, thirty years from now, it's going to be the same shit. He's gonna be making booty calls, only he's going to be married with children."

"Look. I know that," Kitty said angrily, and Orla- one of the most insensitive people Kitty had ever met, which was part of her charm- took the hint and changed the subject.

Kitty felt like she was drowning, so when Peter Park called her and told her he was visiting his parents in Upstate New York and would drop by the city for a visit, she grasped at his visit like a lifeline.

Peter had finally definitively broken up with Autumn. Two days ago, he told Kitty, he left Autumn a note telling her it was all over, along with some money, and drove from North Carolina to New York State without stopping. Kitty was thrilled. She told the judge her relatives were in town and asked for a couple days off. She did not breathe a word about Peter to Ludivine. She told Orla, because Orla didn't really care. If it didn't involve the potential for a banner drop, Orla wasn't interested. She told Paul, because she told Paul almost everything. She told Avi, because she wanted him to know that she had people too. He wasn't the only one with people.

The only cloud on Kitty's horizon was that Peter also mentioned visiting Sonia, his ex-girlfriend from Bowdoin who was working on a PhD in French Literature at Columbia and who lived in Brooklyn. That must not happen, of course. Obviously, this person was Kitty's mortal enemy, and Kitty nursed a deep-seated enmity for her.

Peter was very funny about Sonia in a way that he was not funny about Kitty. Kitty had spurned Peter, and Peter was wary when it came to Kitty. It was Peter who had cast off Sonia, however, and so Peter evinced a fondness for Sonia in his conversation that Kitty found extremely irritating. He felt that he had done Sonia wrong and felt responsible and guilty with regard to her, which seemed to Kitty to bind him to her. It made Kitty want to bare her teeth and snarl.

Peter and Sonia had dated freshman year at Bowdoin. Then Peter had fallen out of love and decided to call things off, but Sonia hadn't taken the hint. Peter, in what was apparently his signature move, let Sonia know it was all over in a note. Which he pinned to the door of her dorm-room. Unfortunately, Sonia had gone to the gym after class that day and didn't get home until evening, by which time she was the last person in her dormitory to learn that Peter had dumped her. The students in

Sonia's dorm called Peter "Martin Luther" for the duration of his college career.

So there was this "Sonia" person with which Kitty had to contend. And as if that weren't bad enough, apparently Sonia had told Peter she would fix him up with a Jewish Columbia undergrad friend of hers who worked as an exotic dancer. Not if Kitty had anything to do with it. Peter was hers. She had claimed him before he even started shaving, and she would be damned if some Jewish-stripper French-Lit major was going to get in the way. Kitty suspected that the whole proposed arrangement was a ruse by Sonia to throw a spanner in the works between Kitty and Peter. The fact of the matter was that Peter was spending his first night in the city at Kitty's apartment. She had time to work her magic, she thought with steely-eyed determination.

Peter Park gave her a call when he arrived, and Kitty met him in the parking garage where he was leaving his car. When she met him she stopped short. He was like a six-foot-something, gorgeous, Eurasian young god.

She hadn't realized he was this gorgeous, she thought with chagrin, while she had been complaining to him about her dating travails over the phone. In her head, she had been talking to the Peter she had known. This Peter she did not know.

Peter Park was no longer the gauche skulking boy in a trenchcoat. Peter Park was a man: a reserved, handsome man who looked like he could kill you without changing expression. And what a way to go, thought Kitty.

The Peter Park she knew was gangly. This Peter Park was not gangly, he was lean and muscular. The Peter Park she knew was sheepish. This Peter Park was not sheepish, he was formal and self-contained. The Peter Park she knew had an insecurity complex a mile wide. It would seem fantastical to suggest such a thing of this young man. This was a fit, together, confident, successful young man whom the United States government had turned into a killing machine.

All the joking with Orla and Paul about three years of foreplay dissipated, and Kitty felt like a fool. And she felt, uncharacteristically, shy. For a moment, contrary to all common sense, Kitty doubted whether she and Peter would sleep together.

But of course they did.

That night Kitty took Peter out in the East Village. They hit all her favorite spots: the Basque tapas bar, the Bavarian pub, the Manchester-themed soccer pub, the Egyptian hookah bar. Kitty was in her element. And Peter Park, a gorgeous heterosexual male member of the American military in Manhattan, was rarer and more precious than an ocelot on a leash. Kitty forgot everything, and simply enjoyed herself.

"You shouldn't drink and smoke so much," Peter told Kitty seriously, as they sat at a table at the hookah bar at one in the morning. He had been drinking water this whole time.

"I'm kind of a hick," he had disclosed unapologetically before they went out, "I don't go to bars a lot." But he liked the tapas bar and the Bavarian pub. He didn't care for the soccer pub, however, and she suspected he did not like the hookah bar.

"I need to be kept in line," Kitty responded archly from the other side of the hookah. Then, ever paranoid, she glanced behind her. "What are you looking at? That table of girls?" she demanded. "I'm prettier than all of them," she said tipsily.

'Yes, but they're not debauched," Peter answered, looking intently at Kitty. "So I could have fun debauching them."

Kitty felt her face get red. Peter Park was like the hottest thing in the world, how was this possible. She covered her confusion by feigning indignation.

"I'm certainly not debauched! That's not fair at all! I would think the *stripper* you're getting set up with would fit that description." She had to get that in.

"Ah, you mean Jew-Ass," Peter said with wry bemusement, using his politically incorrect nickname for the girl Sonia was supposed to be setting him up with. "That's different." Kitty rolled her eyes.

To re-direct the conversation, Kitty asked Peter about the army, about training, about flying. She listened, entranced. He had skills now. He was completely different: confident, competent, comfortable. She saw what a stranger would see: a serious, intelligent, skilled, dignified member of the armed services.

No one would ever have suspected him of drawing a series of cartoons based on the adventures of a clitoris, Kitty thought. No one would ever have suspected him of hiding a dissected rat's tail in his locker. And he was like unbelievably gorgeous. His hooded light-brown eyes, his cheekbones, his lips, and the way he looked at her. Who was this person? And for a moment, contrary to all common sense, again Kitty doubted whether she and Peter would sleep together.

But of course they did.

The desperate, inexperienced, fumbling, rabidly eager novice was gone. In his place was what seemed a cool customer who was used to the upper hand. Kitty's mind reeled at how the tables had turned.

But had they? Because after that first impression, the veneer wore off- the polish lent by experience and porn and success. They were talking afterwards, and for a moment the whole world that was between them flashed into existence, and, with a completely incongruous goofy smile, he fell into her arms like the eager puppy he had been.

The next day they went to the J.P. Morgan Library to look at the Rembrandt sketches. There is nothing so delicious (so *Godard*, thought Kitty) as screwing a gorgeous exotic, whom there is a very good argument is your long lost love, and then taking him to look at Rembrandt sketches in a former *Fin de siècle* Manhattan mansion. It was divine.

Until Peter's phone rang, and it was Dreadful Sonia asking about plans for the night. Peter had called Sonia yesterday when he arrived to let her know he was in town.

It seemed to Kitty that Peter's tone toward Sonia had altered, and that he was being even more gently fraternal with her this morning. Sure, he was in the museum, and he wasn't supposed to be on his cell, so that might account for the hushed tone, but not for its affectionate warmth. Kitty noted with mounting furor that Peter was using the same gentle affectionate tone with Sonia that he used with his mother and his sister- so unlike the mocking, scathing tone with which he so often addressed Kitty. Obviously Peter considered Sonia some kind of a saint, while she, Kitty, was just a whore. Kitty felt her hackles rise.

Kitty gathered from Peter's end of the conversation that Sonia wanted to meet at a Korean restaurant in the small Koreatown near Hell's Kitchen. She didn't bother to pretend she wasn't listening. She loitered menacingly next to Peter, staring gimlet-eyed at him as he talked. Peter said good-bye to Sonia. He had been looking at a Rembrandt sketch as he talked, but he had felt Kitty's eyes boring into him the entire time. He turned to her now, she looked like she was ready to pounce on someone or something and throttle it. Her eyes were narrowed and her shoulders squared. Peter regarded her with cool detached amusement.

"So is she bringing the Jewish stripper?" Kitty snarled.

"Yeah, she's bringing the Jewish stripper. And the Jewish stripper's *boyfriend*, so relax. Relax, Chilly Willy," said Peter draping an arm around the stiff little person's shoulders. It was a nickname he had used for her when she was fifteen. "Relax."

At six o'clock that evening, they showed up at the designated restaurant in Koreatown. The restaurant was two stories and specialized in Korean barbecue. Despite the whole Jewish stripper and ex-girlfriend situation, Kitty was excited to try the food. She was feeling a bit fatalistic about Peter: if she lost him to either his ex or the stripping Jewess, it was just not meant to be. The whole situation was so weird, anyway.

Peter and Kitty waited outside the Korean restaurant. Earlier, after Peter had his phone conversation with Sonia, Kitty had retaliated and called Micah from Cornell, who was conveniently visiting Brooklyn for the week from LA. Micah was one of the three friends Kitty kept in touch with since Holcombe's death.

Kitty and Micah had been friends since freshman year at Cornell when someone brought Micah over to sit with Kitty's table in the dining hall, and Micah quickly and dramatically alienated everyone at their table. He started out by informing everyone present that AIDS was soon to become airborne. They had better make plans for the coming pandemic, he warned them. It went downhill from there, and ended with the table angrily dispersing.

Kitty, after the ensuing disgraceful conflagration, during which Kitty shouted "Bullshit!" to the consternation of some of the prissier occupants of the dining hall, while Michah held his ears and stuck out his tongue at her, became intrigued by the long-haired California weirdo and his spectacular anti-social ability to offend.

When Kitty reached Micah by phone five years after the dining hall debacle, just after the death of Holcombe, Micah's first words to her were: "You were right."

"Yes, I was," Kitty promptly answered. "About what?"

"AIDs didn't become airborne," he said flatly.

Micah was working on his PhD in Biology in L.A. But he was in town this week, visiting Hairy Ben, their friend from Cornell, who now lived in Williamsburg with his girlfriend.

Hairy Ben was called "Hairy Ben" to distinguish him from the other Ben's at Cornell, including but not limited to: "Climber Ben" (a rock-climber), "Pavement Ben" (obsessed with the band Pavement), "DJ Ben," (self-explanatory), and "Big Gay Ben" (also self-explanatory).

Hairy Ben was indeed hairy. And fat. And the mellowest person Kitty had ever met. Hairy Ben was Israeli, and all the Israelis Kitty had met were remarkably mellow, but Hairy Ben took the cake- probably because he was also the biggest stoner she had ever met.

While socially awkward people like Lawrence brought out something very jocular and expansive in Kitty, remarkably mellow people like Hairy Ben made Kitty nervous. Whenever she had conversations with Ben, she found herself talking a mile a minute out of the side of her mouth, like a Steve Buscemi character. The saving grace with Hairy Ben was that he was a big male chauvinist- that was why Kitty's guy friends liked him too. So it didn't really matter to Hairy Ben whether Kitty was talking a mile a minute or shutting up. In either scenario, he benignly tolerated her without taking her seriously, she was just a shiksa. Kitty found his attitude vaguely reassuring.

Williamsburg was gentrifying at the time, and Hairy Ben was among the pioneers spearheading the movement. He had moved to Williamsburg with his girlfriend about a year ago. They had a cool sort of townhouse with a backyard, and when Micah was in town he always stayed with Hairy Ben. Hairy Ben was having a party that night, and Kitty figured that if Peter was going to force her to hang out with his college friend and her crowd, she would return the favor.

Peter and Kitty hadn't waited for long in front of the Korean restaurant, when they were joined by the rest of their party: Sonia and the exotic dancer (whom Kitty had mentally started referring to as "J.A.") and her boyfriend. Peter greeted Sonia with a hug while Kitty glowered. Everyone else just said hello.

As soon as Kitty saw Sonia, she felt an immense relief. Sonia was a raw-boned giantess, almost the size of Peter. But it was Sonia's manner toward Peter that was most shocking to Kitty, and reassured Kitty that Sonia was no competition. Here Peter was this gorgeous, exotic, American killing-machine, and Sonia treated him as though he were a harmless foolish child.

Kitty didn't understand where Sonia had learned this. Was this a WASP thing? Or, like, a New England thing? Undermine menfolk and completely turn them off? It seemed infinitely odd to Kitty. Sonia's tone with Peter was completely castrating. And Peter responded in kind; he acted as though Sonia was his mother or something. This, thought Kitty, is no threat to me. Her inner romantic-power-level reconnaissance team gave the "All clear."

In the dynamic Kitty had going with Peter, if anyone was the harmless foolish child, it was Kitty, and Peter was the authoritative controlling one. She thought this schema appealed more to Peter than Sonia's. It was more natural for women to be infantilized, from a heterosexual relations standpoint, than men, Kitty speculated.

As for the exotic dancer and her boyfriend, Kitty was surprised. They were both these schlubby homely specimens. The stripper herself was a short large-breasted girl with coarse features. Her boyfriend was a laid-back overweight young man with a paunch. No one was prepossessing. No one was a threat to Kitty's hegemony. Kitty internally rejoiced.

The restaurant hostess who seated them was a pretty Korean girl. She eyed Peter with a sideways look from under her lashes, and Kitty glared at her and stuck close to Peter's side. This girl was a greater threat, Kitty reflected, than Sonia and J.A. put together.

They were seated above and climbed the stairs to a round table on the top floor. Kitty was careful not to sit next to Peter, in order to show him and everyone else there how cool she was with the situation. Let him have his fun, she thought. If they were what he wanted, he was welcome to them, and good luck to him. But she would be silently laughing at him, and she knew Peter would be acutely aware of her mockery. She wouldn't even have to say anything.

Kitty seated herself between Sonia and the stripper's chubby boyfriend and sat back and relaxed. Inwardly she was grinning. She knew Peter would be hers again tonight.

The Korean barbecue was fantastic, the conversation not as much. Kitty courteously tolerated the boyfriend's conversation. He talked her ear off, telling her about his job and his commute, while Kitty listened politely, keeping an eye on Peter. Across the table, Sonia's pole-dancer was trying to capture Peter's attention. Kitty shot mocking looks at Peter, but he met her eye and looked away. Kitty attributed it to the presence of Sonia.

Sonia was not the worst dinner companion. She rather charmingly related the Martin Luther anecdote to the table. Kitty didn't understand where she was coming from. She was like a great eunuch of a woman who had, like some kind of contemporary Vestal Virgin, dedicated herself to serving at the altar of academia. Such an unsexy and uninspiring life-decision left Kitty nonplussed.

Kitty, feeling magnanimous due to the delicious barbecue and the lack of female competition, invited the entire table to Hairy Ben's house party. Let Peter foist his former love interest and a Jewish stripper on her. She would turn the tables on him. Sonia expressed an interest in Hairy Ben's party, and Kitty was mightily pleased. Kitty and Sonia joining forces would throw Peter off his game. Kitty shot Peter a look of triumph, but he was absorbed in his barbecue.

The schlub next to her was hitting on her, Kitty figured out about half an hour into the meal. She figured it out after he asked her for her number and said something about "hooking up." Kitty laughed. The ridiculousness of the situation hit her with full force, and she was immensely tickled. Kitty enjoyed ridiculousness. She glanced over at the lap dancer, who was boring Peter, Kitty could see that, with a description of her thesis. Kitty could barely resist cackling with glee.

A few minutes later, the Jewish stripper arose and declared that she had to leave to serve her shift. This news was greeted respectfully by Peter and Sonia, and Kitty bid an adieu that was a bit too glad-sounding to be polite. Before leaving the table, she invited them all to come watch her strip at the club after dinner. Sonia softly demurred.

"I think that would be fun!" Kitty said grinning, forgetting the recent public stand she had taken against strip clubs.

She looked over at Peter, but he was already looking down and eating again. Then, the dinner drew to a close, they divvied up the check, paid the bill, and found themselves at the entrance.

While Peter and Sonia talked about meeting at Hairy Ben's place in Brooklyn, the stripper's boyfriend cornered Kitty and asked her again for her number. Kitty found the whole thing screamingly amusing. She pretended not to understand. He asked for her number again. She countered by asking him for his number, and gravely pocketed it. He said his good-byes and went on his way. Only Peter and Sonia and Kitty were left now.

After the boyfriend took off, Kitty turned to Sonia, "That is the oddest guy. He hit on me! He was asking me for my number!" she hooted.

"They have an open relationship," Sonia informed Kitty in a schoolmarmish tone.

"Oh, I see," Kitty replied with exaggerated respect. "How sexy," she guffawed, rolling her eyes at Peter, who ignored her.

Sonia told Peter and Kitty that she would meet them later at the house party in Williamsburg, she lived nearby. They said good-bye, and Peter hugged Sonia again. This time Kitty did not glower.

Peter and Kitty walked to the strip club, which was only a block away. Kitty had never been to a strip club before. She knew of the club, though, it was a big one, a chain. She had seen the giant ads in the subway. They entered the foyer, the decorations were plain- black, gold, and white. It looked pretty clean to Kitty. Then they had to walk down a flight of stairs.

"She's stripping in the basement?" Kitty chortled. Peter didn't answer.

Downstairs there was a sort of lounge with three stages. It was dimly lit, and there were only a couple other patrons there, it was still early. Kitty sat down primly and expectantly on the edge of a sofa seat, glancing around her surroundings with wide-eyed interest. Peter did not look like he was enjoying himself, she noticed.

On each of the three stages, there were girls swaying slightly and silently, hovering like ghosts. They had no tops on, only "pasties," Kitty thought that's what you called them, glued on to their nipples. The girls didn't look madly sexy or anything to Kitty, but she imagined that just the fact that they were there and would do something for you for money was enough to turn men on.

"Are those things called pasties?" Kitty asked Peter loudly. "Is that what they're called?"

Peter looked uncomfortable and answered in the affirmative.

"Where's Jew-Ass?" Kitty asked Peter in a lower, conspiratorial tone. "Is she out here?"

"She's right behind you," said Peter grimly.

Kitty quickly swiveled to look at the girl on the stage behind her. "That's *her*?!" she exclaimed. She narrowed her eyes and scrutinized the girl for a moment. "She looks so much better! It must be the makeup!" Kitty waved merrily at J.A., who ignored her- not like she was angry, just like she was working.

"Shoot," Kitty said to Peter. "Why would you wanna do that, like a slave on an auction block, like a piece of meat." Kitty had unconsciously grown louder. "Somebody gives you a twenty and you gotta dance around. What a miserable existence."

"Let's go," said Peter evenly.

"But I'm starting to enjoy myself," Kitty protested. "We could pay your friend to dance if you like. I don't care."

"We're going," said Peter firmly, and he got up and waited for Kitty to join him. When she did, he steered her by the elbow to the stairs. They climbed back up the stairs, Peter walking behind Kitty, and Kitty complaining the entire way.

Then they were on the sidewalk in the open air again.

"I'm sorry," said Kitty contritely. She meant it. "I didn't mean to ruin it."

"You didn't," said Peter matter-of-factly. "I go to strip clubs all the time. That wasn't the best."

"Well, I hate them," said Kitty petulantly. "They're depressing."

They took a taxi to Williamsburg. Kitty hailed it dramatically, trying to impress Peter. She stood on the corner and threw up her arm with a grand gesture as soon as a cab came into sight, and was pleased to see the taxi lurch, change course, and make a beeline in her direction as though drawn by a magnet. It was so fun to actually have a companion, it was so different actually having a date to go places with.

In the backseat of the taxi, Peter and Kitty silently held hands. This was Peter's last night in the city, Kitty thought, staring out at the skyline as they crossed the bridge. She wouldn't think about that now.

The taxi dropped them off near Hairy Ben's house, a brownstone not far from the subway. Hairy Ben's girlfriend ushered them in, everyone was on the deck out back.

"Micah!" Kitty exclaimed. It was always so good to see him, he was always up to something. On this occasion he had smuggled some ground-up peyote in with him from L.A., which he was sprinkling on a pipe full of marijuana and passing around. Kitty declined. She gave him a hug (See, Peter, she thought, I have college friends too.) and introduced him to Peter. "We just came from the strip club!" Kitty told Micah triumphantly.

"Were you stripping?" asked Micah sarcastically, looking down at the pipe he was packing.

"Which club?" Hairy Ben inquired with mild interest. Kitty told him shyly.

"Oh, I've been there," said Hairy Ben meditatively. "It was ok." He shrugged.

Peter stepped away from the group on the deck because he didn't want to be around the smoke. He walked into the backyard.

Kitty recognized a few of the others sitting together on the deck. They were almost all from Cornell. These were Hairy Ben and Micah's friends, and they almost all seemed to lay claim to near-celebrity status. There was a girl who'd written a book about following a band and who was friends with a famous DJ.

There was a girl who worked for a celebrity chef. There was a guy who'd interned for a famous artist and whose girlfriend wrote for New York Magazine. Micah was the one who had told her all this, he was very impressed with such things, even though in Kitty's mind what Micah was doing was much more interesting. She was glad these hipsters were there to see her with Gorgeous Peter the Killing Machine. Kitty triumphant.

Kitty joined Peter in the backyard. They gravitated toward the far end of the yard, where Kitty saw her friend Logan from Cornell. Logan was someone she was glad to see. He was a Cree from Montana, and he looked like Johnny Depp. In college, girls were always throwing themselves at him, and he was always catching them. It was true he slept around, but it never really seemed like his fault, because he was to girls like catnip was to cats. It wasn't only because of his looks. Logan had heart, and there was something pure and noble about him that really stuck out at Cornell.

Once Micah and Kitty had been talking about Logan, and Micah mentioned "Logan's girlfriend."

"Who's his girlfriend?" asked Kitty. She saw Logan with so many girls, she was surprised he had an actual girlfriend.

"Nicole," said Micah.

"Really?" Kitty asked. "Uh, serious question. Not to be an asshole or anything, but seriously, what's the distinction? I mean, Logan sleeps with *everybody*. So what makes her his girlfriend?"

"She does his laundry," Micah answered shortly.

Kitty mulled this over. It made sense.

Logan was at the party with his current girlfriend, they lived together on the Lower East Side. Micah, who liked gossip, had told Kitty how Logan met his girlfriend. She was stripping at a club where Logan used to go with a bunch of friends, and Logan fell in love with her. Of course, as soon as Logan fell in love, he wanted her to stop stripping. Now she was working in a department store making much less money than before, but she had Logan. Micah had been mocking Logan with the story, but Kitty found it romantic. Micah could be kind of cynical and heartless, Kitty thought.

Logan's girlfriend was from New York City, she was half-Jewish and half-Puerto Rican and short and curvy and sharp. She was a good complement to Logan, who was lanky and mellow. Kitty was glad the girl belonged to Logan because she had immediately sized her up as Peter's type.

And Logan's girlfriend eyed Peter Park. She was obviously impressed. "Is this your boyfriend?" she asked Kitty point blank.

"This is muh Korean nigguh," Kitty told her gravely.

"And I bet he loves it when you call him that," Logan's girlfriend retorted and winked at Kitty. Kitty and Peter smiled sheepishly.

They hung around with Logan and his girlfriend the entire party, avoiding the deck, because of the smoke, but also because the people on the deck seemed to be their own clique. If Peter hadn't been there, Kitty thought, she would have been with the group on the deck, relegated to second-class status while those around her name-dropped to each other. Kitty didn't fit in any better than Peter did. She and Peter were both small-town Americans, adrift.

About fifteen minutes later, Sonia arrived, and Kitty introduced her to Micah. Micah and Sonia struck up a conversation. Sonia seemed to like Micah, which Kitty found extremely amusing. Imagine treating god-like Peter Park like a kid nephew or something and being attracted to a weirdo like Micah, Kitty thought. Kitty couldn't see the two of them together, but then she couldn't really see either one of them with *anyone*, if she were being completely honest.

Kitty kept referring to Peter as "muh Korean nigguh" to try to get a rise out of the people on the deck. Logan's girlfriend had been right, Peter did seem to enjoy it. Finally, she and Peter decided to go. It had all been foreplay, and it had served its purpose.

They made out in the back of the cab on the way home. Kitty had always wanted to do that.

The cab stopped in front of Kitty's building. Kitty stood on the sidewalk and meditatively lit a cigarette while Peter paid the driver.

When he joined her, she said, "Remember our first kiss, in 9th grade, when you kissed me on the stairs outside the gym, and I pulled away, and I said 'Not on the stairs!'" She laughed.

"I was a nice girl, wasn't I?" she asked him. *Uncle Wiggily in Connecticut* was one of her favorite short stories.

"No," Peter answered, leaning in to kiss her again. "You were never a nice girl."

And the next day he was gone.

They said good-bye in the parking garage. Kitty stood weeping, racked with sobs. She was glad Peter had a girl crying for him as he left.

"I'll be fine," he said, throwing his duffel bag into the trunk.

"Yeah, me too," said Kitty bitterly. "I'll be fine too. We'll all be fine."

"You're the Aging Champ," said Peter seriously. "You'll always be ok. Just stop drinking and smoking."

"Drinking and smoking is less dangerous than going to fucking *war*," said Kitty, weeping.

"I told you, Afghanistan is the dangerous assignment. Iraq is fine."

"I'll drive you to the border," said Kitty desperately.

"Nah," Peter dismissed her. "I balanced all, brought all to mind." He remembered. All those years ago, them hanging out in the woods at the college, her standing on top of the giant rock in the Japanese rock garden, reciting Yeats, smoking cigarettes, so many years ago.

This brought Kitty up short. If he'd balanced all and brought all to mind, there was really nothing that she Kitty could do.

"Here," she growled and started rifling around in her Michael Kors bag. "Here, take my fucking rosary."

"I'm agnostic," Peter told her.

"Then your agnostic ass really needs a rosary. Just take my fucking rosary with you already, will you," Kitty said, angrily holding out the rosary. It was her favorite rosary, the old, cheap, plastic one that still faintly smelled of formaldehyde.

"I'm surprised you're trusting an ex-satanist with your rosary," Peter responded sarcastically. But he took it and put it in his pocket.

"That's what it's for," she said. "Ok, fine, I love you, take care of yourself, stay alive." She sounded like a crusty old father bidding good-bye to the beloved son for whom he had always had trouble expressing affection.

"I love you too," said Peter nonchalantly. "I always did."

"So don't get killed," Kitty pleaded.

"I told you, Afghanistan is the bad assignment. Iraq is about as dangerous as Albany. I'll be fine. Take care of yourself. It'll be fine. Remember, you're the Aging Champ."

And then he was gone. He had parked near the entrance of the parking garage, so Kitty just stood and watched him pull out, pass through the turnstile, drive away, and then he was gone.

"Shit," Kitty said softly when she couldn't see his car anymore.

She called Paul as soon as she got home.

"I fall in love, it's an Orthodox Jew. I fall in love, he goes off to fucking *war*," Kitty raged tearfully. "Gee, what's the next spectacular way my relationship can crash and burn? Ebola? Gets carried off by a fucking giant *eagle* while I'm talking to him? What the *fuck*?"

"Giant eagle," Paul chuckled appreciatively. Kitty was glad she had called Paul and not Orla, Paul appreciated her material much more.

"My fucking romantic life is like the fucking death of *Rasputin!*" she told Paul angrily, waving her cigarette. A half-empty Corona Light sat on her desk in front of her. Peter could go fuck himself, Kitty thought petulantly. If he didn't want her smoking and drinking, he should have stuck around to make sure she didn't.

"The death of *who*?" asked Paul, which was the first sign of real interest he'd displayed in anything Kitty was saying.

"Rasputin, you Philistine," Kitty said with exasperation. "Advisor to the last czar of Russia. They poisoned him, they shot him, they drowned him." Kitty paused dramatically. "He wouldn't die."

## Chapter 21: The Aging Champ

Peter Park's visit unleashed something in Kitty. It acted like Alexander the Great on the Gordian knot.

Kitty supposed Peter had reminded her who she was and where she was from. He had given her a sense of belonging- even if the world they belonged to was gone. It had not escaped her notice that Peter Park had made a pilgrimage to see her right before he left for his first tour of duty. Their lives had meaning, hers and his, and that meaning had been acknowledged.

So, although bereft, she was stronger. Railing to Paul against the injustice of another romantic failure was a way to distract herself from Peter's departure. The truth was that, while on paper it seemed like a romantic failure, to Kitty it seemed like the first romantic success she had since Holcombe died.

The affair with Avi had made her feel depleted and weak: beating her life out against a city that cared nothing for her. Peter made her feel strong and whole again. They were both who they had been, they shared a time, a place, a culture, and an understanding- and that would always be.

With Peter Park, she felt something that was impossible with Avi, she felt kinship. They had teased each other as children, they had grown up with the same people, they had spent hours on the phone together, they had shared books and music, they had mocked the same authorities, they had writhed under the same yoke.

There's an entire country out there, beyond Manhattan, thought Kitty. An entire country where Kitty was not an eternal stranger, but a powerful member.

The barbarians in the hinterlands- because she thought of them as such on some level- were messy, vulgar, rude, careless, ignorant, bumbling, but they were hers. And they offered her a place. She was one of them. She had delved too deeply into the mindset of the others, the city people, those who ran the city, she realized. And she was not of them. How she envied those whose lot it was to exist among their own people. She imagined they were out there somewhere.

Peter called her from his parents' house once before he left. It was anti-climactic. He was chagrined because his mother had found his porn stash on the family computer. Kitty tried not to show her irritation that he had been looking at porn.

The first Gordian knot was Avi. It was Peter who had cut the knot asunder, all that was left for Kitty was to clear the severed remnants away. And it was too easy. Where Kitty had looked at Avi before and seen a star-crossed lover, now she just saw a guy from the Diamond District. Orla was right, Kitty thought flatly, Avi had been exploiting her, although he probably wasn't even aware of it himself.

The next time Avi called her, Kitty told him, "It's over, whatever was going on." He still called her a few more times, telling her he was nearby and asking if he could stop over. "No," Kitty told him firmly each time, and eventually he stopped calling.

The second Gordian knot was the clerkship. Kitty was much more conflicted about the clerkship. Clerkships were treasures people would give their eye-teeth for, and here she was throwing hers away. But every time Kitty's thoughts tread down this path, she remembered Ludivine hanging up the phone when she tried to seek advice about the request for an injunction.

She'd been dropped into hostile territory, Kitty thought. Ludivine seizing the phone out of her hand had been the last straw. It was like some Heart of Darkness shit. Who knew what the judge was doing inside her room for twelve hours at a stretch? Jazzercize? Opera? Alchemy? Who knew? She thought of the goblin secretary and shuddered.

The truth was that it was dangerous. Working in hostile territory when the stakes were that high was dangerous. If anything went wrong, it would all be on Kitty- and the environment was such that something was bound to go wrong. She didn't blame anyone for getting her into this situation. Her elders just didn't understand the degree of dysfunction.

On the Monday after Peter left, Kitty knocked on Judge Jackson's door. Ludivine wasn't in yet. It was nine o'clock, and Ludivine rarely arrived before nine-thirty.

"Come in," the judge answered softly.

Kitty walked in, for the first time not eager to please. She saw the tv and the Blu-Ray player set up across from the judge's desk. There were a couple of pink dumbbells on the judge's desk. Kitty wondered where she kept her workout clothes.

"I have to resign," Kitty said abruptly.

"Oh," the judge responded softly from behind her desk, blinking at Kitty through coke-bottle lenses. "Oh, I see."

Kitty felt like she was RSVP-ing negative to a tea party or something.

"There's been a death in the family," Kitty blurted out. That was always a true statement, she had told herself earlier.

"Oh," the judge whispered, "I'm sorry."

Kitty was astonished at how easy this was.

"Thank you," she said tersely. "Thank you for everything, I'm going now."

The judge nodded, and that was it.

By the time Ludivine got to the office, Kitty was gone

As soon as Kitty arrived home from the judge's chambers, she readied her resume. With something akin to relief, Kitty surrendered herself to the lot of the failed lawyer. She looked up temp agencies and emailed them her resume. And she signed herself up for document review the way men join the Foreign Legion in the old movies: She wanted to work, and she wanted to forget.

Document review was the attorney equivalent of galley-slave labor. Attorneys sat for hours, scrolling through documents, clicking on boxes. In truth, a computer program could have done the work they were doing. Complex configurations of search terms would have done the job. At least galley slaves developed their arm muscles and benefited from the energizing effects of exercise, Kitty would think to herself as she sat there.

Doc review was just a scam firms used to pad their billing, Kitty thought cynically. The firms were billing their clients for the hours logged by the temps at the same hourly rate in-house lawyers would have commanded. They were billing their clients as though they had real lawyers doing real work, instead of an army of drones mindlessly clicking and scrolling, clicking and scrolling. The temps certainly considered it a scam, one that they were grateful to be a part of.

236

A temp agency found Kitty something immediately. Her resume was better than most of their candidates: good schools, good GPA, bar passage.

The doc review Kitty was assigned to had been going on for a couple years when Kitty joined. Half a dozen of the biggest insurance companies were suing each other in a giant clusterfuck of claims and cross-claims. Every party's strategy included drowning the other side in discovery requests, and that's where Kitty and her fellow doc reviewers came in.

These were the days when document review could still pay something. It wasn't like the heady salad days, back before 9/11, when lawyers could relatively easily find good, high-paying jobs, but it was still possible to make six figures with doc review if you landed the right project and logged in enough hours.

Once you broke forty hours, you made time and a half. That was all to know, and that was all you needed to know. The doc reviewers competed for most work-week hours logged. The record on Kitty's project was ninety-six hours; it was a tie between a Chinese girl from Queens and an ex-military guy from Texas. Kitty didn't compete for over-time. She did the minimal and left. If she had wanted to compete, she would have looked for a real job. Anyway, the minimal hours they wanted you to do were fifty hours a week, so it wasn't like she wasn't putting in time.

So the day after submitting her resume, Kitty showed up to work on the third floor of a red-brick office-building on Union Square, where a vast hall full of hundreds of lawyers sat at long cafeteria-style tables, working on laptops. In the middle of the room there was a glass-walled office where a real attorney for the firm that was outsourcing the work could oversee the galley-slaves.

Kitty did not know it yet, but she had been assigned to a document review that was one of the largest and most infamous in Manhattan. There were multiple anonymous blogs describing the work conditions. Attempts by the temp-agency representatives and supervising attorneys to sniff out the blogging culprits was a constant theme at work.

Occasionally, the bosses would pick an employee to call into their glass fortress and interrogate as to the bloggers' identities. The surrounding galley-slaves would periodically look up from their work to cast furtive glances at the overseer's headquarters when this happened, trying to make out what was going on inside. But despite psychological pressure, the authorities' attempts to solve the mystery remained frustrated. There were just too many blogs. Kitty was never called in and questioned, probably because she wouldn't have been gratifying to interrogate- she just didn't care.

Kitty dutifully clicked and scrolled, clicked and scrolled, but other temps got a bit naughty- not porn, you were automatically fired for porn- and someone at Kitty's table actually was. But they played games of solitaire, they read books, they played Mad Libs, they placed bets, they told each other their life stories, sometimes they got in fights. Two Korean girls had gotten into a catfight in the women's restroom right before Kitty started. They were both fired.

The lawyers were a diverse bunch. The vast hall where they sat looked like a United Nations meeting. Maybe India and the Middle East weren't very well represented, but the Far East was accounted for, Europe was present, there was a smattering of Latin America, and Africa dominated.

Kitty accepted her document-review fate in a perfect ecstasy of misery. She had failed at her clerkship, she had failed at life, and now she was in the bowels of hell where she belonged.

> Midway upon the journey of our life,
> I found myself within a forest dark,
> For the straightforward pathway had been lost.

The worst part of document review, the torture, was that it did not occupy your whole mind. You were allowed to wear headphones, that helped.

The second worst part of document review was that everyone was purely doing it for the money. Time was money: you were being paid to sit, and each minute you sat was accounted for. Some of the lawyers had come from as far away as Texas for the opportunity to cash in on this deal where the longer you sat in place the more you got paid. Some of the doc reviewers talked about money all day. Their minds were drowning in it.

Rumors circulated like wildfire. Every once in a while word spread among the lawyers that the project was coming to an end. Another common rumor was that soon all document review was going to be computerized and nobody would have a job. Another story making the rounds was that document review would soon be outsourced to India. Indian lawyers studied English common law, someone said knowingly.

The first week, Kitty was stationed among a contingent of single young women whose sole topic of conversation, apart from money, was a popular miniseries. It was astounding how obsessed they were. Kitty started to think that she was missing something. She went home and ordered it on Netflix, she couldn't believe how boring.

Kitty started to wear headphones while she worked to tune these girls out. A lot of people wore headphones to tune out the people around them. Kitty envisioned the girls around her returning home for holidays to their families in suburbia and impressing their ignorant relatives around the dinner-table with the fact that they were lawyers in New York City. It sounded glamorous, whereas this was the reality.

Meanwhile, Kitty thought matter-of-factly, the girls themselves would have done better to focus their energies on family formation. Then, at least, they would have had something to show for their bird-brained gossipy inclinations, something better than familiarity with the plot of some latest circus for the masses. What a waste, thought Kitty unkindly.

Kitty started to get into a routine. It was relaxing to have an undemanding job, as long as you didn't think too much about what you were doing with your life. She took the train to Union Square in the morning, a short trip. She got a coffee and the paper. She showed up, clocked in, read her paper, worked, had lunch at her desk, worked until evening, then went home, or often, because she was lonely, she went to her parents' apartment for dinner and the evening news. She went out to dinner with Orla. She stopped by Paul's apartment a couple times. She wrote Peter a couple letters, she kept them funny.

Kitty had been working document review for about a month when it occurred to her that she hadn't gotten her period.

She hadn't been keeping track of her period because she hadn't been having sex. Until Peter. And Peter and Kitty, whether because of fatalism or thrill-seeking or romantic sensibility or simple laziness- or perhaps some other undefined instinctual drive- hadn't used birth control, hadn't by some tacit agreement even mentioned it. "I balanced all, brought all to mind," thought Kitty again. And they'd had sex- what?- half a dozen times over the course of the long weekend?

Friday night after work, Kitty, full of dread, went and bought a pregnancy test and took it home and peed on it. She watched with horrified fascination as the second pink line stubbornly materialized. She had seen this before, and it hadn't been good. She sat for a few minutes, staring at the second pink line. Then she got up and called Orla.

"I'll go with you!" Orla shouted as soon as Kitty told her, the standard response among girlfriends.

"Thanks," said Kitty miserably. "But don't you dare tell anyone. No blog posts, nothing, or I'll kill you."

Kitty called a clinic on Upper East Side and made an appointment, mechanically. She was overwhelmed, so she did what she did when she was overwhelmed, she went to her parents' place to sit on the couch and watch tv with her mom.

They sat together, watching Law and Order. Out of the blue, Kitty, who could never keep a secret, said, "What if I had a baby?"

Her mother looked shocked and dismayed. "With whom?" she asked.

"Uh, how about with Peter?" said Kitty hopefully.

"He's in Iraq and you don't even have a job," said her mother firmly, "so I don't see how that would happen just yet."

"You're right, you're right," Kitty said hastily. "I was just throwing it out there."

Her appointment at the clinic was for Monday. Orla met her outside.

"No photos," Kitty warned Orla. "No interviews. And I'm not speaking at your feminist group meeting or whatever."

Orla giggled. Kitty knew her only too well.

They walked into the building together, took the elevator to the second floor, and entered a nice, white, clean, spacious waiting-room, sparsely populated by well-heeled, professional-looking, young black and Hispanic women. Kitty and Orla were the only white women. And there were no men.

Kitty registered, and she and Orla took a seat.

"Note how there's no men in here," Orla whispered to Kitty. "Sistahs are doin' it for themselves."

"Remember," Kitty whispered back fiercely, "I read your blog. If I see any of this on it, I'm going to kill you."

"I wouldn't do that," said Orla, insulted.

"And no banner drops either," added Kitty, irrelevantly.

Then Kitty was called in by the sonogram technician, a heavy middle-aged Hispanic lady, not unkind, but impassive. Kitty imagined the staff were picked for their insensitivity, a quality Kitty envied so much in others. She went into the sonogram room, got undressed from the waist down, and sat back. The sonogram technician did her job.

Kitty looked at the screen. Among the moving shadows, she could see a flicker, a tiny light pulsing on and off. The sonogram technician was taking measurements, to confirm the age.

Suddenly, Kitty thought of Holcombe. How she had willed and willed and willed for signs of life and there had been none. She remembered praying over Holcombe's casket, trying to memorize the pattern of his eyebrows, the flare of his nostrils, the curve of his lips- before they put him into the ground. She remembered how it felt: searching for some spark, some light, some movement, some sign. And nothing.

And here, Kitty marveled, unexpectedly and inconveniently, was life. In a sense, Kitty did not know why Holcombe died, she never would. In a sense, Kitty did not know why this life was here, she never would. Life and death were equally mysterious.

Looking at the screen, Kitty felt overcome with humility. She knew nothing. She was adrift. The future looked bleak and rootless. But here was something definite. Here was someone trying, despite everything. She felt a vague stirring of appreciation for this creature that was daring to live. It cheered her up a bit. A spark, a light, movement. And it was hers. What else did she have? Kitty didn't feel like ending this. Not today.

"I changed my mind," she mumbled.

"What?" the technician asked absent-mindedly, looking at the screen.

"I changed my mind," Kitty mumbled shame-facedly. "I'm going now. Thank you."

"Oh, ok," the woman said, startled. Maybe it didn't happen that often, thought Kitty, that someone changed their mind. Kitty was surprised, she had rather supposed it did.

A few minutes later, Kitty burst into the waiting room, clutching the sonogram photo, cheeks burning. She made a beeline for Orla.

Kitty plopped down on the seat next to Orla and stared ferociously straight ahead. "I'm not doing it," she whispered nervously to Orla out of the side of her mouth.

Kitty fully expected a sanctimonious lecture on female empowerment. It would not have surprised her if Orla had imperiously pointed to the door and loudly commanded her to turn around, march right back into that doctor's office, and reclaim her body from the patriarchy. And Kitty didn't know how she would respond to that kind of command, either. She didn't know what she was doing.

Instead, Orla's reaction was as incongruous as her obsessive-compulsive Hail Mary addiction.

"We'll raise it together!" Orla exclaimed joyfully.

"Orla, have you lost your MIND?!" Kitty shouted. One of the other girls in the waiting room looked at them disapprovingly.

"We'll raise it gender-neutral!" Orla continued happily.

"For fuck's sake, Orla!" Kitty snapped. "You're not a fucking *lesbian*, all *right*? You tried it and you hated it, *remember*? So can you drop the lesbian *bullshit* already!"

Kitty could sense the glares from the others in the waiting room. A couple of wild white women yelling at each other about lesbianism in the waiting room. We better get out of here before someone starts filming us with their phone, Kitty thought.

A few minutes later, they were on the street.

"This is so exciting!" shrieked Orla. She started singing the lyrics to "Papa Don't Preach."

"Shut UP!" Kitty yelled. She didn't feel like serving as grist for Orla's drama mill at the moment. "Is there a diner around here?" she asked desperately.

They ended up taking the subway down to the East Village to a diner Kitty was familiar with. Simply having the waitress fill her small china coffee-cup with hot bitter black coffee comforted Kitty a little. She added cream and sugar and took a sip. Then she put her elbows on the table and rested her forehead in her hands.

"You're making the right decision," Orla said brightly.

Kitty raised her head and looked at Orla with mistrust. "I don't know what I'm doing," she said dourly.

"You know," Orla went on cheerfully, "the collective has a single mother's group that's really strong. Really powerful women. They were at the march on the Brooklyn Bridge. You'd be welcome to join."

"For fuck's sake, Orla," said Kitty, this time wearily. "Is that what this is about?"

"The group's called 'Single Moms for Justice,'" Orla continued enthusiastically. "And the leader's this totally self-actualized lesbian who's had two children through sperm donors. You would love her!"

"I'm not a lesbian," Kitty groaned. "And I didn't use a sperm donor."

But Orla, albeit for the wrong reasons, had cheered Kitty up. Orla saw a future for Kitty, however screwball, where Kitty saw none.

Kitty was tired. She looked at her life, what did she have to show for it? Her parents were elderly and getting older, her brother was a complete wild card, she had her friends for what they were worth, she had Peter Park the Half-Korean Airman Foreseeing his Fate, she supposed (if anyone did).

But she found to her surprise that she wanted this. She already felt lazy and content with pregnancy. Of course there was a lot to come to terms with, but she felt vaguely that she could let other people- responsible people like her parents and Peter Park- come to terms with it. She was tired of having to come to terms with everything. Why the hell couldn't she do as the lower classes did and just get knocked up.

Kitty felt that she had been trying to do the right thing (off and on but mostly on) her whole life. Now she had done the utmost right thing- she had become a lawyer- she had done the above-and-beyond-the-call-of-duty right thing, and Kitty thought she deserved to have a baby if she wanted a baby. She had earned it, she thought.

Kitty showed up to work the next day. The sonogram had said she was 11 weeks pregnant, and she definitely felt pregnant. What would happen, thought Kitty, if she just went with it. Being at work gave her confidence, it made her feel normal. Nobody knew, nobody treated her any differently. It was nobody's business. And so she went on for another month. She didn't tell anyone, and she lived in a dreamworld.

At work, Kitty was selected to work in a group that was reviewing documents for attorney/client privilege, and she was moved to a new seat. On her left was one of the miniseries-obsessed girls. On her right was a young man whom she had noticed before. There were a few hundred people on the document review, but once you had been there a few months, you had seen everyone.

But this young man Kitty had particularly noticed because he was strange-looking. He was very thin, to the point of emaciation, and very pale, but with dark eyes, dark eyebrows, and very dark hair, and he had a lush, thick, reddish beard. He was handsome, but waifish and delicate. Kitty would have thought he was gay, except that his fashion sense was terrible-he dressed like a computer programmer from 1987.

His name was Greg. He didn't talk a lot, and when he did his voice was quiet. Kitty had been sitting next to Greg for several days before she noticed that whenever Greg ate anything at his desk, he would pause first and close his eyes. Kitty watched him from the corner of her eye. His lips were moving. He was praying, Kitty realized. He was praying before he ate. A religious maniac, Kitty thought disapprovingly. She hoped he wasn't dangerous.

Bits of information started to emerge about Greg, as they do when you're locked up next to someone for ten hours a day. He was from Michigan. He had gone to a small law school in Ohio. He learned about the document review online, rented a room in Queens off Craig's list, and was working to pay off his debts. This was a common story.

One day, the people sitting around Kitty were talking about what they would do if they could pay off their debts. This was a routine and recurring theme among the doc reviewers. Most of them didn't want to be lawyers. Almost all of them had gone to law school because it had seemed like a good idea at the time, and now they bitterly regretted it.

"What would you do, Greg?" Kitty asked him, "If you could pay off your debts?"

"Well, that's what I'm trying to do," said Greg. "I'm saving up to go to the seminary."

"You want to be a priest?" Kitty asked curiously.

"Actually, I want to be a monk," Greg said softly.

"A monk?" Kitty was incredulous. "I didn't even know there still *were* monks these days."

"Oh, in the Orthodox Church, yes, yes, there are," Greg nodded seriously.

"Like Russian Orthodox?" asked Kitty.

"Yes, Russian Orthodox," said Greg.

"You're Russian?" Kitty asked, feeling like a low-brow.

"No, I'm American," Greg said, smiling.

"You converted?"

"Yes, three years ago."

"Oh," said Kitty. She didn't ask him anymore. She felt like she was grilling him, and she figured it was personal. But after this, Kitty had a superstitious respect for Greg. She no longer looked askance when he was muttering prayers before eating. He didn't seem weird to her anymore. He wasn't weird, he was just a monk.

A couple weeks later, on a Thursday afternoon, everyone at the table was talking about their plans for the upcoming long weekend. Kitty was planning a trip back home, to Harrison. She wanted to escape, her life felt out of control. She had told her parents she was pregnant, and they had predictably freaked out. The health insurance coverage from her clerkship was set to expire, and private health insurance was going to cost about a thousand dollars a month. She hadn't told Peter- she couldn't talk to him, for one thing, she could only write to him. She hadn't told Peter's parents. She couldn't imagine anything more embarrassing than: "Hey Mrs. Park, remember how I called you a few years ago to ask you for Peter's number, well- Surprise! I'm pregnant now! And guess what? It's Peter's!"

The truth was that work was keeping Kitty together at the moment. Document review was the perfect job for a pregnant woman: sedentary, brainless, undemanding. And Kitty was happy sitting next to Greg. She looked forward to work every day, sitting scrolling and clicking next to a gentle monk who talked to her about the church fathers, the history of the early Christian church, and the Orthodox church in America.

She knew that if she weren't pregnant, she would never have had the patience to be friends with Greg. In the riot of going-out and studying that had been her life for the past few years, she would have marked him as a weirdo and moved on. But for some crazy reason, her friendship with Greg was just what she needed right now. He conveyed, amidst the prison-yard jungle of the document review, a feeling of peace. He was humble. He was kind. Kitty could see that others felt that way too, they gravitated toward him.

When everyone started discussing their plans for the long weekend, Kitty told them she was going back home to Upstate New York, to Harrison. Immediately Greg became interested.

"Is that near Albany?" he asked.

"Yes," said Kitty.

"That must be near Jordanville," Greg said rapturously.

"Jordanville?"

"Holy Trinity, it's in Jordanville. The oldest Russian Orthodox monastery in the country."

"Wow, that's cool."

"You should check it out while you're there."

"Ok," said Kitty. Why not, she thought.

She looked up Holy Trinity at Jordanville online. It looked extraordinarily beautiful, a giant Orthodox church with gold domes.

So Sunday morning, Kitty started out for liturgical services at Holy Trinity. She was nervous. She wore a headscarf as was the custom. She traveled miles on country roads. Familiar, but not her neck of the woods. Then she came to a tiny town with one street, a post office, and a library. She took a road that branched off from Main Street, into the hills. And then, suddenly, like a vision, she saw a cluster of golden domes and white spires nestled among the green fields. It looked magical. The funny thing was she was only about half an hour from her home, and she had never known this was here.

As she neared, she saw that the church campus was like a compound with a bunch of buildings. The church was surrounded by long low buildings that looked like meeting halls or dorms. She parked in the lot next to the church. She was late, the parking lot was full of cars. "Life is precious," someone's bumper sticker read.

Kitty walked with trepidation up the massive, stone, church steps. It's no big deal, she told herself. It's just a church, just be respectful, they'll be welcoming, they're obligated to be. It's in their religion. She didn't know quite why she was so scared. Kitty paused before the massive wooden door, took a breath, opened it, and plunged in.

She was instantly flooded with awe. It was the light, it was the candles, it was the icons, it was the incense, it was the chanting, it was the music, but most of all it was the people. Standing soberly and silently, a flank of women and a flank of men, separate but side by side. The church seemed to be filled with a peaceful low hum.

Where had she seen this kind of communal submission, this gathering of calm, where had she felt this Old World undertow pulling her back to the primal, the ancient, the traditional? Where had she experienced this sensation before? The Orthodox Jews, it suddenly occurred to her. She was reminded of Yitzhak and Hannah's wedding. The same-sex segregation, the mute submissive belonging, the Old World solemnity.

Kitty crossed herself the way Greg had taught her: using the thumb and first two fingers of her right hand and in the opposite direction of how you crossed herself in the Catholic Church, how she had been brought up to cross herself. It felt very awkward, but she wanted to pay her respects.

She remembered what Greg had told her about a medieval czar of Russia sending out emissaries to explore the Orthodox faith, the Catholic faith, and the Islamic faith. His emissaries had traveled to Constantinople, Greg said, and had come back and told him that in the Orthodox Church they could truly feel the Holy Spirit. Kitty felt she knew what they meant. The Holy Spirit was here, she could feel it.

Here was a community of peers who would approve of her decision, who would understand what she was doing. She stood in the back among the women and crossed herself when they did, repeating "Lord have mercy," when they did. She was soothed.

Until the moment when the priest consecrated the host. As she was standing in the back closely watching the altar, Kitty felt a sharp stab of fear- at what she had done and of what awaited her- and shame. She knew she was damned. All she could feel was repentance. Tears came to Kitty's eyes when she thought about how God in His infinite mercy was giving her another chance. She was staggered. Her health insurance problems, document review, her parents, Peter, everything faded into the background. How infinitely loved she must be that God had given her this second chance. She had thought about Peter in Europe, she had brought his letters with her when she traveled, and God had made this happen.

Kitty left the church different. Not perfect or great or anything, but different. She had a glimpse of something that was to sustain her later on. There was a community of believers out there who agreed with her. There was a higher authority. She had seen the big picture. She was doing the right thing.

She went home and wrote a letter to Peter. She told him about Holy Trinity. She told him about bringing his letters with her to Europe, the letters he wrote to her when she was away at summer camp, she had carried them in her backpack with her rosary. And then she told him she was pregnant. She told him not to worry, everything was fine, and she told him she was praying for him.

"I visited Holy Trinity!" Kitty greeted Greg when she came into work on Monday morning. "It was so beautiful!" She had an urge to tell him more, but she didn't know what more she could tell him without getting into Peter, Holcombe, all of it.

Things were still stressful. Kitty had been going to an ob/gyn who ordered sonograms at every visit, and after googling the effect of sonograms, Kitty freaked out and looked for another ob/gyn. Her father asked around, and a family friend recommended Dr. Horowitz.

Dr. Horowitz was a mild-mannered, gentlemanly, elderly Orthodox Jew who always wore a pink tie. Kitty liked him at once. His staff was relaxed and friendly, and there were a lot of expectant Orthodox Jewish mothers in his waiting room. Kitty felt comfortable around Orthodox Jews.

Poor Dr. Horowitz, what he had to put up with from Kitty was terrible.

On her first visit Kitty told him anxiously, "I had an abortion. When I was 19."

Dr. Horowitz made no moral judgements. He was purely a doctor. "In what trimester?" was all he asked.

"In the first trimester," Kitty answered.

"Then it should be fine," said Dr. Horowitz.

Almost every visit they had the same conversation. Each time Kitty anxiously reminded Dr. Horowitz of the abortion, and each time Dr. Horowitz responded "What trimester?" and when he heard "First trimester," he always answered "It should be fine."

But Kitty was still tortured with worry. She feared incompetent cervix. She feared placenta previa. She feared preterm labor. She feared birth defects. Something must be wrong, she thought, something- because it was what she *deserved*.

Kitty got bigger and bigger. At work, people started to notice she was pregnant. As soon as Kitty had told her mother she was pregnant, her mother had given her a wedding ring, so Kitty had been wearing a wedding ring for months. And, really, the people at work didn't really care. No one was curious. No one cared. Everyone had their own lives. So Kitty wore her wedding ring, and people just assumed she was married.

And the more pregnant Kitty got, the foggier she got. She felt like her IQ had dropped ten points. She was suited now to dissecting tv shows with the other girls, she thought. That was about her level now.

Kitty amused herself at work by dreamily sketching Mendel diagrams to calculate the baby's chances of having blue eyes. She was "bb" because she had blue eyes. Peter Park was

"Bb" because, although he had brown eyes, his mother's eyes were blue.

"Big B, Little b, Little b, Little b," Kitty recited to herself as she doodled Mendel diagrams over and over again, in a world of her own. They always came out the same, of course. Bb, Bb, bb, bb. The baby had a 50% chance of blue eyes. Kitty had sketched hundreds of Mendel diagrams by now. She knew what the chances of blue eyes were, but for some reason it soothed her to draw the diagrams again and again. It was funny because she had done the exact same thing in 9th grade Biology class so many years ago. As soon as Mrs. Hopkins had taught them about Mendel diagrams, Kitty remembered, she started diagramming the chances of she and Peter having a blue-eyed baby together.

At about seven months pregnant, Kitty started hating to go to work. Sitting all day was uncomfortable, and she had to pee all the time, but the subway ride was the worst part.

Kitty rode the 6 train. It was full of Upper East Side people going to work in the Financial District. One morning, Kitty got on to the 6 train, and there was just nowhere to sit. It was a little later than she usually went to work, and the car was crammed with people, mostly financial types. It was hard to stand, much less sit.

Kitty cocked her elbows and tried to shield her burgeoning stomach with her arms. She tried to stoop down a little, since she was short. She thought maybe there'd be more room at a lower level. But it was impossible. She was trapped by the bodies of the people around her.

Kitty felt a tap on the shoulder and reluctantly turned her head. A tall, middle-aged, black woman was looking at her expressionlessly. Kitty steeled herself, her face set. She was ready for the woman to tell her she'd stepped on something of hers or tell her to get out of the way. But instead the woman silently motioned to the seat she had just vacated. She was giving Kitty her seat. "Thank you," Kitty whispered. "Thank you." Kitty sat down in the seat, and cried openly all the way to work, the tears rolling down her cheeks. She had been equipped to deal with confrontation; she had not been equipped to deal with kindness.

Soon after that, Kitty stopped working. She moved in with her parents- partially to save money, partially because she was lonely. And she waited it out. It was a brutal winter. It's temporary, Kitty told herself. It's all temporary.

It was really rather providential that she was eight and a half months pregnant when she found out Peter Park had been killed.

Kitty's poor mother was again the bearer of the bad news. It was in the local paper, that was how they found out. Kitty's mother deliberated when to tell Kitty, but she could not foresee a better time. She considered blurting out the news as Kitty gave birth, but that seemed risky. She considered telling Kitty after she had the baby, but she was afraid the birth-certificate paperwork involved would be inaccurate. So Kitty's mother told her as soon as she found out.

Kitty was enormous by this time- and very sedentary. She hadn't taken any dietary precautions, and she was huge, like a giant blimp. It was the tail-end of a long cold winter. She spent her days on the couch watching tv and working on a large embroidery project of a cat. Her poor mother told Kitty Peter was dead just before "Wheel of Fortune" came on, she didn't know what else to do.

Kitty's mother didn't try to psychologically frame the news or couch it or mitigate it or distort it to soften the blow. She just told Kitty matter-of-factly and also told her that she was at a loss as to how to tell her, and she just did not know, her mother trailed off, she did not know.

Kitty covered her eyes with one hand.

*I know that I shall meet my fate*
*Somewhere among the clouds above.*

"A helicopter crash?" Kitty asked in a small voice. Blackhawk, she thought. He was so happy that he got to fly Blackhawk helicopters.

"I don't know," said her mother peevishly. "I don't know, all I know is what the Harrison paper says." And she burst into tears.

Kitty didn't. She had been expecting this. She thought of Eli's mother at his funeral- pale, furious, dry-eyed, not surprised but not resigned. "I've been expecting this," Eli's mother had said. "I'm not happy to be here."

Kitty was experiencing everything as though through a thick fog, and all the news made her want to do was lie down and sleep and try to process it. It was all a dream anyway, she felt on some level: to be this fat and to also be told that Peter Park was dead.

Who, thought Kitty absurdly, would she call now to get back in touch with, now that Peter Park was dead? When Holcombe had died, she had gotten in touch with Peter Park, where would she go from here? And Kitty put down her embroidery and went back to bed. She drew the covers up over her ears and had dreams of Peter, and Holcombe, and Peter again, and Holcombe again. And now the baby was Peter's, and now it was Holcombe's. But Kitty felt loved in her dreams.

When she woke up she stared at the wall for a long time. She didn't have to get up, and she didn't have to go anywhere, and that was good, so she just lay there and tried to get her head around the fact that Peter Park was dead too. Of course, she had thought this would happen, and so had he, why else would he have recited that poem. They had both known it would happen. His baby was the shocker, not his death.

She would have driven him across the border. She didn't know why he had to recite this grisly poem predicting his own death. He might have known she might get pregnant, they'd used no protection whatsoever. He might have given a thought to her.

It was almost impossible to find people who appreciated her, and obviously now she was like a beached whale and felt sure that no one would ever appreciate her again. She knew he would have married her. Peter was the kind of man to marry someone who was pregnant with his child. She wondered if he had gotten her letter.

She was not going to be able to talk to him, anymore, she thought numbly, turning it over in her mind. He wasn't going to call.

Kitty lay in bed, thinking, until it grew dark, and her parents ate dinner without her, and then eventually they went to bed. Her mother checked on her a few times, and Kitty pretended she was sleeping.

Then she got up. She felt terrible because she hadn't eaten anything, she had to eat all the time. She popped a Tums from the container on the dresser next to her bed. She had to take Tums all the time. She had to pee all the time too. She felt like a prehistoric monster. She could feel all her organs being squashed up against her diaphragm. Parts of the skin over her stomach were numb from being stretched. And the baby was kicking one particular spot just under her ribs like crazy. Sometimes she would tap it back.

She got up and went to the bathroom. She stared at herself in the mirror. She had looked lovely with pregnancy a few months ago, and she had wished she had a man to admire her, but now she didn't care. Now she didn't look so much lovely as astonishingly huge. She was wearing her father's sweatpants, they were the only pants that fit.

She waddled into the kitchen, got a spoon out of the drawer, went straight to the freezer and took out a pint of Ben & Jerry's. She hadn't been eating ice cream, because Dr. Horowitz had told her to stop gaining weight, but she was going to eat some ice cream now. What could she do? She couldn't smoke, she couldn't drink. If she had still had her own place, she would have considered screaming and yelling and breaking things, but she didn't want to do that in her parents' apartment. And she was too tired, frankly. Too completely subjugated by the great weight of the baby. Between putting spoonfuls of the ice cream into her mouth, she occasionally let out a self-pitying whimper.

She had, of course, considered the possibility that Peter Park would die. First of all, his whole "Irish Airman Foresees His Death" recital didn't inspire much confidence that this was someone who was completely sold on living. Just as Holcombe driving all night without a pause betrayed a fundamental lack of caring whether he lived or died, Kitty thought. *She* wanted to live, she thought dourly. And now she had a reason to live, she thought, rubbing her mammoth belly. Her reason was she didn't want to be pregnant anymore. Come hell or high-water, she wanted to not be pregnant. That was her reason for living right now.

Once, she had narcissistically thought that Holcombe had died for love of her, that he died because he couldn't have her. Well, she had given herself to Peter Park, and he had died anyway, she thought prosaically, licking ice cream off the spoon. She thought of Eli, he hadn't wanted to live either. Mike, she suspected, would be next. She thought of all the other suicides and overdoses among her high-school and college crowd. Was this normal? This many people? There seemed to be a war of attrition going on. Death was everywhere. She clumsily turned it over in her foggy tired mind. Why did all these people not want to live?

The life cycle that her Orthodox Jewish friends seemed to take for granted as the natural course seemed to be inverted for Kitty's "people." Instead of weddings, funerals. Instead of births, abortions.

Even those who weren't dead, were they thriving? Orla, Paul- trapped in useless graduate programs, bogged down in debts, popping antidepressants, going to therapy. She thought of her other high-school friends, squatting in hovels in Brooklyn, living hand to mouth, a subsistence lifestyle that they kidded themselves into believing was hip. They thought they were hip, but they were just poor, Kitty reflected.

Kitty's civilization seemed to be on the wane, Kitty concluded, taking stock of the situation. She had known she was supposed to be part of the first generation to do worse than their parents since World War II, but she hadn't realized everyone around her would be dying like flies. So this was where the disaffection of post World War II had ended up: in a generation shattered, aimless, dissipated, weakened. Well, her civilization might be on the wane, but, Kitty thought stubbornly, it wasn't *her* fault.

Really, the astonishing thing was not that Peter Park had died, she came back to the thought again. He had joined the others in their class who had died from opioids. Peter Park's opioid was war. They had died deaths of despair, he died a death of nihilism. It was all of a piece to Kitty. The astonishing thing was the baby, that was the astonishing thing.

Kitty saw herself as fighting upstream, against a current of death, to spawn. And it was far from over. She had a horrible medical procedure before her, the ordeal of extraction, and she had no idea how it was going to go, Kitty thought fearfully.

But she was doing her duty. Was it Woody Allen who said 80% of life was just showing up? Well, Kitty was showing up. Peter posthumously was showing up. Whatever happened, they had tried.

"The Aging Champ," Kitty said aloud to herself, alone in the silent kitchen. Saying it made her feel a tiny bit better, so she said it again: "The Aging Champ."

About a week after her mother told her Peter was dead, Kitty was in bed napping, around dinner-time, when there was a knock on the door.

"Come in," she called out. Her parents rarely bothered her when she was in her room. It was her father. Kitty sat up on the edge of the bed. Her father came into the room. His face was set, he looked grim.

"What?" asked Kitty, alarmed. She was ready for the next tragedy.

"I want to tell you something," her father said purposefully. Kitty could tell he had planned what to say to her. His speech was the fruit of deliberation. "I grew up without a father. My mother was a single mother." His father had died in an accident when he was just six-months-old, Kitty knew that. "And I did just fine," her father went on, with a stubborn determination, "and your child will do just fine."

"Thanks, Dad," Kitty said briefly. Her father nodded, and left the room. Kitty remained where she was for a time, sitting on the edge of the bed, lost in thought.

Kitty spent the next week in a miserable limbo. She never left the apartment. She finished the embroidered picture of a cat. She spent her time re-reading Agatha Christies, watching tv, weeping, and googling baby names, in a fog. She hadn't contacted Peter's parents. She and her mother agreed it was better to wait until this was all over. But when would it be over? Her due date came and went.

A couple days after her due date, Kitty was on the couch in the living room, watching tv, she got up to go to the bathroom, and her water broke. Kitty shouted, and her dad, who was the only other one home, came running. Her poor dad drove her to the hospital, he was a nervous wreck. Before she left the apartment, Kitty grabbed a wooden rosary that was made in Jerusalem and stuffed it into her black backpack.

Kitty refused Pitocin, so Dr. Horowitz told her to walk the halls to induce labor. She and her father walked around and around the maternity ward together, while he told her about the cases he was working on. Kitty was in labor for 24 hours, but when the birth happened, it happened quickly.

"It has *hair*!" Kitty's mother shouted when the baby crowned.

Her mother held the baby first. Then the nurse put something into the baby's eyes. It screamed and screamed. Then they were handing the baby to her.

Kitty could feel the nervousness of the other people in the room- her mother, the nurses, the doctor- they all seemed to pause for a moment to monitor her reaction. She imagined they were afraid she would reject it. She wasn't going to do that, she thought- after all this work and all this agony, they needn't have worried. She looked down at it. It was still screaming. It looked very familiar and very strange at the same time. Like it was an alien that had come from a million miles away or another world, but at the same time it seemed like someone she had always known.

"Nurse her," her mother whispered. Kitty put the baby's mouth on her nipple, and the baby clamped down like a vise, she seemed to know exactly what to do. When the baby had been screaming and screaming, her eyes had been closed. Now she opened her eyes.

The baby's eyes were blue.

# AFTERWORD

*This is a personal essay which originally appeared in the online journal* Social Matter *under the title "Cornell, j'accuse."*

*The year is 1994. I am 19 years old. I am a sophomore at Cornell University. I am sitting in the office of a university official. I am in trouble.*

*I don't recall the details of how they got me. Was I retarded enough to go to the Health Center if I missed my period? Most definitely. But I seem to remember I went there with a UTI, they asked me when my last period was, and upon learning the answer, they tested me.*

*So here I was with Roz. I call her Roz because she was a large, grizzled, elderly lesbian. Even given my distress, it was distracting. She eerily resembled Michael Douglas in "Falling Down"- only obese. But I can confirm she was a lesbian because she was the faculty advisor of the LGBT Club (Pre-Q) to which my gay housemate–my confidante, naturally–belonged.*

*As soon as it was discovered I was pregnant, they sent me straight to Roz. Roz was good at her job. I'm not sure what her title was- "counselor" or "advisor" I imagine. But I got neither counseling nor advising. I got Prison Matron. After coldly regarding me with undisguised contempt for a moment that felt very long, Roz told me she was going to make me an appointment at Planned Parenthood. I said I was Catholic. She shook her head, and I shut up.*

*Stop. In that feeble profession of Christian faith is the dormant force that would later save my life.*

*This is my complaint: I was 19 and pregnant, I took this issue to my university, I was "advised" (more like ordered, really) to have an abortion, I protested the decision. "I'm Catholic," I said. The Cornell University official literally shook her head at me, meaning: "No dice. This is Cornell University. We don't entertain that particular fairy story here." Let me ask this: What if I had said I was Jewish? What if I had said I was Muslim? Would the Cornell official have reacted the same way? Would the Cornell official have dismissed my concerns so authoritatively?*

*Of course it's my fault. I have free will. But I was, as you might imagine, very vulnerable at the time. I was 19. I couldn't believe it. I was terrified.*

I was raised Catholic. My family went to church every Sunday. I attended religious education, I received the sacraments. My father, a graduate of Catholic schools and Georgetown (which was Catholic in those days) was very devout, but distant and rigid when communicating his faith. My mother, a Cornell grad and advertising copywriter, was pragmatic: You had to have a religion, and Catholicism was ours. It was a placeholder and a duty. But when they passed around a pro-life petition at church, my mother skipped it. She had friends, career women in their 30s, who had had to make the trip to Puerto Rico when abortion was illegal.

It was pretty clear to me at the time that dropping out of Cornell to have Slocum's baby would kill my parents. Slocum showed every indication that he would assume the mantle of Poet Laureate of the Westmoreland Trailer Park whenever his ne'er-do-well father relinquished the title. But this was whom I loved. Certainly the two-dimensional Long Island strivers I met at Cornell held no attraction for me. They amounted to thousands of slight variations on <u>What Makes Sammy Run?</u>

I attempt to convey my frame of mind in support of this assertion: I thought I was doing the right thing. Like the majority of young girls, I wanted to please. My strong sense of duty was part of what had gotten me into Cornell. Most of the girls I knew who had abortions were good girls who thought they were doing the right thing. To miss that is to miss the whole problem- and to miss the travesty of what is going on here.

So I showed up to my appointment at Planned Parenthood. I went alone. I didn't tell my mother. I figured I might tell her after the problem was resolved, after I had made things right again. The weeks between Roz making the appointment and the appointment I recall as a haze of wretchedness and misery. I felt like I had cancer and I had to have it excised. I did nothing but study. I took 19 credits that semester, and I made the Dean's List.

I was trying to do the right thing.

At Planned Parenthood everyone was breezy and cheerful. My nurse was a Jewish girl from Long Island with a Meteorology degree from Cornell. Fiercely proud of the SJW nature of her work, she expected admiration and gratitude. I weakly obliged. She talked about her dedication to her mission in the face of violent protests by knuckle-dragging bigots whom she scorned. Actually, not a soul was protesting outside the Planned Parenthood that day. The fact is I never saw even a hint of protest outside that Planned Parenthood in all the years I lived in Ithaca.

The doctor was a woman. I bumped into her a few weeks later in Wegman's. She recognized me, I saw it, but she set her face and looked away. I remember the misgivings that moment gave me. But wasn't what we had done all aboveboard? Wasn't I secularly atoning for my sins? Then shouldn't I be absolved? Hadn't we done the right thing? Then why couldn't she acknowledge me?

A few months after the visit to Planned Parenthood, Holcombe and I broke up. I blamed him for what happened.
I studied in Europe to get away. I graduated, then I lived in Europe for a little while. I had a glamorous French boyfriend. He cheated on me, I dumped him. So it goes.

When I returned to the US, my parents had moved to Manhattan for my father's work. I lived with my parents, and I worked in business development for a large law firm.

One night when I returned home from work, my mother met me at the door. She frantically insisted that I eat something. I ate a banana while she hovered over me. "Sit down," she said. I sat down.

It was the strangest thing. Slocum had died.

It is still the strangest thing. He was driving non-stop between Portland and San Francisco, and he fell asleep at the wheel. See, I used to force him to stop driving when he got tired. I'd alternately browbeat, sweet-talk, bribe him with ice cream. I never would have let that happen.

At Slocum's wake I remember his uncle commenting wryly in his thick, flat, country accent: "You look like you want to get into that coffin with him."

I did. I wanted to get into that coffin with him.

That I am alive today, and I am married to a lovely man, and I have children is an illustration of the strength, the power, and the grace of God. That is another and more useful story. My story today is: j'accuse.

People say that universities are "safe spaces"–big daycare centers for spoiled babies. That was not my experience at all. My university experience was Soviet gulag- contempt, submission, humiliation, forced denouncement of God and culture, physical invasion – and then, a lessened person, flung out into the world to face years of coming to terms with the trauma. If you're lucky and strong. Most of the women I knew who underwent abortions in college- that was their permanent induction into the Army of the Left.

*Think about it. What do evil armies do with their child soldiers? They make them kill. Then, after their first kill, the generals say to the new recruits: Your hands are bloody, there is no going back, you are one of us now.*

*Most of the girls I know who went through similar experiences are deeply tortured women who never went on to have children. And I will tell you something, the women I'm talking about would have been great mothers. They were in massive student debt, they didn't want to let their families down, they wanted to be upwardly mobile, they wanted to do the right thing. These girls, like me, were brought up basically secular-mainstream but outfitted with the patina of Christian culture that was de rigeur when and where I grew up. The spiritual torment I have seen these women suffer is demonic.*

*What kind of society condemns promising young women to this fate? What kind of society encourages pregnant girls to kill their babies in the womb? If they had had children, they would have become better people- to society's benefit. Their loss is society's loss.*

*I believe that what allowed me to have a family was the prayers of my ancestors, humility, and a world-view that allowed me to exist as a damned soul.*

*I should note that there are legal issues of consent at play here. But actionable or not, what Cornell University did to that unborn child, to me- the mother, to Slocum- the father, and to my parents- the grandparents was a crime. Cornell, j'accuse...!*

*I am damaged goods because I did what my university told me to do. And I am far from alone.*

*I leave with you with the worst part. After I met with Roz, I left the Health Center, I went home, I called Slocum. I told him I was pregnant.*

*"Let's get married," said Slocum. "I could get a job," said Slocum. "We can do this," said Slocum.*